INTO THE STORM

Axe Druid Book Five

CHRISTOPHER JOHNS

MOUNTAINDALE
PRESS

CONTENTS

ACKNOWLEDGMENTS

This long and winding path has been fraught with crazy adventures, wild times, laughs, tears, joy and pain and would never have happened if it weren't for the real members of Storm Company. Erik, Aaron, Nick, Evan, Jake and Jaken—all of you—this never would have happened without all of my brothers backing me. From the bottom of my heart, and on behalf of everyone whose lives you touched in some way, shape or form, I say thank you.

To my beloved Queen of the Frozen Void, I wish to express my undying gratitude. You've put up with the long hours, sleepless nights and picking up the pieces of what having these stories beat and break me down over and over—and all because you love me. Thank you. I love you too.

My son, this world is as much yours as it is mine, and I hope that some day, you'll be as enraptured and lost within these pages as I was. May you ever find your own journeys and adventures, and may your path along the Way be long and winding, but never alone.

My acknowledgments to those of you who have made it this far in the series only to realize that Storm Company is so much larger than what is portrayed in these pages. It is my absolute honor and with pure adrenaline that I would like to introduce the unsung members of the cast.

Sean Hall, Eli and David Hall, Ezben Gerardo, Tara Mulkey, Nick Kuhns, Jay Taylor, Lucas Luvith, Dawn Chapman and there are more but we have a book to get to yeah?

Thank you to Dakota and Danielle and all my friends at Mountaindale Press for believing me and making a dream come true.

Without all of you, this would have been a pipe dream.
Thank you.

THE WILD RIDE SO FAR

The long of it gets pretty weird, so I'm going to give you the short of it with loads of style.

Oh, I know folks, I got style.

Things have been hard for us, my brothers and I, while we searched for minions and generals of War among the drow elves.

Evil, cunning fucks with shadow magic that rivaled ours. Not Maebe's though, she had that shit on lock. But back to my buddies and me near the beginning, eh?

We were captured by a group of bounty hunters called the Braves of the Thorn. Quite the name, right? I'm teasing, it's awesome, I know. They took us to Lindyburg to face justice for me murdering guards sent to capture and bring back Pharazulla. I hadn't been willing, and she had used me as a means of escape, her mind control making me attack my friends and Muu's trainer Zhavron.

Turns out the Lady Belltree had plans for magic users of the land, and she wanted to kill them all. The Braves, being as cool as they really were, wouldn't stand for it and helped us hightail it out of there.

1

From there, we went to the law of the land and reported her, unlocked water magic in a princess, and marched our way to a dungeon.

Not the kind with whips and chains, no—nothing quite so fun. This is a place as alive as you and me with the ability to create monsters hell-bent on trying to end whoever steps foot inside.

Getting through there wasn't a cakewalk, especially since we had Fainnir, the only living earth mage and a dwarf of the Light Hand Clan from Djurn Forge, tagging along. We tried to guide him into his strength and responsibilities as best as we could, but something about almost being eaten by kobolds and a second chimera that same hour kind of put a brutal stop to that. All of this while I butted heads with my new familiar, Bea —yes, just like the amazing lady of the girls in gold, thank you —who refused to listen for *shit*. Normally. We're working on that.

I called in a favor from the Primordial Earth Elemental, Gorumbal, in order to get us out of there alive, and it wasn't easy. But I digress. The drow were a pain, but they did help us after a vampire attack that saw Yohsuke turning into one of them. The spider queen Lilith has helped us keep him sane by giving him a Vampire Lord's blood so that he could have his independence.

From there, we had to try to kill a different Vampire Lord who harassed and kidnapped patrols of scouts to build an army to attack the drow.

See, ol' Lilith and this lady had a bit of a past and, as sisters, it had spilled onto us.

There was some betrayal, more than a little badass planning on our part, and a major party-crashing by a crew of dwarves from Djurn Forge.

They got their warrior general, Gerty of the Mugfist Clan, back, and we made off with another one of the elemental champions.

Our first morning back, some of the craziest magic I've ever seen came about.

Jafrik, a little drow boy we had rescued, saw sunlight for the first time. And as a champion for the Light Elemental Primordial, he was reborn as a dawn elf. Golden skinned and powerful with light magic, he and who knows how many other people who saw the dawn that morning were reborn.

With that, they were all to come to Sunrise Village. We had no idea how many, or when, but they were coming. Change had come to Sunrise, and with it, a new dawn on that adventure.

But hey, this story is about us, right? We took on a name as a group, probably a little more out of jealousy aimed at the Braves than I'd like to admit.

So, Storm Company it would be, and our company of fine fighters had figured out that our fortunes may be found on foreign soil. Possibly on the continent of beasts.

Well, you're all caught up since our last adventure. Wait, wait. If I don't say this, she may kill me, and I would hate to die.

Maebe and I got hitched in front of all my friends. I'm now King of the Unseelie Fae. Now don't think I'm going to be expecting any of you to treat me differently because of that. I put my pants on the same as anyone else—with superior control over the shadows and a beautiful Fae goddess who is happier to try and prevent that than anything.

Sorry, sorry—to the story now, yeah?

CHAPTER ONE

Covers shifted, snoring in front of me sputtered, then continued. Dust motes fluttered in the thin beams of dusk light filtering through the shuttered window to Vrawn's room.

My queen moved behind me, in her new favorite place to rest, and her breath tickled the flesh on the nape of my neck, making me grin. My wife now.

God, that feels so weird to say. The thought crossed my mind even as her hand meshed with mine, my other arm under Vrawn's head for support.

This had become the new norm, and I was damned proud of that.

I shifted into my fox form and scampered out from between the two of them. Maebe was alert instantly, her head popping up over Vrawn's large shoulder to watch me with her sparkling green gaze.

Her awareness brushed against my skin like it had when we first became aware of each other in the Fae realm.

"Where are you going, my king?" Her cultured voice carried little hint at the stress that we had been going through of late. What with the whole dungeon diving, screwing around with the drow thing and all. But hey, she's a queen, she has to be tough.

"Well, we were planning to go see the dwarves in the morning," I explained again. "So, I was going to take a minute to go and collect a dragon form from Ampharia before we went. Thogan and Xiphyre said that they would be finishing up her order for helping us, so I was going to take it to her."

"And why is she not here to collect it herself?" Her confusion was well-founded, honestly.

"Xiphyre said she grew bored of waiting and that her forest had been left unguarded too long already," I repeated what I'd been told. "So, she gathered her egg and took off."

I scratched the back of my head. "Honestly, that was probably sound. Two eggs would have likely attracted unwanted attention."

"Do you require that I come with you?" Her eyebrows raised with the question.

I smiled at her, crossing the room to stand in front of Vrawn, and Maebe just behind her. "No, dearest, I can handle this. Besides, Vrawn deserves some good sleep for once. You stay here with her, and I'll be back as soon as possible."

"You had better stay safe, Zeke." Maebe's tone turned stern, bordering on an order as she held up her left hand. "I will know if you are not."

I held up my hand, waggling my finger back at her. Our rings glinted in the dull light, the black metal sporting a line of black stones with smaller bright diamonds, rubies, emeralds, sapphires, and other colored stones inside that matched each other perfectly. They also bound us together in more than just legality. I could feel her emotions and her thoughts, to a lesser extent, as well as knowing where she was. I didn't know if there would be greater benefits later on down the road, but it was nice to have now.

I leaned over Vrawn to give Maebe a kiss that made her groan, then leaned down and gave Vrawn a small peck on the cheek.

Last time I had woken her up by being loud, she had almost slit my throat in front of my secondary enchanting instructor, Vilmas. The poor lady had tried to calm the hulking orc woman, and thankfully it had worked.

Vrawn's snoring stuttered again, her beautiful blue eyes opening blearily to stare up at me with sleepy affection. "Hello."

"Hello." I grinned at her stupidly as I swept the fiery orange mohawk from her face, just behind her slightly pointed ear. Her lips curled up, flashing her dainty tusks as she raised an almost seafoam green hand to caress my face. "I'm going to deliver some items to a dragon, she's a friend, but Mae is gonna stay here with you and cuddle. I shouldn't be gone more than an hour."

She blinked up at me with sleep still in her eyes then grinned wider. "If you aren't back in two, she and I are coming after you."

Maebe's light laughter followed me out of the room. I called Kayda to me, and she flitted onto my arm in her parrot-sized form. Her azure feathers were darkened by the falling light, the lighter blue, almost-white feathers that showed her storm roc heritage as one of a kind shone in the dim light.

Normally I'd wait for dawn, but we had spent the majority of the day resting and recovering from the fight down in the Great Below. All of us sorely needed the rest.

Her curious pale yellow eyes probed me, her mind touched mine. *Maebe, and Vrawn okay alone?*

"Yes, my love." I patted her head affectionately, scratching just beneath her beak softly. "Those two are crazy strong, they'll be alright."

I used my earring to send a telepathic message to the others. *I'm going to take these items to Ampharia in her forest. You lot wanna come?*

Hell no, fool. Yohsuke responded first, his gruff tone very much him. *Any word on how long that coffin may take?*

We're still working on it for you, man. Bokaj grumbled tiredly.

Sarah and I are getting pretty wiped over here in her shop, then Xiphyre, Zeke or Vilmas can enchant it to shrink for you, but it takes time.

Jaken, Muu, James, and Balmur were all in the rogue's spell, Happy House, so they were all in a separate dimension at the moment and couldn't respond. The lack of room at the inn was to blame for that, and the thought of sleeping where she couldn't be easily summoned by the guard hadn't flown well with Vrawn. She'd all but begged us to sleep in her room. Mae more than me because I was on her shit list at the moment, but hey—I try.

I checked my inventory for the small black box that Xiphyre gave me earlier in the morning, then closed my eyes to think about where I wanted to Teleport to.

Then I stopped and took out the raven in my pocket. The little purple and green figure activated with a press of 100 MP and my questions. "Hey Ampharia, I have your items from Thogan, and Xiphyre; are you okay for me to meet you in a moment? If so, where?"

A spectral copy of the little item flapped its wings and took off into the starlit night. Moments later, a response came with it as it fluttered into my hand.

"I am in my new den." Ampharia's voice sounded tired as she explained, "It is where the tree planted by Mother Nature grows."

I nodded to myself, I knew exactly where that was, and if I was counting my intelligence up well enough—I'd make it there without need for an unnecessary stop.

But why take my word for it, right? Let's see it all, shall we?

Name: Zekiel Erebos
Race: Kitsune (Celestial)
Level: 42
Strength: 57
Dexterity: 52
Constitution: 50
Intelligence: 95

Wisdom: 50
Charisma: 19
Unspent Attribute Points: 0

Ah, much better. Getting up there in the ol' intel department, folks. Hell yeah. A whole 950 MP at my disposal and that meant I could go farther when teleporting too.

I closed my eyes and selected the destination I wanted, a sort of visual catalog developing in my mind. The forest where I wanted to go, the tree I'd like to see. A deep breath and the intense sensation of the world dropping away from my body later, and I stood inside the once abandoned village of a group of cultists. It had been torn apart and destroyed by a rebellious minion that had taken over a creature possessed by a greater fiend while we had tried to put an end to it. They mixed, and it was a *really* bad time for us. It had been so strong that Maebe had to step in and help out. And even then, it was a hard-fought victory that left a lot of us wounded and me with a broken spine.

That hadn't been fun to heal, but we survived.

"Hello, druid." A bass growl greeted me from next to the tree. My vision at night was excellent, but still, her hulking shadowed figure moving around the wild tree like a leviathan out of the nether made my jaw drop in awe.

"Hello, fierce guardian of this jungle." I bowed my head as a joke, but I think she liked the title.

"You have learned much since we last met." Her pleasure was obvious, and I wasn't about to tell her otherwise. "You bring my treasures?"

I pulled the box with them inside out of my inventory and pressed it toward her. Her great bulky shadow moved toward me, the outline of her head with her antler-like horns lowered toward me until she could manage to get her claw out to lift the lid.

She snarled and moved away from a large oval-shaped shadow.

"It is almost ready to hatch, it just needs more fire energy than is available to me and the enchantment the tiny Fae put on it isn't strong enough."

"Then why don't you look at your loot, and I'll do a little magic to help things along?" I made the offer innocently enough, but she could tell there was something off.

"And what is it you ask in return?" Her large brown iris burned into my own electric-blue gaze. "Nothing is free, and I can sense your bond to the Fae Queen."

"My wife, and I've acquired a new skill." I tried to figure out a way to dance around my question, but with her staring me down, I faltered and just barreled into it. "I can acquire the forms of new creatures, and I believe your form is available to me."

Her head rose to its full height, eyeing me from so far up that I had to crane my neck almost all the way back. "And you wish to acquire my magnificent form?"

I sighed and cast Solar Flare above her head so that the light of day covered the area.

"The whole high and mighty thing looks good on you, sister, but it's a little more intimidating in the light when the shadows deepen across your features." I tried my hardest to sound bored as I stared up at her deep-green scaled face. "That's so much more menacing than before. And now, you can really see the fear on my face."

"A simple compliment would have been nice." She lifted her chin and sniffed. "But seeing as though you know how to be *so* intimidating, I'll have you work for my form, druid."

I sighed and almost rolled my eyes, but I kept my faculties in check. "What can I do for you, Ampharia?"

"Hatch the egg *after* you make me a new lair." She shifted into her humanoid shape, a dragon-kin of shorter height with the same facial features as her other form. "I wish to have something like this tree."

She lifted her right hand and stroked the wild tree.

Now, I know what you're likely thinking—all trees are wild

Zeke, get over your naming system, you schmuck. But that's what we had decided to name it as a group.

The tree looked like the base of it had guardian branches and wood woven around it like a loose basketweave. It had been a gift to symbolize the synergy of the party. My friends protecting me and each other, even as I supported them. Mother Nature had been cool enough to plant it, and now it stood as the tallest tree in the jungle.

The trunk, thick and unyielding, gave me hope that it would stay as strong as our friendship.

"How the hell am I supposed to do that?" I snarled at her, my arms spread wide.

"You are the Druid." She shrugged as she grabbed the box and lifted it to her chest before turning away. She glanced back with a fierce grin. "Figure it out."

I shook my head and trudged closer to the tree before putting a hand on it. I had recently begun to take the time to interact with plants like I did animals. It was a lot more guess-work as trees didn't really *speak*, but they could kind of *feel* things at me. It helped.

"Hello, big guy," I muttered as I pressed my awareness against the large plant, a welcoming presence pressing back. "Tell me about yourself."

My body became connected to the tree. As if we became one, and in that unity, I knew that there were several seeds sprouting on branches high above.

Seeds I could use to grow more trees like this one. But before I went and played with Nature's things, I needed her consent first.

Because consent is cool, and I *really* didn't want Mother Nature to kick me in the metaphysical nuts because I assumed anything about her.

I kept my hand on the tree as I reached toward the world with my thoughts. "Mother Nature? I wanted to ask your permission to give Ampharia a lair here with the tree you planted as a symbol for us. I can feel the seeds above us, and I think I can use them to make her something special. Can I have your permission?"

Wind whispered through the area around us, hissing and shaking leaves and branches before her being touched my mind. Her matronly voice louder in my head than I recalled. *You would use my bounty to create a home for a friend, for personal gain?*

"Well, when you put it that way…" I snorted at her obvious distaste. "We have a lot of unknowns we're getting ready to face, and as awesome as it would be to be able to be a dragon—my thought is my mission. If I can create something that will last a long time and be a testament to your power through me, is that so bad?"

Finally, she whispered and I could hear how relieved she felt, *you begin to truly think as a Druid. Yes, child. Use the seeds born of this tree, my gift to you, and create something splendid. Your power in this craft grows, and I am eager to see your will in shaping my bounty.*

"Thank you," I muttered with a small smile on my face, then tapped the tree with my Fae iron arm, the green and purple metallic hand a perfect copy of the one I had lost when I found out that enchanting can be deadly.

Long story short—I'm less of a boob when I enchant now.

"Will you help me, friend?" The breeze shook the tree's limbs as I asked my question, and several small thuds reached my ears. "Thank you."

I turned and rested my back against the tree, closed my eyes, and focused my mind. My ring, Mage's Well, was full and so was my mana. That gave me a whopping 1,450 MP to work with.

Good. I cast Mass Regrowth, taking 150 MP right away, with the seeds as my targets. I could feel them sinking into the ground. They were about twenty feet or so at the closest to the base of the tree, their roots spreading into the network beneath, but they needed nourishment. The light spell above would fade soon, so we needed water.

Kayda knew my mind before I did and began to sing her song as she took off from my shoulder. A gentle rain shower fell to the ground around us, soaking me and the ground with it.

The water fed into the roots and sizzled against my light spell.

I turned my thoughts to the plants and encouraged them to grow where I willed, coaxing, and gently leading them all in a gentle ark eighty feet above the ground in a domed shape. Then my mana bottomed out. and the tree sagged weakly.

"Not quite the finished product I had in mind, druid." Ampharia sniffed haughtily, her head raised.

I rolled my eyes. "That's not it, I ran out of mana. Give me a minute to rest."

She grumbled something about me not being druid enough for the job, and I found her glaring at me. "Dragons are stronger than this."

I glared at her angrily, and she grinned. "If you want my form, you will need to prove that you are worthy."

I growled as I checked my mana, the ring having not recharged at all and ground my teeth. I had my full amount of mana back by now, so I grinned and bared my soul to my work, hoping I was strong enough to do this in one more push. Otherwise, I would be leaving here with my mission a failure.

My mana funneled into the growths as they moved and shifted, their bending trunks to keep them malleable but strong. Their own branches and shoots of leaves fanning out around the base of the lower branches of the main tree so that they would get sunlight too.

Even as I finished my work, my mana dropped into the double digits, and sweat drenched my body and the ground around me.

"Impressive." Ampharia's appreciative tone took me by surprise. She walked into her new home, the dome having ivy and branches of leaves outside to provide cover. "It will make sunbathing difficult, but I will have somewhere that is mine to guard over my hoard."

I sat down and focused on trying to pull mana into my body

through meditative breathing like Maebe had shown me in the Great Below, but the air here above ground didn't have the same density of mana in it that the air down there did.

It took a couple minutes of rest, but my mana recovered fully, and I spent some time replacing the mana in my ring as well.

"Are you ready for me to try and help this little one?" I touched the egg, large and warm against my flesh.

"If you are, certainly." She sniffed and observed one of the items in the box. "I quite like these. Do as you will. It will be nice to be able to hunt again."

I focused my intent and will as I pulled my mana from the center of my being and used a skill I had called Elemental Tinkering (fire) to give the mana the flame aspect.

The magical essence swirled through my fingertips and into the egg, lowering my mana bar with it. I siphoned the mana in, and tried to evenly distribute it around the egg and slowly increase the temperature. I could *sense* the life inside like I had before, but as the heat built, the little thing grew more active.

By little, I mean large because it's a damned dragon, but you know, whatever.

My brow furrowed under the strain of the constant mana drain. Draining myself for a second time so close together made my head pound terribly.

The cost of mana expenditure.

Crack.

A shifting inside the egg almost stole my focus.

"Almost there," I said, then grunted. "Ampharia, come over here."

"I am here. I can sense her." A deep rumble emerged from the dragon as I fed more mana into the egg.

Another crack, shifting, and finally a burst of heat that backlashed into me where I stood. The egg burst apart in a shower of embryonic fluid and eggshell, some of the red objects landing near me. I leaned down and scooped some up and tossed it into my inventory, some shell, embryonic fluid on a branch.

"Hello, little one," Ampharia almost cooed to the newborn from where she stood.

The tiny dragon barked and cooed back.

"Aww, she's hungry." Ampharia pulled out a large slab of meat from behind her and plunked it into the ground before the little thing.

The baby dragon's scales seemed soft and stubby, like her legs and tiny wings. Orange eyes glared into the darkness, then her nose started to work, and she found the meat at her feet.

Tiny serrated teeth slashed the flesh apart greedily as she gobbled her way into the morsel, and I watched in rapt joy. New life was always a blessing, and I had honestly believed that I would never witness the birth of a dragon.

"What will you name her?" It was impossible to hide the awe in my voice from the elder dragon.

"She will choose her own name." Ampharia rested her head on the ground and eyed the little dragonling with what looked like begrudging affection. "It is a tradition among dragons to let their young choose their moniker. When she is older, I will tell her of herself and her history so that she may make the best possible choice."

"Ah, that's an interesting tradition." I thought about it for a moment. "Close to what the dwarves do with their young."

Ampharia cast a baleful glance my way. "Where is it you think they learned their ways?"

I stammered at her for a moment then fell silent before asking, "Seriously?"

"They misconstrued what was supposed to happen in the naming process for *them* deciding based on the child's actions and history rather than the child choosing. So backwards."

I had to laugh at that. Though I wouldn't be telling that shit to any of the dwarves I'd be hanging out with soon.

"Well, I have upheld my end of the bargain, and you

yours." I bowed my head slightly. "Would you mind if I took your draconic form?"

"Of course, I mind. My resplendent self is far more majestic and perfect than your Druidic magics can manage to copy." Crestfallen, I worried she would tell me no, but she winked instead. "I tease. If you would do me one more, simple favor? A personal one."

"What's up?" I asked tiredly.

She seemed confused for a moment, glancing toward the sky as the dragonling crunched into the bone of the carcass before her.

"It's an expression simply meant to ask what can I do for you," I explained before she grew upset. "What can I do for you?"

"Ask Muu to come and visit me?" She seemed hopeful.

"I can do that." I nodded, then held a hand up to ask her to wait. "Did you mean right now? Or when I see him next?"

"When next you see him." She smiled at me with her overly large teeth flashing in the moonlight. "A personal invitation is *always* better received. Do you not think?"

"It does add a personal flare." I frowned appreciatively at her thoughtfulness.

"Come, take my form." She held out her clawed hand. As soon as I touched her, I felt the normal flash of assurance I always got from receiving a new form.

There hadn't been any sort of notification that my abilities would take less time. Weird.

"She wants your attention," Amphoria whispered as quietly as a dragon could.

I flinched and turned to see the tiny, red-scaled creature stumbling my way with upturned orange eyes filled with curiosity. Her muzzle glistened darkly with blood in the moonlight as she figured out that I was further from her.

"Hello, little one," I found myself talking to her as if she was a baby. "I'm Zeke."

"She thinks you're her mother."

I stood straight up and glared at Ampharia. "No fucking way. Seriously?"

She tilted her head. "I have no fire that she can sense, but she senses it in you." A growl that I immediately recognized as laughter reverberated from her chest into mine. "And you will have no luck convincing her otherwise."

I sighed and reached out to her with my left hand, so she could nuzzle it with her nose and teeth.

"I'm not your momma, but I can be Uncle Zeke, okay?"

Warmth flowed over me, *Momma.*

I must have flinched too hard because Ampharia howled with laughter. "She imprinted upon you? Oh, this is grand."

"Listen here, you green-scaled asshole, I can't take care of a dragon!"

That only made her laugh harder. "Oh, I know, druid. I know. Fret not, I will guide her. Know that she will eventually come find you of her own accord."

Would that be so bad?

Strong, Kayda's voice brushed against my mind as she watched from nearby.

Momma! The dragonling snorted happily; a small gout of flame erupted from her mouth, then smoke burst from her nostrils.

Another sensation of warmth touched my mind, a burning one.

No, no, no! I growled internally.

Yes, little flame. The primordial Fire Elemental made his presence clear, searing my mind and body with his presence. *This one is mine. Along with her brother.*

"Twins?!" I called out loud, startling the little dragonling and Ampharia both. "She has fire magic already—she's a *dragon, man!*"

And she is one of my chosen champions. I could almost feel the flame chuckling at my expense.

"How does that even work?!" I quickly observed our

surroundings. "If she's practicing fire magic in a forest, her protector and surrogate mother will *kill* her!"

"Do you always talk to yourself like this?" Amphalia raised an eye ridge at me as if I had lost my mind. Her head dipped down, her face dangerously close to mine. "And if she burns down my forest, I *will* kill her. And likely come for you, as well."

"I'm not talking to myself, and you're about to have help, I hope." I growled at the dragon, her head recoiling at my ferocity. I ignored her and spoke to the big flame, "What does she need to do?"

She needs to summon one of my children, he explained, the crackling flames that were his voice patient. *She can do it through you, if needed.*

"Fine, but you better send her one that's on the cooler side of the spectrum, because she's already going to be weird for the environment." I sighed heavily. Thinking about how Mother Nature and I were just beginning to be on cool terms again. Fuck man.

I turned my attention to the confused, but mildly entertained dragonling standing at my legs staring up at me.

"Breath fire, and think 'come to me,' okay?" She wasn't thinking that at all as she stomped happily and breathed fire as she stomped some more.

I reached down, tapping her and subconsciously taking her form as well before I held her still and mentally told her to focus. She could communicate with me mentally? I could do the same.

I patiently explained things to her, and she tried to do what I said but got distracted. Finally, I got frustrated and told her to breathe fire as I mentally barked, *Come!*

Once she stopped breathing fire, the flames stayed there, burning brighter and hotter until the elemental took shape. His body burned blue, which just meant that he burned hotter than normal fire, and his eyes were coal black.

"Finally." He snorted. "This is the mage?"

The dragonling sniffed at him and came closer. He patted her head and sighed. "Why do I always get the dumb ones?"

"Excuse me?" Ampharia growled seconds before I made my way closer to the little bastard.

"Your whole mission in life is to see that she understands her magic, and when her twin summons his, it will be someone else's job to teach him." He seemed bored, so I reached out and snatched him up by the chest flames.

It burned slightly, but the gifts I'd received from the Primordial Flame Elemental halved damage from fire.

"You'll treat her with respect, or I send you crawling back to daddy, and I summon someone else." I bared my teeth at him, he seemed unaffected by it, but I continued anyway. "Do you understand?"

Ember meant no disrespect. The Flame Prime explained. *He is my eldest child, and I sent him to the one who seemed to need the most... guidance.*

"Guidance needed or not, you will not disrespect her, and you'll listen to Ampharia." I let him go, and he landed on his feet with a nod.

"I will guide her in her magical ability to the best of *my* ability," he looked like he was going to roll his eyes. If he could. "Just don't blame me if she gets excited and burns things down."

I shook my head and looked to Ampharia, who spoke while eyeing the elemental, "You may go, druid. I will keep an eye on both of them. And if she comes to look for you, pray that she doesn't *eat* anyone on her way."

I cast my gaze at the dragonling, accepted my fate in her life, and sighed before I bent down and scratched her cheek, "Momma has to go, but you listen to auntie Ampharia, okay?"

Momma! She bit at my metallic hand, and I smacked her about playfully before nodding to the adult dragon.

Only one of the primordial elementals had a champion left out there somewhere, and I was that much closer to finding them. All of the other elemental guides, Pebble and Zygnal, really because I hadn't seen Jafrik or Maebe's elemental guides, were cool. Understanding and helpful, if Pebble wasn't a little stony at first, it remained that they genuinely respected their masters and would probably die for them if it were needed.

I didn't have that same feeling for that little fiery bastard, Ember. He seemed the type to shirk his duties because he wasn't being challenged. And now with the threat of Ampharia coming for me, or hurting the little red dragon because her fire magic isn't exactly under the strictest control because she's learning, just seemed like a lot of extra baggage to deal with. Especially right now with one of the generals actively gunning for us.

I glanced back at the dragonling who yipped happily at her fire elemental under Ampharia's watchful gaze. I just hoped that she would wise up and soon. Poor kid would likely have a rough go of it.

I closed my eyes and cast Teleport to get myself back to my room with my girls.

CHAPTER TWO

The next morning, we were up and at 'em! Or as up and at 'em as you can be with your wife, and a giant orc woman laying on top of you.

Maebe had no reason to, other than that she wanted to, and seeing me grunt in discomfort made her happy.

"I swear, if the two of you don't move—I will shapeshift into a dragon right this second and *sit* on you."

"He's so lively in the morning." Vrawn smirked to Maebe, then kissed my cheek. "Good morning, handsome."

"Good morning." I smiled at her despite my grumpy façade. "We need to get to the dwarves, ladies, and eating beforehand would be a great idea."

We dressed, wearing armor and the like more for show than anything else, then headed downstairs to get our breakfast.

Most of my friends waited around a table in the rear of the room with plates of food, eating and laughing in a light atmosphere.

The tavern dining area was middle-sized, roughly twenty yards square, with dark wooden chairs and tables for guests within Sunrise Village.

"Mornin' love birds!" Jaken flashed his small tusks at us. He wore his typical platinum-colored armor, it was mithril dyed platinum by his goddess Radiance, and covered his purple skin.

Jaken, a new dad and one of my best gaming buddies, was the paladin of our group. His black hair looked ruffled, falling over his face and almost covering his bright hazel eyes.

"You got some egg in your goatee, buddy." I pointed to his face, and he flinched, whipping a napkin up to wipe at what wasn't there.

"Good morning, everyone." Maebe gave her winningest smile. "How are all of my knights feeling this morning?"

"Good, my Queen." Balmur stood his grin firmly in place, his left eye an odd color this morning. "Before you ask like everyone else, my eye is gold from an eye that I fed to it. Heat vision hurts man."

The tanned Azer dwarf, fire dwarf for those of us who may not know, had lost his real left eye in the Hells while he had been there under the tender care of a general of War masquerading as a demon lord. A portion of his flaming black and purple beard had been carved away, and the scars covering his body almost as much as his skin did. One of those marks bisected his left eye, where his new eye watched everyone intently. His dwarven features twisted in recognition when he saw me watching him.

"You gonna kiss me?" His snarled question made the others pause, but all I did was snort, and he laughed too.

We worried that his time being tortured and mistreated by demons had done something to him. His humor was a little sharper than before, and he fell into a battle rage unlike anything I was capable of, but for the most part, he was coming out of it okay.

There were some slight signs of post-traumatic stress disorder, but we all kept watch over him to help when we could.

"Ah, humor, I see." Maebe smiled at the man and nodded appreciatively. "I truly am beginning to see how all of you interact and have started to grow accustomed to it."

"Appy to heab bat, baebe!" Bokaj belted around a mouthful of eggs and bacon.

Bokaj, our pale-blue skinned and lithely built ice elf ranger bard grinned while chewing. Some of the crumbs from his face fell onto normal clothes, black long sleeve shirt with black pants, and his black boots, but what shook me was what wasn't there.

"She's not small enough to fit inside your hair anymore, where is she?" I growled as I lifted my tails up further and checked behind me.

"She's around." He grinned wider after he swallowed and brushed his black hair out of his sparkling blue eyes. The sides were buzzed, and the top long and artfully coiffed to the side. "Unlike you this morning. Where is your alarm? Weren't you a Marine? Ass-crack-of-dawn wake up time? Vrawn, you're a soldier, you should know to have an alarm."

"This one's mine," Vrawn advised with her hand clamping down on Maebe's shoulder, then I felt a hand on my shoulder. "As is this one. I usually only wake up when they move, I like my sleep."

"We get it, you're a happy threesome." James rolled his eyes.

The irritable dragon elf raised a mug of piping hot tea to his lips and gulped it down, sighing once he stopped.

His malformed wings settled behind him in the chair, black like the scales along his bare chest, shoulders and parts of his face. He caught me eyeing him and winked, making me turn away.

"Yohsuke asleep?" Concern heavy in my voice.

Bokaj nodded, another bite on his fork. "We finished with it 'bout half an hour after you got hold of me, then he tried to make it comfortable for a bit before laying down. I'm not sure if vampirism sapped his elven sleeping ability or not, but he's been down since."

"AAAAAAAAAAGH! You little shit!" The familiar loud voice and the sound of scampering, heavily-padded cat paws came toward us from the hallway.

A nude but slightly covered Muu, his scaled body rippling

with muscle as he chased his feline tormentor with a pillow held over his groin.

"You tail biting *asshole!*" He hollered while tailing her and gaining ground in bounds around the room.

"Speaking of, we can see yours!" I snarled, sending a Lightning Bolt crashing into his bare backside, making him howl in pain. "Clothes! *Now.*"

Tmont padded toward Bokaj looking proud of herself, I turned so I could watch her pass when the door behind us opened.

"There they be!" A gravelly voice belted out across the room, making me smile. "Told ye, lad. They be here still."

"Thogan, Rowland!" Jaken called happily, standing where he was to wave them over despite the fact that they were on their way already. "What're you boys doin' here?"

"We had a request of ye lads." The smaller dwarf asked, his black beard braided with ornate decorative beads, and his hair slicked back and tied into a small knot.

"What's up, Rowland?" I stepped closer to him and the taller, gravel-skinned dwarf Thogan Swiftaxe. "Let me guess— you both want to come to Djurn Forge?"

They both nodded, but Thogan spoke, "See, lad." He folded a cloth rag in his hands and wrung it back and forth as he went to explain himself, "Been a while since I were with me kinfolk an' I be missin' em somethin' fierce."

"You don't have to explain that to us, man!" Jaken had come round the table to stand next to me. "We get it."

"I appreciate the understandin' lads." Thogan grinned and shook our hands, the rock-like flesh on his palms rasping against the metal grip of mine. "But wee Rowland has a mighty task ahead of him."

We glanced over to Rowland, who blushed, his cheeks rosy red as he muttered, "I be meanin' to ask Vilmas' clan head fer her hand in matrimony."

"Holy *shit!*" Jaken whistled while clapping the other man on the shoulder happily. "Big step!"

"Aye, it be indeed, but it be a hard step." He glanced at me. "Vilmas told me yer her clan head's apprentice?"

"Shellica taught me the majority of what I know about enchanting," I nodded as I spoke.

"I were gonna ask if ye would introduce us?" I frowned at him, and he fumbled to explain. "See, someone with whom the clan head is familiar with needs to introduce me to her. It's the proper way to be about it."

"I'd be honored, my friend." I pulled the smaller man into a bear hug, and he patted my shoulder. "Does Vilmas know?"

"She knows me intentions be pure, but she does nae know 'bout this." Rowland eyed our surroundings. "I'd appreciate yer silence on this, lads. Aye?"

"Yup!" Muu slapped him on the shoulder. "Who let the walking gravel pit and his hideous handmaiden in here?"

Rowland and Thogan howled with laughter, and both turned on the dragon-kin fighter with jabs and japes of their own making for him.

"Teleporting all of you is well within my means, but I need to be sure that she's back to the city under the mountain before I promise anything to you." I pulled my raven from my pocket and sent my question directly to Shellica. "Hey, shitty grandma, you in Djurn Forge?"

The spectral raven lifted from my hand and flew away, the flying spectral image fluttering past Rowland's gawking face. It returned much faster than I had thought it would, and her response was almost distressing.

"No, I ride with a contingent of Dawn elves to the place where they are drawn." She paused for a moment. "We are in a forest, and I think I can hear bears in the area."

My eyes widened. "Did we warn the bears that the dawn elves would be coming here?"

"Willem got a hold of Sam, but I don't know if he acted on it immediately or not." James scratched his chest and stood. "Do we need to go run interference?"

"It's possible; there are dawn elves on their way here from

the high elves, and Shelly is with them." My stride lengthened with the beginning of my explanation of the situation and ended with the last word as I broke through the door to the dazzling sunlight.

It had only been a day since the birth of this new race, how had they gotten here so fast?

The others joined me in the daylight, Balmur muttering, "What do we need to do?"

"Find them and guide them here," I ordered the others. "Mae, Vrawn, if the two of you would prepare the townsfolk and guards for this, it would be a great help. James, Balmur, and Bokaj, you guys help me search the woods. Keep constant comms with each other and note directions; if you see anything, you say something."

Jaken stepped forward and put a hand to his armored chest. "I'll go get Willem and Sam to help the transition. Where will you be?"

"Good man." I raised the raven toward my face. "Shellica, we're coming to find you. Watch for me or one of the boys. Balmur, James, and Bokaj will be out looking for all of you. Watch the skies for a dragon."

The raven fluttered away, and I looked at my friends. "Time to introduce you all to my dragon form."

I focused on the dragons that I had claimed and chose green, then moved away from the others just before I shifted in a glimmer of golden light and energy.

I knew I was larger now, easily rivaling Ampharia in size, but my scaled body was completely black, with the golden dots of light like the same that decorated my fur. But when I glanced down, the light hit my scales, and an emerald tint caught my gaze. So my animal form would be different, but the green still showed, with the exception of my green and purple metal arm. Good. And not so good. People would know that this was me and not a real dragon.

Damn.

NOTIFICATION!

Dragons are beings of extreme intelligence and vocal renown, capable of speaking multiple tongues, meaning so can you!

"This is excellent," I observed out loud, my voice much deeper than normal.

"You are beautiful," Maebe spoke in an awed tone. The others seemed gob smacked.

"Don't stand there—move!" I ordered, growling subconsciously.

"I love it when he takes command like that," Vrawn muttered to Maebe as they rushed away.

"Oh, he has his moments," the Fae Queen purred back.

The raven flew onto my shoulder, and I heard Shellica's surprised reply, "A dragon?!"

I chuckled and leapt into the air as the other members of the party took off to their roles.

It felt so odd to maintain flight with separate appendages like my large wings, but to the dragon, it was natural.

Druid, a light voice that reminded me of Ampharia's, the dragon's instincts that were at my command as a primal warrior, reached out to my mind in a sort of metaphysical nod. *You fly well enough for one so unused to our majesty.*

"Thank you?" I raised a ridged eyebrow and scanned the ground below me. Nothing to see as of yet.

I flew for a few moments when I heard Bokaj reach out with his earring. *T' and I found them. I'm gonna shoot an arrow into the sky.*

I noted the trajectory of an arrow arcing into the sky off to my left and pushed my wings harder. My dragon form was definitely large and strong, but fast it was not.

Speak for yourself druid, the dragon's instincts seethed inside my mind. *You are still unskilled, and I will not allow you to besmirch my kin so. Just as you soar with lesser wings, fumbling and falling from the sky as a newborn, so too do you fly on newborn wings, now. I will guide you, and you will learn to be as I demand. Is this clear?*

I snorted and rolled my eyes in time for my right wing to

snap inward, sending me careening toward the ground in a barrel roll.

You will learn one way or another, the hissing instinct insisted.

I hit the ground and several trees, unable to change form until I came to a complete stop, the instinct laughing with contempt in her voice.

A quarter of my health was gone when I came to my senses in fox-man form with a groan.

"Hell of a way to greet some weary travelers, lad." A mildly cultured observation from Shellica made my blood stop pulsing through my body for a moment.

I opened my eyes and lifted my head to see her squatting down to look at me. Several of her teeth had been replaced and her grin was full at last. Her wrinkled visage was a sight for sore eyes, but she had this way of getting to me in a manner that no one else seemed to.

Loose strands of her gray hair fluttered in front of her bright green eyes as she offered me a hand up.

"Good to see you again, shitty granny."

"I have missed you too." She let me fall and cackled as I landed back on the ground with a grunt of frustration.

I got up and dusted myself off, glancing behind her to find thirty scared-looking people, some of whom recognized me, the others did not.

"They all came from the high elves?" Bokaj asked as Tmont padded through them, greatly improving morale as she received pats and scratches from the people there.

"Not all of us," one of the elves spoke, his gravelly voice familiar, but when I looked at him, he just smiled. "We did not know each other long, but I do wear a new face. It is I, Zell, Questis' elder brother."

I blinked at the shaggy-haired man. Like the others, his hair and body had changed to golden, sun-kissed skin and lighter hair ranging from purple and orange to gray and white on some heads. But he looked younger now and was almost unrecogniz-able save for the silver of his gaze.

"It's good to see you, Zell!" I rushed over to give him a hug that he was *not* prepared for.

"Quite." He attempted a smile but failed miserably somewhere around a lesser frown that showed his perfect teeth. "Some of them came from where we had teleported to, a small village to the south of here that I had grown fond of in my travels as a boy."

"You traveled?" Bokaj asked with a raised eyebrow.

"I did much as a child." Zell sniffed and went back to being quiet.

"Well, at any rate, let's get you all back to the village, yeah?" I nodded to the others and motioned behind me. There were children among the group, those I offered to carry on my back and shoulders if needed as a saber tooth tiger. I padded ahead of the group with my other friends swiftly making their way to us.

We cleared the forest fifteen minutes later to see Jaken standing with the gates and guards, the doors to the village open to all.

"Welcome to your new home, everybody!" The paladin called to us as Sam and Willem jogged forward out of the crowd.

Both human men helped to welcome the villagers to their new abodes, which really had only been tents, but food and water came and went to ensure that everyone was taken care of properly.

"How come you're here and Questis isn't?" I cornered Shellica as she ate her fill of food that Willem's chef had thrown together rapidly and brought to the tent.

"Questis had things to run back with his people and wished to have someone care for his brother," Shellica explained patiently. "Someone he trusts."

"Ah, so he asked his girlfriend to take care of his brother then?" She blustered and flushed, throwing a fist my way with a scowling snarl. "I knew it!"

She looked around furiously. "Tell *no one* Zekiel Erebos, or I swear upon the Mountain I'll hang your tails from my neck, I will."

"You're already a pain in my ass, Shellica; I don't need you trying to crawl into me too." My grin only widened as she rolled her eyes. "An elf and a dwarf—*quite* the scandal. Don't worry, I love it."

She eyed me funnily, her frown lessening as she glared. "Why?"

"Shellica, you likely know me better than anyone, but I would like to level with you." I sat next to her, my gaze off into the distance, watching as the people of Sunrise introduced themselves to the new residents. Children ran, playing with each other while screaming and laughing. Adults spoke in friendly tones. So many people mixing with each other.

"We're not from here, my friends and I."

She nodded sagely, likely knowing since her god Fainne had known we were coming, what we were. "And while here, I found something so precious that I couldn't pass it up. Sorry, several somethings."

"Aye, the bird, and your friends." She smiled and patted my leg affectionately with her small hand.

I watched as Maebe stepped into a ring of children and raised her arms, making snow blast out at them so they would run and giggle from her.

"And her." I reached out and took Shellica's hand with my left. "And you. I'm not goin' soft on you, but I look at you like a… mother. And with that being said, there are some people I would like to introduce you to."

"Well, I already know the Fae Queen Maebe, lad." That made Maebe pause and turn toward us, so I waved her over. She frowned but left the children with a slight bow and another blast of snow.

"Shellica Lighthand." I reached out to Maebe, and she took my right hand without thought. "I would like to formally introduce Queen Maebe, the Empress of all things Dark and Cold, leader of the Unseelie Fae and my lady wife."

Maebe reached out with her free hand to touch Shellica's shoulder, just to the left of her still-dropped jaw. "Hello, lady Shellica, my husband has told me much of you and your ministrations to his education."

She stammered for a second before finally managing a meager, "Hello, dearie."

"Do you need me further, Zeke?" She gave me the look that said everything I needed to know to make me shake my head. "I will see you shortly then."

"You?" She pointed from me to Maebe. "and *her?!*"

"Which is why I believe that if you truly care for him, it'll be okay." She nodded as I spoke, looking out into the crowd. "There's one more person I need to introduce you to. Rather, three people."

She looked at me in shock, and I laughed at her. "Some of them can wait, but two can't."

"Rowland!" I barked, and the Dwarven man stopped inspecting a weapon and handed it back to its owner. "Thogan, you too!"

"Why're ye yellin', lad?" Thogan's gravelly tone from behind me made me jump slightly.

"Fuck me!" I growled and rounded on him. "You're a damned dwarf, stop being so sneaky! Thogan, this is Shellica Lighthand. Shellica, Thogan Swiftaxe, Maebe's champion."

"I thought you all were her champions?" She looked at me curiously, then looked to Thogan, and her eyes rolled back in her head, her body buckling slightly. I stepped closer and grabbed her by the shoulders, lifting her back to her feet with a small, but brutally jarring shake. You know, totally not revenge for throwing hundreds of items into a magical furnace after I worked my ass off on them.

No clue what you're talking about.

"Don't be frettin' lassie." Thogan took her hand and stood her up out of my vengeful grasp. "Been some time, but the hammer falls."

"A... and rises again." Shellica all but whispered back,

taking in the dwarf she ogled. "One of the first dwarves. Here. *Alive*."

"I been with Her Highness' family for nigh on fourteen hunnerd years." He clapped his hands excitedly. "I hold no doubt that me clan may not survive as it was, but I do hold out hope that our people thrive."

"Aye, we do." Her shoulders fell, her face somber and suddenly weary. "But we are fractured. Clans roam the lands, and not all live under the earth as they did."

"Ours be a society who don't hide." Thogan nodded, clearly unbothered by the news. "We were meant to spread news of the Way. Though even in my time, there were those what gave us no end o' gripin' for it. These things happen. So long as our people prosper, I can be happy."

"Then, I look forward to hosting you, Thogan Swiftaxe." She took her hands and placed them on his shoulders before whipping her head into his with a resounding crack of skulls.

Thogan simply smiled and nodded his appreciation to her as Rowland stepped over to us at last. "What be goin' on, Zeke? There's weapons here what I can't see the like of round these parts!"

"Rowland, this is Vilmas' clan head, Shellica Lighthand." He blanched at the introduction. "Shellica, this is Rowland. He's the smith here in Sunrise, and he's a good friend to myself and the others. His weapons have saved lives."

"He be studyin' the old ways of smithin' with me as well." Thogan clapped the younger dwarf on the shoulder and grinned. "Right keen mind, this one."

"I can imagine you're not wasting time on the lad by the look of him and some of the armor and weapons I've seen that the boys carried." Shellica's genuine smile was heartening as she held out her hand for Rowland to take, even as her normal cultured way of speaking fell away. "Though he be a might bit on the weak lookin' side for a dwarf I s'pose he'd be decent at swingin' a hammer for hours on end."

I snorted.

"Well, I'd be givin' ye a hug, but I fear I'd snap ye in half, Mountain preserve ye." Rowland started, and Shellica paused her laughing to see which way the younger dwarf would take the jab. "Ye don't look like you're out of the stone for too much longer."

Thogan and I hollered with laughter for several moments until Shellica clapped Rowland on the shoulder affectionately. "Good sense of humor, too!"

"Aye, I be thinkin' so." Rowland grinned, then looked about nervously. "Lady Shellica, I heared a great deal about ye from Vilmas, an' I feel honored to ask ye this question."

"What question, lad?" Shellica turned sharp eyes on him.

"I've been courting Vilmas for a wee amount o' time an' I wanted to approach ye an' ask fer her hand." Rowland made a motion for Shellica to wait. "Afore ye give me yer answer, know that I promised meself to her, an' tha' I'd sooner stop smithin' than hurt her. I swear on me beard an' swingin' arm."

"You swore this oath before a witness and the concerned party?" Shellica's cautious tone surprised me.

"He swore it before me," I interjected on Rowland's behalf. "While he's a bit rough around the edges, he's as honorable and kind as he is hairy. He took in a small human child as his own and raised her to adulthood. Taught her the Way and to craft with her hands as his god would expect all his children to do. Rowland is a great man and a better smith."

"I have seen the way that Vilmas pines for him," Vrawn spoke over my head, Shellica's eyes widening. "As her friend, she tells me a great deal, and any time she brings this man up, her eyes sparkle, and she blushes deeply."

Shellica marched over to stand in front of me, looking up at Vrawn with an intensity I hadn't seen before. She stopped, her chest just about to crash into my hip as she glared up.

"And who be you?" Shellica growled up at Vrawn. I went to answer for her, but she shoved me aside so I could no longer stand between them.

"I am Vrawn, and I claim Vilmas as a beloved friend,"

Vrawn answered calmly. "I will protect her and her interests as best as I can. She has told me of you, Shellica Lighthand. She looks up to you, admires your craft, and your bravery. You are all that she aspires to be."

"Honeyed words mean naught to me, lass." Shellica snorted, but she leaned back a second later. "She really calls you friend?"

"She does," I confirmed, and both women shot me a look. "Hey look, she's my friend too goddamnit. Hell, more than that, and I'm tired of this whole pissing match between the women in my life. Vrawn's been her friend since she first stepped *foot* in this village, and that friendship stands taller than the hatred I know most Orcs and dwarves have for each other. Okay?"

"Do you have any idea how much I *don't* care about racial tensions, lad?" Shellica actually punched me as hard as she could in the gut, barely registering for me, though the act itself hurt my pride. "My *own* people feared my clan up until but a short time ago. You think I hold a grudge against someone I never met? How little do you think of your dear ol' dwarven ma?"

I rolled my eyes, Vrawn giggling at my expense made me smile though, and I suddenly found it impossible to glare at the old woman. Though she did keep smacking the shit out of my left arm saying something about, "...respect your elders you wee little shite. Answer for me? Put words in my mouth. Ought to have thrown *you* in the furnace. Don't think I don't know why you were so rough, just now. I'll beat your gob if you touch me like that again."

I took her little tirade in stride with a smile, and she just stomped on my foot. That actually hurt for some reason, making me grunt and pull the limb up to me, hobbling away.

"I take it you were taken aback that Vilmas was able to find a friend, let alone one so vastly different from her?" Vrawn smiled down at a nodding Shellica then looked at me. "I like her."

"And I you, sweet child." Shellica patted Vrawn's large hand affectionately before turning back to Rowland. "I respect you for following the old ways, but with my clan, all that matters is their happiness. If Vilmas says yes to you, then you are welcome to marry her. Tell me, what of your clan?"

Rowland blinked at the question and puffed his chest out a bit. "I be clanless."

That took me a bit by surprise. "What about Craglim, and your family?"

"They be a clan." He frowned. "They been meanin' to induct me in when I reached grandmaster rankin' in smithin', but when I chose to teach me skill to those not o' the stone, they cast me out an' I have no family, now."

"*Bullshit!*" I frothed, blood rushing into my face and ears. "Where is that little bastard, I'll beat their whole clan's asses and hang them by their beards!"

"Zeke!" Rowland snapped, his face as red as mine felt, and his hands balled at his sides. "It were their choice to waste what the Mountain taught, not mine. They've lost their Way, lad. An' I'll not make it worse. Not me, nor mine. Aye?"

I grumbled vehemently, and he stomped his way over to me, grasping my shirt and pulling me down. "Not me, *nor mine.* Aye?"

"Fine, but if I see that little bastard, he's mine." I harrumphed as hard as I could, feeling a pat on my elbow from the smaller man.

"No clan?" Thogan grumbled with a frown. "I reckon you could join my clan then, lad."

"Clan Swiftaxe?" Rowland looked shocked.

"It's been dead long enough." Thogan nodded. "We'll share a great many things an' one o' 'em bein' the ancient tradition o' the everyday dwarf. Warrior, creator, thinker, an' drinker. We hold to the tradition tha' a dwarf should be able to do it all. If ye can do tha', I'll take ye in, seein' as though I be the only one left o' me clan, that makes me the head, and this be my choice."

"I reckon I could do tha'." Rowland shook the other dwarf's hand, and they hugged once fiercely. "But why not sooner?"

"Because I needed to know that I weren't poachin' ye from another who know'd ye better." Thogan slapped the younger dwarf on the shoulder affectionately. "Ye been a good friend, lad. I think'd long an' hard 'bout what it would be like to bring me clan back. It'll be long, harder than me head an' gut and take patience, but if ye'll stand with me, we will do it. Together."

"Then, I would be honored." Rowland looked as though a tear had been brought to his eyes, but he sniffed and just hugged Thogan all the more fiercely.

"Then Rowland of clan Swiftaxe, I Shellica Lighthand extend to you my blessing to ask your heart's desire of Vilmas." Shellica put a closed fist over her navel, bowing slightly at the waist. "I ask that you respect her decision no matter what it is. On your clan's honor?"

"On his clan's honor, and my beard," Thogan confirmed gravely, mirroring the movement.

"Then I guess the only question is, where do you want to pop the question?" I blurted before I could stop myself.

"She's a special lass." Rowland grinned and ran a hand through his beard where there was nothing holding the hair. "Somewhere near too many people will spook her. Somewhere too unfamiliar will spook her, though she has taken to a certain tree in the wood near me smithy. I think I'll stay there with her tonight to ask."

"How do you know that she wouldn't like to come home?" Shellica raised an eyebrow.

"Because Xiphyre has her workin' on projects that will keep her here." Rowland's grin faded a little, then he looked my way. "An' she expressed wantin' to stay in the village when Vrawn said that she would be goin' with Zeke on his next adventure."

The large woman's fingers wrapped through mine, and Shellica raked me with a stern look that I ignored.

"I wish you luck, Rowland." I patted him on the shoulder, and we turned to leave, Vrawn and I, but I turned to address

Thogan and Shellica first. "We will be leaving near the inn here in about an hour or so. See you there!"

We turned to walk away, and after a few moments, the silence had lasted long enough. Then I realized why it had been silent.

Vilmas stood in the open flap of the tent, her eyes locked on all of us, her gaze searching the crowd until she saw Shellica standing near Rowland. "Lady Shellica!" Her hands tightened at her waist, wringing her wrists absently before she took a steadying breath, then heaved it out of her body. "I have something I would like to say to you. My friends, please stay."

Vrawn left my side instantly for her friend's, and I couldn't blame her. Vilmas looked pale but determined in a way I had only seen when she was haggling prices with a would-be cheat over some mithril.

"Vilmas! Lass, we were just talking about you!" She beamed and stepped toward the other woman with a smile, and her arms open wide for her.

"I heard," Vilmas stated plainly, though her normally measured speech was gone and replaced by a brogue almost like Rowland and Thogan's. "I were nearby an' I heard some o' the conversation, me name, an' other things. Look—I donnae care tha' Rowland be clanless. He be the most honorable, respectable, and respectful dwarf I ever did lay eyes on. He's been nothin' but good to me, an' I know'd his intentions from the start—"

"Vilmas, it's—" A powerful glare from Vrawn and Shellica stopped my attempted explanation cold, my heart thudding wildly. I knew if I spoke again, I would leave unconscious, so I shut up.

"He be a good man, and I love him." Her cheeks burned as red as lava, her blue dress looking like ice against her chest that glowed red as well. She looked over at Rowland and stomped forward, his speechless shock only growing as she grasped his face and pulled him into a kiss so strong that he almost lost his footing after leaning forward. She stopped kissing him and turned her gaze to Shellica as she panted, catching her breath.

"This is how you feel?" Shellica crossed her arms slowly and carefully.

"Aye!" Vilmas said breathlessly. She turned and reached into her pocket before taking a knee in front of all of us. Audible gasps around the room broke the silence as she opened the small chest in her hands. "Rowland, smith o' Sunrise an' forger o' me bravery, will ye do me the honor o' makin' me an honest woman? Will ye walk yer Way with me as I step to ye along me own path?"

Rowland's mouth opened and shut slowly for a few tense moments, the golden ring in her hands large enough to easily fit his meaty fingers, a stone set where the gemstone would normally be.

In answer, Rowland closed his eyes and lifted his head almost as if he couldn't stand to look at her anymore, Vilmas' eyes grew wide in fright. He reached into his own pocket and hung his head, eyes still closed as he knelt down on one knee before her. He opened the chest and presented a similar ring, though much more intricately carved with runes and engravings.

"Vilmas, temperer of me fire an' enchanter o' me heart, will ye do me the honor o' makin' me the happiest, most blessed dwarf under the Mountain? Will ye walk yer Way with me as I step to ye along me own path?"

He opened his eyes, tears falling into his beard as a smile graced both of their faces. Neither of them said anything for a moment, but a cleared throat captured all of us from the beautiful moment and brought us back to the present. Shellica tapped her foot impatiently before she threw her arms apart and bellowed, "Would one of ye moonstone-struck fools say 'aye' already?"

They flinched and turned back to each other and in unison, spoke the words that bound them together, "Aye."

The crowd burst into cheers, Vrawn was so excited that she

lifted both of them up into her arms and hugged them until we had to drag them out of her joyful grasp. We celebrated with pats on the back and kind words of luck for a solid half an hour.

Shellica shook her head, and I had to approach her as she stood to the side of the festivities staring sadly into the throng. "What's wrong?"

She glanced up at me and nodded toward Vilams and Thogan, who was explaining the situation to her, her face growing more and more red by the sentence. "She was willing to leave the clan and her family, outcast if I so willed it, to be with him. She stood up to me in front of all these people and risked her own name among the clan so that she could find her happiness."

I stared down at her, horrified that this happy moment could have been a horrible thing if she were a lesser person, but she wasn't, and I knew it from her next statement as she grinned to herself. "Sending her off with you was the best choice I ever made. I think I learned something from my once-shy apprentice today. I'll be seeing you at the tavern in half an hour then, lad. Get to going."

She dismissed me and went off to console a tearful Vilmas, Vrawn noting that I was heading toward the door as I looked to her.

"That was an interesting conversation," Vrawn observed aloud as we stepped away.

The village wasn't so much a blur around us as it was less interesting with her around.

"Well, that does happen around dwarves." I chuckled as I remembered all the examples of conversational prowess the dwarves gave me over my time here. Some were amazing. Others? "At least she didn't insult you, and Vilmas will have a real chance at happiness, now."

"I heard that was how they show affection." Vrawn looked alarmed. "Has Vilmas been calling me a pasty, puke-skinned, beefcake just to be mean?"

"That much?" I raised an eyebrow, and she nodded. "It's how they show affection, but there's a good way to know a *true* insult, and she didn't offer one. Though Shellica is a weird one, she's a good person, and I love her like a... like a mother or grandmother since she's so damned old."

I frowned. Why was that so hard to say? Was it the issues that I had with my own family?

I could dwell on that later.

"I can understand that being important." Vrawn pulled me close to her, my steps shifting mid-stride to match hers. "Is this awkward for you?"

"Not particularly, no. Why?"

"You seem uncomfortable." She took her hand from mine but stayed along her own walking path. "And while you were gone, I didn't hear from you."

I went to respond, but she hushed me with a motion of her hand. "Our queen told me what happened, and I can understand that you were stretched thin with training and running for your lives."

I fell silent and let her speak. She deserved to be able to speak her mind.

"But in all of that time, a simple hello would have been better than wondering if you and the people I care about were dead or not." Her face was stoic, free of all emotion, but it was that stillness and perfect bearing that let me know something was truly wrong.

"You're right," I admitted softly, upset with myself for screwing up like that. "I wouldn't have done the same thing to Maebe, even with the time difference between the planes. There's no excuse I can give you. No reason I can think of to try and fool you into thinking that I wasn't an idiot too self-absorbed to care about how you might feel. I wasn't thinking, Vrawn."

I stopped walking and turned to face her, her stride carrying her a little further away from me, where she stopped and watched me passively.

"The only thing I can think to do is beg your forgiveness and hope that I can have an opportunity to prove to you that you do matter to Mae and to me."

"I know that I matter to her." Vrawn crossed her arms across her stomach and took a more relaxed stance. "She was the one who had been kind enough to speak to me when she could, how she could."

She sighed and stepped closer to me, completely invading my personal space but I was fine with that. She had a right to hurt. A right to be angry.

"I know I matter to her, Zeke." She pressed her soft lips to my forehead, carefully looking me right in the eyes after. "What I need to know is if I matter to you. I've tried to fight how I felt, this rising hurt and just ignore it because I thought that it was all right. That it *should* have been all right. I just can't anymore."

She stepped away, turning to stride off toward the tavern with a call to me from over her shoulder, "I'll see you in a while."

CHAPTER THREE

The time passed swiftly as I took care of Kayda and Bea, who was *not* having my shit today.

Her green and gray scales almost glowing in the daylight, her brown left eye and the right crimson, with both of them glaring at me.

Hungry and mad! She snarled at me once more as she watched the people around us skirt the area again. The first person to try to pet her had—thankfully—been me. Her snapping at my fingers had resulted in my smacking her snout and reprimanding her, but she wasn't having it.

Finally, I fed her something that I could find from the kitchen in Willem's tavern and got her back into the collar that encircled my throat and sighed with relief. What a dick.

That did make me wonder, the last time she had been docile and obedient. Now, she was acting angry, and her eye was red. Her personality was changing and being affected by the mutation obtained from the chimera.

Shit.

That left her with, what, four potential personality types to cycle through at who knew when? That wasn't going to be fun to deal with. But she had earned my love, that was for certain, and I wasn't going to abandon her here.

Kayda snapped up bits of meat that I tossed her absent-mindedly as the conversations from earlier played through my head. The things I should have said or done coming to mind, then filtering out as if they had never come because they were useless, now.

"Ah, there you are!" Thogan grinned as I glanced up at him from where I was. Kayda flapped her way toward him in parrot form, and he caught her easily on his shoulder. "Still getting used to that. Here, this is from Xiphyre. A gift for Yohsuke."

The dwarf tossed me a cloak that weighed next to nothing, and the stats blasted into my vision.

Living Night's Shroud

Protects the wearer from the light of day for a small mana cost. Cursed: once put on, the wearer must bear this shroud until they die.

There is something to be said for what goes bump in the night. But little is said about what sticks with those who bump first.

Shroud woven by Adept weaver Sindri Vex and enchanted by Xiphyre.

That was still weird. My hand had shown the same thing. What was Xiphyre's enchanting level? He was obviously high enough to be a grandmaster. Was there something above even that?

"Thogan, what are you and Xiphyre?"

Thogan cocked his head to the side a moment before answering, "Well, I be a proper dwarf, handsome as they come I reckon, and him a fluttery shite—why?"

I had to laugh, Xiphyre would likely beat the dwarf's ass for saying that.

"No, I meant that any time I see items either of you have made or enchanted, all it shows is your name." He eyed me carefully before his gaze turned to the area around us. We were still alone for now, and that was enough for him, I guessed.

He stepped closer with Kayda contentedly resting on his shoulder to speak in a low tone, "We be higher than grandmaster. Centuries o' work put in to levelin' an' honin' our skills. I reckon I may be one of the few livin' smiths of legendary rank in this plane o' existence. And Xi? He be well past legendary in enchanting. Though he hates what it makes him do."

"The curse?" I asked as an example, and he nodded gravely.

"If he works with anythin' but the finest materials, his magic can pervade it." He tried to find the right words, struggling with the idea, then snapped his fingers and pointed excitedly toward me. "He telled me tha' if it be less than master quality, there be a curse effect and above, a heavy toll. It be a double-edged sword. Powerful enchanting for a high price."

"That makes sense, but how can so few people know about the legendary rank?"

He pulled out a long pipe and lit it with a match, pulling on it in thought before answering, "Reckon it has to do with loss of ancestral knowledge. See, we dwarves be smithin' almost all our lives if it be our callin', but the old legends choose who they passed their know-how to, carefully. I learned through sheer stubborn will an' needin' to be of use an' close to me god. When I were a wee lad, the legends were few then, as well, but took students less and less because they grew vain. Took away from their craft and 'polluted' the potential of the next generation."

I frowned. That was like a teacher telling kids to do something in class like teach themselves. Without guidance, only some would learn, but the majority would stumble and fall.

"Never understood it meself, but I was a fighter first." He patted the large axe at his back and shoulder. "It were only in me time at the forges within the Fae realm when I found meself at home. Though I were still only a master at the time."

"I see. Is this a closely guarded secret, still?"

Thogan thought, and as he continued to do so, other voices rose around us. People were coming.

Finally, he nodded at me once, and I understood that I was to keep this to myself, for now.

The boys had all come to stand nearby, but I passed James the shroud for Yohsuke. "Go wake that lazy bastard up."

He chuckled and ran into the tavern to do as I had said while the rest of us waited patiently. Finally, James stepped out of the building with a figure wrapped in living shadow behind him.

"You finally awake, vampire boy?" Jaken called teasingly to the other man.

The figure just flipped him the bird and continued to move forward toward us. "If we're going to go, let's go. This sunlight is painful."

Darkness enveloped where we stood as Maebe joined us with an entourage of children playing around her feet in a circle of joyous cries and energy. Her radiant smile contrasted well against the void-like blackness that burst into existence over our heads.

"I must go now, children, but if you listen well to young Kloee, I will be certain to tell you all more tales of Storm Company's exploits." The children were sad that she was leaving, one little boy brazenly clinging to her leg and refusing to let go for a moment as Maebe eyed him as if he were the most precious thing.

"That's my wife, little man," I called with a playful tone of warning. "I'll keep her safe, don't worry."

He narrowed his eyes at me, and I winked at him with a grin, and he grinned back, his little teeth flashing as he called to the others, "I got to talk to King Zeke! Ha!"

He let Maebe go and scampered away with the other children hot on his heels, calling for him to slow down.

"They really do adore her." Bokaj frowned thoughtfully as he patted Tmont's head.

"And I, them." Maebe's serene, soft smile let me know she was being honest, but there was almost a hint of sadness there. I would have to talk to her later about that.

"Are we ready?" I asked everyone as I took a count of those joining us. Me, Maebe, Vrawn, Jaken, Yoh, James, Bokaj, Balmur, Muu, Thogan, Shellica, Tmont, and Kayda with Bea in my necklace. Well within the limits of my Teleport spell.

Everyone nodded, the ones who had the most experience traveling by this spell's method grabbing hands and motioning for the others to do so as well. Kayda still perched on Thogan's shoulder, and Tmont had crawled into Bokaj's hood where she could hide comfortably.

"Let's do it!" I grinned at the others, their smiles and relaxed glances fixated in my mind as I reached within and focused on where I wanted the spell to take us. The entrance to the city of dwarves, Djurn Forge.

The ebb of my mana accompanied by the customary loss of footing was familiar to me, followed by the also familiar sucking sensation before our feet touched the ground at our destination.

"I hate that!" Thogan spat vehemently as he tugged on his beard.

"You get used to it, dear Thogan." Maebe comforted the dwarf with a soft chuckle and a pat on his shoulder. "It took some of them a while to get used to it, as well."

Three loud bangs on the metallic doors drew my attention to Balmur. He stood back from the wall of metal and put his hands on his hips while waiting.

Three dwarves pushed the door on the right-hand side open, somber and respectfully bowing their heads to Balmur.

"We offer nae the typical greetin' o' those familiar with our ways, but tha' o' humble men in the presence o' heroes." The lead Ironnose guard spoke clearly though his head was bowed still. "Glad be we that ye returned from yer time in the Hells, cousin Balmur. We hear'd o' yer feats o' glory, an' we will hear more this night at the feast. All o' ye—be welcomed as heroes an' dwarves to yer humble home o' Djurn Forge."

Balmur was the first to step over to them, thumping each of them on the backs of their heads so that they would look up at him. He eyed each one, giving a small nod to each, then broke out in a huge grin. "Pretty words from such an ugly gob! Who would have thought you capable of all that?"

The Ironnose standing before him reared up and belted out a peel of laughter so loud I thought the whole of the Great Below would know where we were.

"Oh, lad, yer well along the Way, be ye." The guard sniffed and used his red beard to wipe away the tears flowing from his eyes before he wrapped Balmur in a great hug. The other two dwarves moving out and pulling members of the party into great bear hugs.

The one who grasped me by the stomach and pulled me close muttered, "Welcome home, brother." I clapped him on the shoulder, and all three dwarves found Thogan, who stood silently, still as stone—almost as if in shock.

"Cousin?" The leader of the guards called back, "Be this a prank?"

"Nope!" Balmur rushed over to stand next to Thogan and slapped the shit out of the side of his face to make him blink and shake his head. "This is Thogan Swiftaxe, clan leader of the Swiftaxe clan and an ancient dwarf from the Mountain himself."

Shellica put a hand on Thogan's shoulder. "It be true, lads."

The three dwarves took a knee before Thogan, his surprise evident, and all three of them spoke in unison, "Long has yer path taken ye away from us, but the Way be long and windin'. Let we who walk together welcome ye back to the path among yer kin, Thogan Swiftaxe."

They looked up at him, and the leader offered, "The hammer falls."

Thogan, stricken with tears flooding from his eyes bellowed, "and rises again!" He leaped forward and pulled each of the younger dwarves into a fierce hug that lasted almost uncomfortably long for us, but we waited. This was his first time being surrounded by his kith and kin in centuries. Dwarves weren't solitary people—they needed their clan and others to be okay.

And Thogan would finally be okay, it seemed.

"Come on, lad." Shellica gently pried the dwarves apart with a soft touch and caress to Thogan's back. "There are a lot of dwarves here who need to see their ancestor. Let these ones get back to their duties, and we will see them tonight."

Thogan used his beard to wipe away his tears and blew his nose into a handkerchief. "Aye, I thank ye lads, I truly do."

"It be we who are grateful, for we have regained so much at the hands of these lads here and their deeds." The lead Ironnose sighed, then cut to attention, his right fist crossing his beard and resting over his heart. "When I raise a tankard, I raise it to ye, me and mine are with ye lads. I'll be singin' yer praises longer'n anyone, don' ye be doubtin'."

I grinned at him and winked. "We welcome the love, but you be sure to stay safe, okay?"

"Not shite out here what could threaten an Ironnose, lad!" One of the other guards guffawed good-naturedly.

"Get ye inside now, the lot of ye." The last dwarf motioned toward the door. "What a sight we be, buncha blubberin' belles the lot of us. Me wife finds out, she'll be puttin' bows in me beard and callin' our kids home ta help!"

Maebe stopped to look at the dwarf, leaning down a little to look him deep in his eyes. "I wish to show my respect in the dwarven manner."

The Ironnose seemed taken aback but curious, so he nodded his head so that she would know to continue.

"I think you'd look prettier with the bows, but only if they hid the majority of your face."

Silence fell over all of us, then the other two Ironnoses burst into fits of laughter that made them double over as they relentlessly beat on the other dwarf's shoulders as he snorted and nodded his head.

"That were a great greetin' Majesty," Thogan rumbled proudly as he collected Maebe from in front of the other dwarves.

"Balmur taught me the way of the dwarves, with young Fainnir to assist him, while we were in the Great Below and the dungeon," Maebe explained as she walked. "It was a wonderful learning experience. I find that I was remiss in not asking you more about your culture before, Thogan. I apologize."

"Donae fret, Majesty, I likely would have been sad knowin' I could talk of 'em but nae see 'em."

"Get ready everyone, we will likely be mobbed by people in here if those guys were anything to go off." Yohsuke warned the rest of us.

Djurn Forge was not what I remembered, and I was almost worried that we had been trapped. The streets were almost barren. No one called out wares, no one walking except for those who were going into homes or shops.

I turned back to the Ironnoses, who still teased their friend and asked, "What's going on?"

They seemed confused until Balmur pointed to the streets, and one of them perked up. "Oh! Aye! They all be preparin' for tonight. Not a one family in this whole city is gonna let any o' ye be drinkin' yer own mead or eatin' yer own food. Get ye to yer clan, lads. We will feast an' party like ye never seed tonight!"

We chuckled and meandered through the quiet streets of Djurn Forge. The only thing that I could hear was a distant thrumming of the true heart of the people here. The echoing sound of hammering somewhere off in the distance.

Maebe and Vrawn found themselves drawn to many of the different shops and stands that had been abandoned for the celebration, vowing to come back and check out the wares.

Yohsuke dropped his shadow shroud and revealed his gray skin tone, not because he was a vampire, but because he had chosen an abomination elf as his avatar's race. A mix between a drow and high elf with all of the disdain both could manage for the other aimed at it. His yellow eyes seemed sharper than normal, and his shaggy white hair a little more unkempt than his usual self, as well.

You hungry? I asked him telepathically through our earrings.

He sighed, nodded, and looked my way. *Is it that easy to tell?*

You have the same kind of predatory look I imagine I may have when I'm pissed off, and the Wolf was threatening to take over.

I'll need to feed soon, was all he would say after that.

We would find him something. Well, some*one* and soon, if not one of us. Not me, though, my blood would kill him with the lycanthropy running through it.

But any of the others would be able to bleed in a cup for him.

After walking a little while longer, we made it to the fenced-in, squat buildings and training grounds belonging to the Mugfist clan. Silence was no longer all that we heard, as there were dwarves outside in the yard who fought furiously with each other.

Axes flashed in the torchlight, dotting the walls of the buildings and outside of the training grounds. Dwarves wearing only their breeches and weapon belts fought inside a circle of equally dressed bodies as a thrumming sound of low voices and the rhythm of feet falling in time.

"What the Hells is going on over here?" I called, shoving my way through the bodies before me. Inside the circle, I found Brawnwynn and Farnik in the middle of a fight, both of them bloodied and cut. Farnik's stubble looking a little more toward a beard than it had days ago.

Brawnwynn and Farnik fought on, but a dwarf to my left took pity on me and answered, "It be a challenge for the right to be head o' the clan. Brawnwynn thinks it be time for Farnik to step down so that he can be with Gerty. Farnik says he can do both. An' right now, no one better be interferin'.'"

"Thank you." The others piled in around me, and we watched together as father and son fought for the fate of the clan.

Farnik and Brawnwynn each held only one axe, eyeing each other from twenty paces away. Both of them huffed and puffed, their bodies covered in cuts, welts, and bruises. Farnik sported a slowly swelling cut above his right eye, bleeding steadily, and

Brawny had a gash under his ribs that made me wince when he moved.

Neither dwarf looked anywhere close to giving up.

Brawnwynn took the fight to Farnik, his axe held low in his left hand with a savage expression of rage on his face.

Farnik leaned forward, then sprinted toward his son with his axe in his right hand. When they had five feet left, Brawny's axe sliced up, and Farnik dropped into a slide with the beard of his axe snapping out around his son's left leg. When metal met flesh and cloth, Farnik yanked with a grunt, and Brawnwynn fell forward onto his face.

In a flash, Farnik held his son's leg in a lock between his own with his axe poised under the younger dwarf's beard.

"Under the eyes o' the Mountain, our brothers an' the forefathers within the stone, you have been found unworthy for the right to rule Brawnwynn Mugfist." Farnik growled with his axe still dangerously close to Brawnwynn's throat. "I rule here, this family of strong men and women. Your Way is guided by my honor and mine by your commitment to this clan. Will you stand with us and protect Djurn Forge, or will you walk your own path?"

Brawnwynn grunted with pain and frustration. "I will never betray me clan, da. I stand with clan Mugfist above all else, second only to the city. I do swear on me honor."

Farnik nodded once, releasing his son's leg and standing with a hearty grunt of effort.

He looked to the crowd around him, raising his arms in challenge as he shouted, "Be there anyone else among ye here today dwarf enough to stand to his convictions who thinks me unfit to lead this clan? If ye do, get ye in here an' take yer lumps!"

I found myself laughing harder than I had in a while, as Farnik whipped around and glared. He stepped closer swiftly, then realized who was laughing.

"Hail, Storm Company!" Farnik grinned, and the dwarves

around us turned and cheered rabidly. "Our brothers in arms and our cousin, home at last!"

"I see we stepped in at a rough time, Farnik." Jaken stepped forward and cast a mass healing spell on the area, catching both Farnik and Brawny in it. Their wounds almost melted away under the golden light. "You want another go at the kid?"

"Bah, he learned his lesson, aye?" Farnik looked back to see his son grinning, and a shake of his head signaled he was good. "Well, he will eventually then. For now, we get ready to celebrate, but it seems we have guests with us this day. Tell us, lads, who be with ye?"

Jaken turned and motioned for the ladies to step up first. "Clan Mugfist, this is someone with whom some of you may be familiar, we have our Lady Darkest and Queen of the Unseelie Court, Maebe. Next, we have the lovely lady in green who could likely rip someone's head off and look pretty doin' it, that would be our lieutenant of the guard of Sunrise Village, Vrawn."

Both women cut a nice, strong figure as they smiled at everyone. To my pleasure, not a single utterance of the words "elf" or "orc" could be heard.

"It is a pleasure to meet members of my husband's clan." Maebe bowed her head politely, but that was when shit hit the fan.

Or, rather, the dwarves had found an in.

"One o' ours be courtin' royalty?" One loud bellow of surprise called over the crowd. "He can barely lift an axe an' he has such a lady ta call his own?"

I snarled and paced toward the crowd. "Which of you little fuckers thinks I can't hold an axe?" It was really all for show, but the crowd moved forward en masse and started to poke and prod at me with fingers and jabs to the gut.

"Think ye'self too good for a proper dwarven lass then, ye wee shite?" One of them called playfully. "Bold thought for a beardless gutter welp like ye'self!"

The boys waded in, and a brawl almost broke out when

someone whistled and took our attention. I turned from the red-bearded dwarf I had lifted from the ground to punch, my fist bunched in his belt as he chuckled heartily, and saw Gerty.

"Lads!" She hollered, and the dwarves broke ranks and filed into squads like a formation. Well, all for the one I held, of course.

She walked down the path, joined by her husband with whom she exchanged a brief nod as she made her way toward us.

"Hey, how're you feeling?" Jaken almost ran up to her but managed to make it a saunter instead. He stopped to look her over, making it easier for me to take in the details I'd been forced to overlook last time.

She had rosy cheeks covered by wafts of long brown hair that framed her stout face even though she had tied it in a tight bun like she'd left those strands loose on purpose. Her black eyes seemed clever as she took in everything around her, her simple clothes giving us a view of the wrought-iron musculature that rivaled some of the men in our company and her clan. The way she moved was purposeful, and almost primal in itself as if each step could lead to an attack if she so willed it. At the back of her waist, poking out on each side perched two axes. Her weapons of choice.

She smiled at Jaken. "I be a'right, Jaken, thank ye fer askin'." She moved to Muu, who looked at her hopefully. "Ye armed me when I had nothin' to offer ye in return. I did nae ferget ye, nor yer weapon. Here."

She reached into her inventory and offered him his hammer back, and he cradled it against his body lovingly while stroking it. She frowned at him before chuckling and shaking her head.

She eyed the rest of us. "I cannae thank the lot o' ye enough fer yer bravery an' service to this clan. I can only hope to repay the kindness ye gived me an' mine."

"What else is family for?" Balmur grinned, his smile seemed almost practiced and frail.

Gerty walked straight up to the Azer dwarf and took him in

her arms, muttering, "I hear'd what ye went through, lad. I understand yer pain. If ye ever need a shoulder or an ear, ye come ta me, aye? On yer beard, now."

Balmur hugged her back, a flash of true pain flickering across his face. "I will, I swear it on my beard."

"Good lad." Gerty pinched his cheek and winked at him before stepping back. "Tonight, my husband and I mean to adopt all of ye into our clan. Now, I be know'n that we had made it clear ye belonged with us, but we mean to make it clear to the world that ye *are* us. And we are ye."

"Does that mean I'm gonna get shorter?" Muu called his question with mock concern. "My brand of handsome doesn't work with being short."

Gerty snorted and laughed as the dwarves in formation eyed him cautiously. Good, their bearing was on point then.

"All it means is tha' each o' ye will be like sons to us, an' for the rest o' yer days, all o' yer lines will be Mugfist, as well, by birth." She took her fist and pounded her chest with it, the dwarves in formation doing the same. "Lady Shellica, I take it ye have no concerns with our plans?"

Shellica shook her head with a smile as she advanced on Gerty. "Not in the slightest, old friend. I knew these lads would be destined for great things, but bringing you back to us was something beyond even my wildest dreams. I'm proud to welcome them."

Shellica and Gerty took each other and cracked their foreheads together loudly before embracing. The hug lasted until both were nearly in tears, such was the joy they felt.

"We have one final guest for you all, for all of the dwarves of Djurn Forge, rather." Bokaj made a motion to Thogan, and the stone-faced dwarf marched his way to the front of our group. He had secreted himself behind all of us as if the love he had been shown earlier had done nothing to quell some of his nervousness at being with his people once more.

If only you could have heard the sound of more than a

hundred dwarven jaws hitting the floor in shock. It was quite thunderous, I swear.

"I am Thogan Swiftaxe, champion o' the Unseelie Court, an' leader o' the re-emergin' clan Swiftaxe." Thogan squared his shoulders as he addressed the dwarves around him. "I am from an era past, an' while I love that our people thrive, I would see that they have the benefit o' the ancestors with them still. Our old ways should not perish, an' through me an' mine, dwarves can continue to flourish as they have. If ye would take me as an ally, I would see that all of ye be treated as well as can be treated. What say ye?"

"I think I speak for all o' me clan when I say that we would be honored to lift our mugs with ye, friend Thogan." Farnik stepped forward, and the dwarves clasped forearms, gripping tightly with grins in place. This time the dwarves couldn't hold their tongues any longer and howled in delight and support.

"Is there anything you lot cannae do?" Brawnwynn muttered as he shoved his way through the dwarves that had flooded the two leaders.

"I can't be ugly," Muu quipped before any of us could answer, eliciting a few snorted chuckles.

"Ye bring back not just the dead, but our history." Brawn-wynn shook his head as he stared out into the clan. "Magic, history, an' me ma. We owe ye everythin'."

"Think nothing of it, man." Jaken grinned at his dwarven brother, and they meandered away to discuss things themselves.

"What time does this shindig take place?" Bokaj called loudly, some of the dwarves turning to look at him. "Tmont is getting hungry, and there are a *lot* of tails here."

The dwarves howled in delight at the joke, and a cold chill swept through me at the thought. "No, seriously, when is it because if she bites me, cat is on the menu."

More laughter rang out, and the dwarves pulled all of us toward the living quarters of the compound. There was much left to prepare, and that included us.

CHAPTER FOUR

Warm water doused my head, and I growled at the dwarves around me. "I asked nicely for you to watch my ears guys."

"Oh donnae fret, Majesty, we were watchin' 'em fer ye." One of the dwarves snorted teasingly, scrubbed my back and lifted my arm.

"Do you really have to wash us?" Balmur muttered almost bashfully. "I can seriously do this on my own."

"Traditional hero's cleansing!" Muu barked pointedly from across the room in his own tub. "It requires the clan to wash the sins and past transgressions of the hero away so that we can be seen as we should be in front of the whole city. All that we need now are rubber duckies and a shower beer and we would really be heroes."

A mug of something amber and delicious smelling found its way into our hands, and he grinned. "Now *that's* service."

"Cleanses the insides too," the dwarf washing the sole of Muu's foot explained, and Muu immediately spat the liquid out. "What'd ye do tha' for?! That's our best mead!"

"Is this going to make me shit myself?" Muu eyed the

dwarf, and the ones around us just muttered murderously before his attendant shouted a negative back. "Oh, okay."

He tilted his head back and drained it in one go, finishing with a loud belch that seemed to go a long way toward calming the dwarves around us.

This room was a simple washing chamber that only had three tubs in it, occupied by Balmur, Muu, and I. The other guys were in another building getting the same VIP treatment, along with Maebe and Thogan. Vrawn opted to spend some time with Gerty and Farnik getting to know the place and learning about what would be going on tonight.

Because they sure as hell weren't telling us anything other than what they thought we needed to know.

I took a small sip of the amber liquid in my cup, the bitterness of what I expected immediately destroyed by a delicious, sweet burn of fruity goodness with a hoppy undertone that I found quite enjoyable. I drank more, the beginnings of a buzz coming on as I finished the cup.

"There, ye be clean now, carefully, hop out, an' we will dry ye off." The wizened dwarf who seemed to be leading the cleanup crew oversaw our cleansing thoroughly, even going so far as to press a wrinkled finger into the fur on my shoulder to assure himself I was completely dry.

"I can't imagine this went as smoothly for everyone else." Balmur smiled at the thought.

"Yeah, I wonder who Yoh threatened to stab." I could imagine the man, a true thoroughbred Texan not enjoying the idea of anyone touching him while he was naked except his wife. "I can almost hear him now."

"Pretty sure that was him, does the phrase, 'touch me again you little fuck, and I'll see that the hand you use goes up your ass' ring any bells?" Muu asked with a smartass look on his face.

Everyone chill the hell out, we have to do this. Jaken groaned.

He tried to touch my junk! Yohsuke growled savagely.

"Shut up, Muu." I pointed at him, and I could see a look of pure disappointment take over his features.

That makes one person on the whole planet. James chuckled.

"My will be done anyway!" Muu shouted triumphantly as he threw his arms up into the air and his towel dropped onto the ground.

"Damn it." I sighed and looked at the dwarf. "Can we get dressed now?"

"Aye, but no armor, and no weapons outside yer inventory." The wizened old man advised before stepping out. He stopped to crack a grin at us, "We know that things can happen, and we like to be prepared too. But only should they happen should you bring out any weapons. Aye?"

I looked to the others, and they nodded, forcing me to relay, "seems fair."

They led us to the training grounds, them in their normal clothes, and us in what we had that wasn't armor. So that left me with a green shirt with no sleeves, simple brown pants, and my black boots. Balmur wore a simple silver shirt with gray pants and no boots like the dwarves around us, and Muu wore a brown shirt and black pants with no shoes as well.

The others wore simple clothes, and Yohsuke still wore his shroud, which the dwarves allowed since it wasn't technically armor.

The whole of the clan marched surrounding us like an honor guard toward a section of the city we hadn't been to before.

This part of the city had large pillars with carved art lining the roadway. Depictions of the forging of the first dwarves, their crafting by the god Fainne, whose desire to make someone in search of things to create themselves led him to breathe life into the dirt and stone to make his children.

The Mountain, Fainne, bestowing materials upon his children by creating veins of precious metals and gems to mine and use to create as he did.

The next pillars illustrated the beginnings of dwarven civilization, the people themselves coming together to form the first clans. And from there, cities under the ground, sprawling cities unlike anything even conceptualized by the other races.

Then it showed a huge cavern where the city once was, making me stop. "What happened here?"

The dwarves stopped their marching, and the elder that had led our cleansing spoke, "We do not know much of that time in our history, there is much confusion and worry over it. The clans who survived adapted to the world around them and grew closer and stronger than ever."

"Lost because o' our hubris maybe," Thogan muttered darkly, and when all eyes turned to him, he shuddered. "Odd, now that I be round me kin again, I have to be narrator of our greatest sin."

Thogan pointed to the cavern and explained, "This be accurate because we toiled with what we knew precious little of. When we dwarves, the first o' our kind, had been tasked to create, we did so with fervor. Some created weapons the like I never seed before. Others, armor and monuments that would make a man weep to look at 'em. But it was those who sought to create life themselves what brought Fainne's hammer on our heads."

His fingers wove nervously through his beard, fidgeting with his eyes closed as he continued, "Dark magic, nothin' like the light and heat bestowed upon us by the Mountain. Not purposely, mind ye, the rest of us were in the way. Not one o' us had know'd what were happenin' but learned of it in the aftermath. The survivors o' the clan at fault, may their names never be written in the stone of our memory so long as dwarves breathe, told us o' their misdeeds and we judged 'em as Fainne had. Swiftly. Deadly."

"And from there, you moved on?" James asked quietly.

"I donnae know the rest, as this was about the time I found a tear in the veil between worlds, and the queen of the Unseelie found me wanderin' her lands."

Maebe smiled. "Mother did say that you were one of the most interesting fighters she had ever come across."

"High praise, Majesty." Thogan bowed his head in return. "Forgive me, my tales. I'd be happy to sit with one o' yer historians an' fill in the gaps."

The dwarves around us watched the older dwarf with rapt enthusiasm, some of them skeptical, but I couldn't help wondering if that could have been why dwarves seemed so resistant to the idea of their people using magic. Because it had almost destroyed them once.

"We would be delighted to have ye do so, Thogan." Farnik's voice returned me to the present and so too his order, "Let's move."

The pillars led us to a large area hundreds of feet high before a blackened stone ceiling came to view, and at least a hundred yards squared where dozens of dwarven families stood waiting around a stone platform with two small figures on it.

Dwarves of all ages and sizes stood together around the platform with looks of somber recognition on their faces. The scent of food and drink wafted into the air around us, but we couldn't find any of it, at least I couldn't.

"Up on the platform lads, Queen Maebe, you too!" Farnik encouraged with a look of pride on his face as we mounted the stair.

We clambered up the stairs and found Fainnir and Pebble waiting for us. The young dwarf wore a simple pair of black pants and a brown shirt. His sparsely growing beard hairs poking out of his chin well on display. He nodded to us stoically despite the boyish grin on his face. We gathered around him with hugs and pats on the shoulders, no words needed. He was an honorary member of the party, and he knew it but was proud anyway. Pebble just stood and waved at us soundlessly, his stumpy arm working back and forth slowly.

Farnik's pride seemed to swell as murmuring took those gathered, their attention rapt one moment and seeming scattered the next. He mounted the platform after us and waited for the muttering and noise to calm.

When it did a few moments later, the leader of the Mugfist

clan raised his arms over the crowd, and all eyes came to rest on him.

"Clans of Djurn Forge!" Farnik shouted and the crowd went nuts, hooting and hollering with abandon for a long minute, then fell silent. "We come together today to raise up the heroes what brought home me Gerty. *Our* Gerty!"

Once more, the dwarves of Djurn Forge cheered together, shouts of "Aye!" "Heroes!" And "GERTY!!" Rang out all around us in a near-deafening burst of sound.

"Heroism what deserves to be noted in the collective memory o' the clans, so that all may know the glories what need be sung about the return o' our most vaunted defender!" Farnik continued, and many of the dwarves nodded enthusiastically. "They fought their way to the Great Below, riskin' life and limb to get to the drow to do their duties when they happened upon a captive who struck them as one o' ours. And confirmed that it were Gerty."

"*Betrayed* by the drow scum, they fought back an' rescued her from the evil queen's clutches, her prison of lies and shadow." Farnik slashed with his arms as if he were fighting something. "Joined by me an' little more than a score o' me kin, they fought through drow an' vampires alike to join us an' reunite kin an' clan. I stand before ye today, claiming that these lads an' lasses deserve to be heralded as some o' the greatest heroes o' our time!"

"They be dwarves!" One of the clan leaders bellowed from his spot, his flaming head of hair and beard down to the ground were impressive, but he had a piece of iron on his face. We knew who he was. "O' course they be heroes!"

A resounding cheer of agreement rang out around us, causing me to grin at my brothers and wife.

"Be there any here this day who donae think their deeds were heroic?" Farnik raised his voice, almost like a threat. His scowl turned on all of the dwarves below us.

"Me." Jaken snarled and stepped forward.

Farnik didn't seem surprised when he glanced back and saw

the paladin striding forward. "Speak yer piece lad. Tell all here afore ye what be on yer mind."

Jaken came to stand next to Farnik and raised his own voice, "We did what any good dwarf would have done themselves if they had known. Any one of you would have brought this whole city down on their heads if you had known that Gerty was down there. Hell, we would have been right there with you if we could have been!"

It was hard to argue that logic, and I'd be damned if it weren't true. Watching the area, I could see the dwarves reflecting on the information before one of the other clan leaders limped forward. His bald head reflecting the bright fire-light around us as his long, wispy-gray beard waved like a flag before him. Several of the dwarves around him went to aid him, but he battered them away with a thick metal cane.

He stopped halfway between the stone we stood on and his clan and glared up at us with nearly-closed eyes as he spoke something in dwarvish. His raspy voice lost before it could reach me.

Farnik leaned forward, and one of the younger dwarves from the clan asked the old one his question and took a whack on the backside as she ran the question to Farnik.

"Ah, a fair question." Farnik turned back to us, Jaken in particular and related the question, "Knowin' what ye know now, would ye change yer actions?"

I blinked. A fair question was right, and other than maybe a little better planning on our part and maybe a more brutal end to a certain spider queen, I don't think I would have.

Jaken looked to us, our heads shaking collectively, then turned to the crowd and announced, "No. We wouldn't have."

The elderly dwarf cracked a smile, his single yellowed tooth moving up and down as he lifted his metal cane and cracked a rhythm on the ground.

Not a heartbeat later, every dwarf in the room, including Farnik and Thogan, stomped their right foot on the ground in unison.

"What're they doing?" Jaken whispered loudly.

I couldn't help the laugh that bubbled out of my throat. I'd been there for this once before.

"This is the Heart of the Mountain, guys," I explained with a grin and pulled Yoh and Jaken close to me. "It means they approve of us, and we're heroes!"

———

The party itself was intense. The food smelled so good once the clans brought it forward that my stomach gurgled almost as loud as a dragon. Keg after keg after keg of the best alcohol any of the clans could manage to muster rolled across the stone tables around the outer rim of the area with the food in the middle on display.

The heroes sat at a stone table near all the food while the clans sat around them in no particular order with no partic- ular arrangement by clan. Ironnose dwarves mixed with Lighthand and Mugfist, and everyone ate and drank in harmony.

Up until the tenth barrel of booze had been opened.

That's when things got a little hairy. Or should I say scaly? I could swear I turned into a dragon at some point, but I wouldn't know much for long.

I woke up to dull pain in my side and crick in my neck. And also in my ursolon form. Laying with my ass on top of the table. My head on the ground and a leg in my mouth.

"Graah!" I mulled, the noise making me wince and fight not to tighten my jaws.

I gently extricated the leg and shifted to my typical fox-man form, casting Regrowth on myself groggily. My bleary eyes failed to comprehend the scene before me.

"Good morning, my love," Maebe's voice greeted me from the shadows beneath the table. Her eyes and smile were visible, but nothing else.

"Whah happen?" My dry throat cracked, I grabbed the

nearest tankard and pulled it to my lips then almost vomited as the taste of alcohol hit my throat.

I looked down to see that the leg belonged to Vrawn, the orc woman snoring happily with a dwarven teddy bear in her arms. Well, it looked like Fainnir, snoring just as happily in her arms as she slumbered.

"Here." Maebe giggled, appearing on the table. "Let me show you."

She held her hands out for me to put my head into, and I did. Memories and images, chaotic and bright, flooded into my mind.

The sixth toast to Gerty's continued health and return had given way to a call for music and dancing to which all of the party had acquiesced. Even Yoh had come out to cut a rug.

By this time, I was well and truly gone, and people wanted to see animals dance, so I turned into a dragon, of course. I stumbled to and fro, the alcohol inhibiting my movements a bit, but I was having fun! At least it looked like. Children wanted to jump over my tail, so I flicked it back and forth over the ground so they could do just that.

Then the dwarves, hell even my friends, began shouting requests for different animals. By the end of the night, I was an ursolon doing the waltz with Vrawn in my paws as my friends sang a song.

"Oh god, not that Jungle Book shit." I groaned sadly. "Really?"

"Oh yes, that was the highlight of my night, right there," Muu grunted as he shuffled over with a yawn and a wince at the noise. "Remind me to drink water next time?"

"Shut up." Balmur growled quietly from beneath another table ten feet away. "This hangover is trying to find me. Hushshshs."

"Well, lads!" Farnik guffawed, and the collective cry of pain made him laugh harder. "We have heroic items to bestow upon ye!"

"Can it wait?" Bokaj moaned at the small man. I glanced

up and saw him hanging by a rope noose tied around his ankle from a lantern pole.

"What the fuck happened to you?" I asked as I ordered the shadows around us to cut it so he could fall, and I could catch him.

I honestly thought I would catch him, but him hitting the ground from nearly fifteen feet in the air proved me wrong.

"Sorry." I hiccuped and shook my head, my vision splitting momentarily. "I thought I could get you."

I cast Regrowth, and he flipped me off as he stood and dusted himself off. "I don't know. I think I lost a bet?"

"It be likely." Roslyn snickered, her pants and blouse dirtied, and her hair tousled. She eyed the elven ranger longingly before sighing. "You do sing such lovely songs. And you move so well."

I found myself blushing at the implications and turned to see Farnik scowling at the two of them with a look of concern on his face.

"So!" I tried to get between them to keep him distracted. "About those items?"

"No need to worry, Zeke." Roslyn grasped my shoulder tightly. "Though ours is a stuffy lot sometimes, no dwarven woman needs be a maiden when she marries. We're free to do what we please. No one owns us."

"She be right, lad." Farnik grunted, eyeing his daughter strangely. "Though I be wonderin' why tha' one. No disrespect to ye, Bokaj, but I always figured me daughter'd be drawn to the stouter type. Like Balmur."

"He's a musician, da." Roslyn shook her head and grinned. "There be more to life than muscle an' the skill to wield an axe. An' Balmur be betrothed already, an honorable lady doesnae dally another woman's man."

Farnik chuckled and patted her shoulder. "Good lass. Good. Go an' see to the armory for us before we get there. Lay out the pertinent weapon sets for us, and we will see about outfittin' these 'uns for their journey, aye."

Bokaj blinked, then frowned as she walked toward him. "Did we? You and I…?"

Roslyn winked at him as she passed him, then turned and smacked his rump before sprinting away.

"Good on you, man." Jaken grinned, looking a lot fresher than the rest of us, clean clothes and all. "She's a looker. You all ready, or what?"

"Yeah, yeah," James grumbled as he glanced around. "Where's Yoh?"

"Hungover." The sounds of retching and something splashing on the other side of the table reached my ears.

"How?" I asked the vampire, his face popping up over the stone of the furniture.

"Alcohol infused blood from the smell of it," Muu gagged, covering his nose with a hand. "Let's get the hell out of here and get cleaned up."

I nodded even as I called the shadows to come to my aid, lifting them as we walked and using them to wick away the grime from my body and clothes. The scent of alcohol and sick was much less overpowering than it had been, and I felt much more refreshed.

"You grow more adept, husband." Maebe touched my shoulder, pointing with her chin toward where we had been. "Please, collect our lover. It will go a long way toward repairing the small rift between the two of you."

I kissed her forehead softly, more for my comfort than hers, and went about collecting Vrawn. The large woman wasn't heavy, not surprising with how high my strength was. But Fainnir fought like hell to stay cuddled in her grasp.

Finally, Muu lumbered over and grasped the boy by his shirt and tugged, his grasp slipping from Vrawn and leaving her open to my lifting.

I stood, the woman balanced in my arms precariously, before I whispered, "Hang on to me, sweetheart. I've got you, but I need you to put your arms around my neck."

Vrawn's lips curled, and her snoring paused for a mere

heartbeat before her body leaned toward my own, and she wrapped her muscled biceps around my neck loosely. The ground swayed a little as I walked; eventually, Maebe had to help me a little by leaning against my shoulder.

I kissed Vrawn's cheek, and her snoring went back to normal as Farnik led us toward the back of the area. Here, a large tapestry woven through stone and wooden towers told the same tales but featured certain dwarves.

"Heroes Hall," Farnik muttered, then turned to us, motioning to the art above him. "These are the dwarves throughout our history who have been deemed heroes by their peers in the clans. You'll see Granite, meself, and Gerty as the latest additions, but we be plottin' to add to it lads. And yer all in that addition."

Bokaj scratched his stomach and yawned. "That's awesome, Farnik, but why are we over here?"

Farnik growled. "Patience!"

Stone rumbled in front of us, grinding and rolling away. Roslyn strode out of the opening left in the wall off to our right, and motioned that we should come to her.

Our footsteps echoed around us as we ducked into the room.

"This be the armory," Farnik explained, opening his hands and motioning to the room. "Not just a selection o' weapons an' armor, no. This is *the* armory. Where our greatest weapons and armor forged in these halls are stored for the heroes o' the dwarves to select from should they be nominated."

"So, we get to pick a piece of gear from this?" Jaken asked with a smile and a more than hopeful look on his face. His hands raised and fingers waggled over a set of armor.

"Any one piece." Farnik grinned and turned to Bokaj and Balmur. "I know ye be o' the sort who enjoy odd weapons, we got a few odds and ends what may be up yer alley."

I grinned and laid my lovely orcish lady on an empty stone table where Maebe had perched with her legs over the side. I made it so that Vrawn's head rested on Maebe's thighs, where the Fae Queen could softly play with her hair.

"Pick something for me?" Maebe raised a brow and motioned to the piles of things. "I trust your judgement."

I grinned at her and went to work perusing the items on the tables. My current items were pretty boss, and my great axe Magus Bane could steal mana from whomever, or whatever magical thing, I hit. Not to mention, break magical barriers. And who didn't want that?

If I found something that would be a great match, I'd get it, but I had a good enough great axe at the moment to be picky.

Armor looked great, but metal gear like plate mail would inhibit my movement and weigh me down too much to be of any real use in a fight. It would likely need to be a weapon of some sort.

Nothing stuck out to me right away at the table I currently browsed. Hatchets, a long knife made of bone, a double-sided axe with a skull on top of it. The next table didn't have much either, but something did catch my eye, a ring that looked to be crafted of a metal that seemed to move and change color in the light.

Encorn's Signet
+18 dmg with magic spells and increased control of the elements.

Encorn's delight in magical manipulation met no end until he did. There is still much that shrouds his fate, but nothing of his life is left in this plane, but for a ring and a saying: He who controls himself, controls his fate. He who controls fate—controls nothing.

That was an odd statement, not to mention the fact that there wasn't any crafter information like there would normally be. That aside, the ring was amazing, and I pocketed it for now, either to give to Maebe if I found something better or to keep for myself if not.

Hey, she would want me to have it, right? I mean, it's not

like I wasn't going to tell her about it, and it *did* seem to be something I could use.

Several bladed weapons stuck out to me, nice as they were, I wasn't a sword guy in this world. They could do some wonderful things for my friends, but not me. After a while, I'd begun to lose hope of finding anything else of use.

That had been until I spotted it at the back of the room leaning against a wall with a sheet over the top of it. Drawn as I was to many things around us in this world, whether from a sense of curiosity or a child-like wonder I'd had since I was a child, I found myself storming across the room toward it.

I shoved Muu out of the way when he stepped in front of me.

"What the hell, man? It's a wall."

I walked through the "wall" he had been talking about, my True Sight allowing me to see through the illusion as if it were just a screen.

I lifted the sheet away and found a simple looking wooden scepter, ashen gray with ghostly runes carved into it covered in dust. Breathing deep, I blew on it mightily, the motes falling away and littering the air around the item and I. Glowing runes of spectral silver, purple, green, red, blue, and black dotted it in a flowing pattern from top to bottom with a knob at the top of it.

Take me up.

The siren song of the weapon whispered through my mind temptingly. Every fiber of my being burned for the object before me. I needed to touch it. To wield it. Why wasn't I reaching out to it the way it reached for me?

I glanced down at my hands and found the right held by Maebe, my left in Vrawn's hands.

"Zeke, calm yourself," Vrawn whispered against the top of my head.

Calm? I was perfectly calm, well, that was a lie. I was excited at the prospect of finding something else that could be useful.

Claim me as your own.

My tails flicked in agitation. "Guys, I'm cool, it's fine. I just want to see what the stats for it are. I'm one of the more powerful casters in the group—a staff seems like a great idea."

Farnik appeared as if from nowhere and pressed a thick hand against my stomach and pressed against me, my feet sliding a little. "Easy, lad. Stay yer hand."

"It's just a staff, guys!" I reasoned again, my voice growing slightly louder.

"A hidden staff?" Maebe asked with her arm suddenly across my chest. "One that not even Farnik knew was here?"

"They didn't know that their people had magic until we told them, this could be something from their past that they had forgotten." I reasoned with her. Why didn't this make as much sense to them as it did me?

"We what?" Farnik seemed thrown by the realization. "Magic from Fainne is all well an' good, lad. An' I admit, I be keen to learn more from Thogan, but we don't know what it be doin' here, it coulda been sealed here for all we know! I... be unsure ye should touch it."

Until someone worthy came along.

Call my name.

"He's not exhibiting any weird signs, and his ring isn't glowing, so it's not some kind of spell. What's the harm in one of us trying to see what it does for him?" Jaken offered, and walked through the illusion to touch the weapon.

A charge of magical energy so strong the fur on my body and the hair on Maebe and Vrawn's heads stood wholly on end and sent the paladin careening away from it, violently flailing as his momentum carried him out of the door into a stone pillar. A thunderous crack from outside drew our attention, and we rushed to see what was going on.

We rushed out to see Jaken lying unconscious under one of the large pillars, it was cracked to hell and looked about ready to splinter and fall on the Fae-orc. A larger section of it just above stood out to me as well.

"Muu, get over there and hold the stone in place, go," Yohsuke said tersely, taking command. "Zeke, shift to dragon and hold the higher portion steady so that it stays still. Vrawn, you're strong, go get Jaken, and drag him back here to us."

We moved into a flurry of action. I towered over Muu as he held the pillar in place, the pressure of thousands of pounds of stone further splintering the pillar sending several motes of dust and rubble crumbling down on us.

Ice froze the cracks and portions of the pillar that seemed closest to falling down, but it didn't seem to be enough.

"I'm still weakened from that fight with Lilith!" Maebe warned loudly as she ground her teeth and flexed her arms closer, shadow and ice packing up the sides of the pillar. "My magic wanes, we need to hurry and evacuate this place!"

"James, Bokaj, and Balmur." I grunted, the strain of the pressure taxing me more and more. "Go warn the dwarves. Do what you have to get them away from here."

"What about you guys?" James retorted, he was already in motion leaping above my head, kicking away large chunks of stone and rock that could brain me and render me useless.

"Did I fucking stutter?" My roar reverberated in the air around us. "Go! Take Mae and Vrawn, too. Maebe can protect you all with shadow and ice."

"I will not leave you!" Maebe and Vrawn snarled in unison.

"I can buy you time, so *go*!" A hiss of pain escaped my clenched teeth as a large chunk of ice and stone sliced into my shoulder.

"You heard him, move!" Yohsuke called, I could see him hesitating, but I nodded to him, and he was gone. Vrawn had Jaken over her shoulder, and the other swifter members of the party led the charge toward the dwarves.

Let me help you.

"How?" I hoped that whatever was speaking to me could hear me where I was.

Call my name.

The insistence that I knew the thing's name was silly. I

would be perfectly fine if the place went down, I could turn into an earth elemental and move through some of the looser earth, though the bones of the mountain would be unacceptable even if I had permission from the primordial earth elemental. If nothing else, I could teleport away from here.

But that was if whatever happened here didn't bring down the roof to the whole damned dwarven city. Shit.

Maebe, Vrawn, and all of my brothers were in danger. Mortal danger.

Call my name.

"What is it?!" I shouted, the strain on my muscles continued to build, my draconian knees wavering and shaking like I had just squatted my max six times in a row.

Call. My. Name!

"Damn it!" I racked my brain. Searched my heart and came up empty.

"Dream eater?" No. "Captain Cru—FUCK!" Another chunk of ice hit my shoulder and my tail, knocking 20% of my health bar away.

"Hubris!" I snarled, something flashed into my clawed hand and calm descended over me. I shifted into my fox-man form, and the pillar threatened to crumble and collapse onto my head.

Master.

The knob at the end of the weapon burned white-hot, then cooled until the wood became a large gem the size of a softball. I took my left hand with Hubris in it and lifted it into the air, channeling the energy in my body, my mana funneling in and seeping into the world around me. The mana fixed cracks, the shifting of the stone stopped, and my straining muscles collapsed so that I remained on one knee, but continued to pour my magic into the weapon, willing the world around me to right itself.

Stone lifted into the air and back to where it had been. My mana soon ebbed, and the ring on my finger fed the hefty spell before draining dry. Even as what mana I had came back, it all fed the scepter in my hand. My life force drained, blood seeping from my nose and traveling down my arm to feed into the glowing gem.

More.

More of my health drained, further and further.

Almost whole again.

Darkness ebbed into my vision, the edges of my sight fading as the scepter fed hungrily. My knees grew weaker, and suddenly, I found myself sitting and staring up at the ever-darkening ceiling of stone. Cold. So very cold.

CHAPTER FIVE

My awareness of my body was off. I had been snoring again, my throat was dry and my tonsils slightly swollen, then I was going down once more. Something seemed to be ferrying me, grasping me beneath my armpits like a parent carries a child, the light-lit doorway of my room fading from view slowly as if it were never meant to reveal my comfortable bed and red comforter at all.

Light faded further until darkness surrounded again, different from the void I was used to, I had no power here. Alone with this sensation of being carried and the sound of slowing flapping wings that I never got to see. Then I knew peace.

"Return to me, my love, please?!" Moisture found its way onto my cheek.

Odd, I thought belatedly. I touched my cheek in the darkness, the moisture glowed radiantly against my fingertips.

Come on, Zeke! More voices of encouragement reached my ears, their hollow echoes as if thousands of miles away, but right next to me, too.

It is not yet time to return, friend. You must go back. I blinked, light suddenly arching the distance toward me at hyper speed. The darkness was eaten away, slowly at first, but then gone in a painful white that made my whole being ache.

"Ahhh!" I cried as a sharp *whumpf* forced my lungs empty, like I had been slammed back into pain and something constraining.

A pounding headache erupted from my head, and my mouth felt like I had decided to try and eat sand.

"What happened?" I groaned, my voice rasping out of my throat. The light flooding my gaze blinded me, and the shapes I could make out were heads and shoulders made of shadow.

"Oh, Zekiel." Small hands grasped at mine, larger ones cupping them, and a third set of arms lifting me.

"Let's get him back to the compound, we can talk it out there," Muu said from nearby.

"I can walk myself." I said, overcome by everyone's sudden distraught act. I was fine. "I've passed out before, I'm fine."

We stopped moving, the motion sending the world toppling dangerously as Maebe swam into view. "Zeke, you died."

"Bullshit." I blinked, the light a lot easier to deal with than the still red-eyed woman before me. "There's no way."

"Yes, way." Vrawn snarled, jerking my chin toward her, her eyes serious and worried. "You used that item we warned you about, and it killed you making things right."

We began to move again, me still being carried like I was a damned damsel in some old movie.

Did I really...die? I asked the others. None of them answered outright, but their silence was enough.

I had died. And it was because of Hubris.

We will be better when you have more mana to offer, and when the desired magic is less...unrefined. I can help you.

I closed my mind off from the whispering weapon and let myself be returned to the compound in near silence. The echoing sounds of footsteps masking the whispers from onlookers as we passed by.

By the time we arrived at the compound, I was strong enough once more to truly walk on my own.

Muu took pity on me and let me down gently. Maebe and Vrawn sandwiching me between them protectively.

"What made you use that item, Zeke?" Vrawn's question wasn't anything I hadn't expected, but the force behind it was.

"I was flagging." They seemed confused, so I explained, "I was tiring, and once all of you were out of harm's way, it occurred to me that if that pillar fell, there could be more of the structural integrity at stake than simply that room. The scepter speaks to me. *Calls* to me. It helped me fix the room, and it told me that I could use it better with more mana."

"A sentient weapon can be a dangerous thing when you don't know what the weapon wants," Maebe spoke softly, her troubled frown forcing her gaze away from me.

"I found this for you." I held out Encorn's Signet, and she took it.

"This is quite powerful, but I'm afraid I cannot accept it." Maebe pressed the ring toward me. "That ring would be most useful to you since you can control multiple elements. Who knows what you would be capable of with it."

"I can only have one item from there, though." I shook my head, and she smiled as she shook her head back. "And while I don't know where it is, I think I still have it."

"I planned to give you whatever I gained from there." She grinned, though it seemed sadder than anything. "I am a queen, my love. I have many interesting baubles and weapons. I find that news disconcerting, but while I am... weakened as I am, I worry that my trying to interfere with it could drain me further and I would be unable to muster what little strength I have to return home."

"You do indeed." I kissed her hand and I could feel her aching sadness through our bond. "It's time for you to go home, isn't it? I mean, I did just die."

"My strength wanes too deeply here now, and I worry that if I do not recover, it will not be the last time you die." Soft tones for something so detrimentally painful. "I need to return to our kingdom to recover and see to our people. Next time, Jaken may not be able to bring you back."

Crestfallen, I pulled her close and shifted into my human form to kiss her deeply before stepping back. "Be safe, and send to me."

"I will." She brushed my cheek with her knuckles and smiled pleasantly. "Vrawn, come to me."

Vrawn stepped toward Maebe and hugged the other woman goodbye before dipping down to give her a chaste kiss. "I will miss you, little one."

Maebe chuckled at Vrawn and brushed a hand over her cheek. "I shall miss you as well. I need you to take care of our Zeke while I am away."

Vrawn eyed me from where she stood, slightly bent over Maebe. Her piercing blue gaze penetrating mine, and I could see indecision there.

"He seems to stubbornly hold to the idea that he needs no help and listens to no one." Vrawn's ire was well deserved.

"He listens to me." Maebe growled as she lifted her hand and yanked on my shadow. My body slid toward her without a fight. Her hand landed on my cheek, the soft sting of her flesh slapping against mine. "And I say that he should be a little more receptive to things now that he realizes what can be taken from him if he doesn't tread carefully from here on out."

"Yes, dear." The rumble in my chest traveled farther than I meant for it to, and her eyes half-closed.

"I love you, do not continue to be foolish about things, for my sake?" Maebe's question got a nod in return. "Goodbye, and do take care of each other, will you?"

"Yes." Vrawn huffed and stepped back.

"I love you." I returned her affection by rustling her hair and grinned. She smirked, reaching into the air before her and pulling out a single small vial of something that flowed almost like mercury inside of it, but it moved of its own volition in the glass. "Before you ask, this is a special elixir that will give me enough strength to tear the veil, but after that, I will weaken rapidly. I will be home, so my power will return more swiftly, but even then, I will be down a while. Do be safe until I return."

Sighing, I stepped over to Vrawn and pulled her to my side, a small gasp escaped her lips as Maebe's hair fluttered in an unseen breeze. The shadows tore the veil apart, and she walked into the Fae realm, a single glance back to smile at the two of us.

"Presumptive of you, Zeke," Vrawn observed with her arms crossed before her.

"I wanted her to go knowing that you and I would try to patch things up." I let her go but stayed where I was, glancing up at her. "I wanted *you* to know that."

Vrawn simply watched me a moment. "Why?"

"Because before I died, when I was trying to figure out what to do…" I ran my hand over my head, still trying to cope with what happened. "You were one of the people I thought of. You matter to me. Your safety. Your happiness."

I brought my hand up, staring at it, the two rings on my metallic right hand glinting in the low light.

"I'm stupid, I'm brash and headstrong." I clenched my fist as hard as I could. "I will sacrifice everything to make someone else happy, or to be there for someone else, and my own happiness means less to me than anyone else's, usually. I figure if I do something like give you things, or make grand promises, that the gesture will just hurt me trying to do what I truly want to do, which is to prove that you are worth more to me than that. "

"Why are you telling me this?" Vrawn sounded genuinely worried.

"Because." I turned to look at her, and realized what was going on. "I've been doing everything for everyone else. And I found someone to be there for. So I'm going to do that. For you. For Mae. For me. And my friends will understand."

I reached out my right hand, about to speak when I felt something in it. I looked over to see Vrawn's hand in mine, a soft look on her face.

"Good." Her dainty tusks flashed at me from where she stood. "That's a start."

"He also forgot to say that he's ugly as fuck, has a shitty temper, and smells like a wet dog at all times." Yohsuke stood grinning off to my left. "So, you finally decided to do your own thing?"

"You been expecting it?" I tilted my head at the man, and he shook his head.

"You forget that other than Muu, I've known you the longest out of all of us." Yoh paced around Vrawn and me. "Not to mention, I've died too. No one knows you better than me, right now. So, how is it you want to grow?"

"I think I'm going to up my magic, for now." I ran my fingers over my smooth chin. "And maybe work more on enchanting."

"Good. Let's make sure we have what we need before we get going to this new city that we're to leave from to cross the ocean." He went to turn away, then stopped and walked over to me, pulling me into a fierce hug. "You ever scare me like that again, I'll beat your ass."

I snorted, and he punched me in the bicep for it, which was pitiful, but I understood where it came from. Taking a mental inventory of the rings I wore, two of which were crazy important for me to keep. Spell storing and Mage's Well, like I could give up that much. That left Radiant's Binding that increased my healing ability and range that it took for the spells to take effect and my charm resistance ring. We had been using that lately, and if I was to go more caster intensive, then the signet would help.

I took off Radiant's Binding and stored it before slipping Encorn's Signet ring onto my metallic right hand. The ring shimmered and turned black, spreading along my fingers, then up my forearm until the metal was completely hidden from view.

"What the hell is this?" I touched the arm, and it felt like my normal skin. "That's weird."

"It makes you look like you're whole, and at the same time hides that you wear the ring," Vrawn observed, taking my hand in hers. "Can you feel the effects of it?"

I shrugged, then reached out to the shadows around us and coaxed them toward me. They were normally eager to come, but now they whipped toward me like a rubber band.

"Oh, that's going to take some getting used to." Shaking my head and sending the shadows home, I grasped Vrawn's hand and walked with her toward the others as they gathered. "Before you guys ask, yes my arm has changed, yes it's still metal, but the ring I got makes it look like my skin."

"I was mainly staring because you look weird in human form." James blinked at me honestly, the mischievous glint in his gaze making me flip him off. "We need to go say goodbye to Farnik or anything?"

"He said that once we were good, the clan was good to say goodbye together; we just had to let them know." Balmur whistled, and the clan came around the corner from where they had been hiding. All of them looked completely fine, the bastards.

"Taking off already, lads?" Farnik and his family stepped closer to us than the others and looked over us. His gaze halted on me. "Well, ye donae look dead."

"I'm a ghost?" I tried weakly, and he just snorted at me.

"What all did ye pick then?" Roslyn's excitement shone from her rosy cheeks. "From the armory?"

Jaken held up a new shield of softly glowing stone, the red jewel in the center of it pulsing slowly. "Remembrance, it should do me well. Thank you."

"Oh aye?" Gerty stepped forward and touched the craggy item. It looked like tectonic plates that had crashed into each other amid a magma rise with the jewel. "It be one that can cast a hostile spell on it?"

Jaken nodded, and all eyes turned to Bokaj, who grinned and held up a metal drum with an older looking brown skin pulled tight over it. "Bongo's Spectral Drummer, tap it three times and a spectral drummer plays a song. I can't wait to see how it works."

"That does sound really awesome man, it's like having a band!" Balmur gave his best friend a high five, then held up a hatchet that looked surprisingly normal. "This'll do me just fine. It's kind of like Storm Caller, but it just returns to me when I throw it."

James held up a vambrace that he wore and smiled. "Should be handy in a close combat situation."

"Don't you have scales to protect you?" Jaken asked with a look of scorn leveled at the monk. "That's a waste, man."

James just punched toward him with that arm and a small blade of light erupted from the bottom of his wrist and sliced the air next to the paladin's ear. "Okay, never mind, that's dope."

"Yohsuke?" Brawnwynn raised a brow and pointed at the distracted vampire. "What'd you get?"

"Oh, I took this grappling hook." He pulled out a chain with a three-pronged hook on the end. The chain was no thicker than an average gold necklace, but the links looked to be either platinum or silver. "It grows and grasps anything so long as my aim is true. I was just thinking about how to attach it to something, so I could throw it unexpectedly."

A clanking and clattering sound crashed through the area, and everyone turned to see Muu donning his new armor, spikes lifting from the shoulders and flaring out from his elbows and knees, sharpened like blades.

"Dragoon armor, guys!" Muu cackled as he lifted his legs to stomp his way into the boots on the floor before him. "Finally, dragoon armor for li'l ol' me!"

I shook my head, unsure of whether to be mad at him for it or just surprised that I hadn't suspected this would happen sooner.

"Maebe had me choose a ring for her, though she's making me wear it for now since she had to return to the Fae realm."

The dwarves nodded almost knowingly but seemed to be waiting, so I held my hand out and called. "Hubris!"

The scepter appeared in my hand, and I closed my fingers, grasping it. The wood no longer looked old and gray, but bright white like ivory with the runes shimmering and shining.

You called to me?

I ignored the question, I would need to sit and look at the weapon soon to see what it did.

"You kept that thing?" Yohsuke hissed at me, clearly angry.

"It was my fault that I died, and it seems to be tied to me somehow." I shrugged off the hateful glares from the others. "Magic is where I want to take my progression for now, so why not have a weapon that can amplify my magic?"

Is that what it did?

I will explain if you ask me.

I thought, *Later,* and it seemed to take that at face value, falling quiet.

"I will not require you to leave it behind, but you will be careful using it," Vrawn stated wearily. "I support you trying to better yourself, but if that thing almost kills you again, I will throw it into the ocean, and it will rot there."

No threat, just promise. Got it.

"Well." Farnik cleared his throat and clapped his hands to get our attention. "Then, all we would like to do now is ask if ye wish to truly be part of the Mugfist clan in more than just honor?"

"I thought that the party was to do that?" James shifted his feet a little bit and came forward.

Farnik blushed furiously. "So taken were I with the crowd an' their adoration that I forgot to do the ceremony to induct ye, if ye be willin'."

Yohsuke perked up and seemed to blanch a bit. "Does that mean we have to do the bath thing again?"

"No!" Gerty laughed at his discomfort. "That were to prepare ye for the clans to witness yer ascendancy into the histories as heroes. All we need to do is ask the questions an' yer to give yer honest heart's answer. The Mountain will name ye clan if it be so."

"Brawny, ye start us off, lad," Farnik ordered, and his son stepped forward and closed his eyes.

"Be yer heart true?"

"Yes," All of us answered aloud. Vrawn stood close to me, silent but interested.

Roslyn stepped forward, her hands loosely clasped before her. "Will ye stand with the clan in its brightest moment, an' darkest hours?"

"Yes." No hesitation from any of us.

Gerty tread forward, her daughter stepping aside. "Should a brother, or sister of the clan come to ye for aid, will ye give it? Should a person in need ever call out in fear, will ye rise to stand against the threat?"

"Yes." Chills swept down my body, my fur standing on end as my adrenaline spiked.

Finally, Farnik stepped toward the members of the clan and motioned toward the others. "Should ye dishonor the clan, these are the ones whose pride will pay. Should yer heart be false, an' yer stride along the Way falter, their lives could be forfeit." He walked toward us slowly, arms out to his sides. "Know'n tha', could ye walk with us?"

The others seemed at a loss for words, but this was my family, these dwarves had done so much for us, that I couldn't not be part of something like this.

I spoke softly, but firmly, "The Way is long and winding, but never are we alone. I will walk with you as your brother. And I know I speak for my wife when I say that she would, as well."

Pride swept over Brawnwynn, Roslyn, and Gerty, but Farnik turned to the others and waited.

Muu nodded. "Aye."

Yohsuke did the same. "Yes."

"Never doubted I would." Balmur grinned. "Yes."

"You guys are too cool not to want to hang with." Bokaj winked. "I'm in."

"Yup." James crossed his arms with a wink.

Jaken grinned at the smaller man. "Brawny's my brother, of course, I'll stand with the clan."

CONGRATULATIONS!

You are now a member of the Mugfist clan! You are one of a proud line of soldiers, generals, and protectors. Your standing with the Mugfist clan has greatly improved. As a clan dwarf in name, your honor reflects on the clan's honor. Be careful!

"I think there's been some sort of mistake." I turned to see Vrawn visibly shaken and on the verge of panicking.

"What's wrong?" Roslyn stepped forward to stand near the other woman and froze, a look of equal parts fascination and confusion on her face. "Yer clan, lass."

"A full-blooded orc is clan?" A loud voice rang out from the far side of the group of dwarves. A grizzled dwarf with scars all over his body swaggered through the dwarves around him. His muscles made the rest of the dwarves around him look small and likely would've given Rowland a run for his money on bulk. "How can it be possible?"

Roslyn glanced up and reached out to take Vrawn's hands. "Did ye answer the questions, Vrawn?"

She shook her head, then stopped. "Not out loud." Grunts and cries of wordless sound came from the dwarves. "I'm sorry, I didn't mean to. Vilmas had been telling me so much about what it was like to be in a clan, and when she spoke so highly of the Mugfist clan that you all had been so involved with, I couldn't help wanting to be a part of something so grand."

"The words need nae be spoken fer the Mountain to hear what be in the heart, lass." An elderly dwarf, his mouth working where his teeth were missing as he shook his way forward out of the crowd. "The Mountain know'd ye be earnest child."

"Earnest or not, an orc has no place in the clan!" The same grizzled warrior snarled. "Jaken be enough, and I be proud to call the others clan, but that one don't even belong!"

"Yer steppin' on yer beard, Vlegen!" Farnik growled dangerously. "Ta say tha' be nigh on blashpemin' the Mountain!"

"Then I'll be the one to be sure tha' the Mountain knew what he were bein' offered!" Vlegen's face split into a menacing grin. "I challenge the length of her beard!"

"No!" Brawnwynn shouted and bolted forward before the dwarf could move too much further.

"What does that mean?" I muttered to Roslyn.

"It's a challenge to a duel, by the old way, almost like challenging the head of the clan, but the loser has to shave." Roslyn's entire body was rigid, and her scowl grew progressively worse.

"That doesn't sound so bad." Vrawn shrugged and stepped forward. "I accept."

Roslyn spat a stream of curses so virulently that I had to stop and make sure she was okay. "What?"

"If the loser doesn't have a beard, they can be killed for the dishonor!" She plodded forward and stood in Vlegen's way. "She has no beard to challenge!"

"Were she a dwarf, we would settle for cutting her hair, but the norm donae apply, an' she hasn't much anyway." Vlegen sneered, and drew his own double-headed axe. "The challenge be accepted. Step aside, lass."

"Can anyone stop this bullshit?" Muu smacked Farnik on the shoulder urgently. "You're the clan head, can't you?"

Farnik shook his head. "Only Fainne can stop a challenge of this sort." Farnik plodded forward, his jaw set and ticking as he faced Vlegen. "Ye survive this, an' I'll personally see ye thrown into the hole."

"Once I win, I mean to take the clan. I were fine with ye leadin' when she were to be leavin' hopefully ne'r to return. I'd have said me piece once she left and been done with it, but this? To be made *clan with a beast?* This be a travesty I cannae bear anymore." Vlegen winked and turned to the others. "Too long we been dealin' with the soft heart o' Farnik an' his ilk. It be time real warriors like the ones what we celebrated last eve be leadin' us to glory again!"

Not a single dwarf with the clan raised a cheer or even a voice of agreement. This guy was alone in a sea of enemies right now, and the only way to keep from being killed was to be the leader.

"Can we use any weapon we want?" Vrawn asked Farnik quietly.

"Aye, do ye be needin' one?" He offered her his axe, but she smiled and shook her head. "Then good luck, lass."

Gerty and Farnik waved the clan to two sides of the training grounds to spectate, and then Gerty stepped back out. "The rules be simple, yer not to kill each other, an' anythin' goes as for ability. Once one o' ye falls to a fourth o' yer health, then ye stop an' the winner be declared."

"He can't win if he's dead." I shifted into my ursolon form and padded forward, but Gerty stepped in.

"She accepted the challenge lad," Gerty tried to reason, pressing her palms to my chest and slid back in the dirt as I pushed on undeterred. "Do ye not trust her to hold for herself?"

That stopped me cold. I'd seen Vrawn fight once before, and I knew she was capable. But the thought of her risking her neck for something like this? I shifted back and felt a hand on my shoulder, Muu stood there and stared into my eyes.

"She's going to fuck him up." His soft-spoken support meant a great deal to me, but how about Vrawn? "She signed up for this when she asked to come along. She's got this."

I nodded once, then turned to the orc. "Hey, Vrawn." She turned around and motioned for me to speak. "We're on a timetable, dear. Don't go too easy on him."

Her fierce expression from there gave me the confidence I needed to step away from her side and watch with my brothers around me.

"Ye may begin!" Gerty snarled, the look of frustration and acceptance she had more telling than not.

Vrawn withdrew a sword from her inventory, crudely made

with bars attached to it by welded strips, but the sharp tip of it was still there, and if anything, it would act like a club with how many bands were around it.

"Is she really using a training weapon in an actual fight?" James frowned and crossed his arms while observing.

"That'll bring a good deal of shame on his head to boot," Jaken observed loudly with a smirk firmly set on his face. "Not that he has much, to begin with."

Vrawn stood in a loose, ready stance and watched Vlegen closely as he paced forward with his axe clasped in both hands. The sneer he had as he watched her in return seemed cemented.

Finally, he roared impatiently and sprinted at her with his axe held in a high guard. Vrawn lifted her arm as if to block and Vlegen just shouted again wordlessly as he brought the weapon down short and used it to pivot and drive his left foot into a sweep aimed at her legs.

Vrawn widened her stance, and instead of letting the sweep take her leg, or lifting it to get out of the way, she drove her practice sword into the stone on the outside of her leg and used the limb to support it as Vlegen's shin crashed into it.

A meaty thud and a slight crunching sound echoed from it, the small man grunting but making no other sound as he tried to recover by hobbling away from the orc with a hateful glare.

Vrawn lifted the sword into an easy guard, her left hand held casually to her side as she began to pace around him counterclockwise. The sword tapped a rhythm with each step, bobbing up and down and side to side as if pointing to a few spots but never seeming to fall out of that same easy guard.

The dwarf fiddled with a gourd at his hip that I hadn't noticed before because it had been tucked under his beard, then took a mighty draft of it.

"That's no fair!" One of the dwarves called from our right, his face paling.

"It be an ability he has, an' has the right ta use in the challenge." Gerty sounded more than pissed off, but she remained where she was as she quipped, "Though to see him pull out this lit'le number on someone he thinks be inferior is most tellin', aye Vlegen?"

The dwarf simply drank on, his cheeks growing flushed, and his eyes glazing over. Finally, he finished whatever it was and belched loudly before stumbling over to where Vrawn was.

Vrawn set her guard as the drunken man threw a haphazard fist in her direction that she caught easily. She brought her sword down where his head should have been in an overhead chop. Vlegen fell where he was and used her grasp to swing himself out of the way of her strike and had somehow managed to get himself caught up in her legs where he beat the limbs with the haft and butt of his axe. Small portions of her HP bar began to fall away as he did so, but Vrawn remained in control of herself.

"Some drunken master type fighting?" Muu whispered excitedly so as not to alarm Vrawn. "Is she going to be able to figure that out?"

"I couldn't tell you, but she has to, or I have to be okay with dishonoring us and killing him before he can do the same to her." I looked at the others, their own grim countenances giving me a clear guess as to what most of them would likely be okay with. They liked Vrawn, and seeing her die over something like this wouldn't sit well with any of them.

Vrawn seemed to have decided that enough was enough and reached down to grasp the slippery little shit by his beard, eliciting a gasp from some of the dwarves in attendance. "It be fair!" Hollered one of the ones across the circle, only being met with mutters of assent.

She lifted him and head-butted him across the face, his head turning somewhat with the force, allowing him to minimize the damage and use the momentum to drive his knee into her solar plexus. What would have left a normal person stunned and gasping for air just pressed the air from her lungs harder as she forced the air out in a concentrated burst and flung the dwarf into the air.

With nowhere to go and no way to dodge, she took her sword and used it like a major-league batter and swatted the dwarf in his already damaged leg, breaking it completely and stealing more than 15% of his total HP.

He landed ten feet away in a heap and grunted painfully as he sat up, tugging the leg straight with both hands and his other leg, pulling the milky white and pink bone back through the skin with a sickening squelching sound. He pulled out a small red vial and downed it, his health replenishing and the bone healing with it.

"You little *cheater*," Balmur howled stepping into the circle, his rage making his hands shake with the beginnings of one of his murderous episodes. "Using a potion in the middle of a duel is the *lowest* thing anyone can do."

"But it ain't against the rules." Vlegen grinned as if he had no worries. "I had the ability to drink it."

Fuck this, I sighed to myself. "Vrawn?" She looked back to me, and I stopped what I was going to say instantly.

There was a look of absolute, cold fury and determination on her face.

I gave her a small nod, and she walked over to me, staring down at me, "Your support is appreciated, but I have been fighting a long time. I will be fine. And he has worn down the last of my mercy."

I almost found myself grinning, and if it hadn't been for the fact that she looked ready to seriously beat the hell out of someone, I might have. "Fight hard, then. And know that we have your back."

She turned without a second thought and marched back into the circle where the crowd booed and cajoled the dwarf, but Vlegen would hear none of it.

"Balmur," Vrawn's voice was tight, but cordial. "Please leave the circle. I have a fight to win."

"He cheated, this shit show is over." Balmur insisted, but Vrawn shook her head, making the rogue growl in frustration. "We have shit to do!"

Vrawn stopped and regarded him coldly. "I am well aware of that, Balmur. But I have been accepted by something far greater than me, and that acceptance has been challenged. I will defend myself because I haven't been able to before. I will not ask again—leave the circle as my friend. Please?"

Vlegen made to act on her momentary distraction, but a dwarf nearby stuck his foot out and tripped him, the sneaky little bastard falling on to his face from the sudden slight interference. His calls of cowardice and rage buying us more time.

Balmur paused, his hands still shaking as he took a deep breath, let it out, then another one before looking up at her. "I'm sorry. I hate it when people cheat during duels. My time in the Hells was rife with it, and it still drives me nuts."

"I will see that he pays for it, dearly." Vrawn reached out and brushed a hand over Balmur's. "We will talk later. Go now."

Balmur returned to his spot, Tmont coming out of her hiding spot to purr at him like a small motorboat. "I'm okay, T', just not in my face, I have a fight to watch."

The cat mrowed angrily but laid on his shoulders in a way that allowed her to see what was happening as well.

Vrawn pulled her weapon close to herself and set her legs before adopting a different style of fighting stance. Her weapon held above her head in her right hand, the arm behind her body with her left side presented to Vlegen. "Come."

The dwarf had all the encouragement he needed and bounded forward, less wobbly than before, but rather than attempting to drop her onto her back again, he attacked full tilt. His axe whipped out, aimed straight for her head in a tight pass as he lifted his knee toward her sternum. Vrawn stepped into the swing, the haft of the axe bouncing harmlessly off her thick neck, and her sword whipped forward like a scorpion's tail. The score across the dwarf's face carved away a small chunk of his beard, leaving a bloodied mess where it had been.

Vlegen bellowed in outrage. "Beard cutter!"

"And I mean to shave you completely by the time this fight

is over, Vlegen." Vrawn grinned savagely as she settled into the same stance. "Come at me, coward."

Vlegen looked to the rest of the clan, all of them watched in a mixture of horror and fascination at the fight that was taking place before them. No one raised a voice to stop them. This was their fight.

Rather than allowing him to gain any sort of advantage, or to do something else to cheat, Vrawn shifted forward slowly and maneuvered herself to be able to fight more easily in the same stance.

Her dwarven opponent snarled and came at her with a wicked right hook toward her jaw, but slashed at her knee with the bladed portion of his axe. Vrawn speared her training sword down behind the beard of the weapon and whipped it away and out of Vlegen's grasp, his gasp of anger telling as to his frustration. But nothing compared to the swath of his beard that fell away from his face when she pulled a small carving knife from her belt. Half his face was a bloodied mess, and hairless as well.

From there, Vlegen devolved into a screeching mess, his movements filled with desperation and hatred while attempting to batter the orcish woman with his fists and feet. His only weapon having disappeared into the crowd of dwarves around us and not one soul was willing to assist him.

"Enough!" Vlegen spat, his face more carved up and bereft of facial hair than it had been before, only a slight wisp remained. He glared hatefully around the area at the spectators. "Ye stand with an orc afore ye'd stand with yer kin?"

"You would stand against a chosen clan member, so named by Fainne?" I countered and stepped into the ring, he was only at 60% health, and this was growing tiresome. "You would leap off the Way over hatred?"

"Over what be *proper*!" Vlegen howled, spittle flying from his lips, the whites of his eyes almost bursting from his head. "No one would allow a gods-forsaken orc into their clan without proof of honor! With Jaken, he fought his way in an' won under the gaze o' the Mountain, an' proved hisself to be honorable an' heroic!"

"Excuses, Vlegen!" Farnik shook his head. "Ye cling to the old ways an' times, the orcs have done nothin' to us in hunnerds o' years."

"Yer memory may nae be long, but mine be!" Vlegen snarled, his breathing labored. "Watchin' brothers and sisters felled by the clans o' orcs who sought to appease their war-lovin' god by slaughterin' those they thought weak—his rival's people! That be us!"

Vrawn stilled, listening as the dwarf continued his hate speech. "They came in droves, driven mad by their smoke an' fire. Bringin' their wargs an' beasts to the fore as our families fought to hold the line so we could escape! An' here they be again! Infiltratin' our ranks an' sewin' discord an' contempt among the finest warriors Djurn Forge ever know'd!"

"I was adopted by humans and taken in by them," Vrawn explained solemnly. "I was raised where people hated me and given the power to change that hatred into respect by serving the country who accepted me. That didn't last because of my failure, and here I am, once again, trying to show people that I can belong."

Angry tears fled from the corners of Vrawn's eyes as she stared down at Vlegen. "I didn't ask for this, but for a second time in such a short period of my life, I felt truly welcomed by a people and finally a god. I may not serve Uk'Beth, but I will have you remember that I am a warrior, and I am worthy of respect." Vrawn's face hardened, her nose wrinkling, and her tusks flashing in the firelight. "If you will not respect me for my skill, then you will fear me for my wrath."

She stepped forward and clobbered him over the head with the weapon in her hand, the bands keeping it from cleaving him in two, but the crunch of it saw him to the ground unconscious. Vrawn dropped her weapon to the ground, where it clanged against the stone loudly.

The dwarves surged forward to lift Vlegen and carry him

away, but the leadership stayed behind, barring Vrawn from having to see the dwarf again.

"You guys protecting him?" Bokaj asked warily, with a look of concern in his gaze.

"No." Farnik shook his head forlornly. "We bar the path to our shame, an' stand before our newest member humiliated. We knew he hated orcs, an' tha' isnae an emotion that most dwarves are far from with the memories of the clan wars so fresh for some, but we had no reckonin' it ran so deep as tha'."

"We be sorry, lass." Gerty bowed her head as well. "Ye have a place here amongst us, an' as a warrior of such skill, we'd be hard-pressed not to appreciate yer abilities."

"Thank you." Vrawn tried to smile, but she still seemed a little ticked. "I understand that the voice of one does not speak for everyone. I will stand by this group for their mission and think on my time here with fondness. Should you have need, call on me, and I will come to you how I can, to aid you."

Both Farnik and Gerty seemed to understand that pressing the matter would be an issue and decided to settle for hugs and pats from the rest of us.

"What the blasted hells is this thing made with?" Brawn-wynn grunted. I glanced over to see him lifting the weapon but straining to do so.

"It is normal metal with a much heavier banding around it is designed for training." Vrawn's attempted smile seemed to grow a little more genuine. "It was exceptionally well made. Each band weighs around ten pounds. And there are ten bands, so roughly one hundred and ten pounds total if I recall correctly."

"And you swing it so well and so fast?" Farnik blustered loudly as he booked it over to try and lift the weapon. He could, relatively easily, but trying to maneuver it was difficult, and he had to use both hands. "How?"

"I trained with a weighted weapon from the time I was a child, and still carry one with me to train every day if I can." Vrawn reached out and took the weapon into her grasp with ease. "I would recommend doing the same for yourselves if you wish to remain competitive. Weight training can be as important in developing stamina as running or fighting."

"We be puttin' in an order for weighted axes right his second!" Farnik hooted and clapped his son on the back. "Go and get it done, Brawny. I trust ye to see it to perfection."

"I would start off on a lighter weight and work your way to a heavier," I offered. Vrawn nodded her agreement. "That way, you cut back on injury, and you can keep people from growing accustomed too quickly."

"Good idea!" Gerty grinned at us. "This ought to be fun! We wish ye the best o' luck on yer travels, the lot o' ye. If ye need us, ye send the birdy to us, and we will get to ye."

I nodded, and Muu wandered over. "Hey, I just wanted to let you know, I'm glad you're back. And Farnik can tell you about the joke I told him."

"Muu, he has already." Gerty grinned and smacked him on the arm. "That were a funny jab, lad. I'd have taken ye in then an' there were I there to hear it. Keep yer humor up, an' come back safe, aye?"

Muu nodded, and the others said their goodbyes as they were wont to do. After that, we walked through the streets of Djurn Forge with dwarves hailing us as heroes and shaking our hands. It was about another hour and a half in getting to the edge of the city closer to the exit. Though it was here that we stopped for Vrawn to browse some of the wares at a couple stands. The vendors wouldn't even let her pay because she was with us. Some of them even offered us items for free, but we declined as it was the right thing to do. Though I did purchase something small that I thought she might like for later. I kept it close, though, not letting her see it. Vrawn took the two necklaces that she had picked out and put one on before pocketing the other.

"That's really pretty," I observed on our walk away. The necklace was a simple thing, a golden-hued metal wrapped around a small branch of dark metal with an emerald leaf at the end. It was beautiful, and even against her green skin, the gem sparkled visibly.

"Thank you." She smiled softly back, she held up a match to it and offered it to me. "This is for Maebe."

I pressed it back toward her. "I'm absolute crap at giving gifts, she can tell you for sure. So can the others—"

"He is!" Muu interrupted. "One time, I came home from work, and he had sat my gift on the table with no wrapping paper on it. Then pointed to it and said, 'there you go, buddy, happy birthday.' Like a schmuck."

"She doesn't know what that means!" I hissed angrily, but the story was true. "See what I mean?"

Vrawn laughed, and she seemed to relax a bit more. "Thank you, all of you, for sticking up for me back there."

"Of course!" Balmur grunted as he took the fifteenth head-butt from a passerby in the last ten minutes. "You're coming with us, and we know how important you are to Zeke and Maebe."

Vrawn tilted her head and regarded the man as another dwarf made their way over to him while he rubbed his head. "Do you?"

"Of course we do!" Bokaj chuckled and wrapped an arm around her waist loosely while he waggled his eyes suggestively. "We've been trying to get the two of you hooked up since we first met you and knew that you were sweet on him."

"Hooked up?" Vrawn's brow furrowed in confusion.

"Yeah, together, you know?" Jaken offered with a slight grin on his face, his own tusks flashing at us as I glanced his way. "It wasn't as much to mess with him as he likes to think. You seemed nice from the first time we met you, and we weren't sure how things would turn out. You're beautiful and strong, so we figured why not? And now, here you are!"

I rolled my eyes at my lovable, if not affable, idiots.

"You did not know me well enough to truly pursue this." She seemed confused. "Why?"

"Dating is a thing that is designed to help you learn about

someone and to see if your personalities will mesh," Yohsuke explained patiently. "My wife and I had dated for a long, long time before we got married, and even now we learn more about each other all the time."

Yoh's face fell a little as he thought of his wife, but Vrawn put a comforting hand on his shoulder. "I am certain she is a good woman."

Yoh snorted. "She is, and I love her to death even though she can be a friggin' pain in the ass at times. But she's my pain in the ass. And I wouldn't have it any other way."

"So you see, every chance we got to try and bring the two of you together so you could learn about each other, was one we took." Bokaj grinned up at Vrawn, and she smiled down at him. "I'm glad it worked out because both of them care about you a lot. Watching you watch him and Maebe, or them watching you, you can see it."

My cheeks burned fiercely as I stared ahead, the metal barrier to the outside looming closer.

"I see, thank you for enlightening me in this." Vrawn lifted her head in thought and stared forward as we walked, no longer talking. Though I did peek at her occasionally to ensure she wasn't quiet just because she was upset. Her looking around and taking in the sights the city had to offer made me smile, and I had to stifle a grin when she found a little dwarven girl motioning at her then her tusks in a comedic sort of way.

As we went to leave, a large crowd of dwarves stood before the door, all of them Ironnoses. They lined up on each side of the door as we prepared to leave and saluted with fists over their hearts.

As we reached the end of the group, the clan head that we had seen at the party stepped forward and bowed at his waist. "Ye be safe out there, lads and lassie. And if ye ever need us, ye holler for the Ironnoses. Aye?"

I smiled at him and nodded, "Of course we will! Who knows when and where we might need some of the ugliest dwarves to grace Djurn Forge?"

The leader raised his head with a glint of mischief in his gaze as I grabbed his shoulders in both hands and whipped my head into his with a crack, and my health lowered about 7% from the strike.

The leader guffawed and patted me on the shoulder affectionately as we all filtered out of the doorway to the tunnels outside the city.

"We know where we're headed?" James asked, then facepalmed. "We forgot Thogan!"

"I think he was supposed to be with the historians or something, Zeke, you want to check in with him?" Jaken asked quietly, uncertainty coloring his features.

I used the raven in my pocket and used it to ask. "Hey Thogan, we're getting ready to leave, do you need anything? Are you okay?"

The raven flew off and fluttered back a couple minutes later. "Aye, I be fine here, lad. I missed me people, and there be time now to talk to 'em and explain our history. I'll be doin' tha' a while, then I'll be on me way with Shellica to the village to check on Vilmas and Rowland. Ye be safe now."

I nodded to myself, then turned to the others and smiled. "He's good for now. He and Shellica will head to Sunrise in a while. As to where we're heading, I was thinking that city that we had seen when we had traveled from the forest to the beach near the island. I think that could be the port city we need to get to, to head eastward for the Continent of Beasts."

"Seems sound enough as far as plans go, did Queen Chareen ever say how she got back and forth?" Yohsuke muttered, then sighed when I shook my head. "Send them a message and ask how things are going. Do they need our help with Lindyburg?"

That was a great idea. I lifted the small raven out of my pocket and spoke into it in a genial tone, "Greetings, King Westwind, this is King Zeke. I wanted to check in with you and see how things in Lindyburg were coming along? If you need our assistance?"

Was it a little late to ask that? Sure. Did I hold out hope we would be able to go back and put that evil bitch in her place, then hopefully get some kind of royal escort across the ocean? Also yes. All you following along, cross your fingers.

The spectral raven flew off, and we waited patiently for it to return with the King's reply.

A brief flash of motion near my hand several moments later caught my attention, and the spectral raven had returned, the King's voice greeting me, "Yes, my friend, things seem to be going well. She has returned a missive stating that she has no idea why you attacked her so ruthlessly, but if she is to be treated as a traitor, then we are to come. We march on her as we speak with your friends, the Braves of the Thorn to assist us, as well as some of the dwarven druids Nick has spoken of. We will root out this evil and set things to rights. I hope your mission goes well, and have you need of Zephyth, contact my family."

His voice disappeared with the raven messenger, and we were quiet for a moment until Jaken grunted, then said, "Seems they've got it under control."

"Well then, I guess I need to get ready to face the sun." Yohsuke sighed heavily and pulled his shadow cloak's hood up over his head.

"I thought the shroud helped?" Balmur tried to lift the living shadows, but they washed over his hand and fell to the ground again. "She kind of never talked openly about it, but Jay said something about travel by ship as well."

"It does, but it still kind of sucks." Yoh pulled the hood of the shroud up around his head and face so that his whole body was covered and stepped over to all of us. "Let's go find us a ship then. Fuck."

I held my hands out and so did the others except Yoh, he allowed Bokaj and James to reach into the shroud and grasp his shoulders so that there was no exposed skin. Once all of us were touching, I cast Teleport, and we were on our way to the open-air once more.

CHAPTER SIX

The sunlight beat down on us almost in waves after being underground for only a short time, I heard Yoh growl at the sun, but that was it.

I allowed Bea to come out into the warmth so that she could stretch her legs and eat with Kayda, as soon as the light touched her, she blinked. Her beautiful brown eyes stared out at me.

I reached out to her, and she tapped my palm with her muzzle, I could feel her discomfort.

"You okay, sweetheart?" I pulled her head close to me so that she might feel a bit more comfortable.

I remember all of it. Her voice was somber, lighter almost and she sounded so much more put together. *The voices took over.*

"You're okay, baby. I'll help you learn how to deal with it and remain more in control."

She licked my palm, sadder than she had before. *You don't know how these voices shout.*

I leaned into her, pressing my forehead to her jaw and sent her memories of the voices I heard as instincts in my head. The alpha's voice howling at me. The elementals and Mother Nature herself.

Bea whimpered against me, her huff of sadness shaking me a bit, making Kayda drop down and grow to the point that she could cover us both with her wings. *I love you both, voices and all.*

I chuckled at her and patted Bea's thickly scaled hide, "I'm not going to put you back in the collar for a while if I can help it baby, but I do need to let you know that we're going to a city so I may need to just before we get there. Okay?"

Okay. We hunt? Bea looked up to Kayda, and the large bird nodded and puffed her chest out defiantly.

Kayda spread her wings, and the sound of crashing thunder washed around us, the sky darkening with her presence. *We hunt!*

I snorted at them and lifted my hands in defeat. "You can hunt, but you need to stay close to each other, and nothing on two legs. You be safe, and you communicate. Bea, I need you to listen to your sister, okay?"

They took off, almost as if they were competing with one another as they raced southward.

"Where the hell are they going?" Yohsuke shouted as he held out a leg of meat.

"They want to hunt because Bea's upset that the chimera's personality is taking control of her," I explained while observing our surroundings. This was the place that we had passed the city, but it had been about a day or so east of our position at the time. Striking my gaze easterly, I found the haze-covered city against the sea. "Think we need to come up with a story for why we're heading to the C-O-B?"

"The what?" Jaken grunted and pulled some jerky from his pocket, then flinched as he realized, "Oh, the Continent of Beasts, I like that. Yeah, it's likely that we may need one. I'm not sure how we will be received for wanting to go there."

"Is it a bad place?" Balmur asked, his book of spells in his lap with a pen in hand as he glanced about. "Like, how bad can it be?"

"It's not a bad place per se," James explained while pulling his notebook out to read from. "All that I've read leads me to believe that whatever is on that continent is powerful monsters and powerful people who have to compete with them for land and survival. The cities of the drow that are above ground are covered in domes protected from the sunlight there, and the Queen of Zephyth's people who she wouldn't tell us all that much about."

"So the types of people who go there are on either diplomatic missions or to hunt." Bokaj frowned in thought and scratched his eyebrow. "Well, why don't we claim to be going there to explore and see what we can bring home to our people on this continent? Like Manly had said, she went there on an expedition to find things like Bea's egg and whatnot."

"That could work." Jaken grinned with a chunk of jerky hanging out of his mouth, chewing noisily.

"I feel like that will be a good idea." Yohsuke nodded his assent then looked over to Vrawn. "You know anything about the city we will be walking into?"

"I cannot recall the name, but I have heard rumors that it is a den of thieves, liars, and cutthroats despite naval occupation." Vrawn stepped toward me. "I got a decent workout in this morning, but I think I might need something more. Should we move while the girls hunt, or would it be a better idea to stay and train?"

"It would likely be a good idea to stay and train, I don't want to be moving too far from them while they're out there in case they need us." I looked to the others apologetically. "Sorry, guys."

"What're you apologizing for?" James raised an eyebrow. "We're just as attached to your pets as you are. Though, I am surprised that Tmont isn't out there hunting with them."

"Oh, T'?" Bokaj pointed to his hood, likely where the cat slumbered. "She's too lazy to hunt for herself."

A small black paw slapped the back of his head, an indignant yowl coming from the inside of the hood. "What? It's fuckin' true, you lazy cat."

Another slap, and he fell silent to rub his head.

I looked to Vrawn and held a hand up. "You want to reach out to Maebe with me?"

"Will I be able to see her?" I shook my head, but she shrugged and offered to come stand with me regardless.

I took a steadying breath and drew on the shadow around me to form a small pool of the inky darkness, then cast Shadow Speak.

My mana drained, and the shadow rose and shaped itself to form a likeness of Maebe.

"I see it is finally time for you to call on me." Maebe sniffed. "Where have you been?"

"With the dwarves, sweetheart. We just left them this morning, why do you ask?" I explained what was being said to Vrawn as she spoke, and she could follow what I was saying well enough.

"It has been *days* since I last spoke to you here, Zeke." Her likeness frowned deeply. "And you say you only just left them this morning; this is the same day that I returned home?"

"Yes, dear, it is." I frowned in return, then it struck me. "Is the veil growing thicker? Does time speed up and slow down as the worlds come closer to each other?"

"I think that it does." Maebe sounded tired. "So, where are you now?"

"We're about a day or so outside the next city, where we will recruit a ship to go to the Continent of Beasts." I watched her nod, then added. "How go things at home?"

"Not well." Her voice grew harsh. "The Seelie grow bold, and they have begun to draw their forces to themselves. I am still… unwell."

"Even after a couple days?" My heart thundered in my chest at the realization. "Have you been looked after by a physician?"

"I have, they say that I am perfectly healthy, but the strain on my magic in a realm not my own has drained me deeply, I think." She did sound more tired than I had ever heard her.

"I think you should stay there until you're completely

better," I blurted. She didn't seem surprised, a small smile gracing her lips. "What?"

"I knew that you would care more for my wellbeing than anything else." She smiled wider. "I will stay, but only if you have Vrawn with you to help you in my stead. And as long as you reach out to me daily. My mother and I are needed here, and I fear that there is a battle coming between the Unseelie and Seelie."

"Can't we come to help you?" I implored her, but she shook her head. "Samir won't allow me to return to help our people?"

"No, though I did surprise him with my proposal." Her smile turned into a grin. "He rewarded me greatly for it, and before you ask, I cannot tell you."

"Was it a good thing, then?" Vrawn asked after I explained.

"It was the *greatest* thing." Maebe giggled and then sighed. "I will never forget the look on his face when he found out. Priceless."

I found myself laughing, then held up my hand with the ring on it. "I wear your ring, and I will continue to do so until you are here with me once more. Vrawn also has a gift for you, so she will be keeping that safe for you, too. I love you."

"I love you, too." Maebe smiled, then held a hand up to stop me from speaking. "Do not say this before her, but I want to teach you the name of another Fae to Call. Her name is Tan'rbleth. She is powerful and has expressed an interest in serving you after hearing that you were my husband and that Servant was so fond of you."

"Thank you, my love." I bowed my head and committed the name to memory as best as I could. "Vrawn, would you like to tell Maebe goodbye, for now?"

"Goodbye, Mae, I miss you." Vrawn seemed sad, but raised her arm to put over my shoulder. "I will keep our Zeke safe."

"See that you do," Maebe warned playfully. "Zeke, I want you to kiss her for me, and tell her that I miss her, as well."

I shifted into my human form and pulled Vrawn's lips to

mine in a kiss that I felt would be worthy of Maebe's affection for the other woman, leaving Vrawn surprised and breathless.

"Wonderful." Maebe clapped once. "Be well, husband."

She dismissed the spell and was gone as Vrawn leaned down to kiss my forehead. "I know it took a lot to have her stay like that."

"It surprisingly didn't," I corrected her with a smile. "I need her to be safe and whole. I need our people taken care of, and I'm surrounded by friends she and I trust. I'm fine. I worry about her and the dumbasses who threaten us."

Vrawn seemed to take that news oddly and stopped to mull it over for a moment too long. Longer than what was necessary, I thought.

I grinned at her. "You ready to scrap or what?"

"Scrap?" She glanced around us. "There is no waste here. What scrap?"

"It's a term people use where I'm from to mean 'fight'." I shook my body out and rolled my neck. "But we don't have to spar. We can do pretty much anything you like to work out."

"Anything?" She smiled, her green skin glowing in the light around us, her smile radiant as her glimmering blue eyes.

"Oh my." my eyebrows shot up and she chuckled. "I take it that was a joke?"

She nodded, and I shook my head. "I don't really have anything I can use for weighted training. So maybe we do something else?"

"Fighting and forms would be welcome." Vrawn pulled her weighted sword out, and I pulled out Magus Bane. Together, she and I slowly went through different types of strikes, the others joining us as they would. Eventually, the girls returned from their hunting victorious, Kayda hauling a large antelope-like creature in her claws.

"What the hell is that thing?" Yohsuke looked it over as if trying to decide what it was, but Muu just shrugged and went to work skinning the pieces of the hide that were salvageable.

"You know, pretty bird, if you would just slice a single time in the guts and eat your fill, we could have a whole mess of these?" Muu grumped at the bloody bird as Bea watched curiously over his shoulder.

There were many, I can bring more if needed? I relayed Kayda's offer, and Yohsuke frowned in thought.

"Having food to offer for part of the travel could endear us to whomever it is that we charter." Jaken rubbed his chin. "Can we make meat last a longer time like that?"

"I have a skill that allows me to treat food for longer travels, but it will only last like, a week longer than normal in perfect conditions." Yohsuke sighed.

"What if we got a barrel or something to store it in, and Zeke enchanted it to last longer and keep food fresher?" Vrawn offered with a finger pointed to the carcass, flies beginning to buzz through the area.

"Can you do that?" Jaken asked skeptically.

"Dude, I made the Mobile Spring Rod." I made to flip him the bird, but James stopped me with a rebuttal that it had broken. "That was from the wrong kind of use!"

"If we can manage to find a good power source, and convince them that we had come across it in our travels rather than making it ourselves, then maybe it could work." Yohsuke grinned, his fangs flashing beneath his shroud.

"Then we spend a couple days in town, acquire a barrel, enchant it, and use that time to find a boat to get overseas." Balmur sniffed and scrunched his nose up at the fly-infested scene before him. "Something fresher than that would be great. Maybe still alive?"

"Alive is a great idea." Yohsuke snapped his fingers and looked to the city in the distance. "Mount up, boys, we ride to the city!"

"What about Vrawn?" I glanced over at her, and she shrugged. "You don't have a mount?"

"I do not." Which made all of us pause. "I am but a simple guard lieutenant, and I only rated a mount while I was with the army. I have yet to find a suitable one."

I couldn't let her ride Bea, could I?

I will carry her. Kayda craned her neck and leaned down. "You can't carry her and get close to the city, hun." I ran my fingers through her facial feathers, the fine feathers brushing against my wrists.

Sister carry? Kayda glanced over at Bea, her muzzle in the remains of what leftover antelope that Yoh had left her with Tmont growling next to her as she ate. I knew she was capable of saying more and more intelligently, but she preferred to speak this way, it seemed, and as much as I could complain, the effort wasn't worth it at the moment.

Bea's gore-covered muzzle snapped up as chunks of meat fell into her gullet, and she swallowed happily.

"Bea, come here, sweetheart." I motioned to her, and she seemed content to listen. Her comforting weight bumped against my shoulder, and she listened with one of her brown eyes on me. "You think you could carry Vrawn for me? To the city?"

No collar? Her mind touched mine in excitement, images of her as a hatchling experiencing things outside for the first time.

"For as long as we can get away with it, how's that?"

Carry! Her feet stomped the ground as she trotted toward Vrawn. They didn't have the bond that she and Maebe did, so I worried a little.

With our connection still open, I could feel the sensation of her breathing in and tasting the air around Vrawn and it reminded her of home, somehow. Her scent was the opposite of Maebe's, a deep musk that held sweet notes and spice to it.

A ululating gurgle came from Bea that I had never heard before that left me speechless.

Like her. Bea's scaled muzzle and the side of her head brushed up against the orc's shoulder, and Vrawn laughed.

"She… likes you?" Muu whispered, almost to himself. "She tries to bite me if I touch her!"

"In her defense, you called her armor-in-the-making." Bokaj pointed out with a grin.

"It was a *joke!*" Muu blurted, and Bea eyed him warily.

"Animals don't get jokes the way we do, man," Balmur teased before blowing his whistle and summoning his horse-sized chameleon.

Tmont chose that moment to pounce on Muu's back and bite his tail before prancing away, the rest of us cackling with laughter as the dragon-kin chased after her for a moment.

"Let's mount up and move out!" Bokaj hollered, the rest of us blowing the whistles for our mounts and preparing to move out as was stated and heading toward the city at speed.

Thor, my black and gold kirin mount surged forward, his strides trying to match Bea's as she ran. Even with Vrawn's bulky frame on her back, the Gust Raptor ate up ground as if her legs were the fat kid and the ground a big, delicious cake.

I should know, I've been that kid.

With our mounts beneath us, the miles flew by, and we were to the city in a day and a half, stopping to eat and sleep at night training often while the girls hunted. Kayda and Bea brought two more large antelope in perfect condition to us to slaughter, I took their form, and then we butchered them for their meat and hides.

When the city came into full sight, we rode straight to what seemed to be the entrance to the city where a small cadre of armed guards with heavy crossbows and bows stood watch at an arch. Their somewhat scaled armor glistening in the sunlight like fish scales would.

Each of them looked different. Half-Orcs, dwarves, humans, and elves guarded the arch.

They would give people a tertiary glance here and there, stopping subjects that seemed to be entering with shadier materials and speaking with them in low tones before letting them go.

One of the elves stopped us, her dusky skin almost a wooden brown color and her gray eyes searching.

"Welcome to Feltgeor, travelers, what is your business?" Her brisk tone seemed odd with how relaxed the other guards seemed.

"We came seeking passage across the sea." Bokaj smiled, his charming personality taking over as he began to step closer. "I'm Bokaj, and you are?"

"Bored." Her smile seemed interested, but cautiously so. "But if it's passage you seek, try the dives by the docks."

"We'll try that." Bokaj's smile upped to a grin that he passed her way.

"The inns down there can be a little seedy if you don't know anyone." The guard stepped closer. "Maybe I could come by and give a little... extra protection?"

The rest of us began howling through our earrings, and he shook his head. Her smile faltered a little, but he recovered with, "If you think it necessary, I imagine I'd be grateful for your attention and guidance."

Her eyes sparkled, and the guards around her seemed decidedly taken aback, even one of the half-Orcs grunting in distaste as she offered Bokaj a nod and said, "I'm Nerine, I'll come find you after my shift."

"I look forward to it." We walked by with Bokaj in the lead, and then all hell broke loose over him.

"You *dog!*" I chuckled and ruffled his hair playfully.

"You still got it, man." Balmur snorted, his eyes darting about. "Those weren't guards, though."

That stopped the rest of our teasing quickly. Vrawn stepped closer to us. "How can you tell?"

Balmur nodded back toward the wall next to the arch, where stood a man in white clothing that reminded me of a sailor.

"The navy should be running a town this size, but they aren't, and the rest of the guys at the gate looked more like thugs and hired muscle than classically trained guards." His explanation halted as a few people grew too close to really talk and not raise suspicion. Once it was clear to speak, he continued softly, "I'd wager this town is run by a thieves guild or smuggling syndicate who allows the navy to operate so long as they stay out of the way."

"How the hell can you guess all of that?" Jaken was dumbstruck.

"Oh, Balmur used to play a lot of uh… less than favorable characters in a lot of games," Bokaj explained as our rogue grinned. "The criminal underbelly of these crazy places is always interesting, and not everyone wants to be the hero."

"It's boring and played out sometimes." Balmur shrugged and waggled his fingers toward the area. "There are times when the heroes are cool and necessary, but being able to successfully navigate the dark side of things is as necessary to get things done."

"So then what does this mean?" I wondered aloud, though I kept my tone low.

"Same as we planned, but we keep an eye on each others' backs and wallets." Balmur turned toward my right. "Muu, left hand down three inches and grab hard."

I turned and caught sight of Muu snatching ahold of a child's wrist as he went to pick the dragon-kin's pocket. "Good call, man."

The child darted off, as several other sets of hungry eyes followed us around as we walked through the city toward the docks. People gave us a wide berth, Bea not wanting to leave Vrawn's side, and I had given my word to her not to put her into the collar if she carried the woman, and they were cool with her being out.

Apparently, they had been cool with her or hadn't cared. Either one, and I was still a little on edge about that. That had to mean that either we would be watched or that they had more dangerous things in this city than a damned raptor.

We would need to be on our guard. And we were, for the most part. Despite the fact that the homes and buildings in the area grew progressively nicer the closer to the docks we went. Which was weird.

"The money has to be here." Balmur said, then grunted,

looking around excitedly. "Keep an eye out for any thugs you might see."

"Dude, it's the mid-afternoon," Muu grumped, then sighed. "Ten o'clock, three bodies and one above the door with a bow. The others armed with bludgeoning weapons. How does he do that?"

"Skill, baby." Balmur winked and glanced about. "Don't look at them, and whatever you do, do not talk to anyone in the navy outside. I'll find us a nicer inn to stay at while the rest of you get what is needed."

With that, he was gone, and the rest of us were left to wonder what to do, then set about looking. Carefully, we inquired about where to find barrels until Kayda took off and signaled to me where to go.

I led the rest of the party to where she perched above a large building of wooden slats nailed haphazardly together with a door to the road and a large workshop on the other side with a small fence surrounding it. On this other side of the building was where I spied several barrels and called out to see who owned the place.

A large, grayish-skinned orcish man in plain clothes and a leather apron took the time to bind a ring of metal around a set of wooden slats that bowed outward slightly from bottom to top, and he tapped them into place. It took him five minutes after the piece was finished to realize that someone was there with him.

He turned, scratching his bulbous stomach, and jutted his chin out at us. "Need a barrel?"

"Yes, we do." I smiled at him and motioned for Bokaj to step forward for his advantageous dealings with merchants due to his high charisma.

The man began to speak in a guttural language that seemed almost harsh and grating, but our linguist was out.

Vrawn stepped forward and began to converse with him, though haltingly at first, her deeper voice taking to the guttural noises easily enough.

"You speak like a child, where did you grow up?" The man inquired, his gaze longing and curious.

"I was raised by humans in Zephyth, the orcish I know is rusty, and I have been learning to refine it by speaking to a friend," Vrawn explained herself, but I noticed that she didn't apologize. Good.

"So you know little of our people other than what you've been spoon-fed to believe?" The orc shook his head and returned to what he was doing, then stopped. "What kind of materials do you need to store?"

"We need to store meat, and maybe another one to store fruits and vegetables. A slat to separate the two would be good." I thought for a moment after looking back at my friends and silently admonished myself. It was my craft. "And I will need them to be the best materials that you have."

"I make things for function, not pretty." The orc's harsh tone, deep with anger, belted out.

"I don't need pretty, I need it to be the best so that I can work with it," I said, then growled in return. "You capable of that, or do we need to go elsewhere?"

The orc rounded on me and stomped over until he towered over me by more than a foot and a half, his tusks sharp and capped with gold flashing down at me. "You must think you have some big balls to come in here and demand shit from me, little fox."

I simply smiled and silently cast Aspect of the Ursolon, growing taller and stronger as I stood there until finally, I was seeing at more than eye to eye with him. "I know I do, but I have the strength to back my demands. Do you want my business or not?"

The orc nodded, more to himself than anything else, and grinned. "I'll take up the challenge. Give me until morning two days from now. I keep the good stuff out back, and it's already cut. It'll be expensive, twenty gold each, but it'll serve you well."

I took out twenty gold and handed it to him. "Half now, half on receipt."

"Good business, get out." The orc snorted and returned to what he was doing.

We walked outside, and I looked over to Vrawn. "What did he say to you?"

"He greeted me kindly, but wondered why I traveled with all of you and no orcs but a half one." She shrugged, and we were on our way toward the docks while we all watched the shadows. "I explained as best I could that I was with you, and he seemed to find that offensive because you look weak."

"Ah." I dismissed the aspect spell and instead cast Aspect of the Eagle, a new spell that made my vision sharper and improved my dexterity by fifteen. I could feel my body becoming more lithe and sinewy, my eyes growing sharper, things at a distance became much clearer. "I apologize for looking weak."

"We all know looks can be deceiving." Bokaj sighed with obvious despair. "I mean, take Muu, for instance, he looks cool as shit and is as dumb as a toddler."

"Oh, I'll show you as dumb as a toddler, Elton John." Muu huffed and shoved the man gruffly.

Bokaj flew into a stall where someone had been selling fruits and veggies, the wood buckling under the newly added weight, and caving inward.

"Uh, I am so sorry, miss." Muu rushed over to help clean things up, barely taking note of the pissed off ranger or the cat who stalked out of his hood.

The human woman was mildly distraught. "I just paid for today's permit to sell, and now my stall is ruined. I'll never be able to feed my family now and pay for the goods I'm selling."

Rather than seeking revenge, Bokaj took a deep breath and waved Tmont back as she looked ready to strike. "Tell you what, ma'am: Muu, the dragon-kin in front of you is going to help me rebuild your stall better than it ever was, and then we will pay you for the damages. How's that sound?"

His winning smile and apparent sincerity seemed to be

winning her over, but Muu sweetened the deal. "And we will cover the rest of the permit fees for the week, if you'll let us?"

She nodded once, still looking like she was on the verge of tears as she brushed her brown hair aside. She wasn't a bad looking woman, a little on the frail side, but she seemed strong and had smile lines on the sides of her mouth and eyes.

You guys go find Balmur, we can handle this. Bokaj began to take stock of the wood he had access to and shook his head. "This stuff is nearly rotted out, it's not fit for use. Don't cry! I have some wood I'll use. I'm quite the carpenter, you know."

Muu looked at us and nodded, his eyes flashing to the alley behind us. *Tmont is over there watching our backs, so we will be able to know if something is amiss.*

Okay. Be safe. I motioned to the others, and they fell in around me.

We walked to the docks, and a familiar rogue figure separated itself from the shadows and waved us over.

"I got us some rooms here." Balmur jerked his head to the nice, white-painted building behind him. "And I think I may have a lead on one of those demons we're supposed to be hunting."

"The Demon's Day Out quest?" Yohsuke scowled. "How on earth did you figure that out?"

"The syndicate here has ties to all the cities and a crap ton of lesser mages in its employ," Balmur explained in a low tone, his eyes shifting back and forth to watch our surroundings. "Using them, they've discovered a large nexus of shipments that have demon summoning components smattered in."

"And where's it headed?" Vrawn asked suddenly with her back to us.

"Overseas somewhere." Balmur confirmed my suspicions, then glanced toward Yoh. "I'll answer that later. Where are the others?"

"Helping to fix a stall, Tmont is watching over them, and the barrels should be done in a few days," I answered. "What the hell is going on with you, man?"

"I'm finally in my element." Balmur grinned excitedly. "This is what my trainer trained me to do, but there was never an organized criminal element to any place we went, but here? There's an entire playground I get to wander, and I'm having a blast."

Suppose that's fair, I growled to myself. "Let's get inside and get some food. Bea, baby, I have to put you in my collar now because it's inside. Okay?"

The raptor dipped her head and nuzzled Vrawn's shoulder affectionately before tapping my collar and filtering inside in a plume of smoke.

We walked inside and sat. The interior was as nice as the exterior, bland, and coated in white paint. The black chairs and tables seemed decently put together, though, and the bartender dressed well. Her spiky blond hair stood up from at all angles around her head, angular cheeks, and a pointed chin greeted us with a smile. Round, human ears stuck out from the side of her head, and gray eyes watched us intently.

"Hello." Her thick accent sounded almost Russian, which was surprising. "How can I help you?"

"We rented rooms earlier and wanted to see about food?" Balmur sat at the bar and smiled at her.

"You, I remember, mister cute dwarf." She tilted her head at Balmur with a wink. "These ones, I do not. Will you be vouching for them, fiery one?"

Fiery one? Jaken snorted, his grin unabashed and plain to view.

"I'll vouch for them, I work with them." Balmur's smile was untouched. "Katja, my brothers. Guys, this is the owner of the Albatross Nest Inn and Tavern."

"Nice to meet you." Vrawn offered her hand, and the woman shook it lightly. "Thank you for hosting us."

"You are welcome." Katja pulled out several glasses. "It is customary for my customers to share a drink with the owner."

"I don't drink alcohol." Yohsuke grunted, pointing to a bottle of what looked like water. "You have water?"

"I do." She grabbed a dingy looking bottle with a brown liquid in it and set it in the bar.

"We will pour his." James offered quickly and poured water from his canteen into the glass meant for the vampire.

Katja nodded once and poured a silvery liquid into a cup in front of her, then the others, and lifted her cup. "To your health and honor. May one never impede the other."

"Health and honor!" The rest of us raised our cups and knocked back the strange alcohol. It burned something fierce but in a delightful way. My lycanthrope metabolism kicking in to destroy the booze that might affect my system. I could get drunk, but it took a *lot* of alcohol. I'd really learned that at the party with the dwarves, but this was a decent place to note it too.

The others had sour expressions and smiled, Jaken venturing, "Thanks, Katja, can we order some food?"

"Food will begin in one hour, it is self-serve style. I do not care to wait on many people, so you will care for yourselves."

Yohsuke offered a nod. "See you then." He made to leave toward the stair at the rear of the bar opposite the entrance and stopped when we all looked at him oddly. "I'm tired. I'm going to sleep."

Several "oh," faces greeted him, and Balmur took him upstairs to find the rooms that we would be using while we stayed.

"Katja, do you know any ship captains who we could speak to about passage overseas?" James requested softly as a group of people made their way inside, it looked like the lunch rush was starting.

"No captains here." She motioned to the people who had walked in, looking like the majority had been merchants. "They prefer to be near their ships on the other side of the docks. I know of a place, look for the mermaid on the wall, it is called the Schooners' Screw. Captains and first mates only there."

I glanced over at the others. *Food then go see about trying to set up passage?*

Don't you think we should wait until the barrels are done? Balmur returned as he plodded down the staircase.

Passage should be procured as swiftly as possible. If they know we're waiting a couple days, then they might delay their departure time so they can make more money, Jaken reasoned, his hand on his stomach. *Anyone else feel like the booze was a little potent?*

Sensing something was off, Katja called out, "Novasti alcohol is very potent, my friend. We brew it in house, you are not poisoned, but you should eat a belly full to be safe." Her smile was one of pride, and I knew we would be okay here.

We ate our fill, leaving a generous tip for Katja and her employees before we took off to secure passage. Out the door and into the light once more, the sea breeze ruffled my clothes, and I took in a deep breath and sighed. The place kind of reminded me of San Diego with the way the heat and sea scent played together, making me a little homesick.

We continued on our way down the docks and toward our destination. We took in the sights, wooden planks, and what looked like stone piers struck out into the bay where crystalline water met the gravel shore. A few tall ships docked in places, none of them really sporting any sort of flag or moniker, which seemed odd, but I was a Marine—not a sailor. What little I knew about boats was that they sucked, and got my brothers and me from point A at home to point B anywhere in the world in time to kick ass and take names so hard it was like we stole them.

Yeah, I was proud of that. Thank god I'd never been on ship more than a few hours, though. Screw that underway shit.

A hand on my shoulder startled me and I turned quickly to find Vrawn watching me with concern offered a small smile, "Are you well?"

I nodded. "I've never been one for the ocean, and seeing all these ships reminded me of an aspect of my life that I thought I may never get to experience again. Let alone need to."

"Can you not swim?" She looked at me, curiously.

"I swim great, all of the people who make it through the

training that James, Yoh, and I did need to be able to swim well." I smiled at her, and she seemed to take it better than before. "It's more a matter of what is beneath the water that I don't know of that concerns me. Always has."

"You're afraid?"

"I prefer the term, respecting boundaries." She snorted, and a couple of the guys laughed. "See, if I was meant to swim with the fish all day, I'd have been born with gills."

Vrawn laughed then, her chuckle making me grin wider. "How about you? Do you like the ocean?"

"Growing up near Zephyth as I did, I would go to the beach with my mother and siblings to train in the sands." Vrawn's wistful expression left her with a sad look in her eyes despite the small smile on her lips. "I remember the time my brother and sister went into the waves to fight a dreaded sea dragon as children. They giggled and carried on for hours as our mother watched them proudly."

"I take it they were playing, and the sea dragon was fake?" She snorted and nodded her head, as we rounded a bend in the docks with buildings creeping closer. "Why didn't you join them?"

"I also have a fear of the unknown in the water, and never learned to swim because of it." She crossed her arms as if it would protect her. "While they played, my mother took the time to show me how better to attack a foe and prepare myself for battle. She offered to teach me to swim, but I was stubborn and refused. My answer was always, 'what need have I of flailing in water when my enemies will be on land?' She was proud of my pragmatism in this, and showed me many things."

"So we need to teach you how to swim then," Jaken's cheerful assumption made Vrawn pause and shake her head. "We'll be on a boat, Vrawn. If you can't swim, you won't be able to keep up with us. And someone could get hurt trying to protect you or save you."

Vrawn stopped in her tracks, consternation and fear taking her features. Her brow furrowed, and her nose crinkled before she sighed heavily and looked at us all. "Please teach me how to swim."

"We would be delighted." I took her hand in mine and we continued on toward the tavern.

This place looked much more run down than I had expected. The grayish-green stone walls and wood boards above the structure looked pitted and worn from time and exposure to salt air and water. Honestly, it may as well have been on the damned beach with how close it was to the water.

"We sure this is it?" I muttered to my friends. "I don't see a mermaid on the wall."

"That's cause she be on the starboard side o' the buildin' close to the sea," a gruff voice made me turn, and I found a small gnomish man limping our way. "That be the Schooner's Screw sure as I be Cap'n Fredric Filthyfeet."

I frowned at him for a moment, then realized he wore no shoes despite the rest of his well-made attire. The white shirt held a fringe of ruffles on the front of it like a lapel, and his pants were black as the night sky. He looked every bit a ship captain, though he wore no hat over his tanned face or bald head. His right hand fell to a cutlass almost as long as he was tall that dragged on the beach behind him as he walked forward to stand closer and leer at us.

"Nice to meet you, captain." Jaken was the first to step forward and offer his hand. The small man clasped the paladin's wrist, and they shook once. "We were wondering if we could interest any of the local ship captains in some work. Do you and yours sail to the Continent of Beasts?"

The gnome snorted. "Not many here be crazy enough to venture there, but I s'pose ye could ask about." He motioned toward the building. "Sailors and crew be barred, and normal folk be tolerated, so mind yerselfs and ye'll be a'right."

"Thank you." Balmur smiled at the shorter man, the captain looking at him oddly, then limping away.

I nodded and we headed inside the building to a warm

room and beer-infused air. It was almost enough to give me a headache, like some of the bars I'd been in as a child.

There was Filthyfeet speaking to the barman, a human man with a greasy mop of hair who didn't seem to pay us any mind as we filed in. Several men in white hung around in the far corner of the room with a table, smoke billowing from their pipes and ruckus chatter pausing for a second, then continuing.

There were several other figures watching us carefully, some of them wearing normal enough clothing, others not so much.

"Ye don' look like any ship cap'ns I ever did see," a gruff voice reached us from our left. A lone figure sat at the only table on that side of the room with their back to the wall, a hood lifted over their head despite the dark surrounding them. There was no window here on this side of the door to shed any illumination for us to see with.

"That would be because we aren't," I spoke, my charisma being the highest of those of us here. "We're hoping to find passage to the continent of beasts. Know anyone who might be able to help us?"

The figure chuckled, a rasping wheeze emanating from the void of his hood. "Not many choose to go there of their own accord, and not many more come back."

"We're thinking we'll be okay." I tried to sound nonchalant, but the unknown was… well, the unknown.

"I see, and how you meanin' to make yer way there?" The figure motioned to the chairs around the table. "Funds? Employ? Trade?"

"Depends." Balmur shrugged as he took a seat across from the figure. "Who are we speaking to?"

The figure stilled, then lowered the hood from his face. Burn marks covered the majority of his features, the scar tissue looking like claw marks over the majority of his head. Tufts of hair grew where the scarring wasn't too bad, strawberry blond locks growing haphazardly. Once we had a good look at him, he lifted his hood back up and coughed.

"I'm Scar, a broker of sorts here for the cap'ns, so their precious revelry be safe and sound."

Balmur nodded appreciatively. "I don't know how you got 'em, but that's a nasty scar. I'd like to buy you a drink in brotherhood." Balmur showed his own scars, lifting his arms and showing his face. "As to the business? We can offer funds, protection, and food storage."

"Protection?" Scar snorted, his wheezing laughter surprising. "Ye think ye can beat the oceans? The beasts that lurk within?"

It was my turn to smile and laugh. "No, but Storm Company is capable, and we can do a little of all of it. We're pretty handy."

"I think I'll be needin' a show of strength, then." Scar sat back. "However, ye prefer to do so be fine, but do not harm this place."

I blinked and looked at the others, Vrawn shrugged and let us think.

You want to show off, or you want me to? I asked the others.

I think we all should, James offered. His plan after that seemed interesting enough.

"I'm waitin'." Scar's voice rang out in irritation.

The first thing that happened was that I held my hand up and flexed my will, pulling the shadows in the room to me with a mental yank. As the shadows passed toward us, Jaken's body pulsed red, taking Scar's attention. James hopped onto the table with lightning crackling around his fists and ki cycling through his body.

"How's that for a show of force?" Balmur asked from beside the broker who flinched visibly.

"Ye used yer other skills to distract me?" Scar's question seemed more accusation than anything else. "That won't work on the beasts of the sea."

"That's okay, we have other means." James sighed deeply, and the ki in his fists dissipated, slowly. "But, our request remains."

"I will inquire." Scar motioned for us to leave. "When do ye wish to leave?"

"Three to four days from now," Balmur answered readily. "We're staying with Katja."

Scar stilled. "Katja?" Balmur nodded, and the broker whistled. "Ye do have balls. Good, I'll inquire for ye and come to ye with the deal. I require a ten percent fee if I can find ye someone to take yer deal."

"Sounds good to me." Balmur looked at us, then back at Scar. He laid three silver on the table in front of the man and motioned to his magical eye. "We'll see you then."

Scar nodded, and we got up and left for Katja's.

CHAPTER SEVEN

"How was the rebuild?" I asked the next morning as we ate breakfast together. Yohsuke had spent most of the night awake and out of the city with Bea and Kayda collecting antelope to store once our commissions were completed.

"It went well enough, but Tmont noticed we were being followed." Bokaj took a bite of some fish and grimaced. "Nowhere near as good as Yoh's, man."

"That's fair." Balmur grimaced as well. "Needs something. Less salt and more lemon, maybe?"

"Can we get back to the fact that we were followed?" Muu growled softly, his teeth still covered in bits of food.

"They just followed us to the area before the docks, there's no reason to be too concerned." Bokaj waved the worry away with vigor. "And that 'guard' came by last night. She seemed nice enough."

"Oh, I bet she did, and it could be," Balmur sighed thoughtfully. "I have a plan. Some of you may not like it, though."

"You want to lure them out and use these two to do it?" James yawned and took a sip of water before stretching. "It's predictable of us."

"A little bit." I grinned, but Balmur shook his head at me.

"We need you to make sure that Vrawn is ready to go, so take Bea with you to the island you stashed the hoard at and collect more loot for us to use as a payment," Balmur explained and stopped me before I could gripe about it. "I know you guys have a lot, and I have my share too, thanks to Bokaj, but we may want more. Money never hurts."

"And what, while I'm away, you guys get to play?" I snorted indignantly, shaking my head and pointed at all of them. "There's no fucking chance."

"I agree with Zeke." Vrawn put a hand on my shoulder in support. "Splitting everyone up like this isn't a good idea."

"We're big boys, guys." Jaken chuckled, his easy-going grin, then he cut a stern look at both of us. "You still haven't gotten over that fight in T'agnolian Val. That would've happened whether you and Balmur had been there from the beginning or not. And *you…*" He pointed at Vrawn. "You're just afraid to learn how to swim. If we have to turn it into a vote, we will, but you will lose."

I growled at all of their smiling faces but saw the wisdom of what they were saying. This needed doing, and no one else would be able to be there for Vrawn the way that I could.

I held out a hand to Balmur, the raven I used to message in it, and he took it with a smile. "We got this, and don't worry—we won't be heroes."

Muu grinned. "Because we already are."

"Jaken, you think we're heroes?" James snorted as I rolled my eyes.

The Fae-orc shook his head. "Nah, man. Heroes do the shit we do and make it look good for the glory of it all. We just do our best not to get killed or look too stupid doing things."

"Then that means Muu is sure as fuck, not a hero." Bokaj howled with laughter at Balmur's jab at the dragon-kin.

I rolled my eyes at their antics and mentally told Kayda what she was to do while I was away. She wasn't too worried about the others but knowing how Vrawn and I felt about the water, she knew what I was doing was necessary. She did, however, send Bea racing through town to get to the inn.

We will not leave you completely unprotected. I could feel an air of superiority from her and rolled my eyes as a knock on the front door resounded through the building. Katja opened the door, and Bea made her way in, the woman cursing in surprise.

"She's with us, Katja!" Balmur called as she produced a blade to strike. Bea made a straight line for me and tapped the collar at my throat and filtered in.

"We're going upstairs to get out of here," I explained to the others, their breakfasts in various states of being eaten, though Muu piled more food onto his plate as I spoke. Katja's discomfort having been forgotten. "You had seriously better get a hold of me if anything goes wrong, and wait half an hour for my cool down before you leave, get it?"

The others muttered, "Got it."

And I finished with, "Good."

I stood with Vrawn, and we made our way upstairs into our room. I had spoken to Maebe last night and according to her, it had only been half an hour since our last discussion. The veil had thickened, and it seemed like time was passing faster here than it ever had.

"I hope to be fully recovered soon, my love. Please be safe," she had implored me simply. I had nodded and told her I loved her before I had gone to bed beside Vrawn.

Now, we stood together with our hands clasped and I cast Teleport to get to the island. Thank god for my higher intelligence because I was able to make it there with ease now.

Our feet lifted as a veil of darkness overtook us, and the sensation of being weightless for a second took hold of me. Then the squeezing began and ended as abruptly as it had come, leaving us standing next to where the cave with our hoard inside.

Business came first, and that meant going into our prehistoric bank and making a withdrawal. The cave was as we had left it, plenty of gold and coin littering the floor, at least there seemed to be a little less than there had been before. Some of the armor and weapons appeared to be missing.

"Damn, someone found the hoard," I muttered to myself as Vrawn wandered around the pile that was still there. "Okay, I'm going to gather all of this that I safely can. Feel free to take out anything you like, it's more than we need, and you'll need to care for yourself."

She nodded, her face slack in shock from the amount of loot before her. "If I see something I like, I can take it? What if one of you can use it?"

I shrugged as I began to press pile after pile of coins into my inventory. "Let me know, and I can tell you if it might be something we can use. Also, any weapon you find that you like, I can enchant for you. So keep hold of it."

We pored through the place for a while, but the amount seemed to still be present. No matter how much I tried, I couldn't seem to hold enough coin to get it all. And that was with more than two hundred thousand coins in my inventory. After that, there wasn't a way for me to have any more money go in at all.

That wouldn't do, and no matter how much money we had, there would always be a call for more.

I found a wooden chest with a small clasp on it that looked to be unsecured. I touched it, my fingers sliding all over it to ensure there was nothing odd about it. I lifted the clasp slowly and cast Diamond Skin on myself, one spell I didn't use nearly as much as I should, and opened it all the way.

Inside, there was a large gemstone on a pillow, the blue of it enticing and wishing for me to touch it.

Do not touch it, Hubris chided me in my head.

"What?" I blinked, and my ring glowed a bright blue on my hand.

It will siphon your soul away if you touch it. That gem is meant to be used in another manner, and you are not strong enough to touch it. Only someone of supreme strength can get past that enchantment to the real treasure—or a chosen person.

"So then what do I do with it?"

Close it, and secure it before you put it into your inventory, I have found another vessel you may use for what you desire.

I checked the area around me, the scepter nowhere in sight. "How did you know?"

We are bonded, I know your mind, master. And I wish simply to aid you in becoming great.

Ah. I thought to myself. That made sense then, I suppose, just weird that this item could anticipate my needs.

It is because we are bonded, and my sentience allows me to know my master.

The cool tone seemed less sarcastic and more matter of fact, which went a long way toward easing my mind.

I closed the box and set it into my inventory with a desire to touch it spiking and then did my best to forget about it. I felt a small pulse off to my left, at about ten o'clock from where I stood and found a large, leather sack.

This will do you nicely, master.

I frowned and muttered. "I need you to not do that so much. It freaks me out a bit."

Silence greeted me, and the relief I felt was lovely. I thought about what I wanted to do, the way I would need to enchant this bag to ensure it was right.

The leather of it was well made and a deep brown that reminded me of some of the cows I had grown up around. I took a couple pieces of platinum and held them in my disguised metal hand, channeling flame-aspected mana to heat them up and melt them together. Then I pressed the sides and edges to make a small placard for me to place on it. It didn't look like it would work well, so I used my claws to punch a hole through the top of the sack and the placard.

I found a bit of leather cording in my inventory that I pulled out and used to attach the small piece before engraving a funneling cloud of money signs to a pile below it in the shape of an infinity symbol.

Next, I gathered my wits and will to begin the enchanting

process. My idea was to pull the coins into this bag that would act as a bag of holding of sorts. Hopefully.

Master, the secondary half of your engraving will kill you.

I stopped, having just begun to pull my mana down the channels in my body.

"You have a better suggestion?" I raised an eyebrow, uncertain as to how to do what I wanted.

Call to me, and I will assist you.

I frowned. "Won't I need both hands?" I looked at the item and how oddly shaped it was. "I feel like I'll need both hands."

Call me. I will help you.

I growled and spoke the name, "Hubris."

The scepter appeared in my hand, and a warmth spread from it. The voice showed me how to cover the error the same way I had made the placard and now in its place were runes for holding and a rune that looked kind of like the pi sign, but small lines bisecting each different line of it. In the center of that symbol I engraved a circle with my own for money, the dollar sign.

"What is that rune?" I asked softly.

That is Naberious' Incarceration, a rune that allows immeasurable weight to be held inside a container with minimal weight on the outside, though your rune does not make sense to me your intent will power the spell and the effect you desire should be possible. Hubris's explanation was interesting. *I will teach you many more of them if you will work with me to assist you. It is time to enchant the placard master. Is the item secured?*

"It is." I ensured that the leather cord was woven through the several other holes I punched into the leather so that it would synch closed when tugged shut.

Excellent, I will assist you with this if you like? I didn't see the harm in it, so I nodded. *I want you to envision a wind that will pull loose coinage to this bag and store it for you to withdraw from on-demand by placing a hand into the bag and thinking of a sum. Once you have this sequence of events in your mind, begin to funnel your mana not into the item, but into me, and I will direct it in a more controlled manner.*

"My control is awesome, what're you talking about?" Vrawn had joined me by now and eyed Hubris with clear disdain. "You had better know what you are doing with that thing, Zeke. Nothing like what happened last time, or I leave. Am I clear?"

Your lack of it as you bled mana into me is what stole your life. Your survival and quenching my thirst was what bound us together. I am now an instrument for you to conduct your will into the world, and as such, I can more finely inscribe your intent into items. Will you trust me?

"I do, Vrawn, thank you." I turned my attention to Hubris. "That's all fine, but if you try to kill me…" I gripped the wooden handle as hard as I could. "I will straight up give you to the primordial fire elemental. He and I are on good terms."

The scepter remained silent, so I took that as an assurance that it wouldn't kill me and began to channel my mana into the weapon from where my hand was.

Once the mana hit Hubris, the gem at the top began to glow slowly as I filled it continuously.

Lower me to the item and tap the placard with my gem, and allow your mana to flow through me more vigorously.

I almost lost my focus as I rolled my eyes, but the interest I had in seeing this through was a reliable focal point to keep me on task.

I lowered Hubris slowly and tapped the platinum placard with the gem, and a peal ringing like a soft chime echoed out around me. More than five hundred mana funneling from me in the span of a heartbeat when I knew the item was completely done.

Bagged Avarice

When opened near loose coins and items of value, this bag will consume them for later perusal at the holder's discretion. Only works if items are not on another living being's person, or held down by a spell.

At times one's lust for riches becomes the better of them, and their fiendish desire to possess is given form. Be careful what you wish for.

Item enchanted by adept enchanter Zekiel Erebos.
That is good work, now to test it.

"Stand beside me, Vrawn." I motioned her next to me on my right and opened the bag.

A rippling suction sound emanated from it, a soft wind whipping out and lifting coin after coin into the air before the small items began to fly toward the open mouth of the sack. Thousands of coins of all types and items twisted and floated on ghostly gusts of gathering air and funneled into the mouth only to disappear. The sack felt no heavier than what a small bag might if I had shoved a lunch into it.

"This is awesome!" I couldn't help my grin, and Vrawn drew closer to me.

The bag had cost me only 839 MP total, including the engraving, and *this* was the effect! Amazing!

"Thank you, Hubris." The scepter warmed, and I dismissed it to wherever it was that it stayed.

"This is quite impressive." Vrawn's tone was careful. "How are you feeling?"

I took a quick mental check of myself and shrugged. "Other than a slight mana headache, I feel peachy. Why?"

"I wanted to be certain that it hadn't harmed you," she answered, and we moved forward so that the rest of the coins and goods would be lifted by the winds and carried to the bag.

Ten minutes later, we finished, and the items that remained were a sword that was rusted and useless and a couple of other small trinkets that looked worthless. I touched each of them to ensure that they were, and found that not only were they worthless, some of them may have been why the dragon killed people. Who carried such rusted garbage?

"I think that's all that she wrote here, babe." I grinned, and tossed the now-closed Bagged Avarice into my inventory. "You ready to go learn how to swim?"

She shook her head with a small smile. "No." she reached out and took my hand then squeezed it softly. "But now is the time for bravery."

"Good answer." I smiled at her and we left the cave to search for a small bit of water. The island was much larger than I thought it was, the area around the cave entrance having been destroyed by the black dragon Riktolth's influence and presence. That and his fight with the red dragon whose children still lived thanks to us, but no time to pat myself on the back there.

It took the better part of half an hour for me to find the scent of water with Bea's help. From there, we headed straight for it and would've started training immediately if it didn't look like the water was almost too still. I closed my eyes and willed the shadows around us into it. I felt things down at the bottom of it. Living creatures, things that could breathe water, it seemed.

"We may need to fight." I pulled out my axe, then frowned and whispered Hubris's name.

"What are you doing?" Vrawn hissed, "I thought you said we were to fight!"

I glanced at Bea, then her. "We are, and we will, but I want to be smarter about this. I can tell there are a few of them down there, but I don't want to just rush in headlong in case they're stronger than us."

Vrawn took out her weighted sword and nodded assent to my reasoning. "What would you have us do then?"

"Bea, you go 'take a drink of water' then be ready to bolt as soon as you see something, while Vrawn and I hide and wait to spring a trap on them. Okay?" The raptor nodded once and trotted over to the side of the pool. I glanced from Vrawn to the tree she stood beside, and I stealthily made my way toward the tree on my left.

Bea took a drink of water, then another, her thirst taking over for a moment as she lapped it up greedily.

I felt movement through the shadows I'd sent beneath the water and mentally tugged at Bea. *You gotta move sweetheart, they're coming.*

She stopped drinking, and grudgingly stepped back from the water as five frog-like men silently hopped out of the depths, the water wicking away from them easily. Crude spears gripped by three-fingered hands aimed directly at Bea's back.

I coached her toward us so that the attackers would stalk forward a little more before I cast Lightning Bolt at the first one who looked ready to throw his spear. The electrical lance almost pierced his chest and flung him back toward the water.

The frogmen froze, then one of them gurgled a shrieking war cry and threw his spear at Bea.

Cast your next spell through me! Hubris ordered, and I did just that. I willed the shadows to form a wall like a shield, Void Shield for 203 MP, and the solidified mass stopped the spear and a globule of mucus with it before it dissipated.

The reaction had been so fast that I sent another arcing blast of electricity at the offender just before Vrawn hurtled into the remaining three. Her heavy weapon caught one under the ribs where a set of gills assisted it in breathing and tossed it into the water fifteen feet behind it.

I growled and sprinted forward as one of them prepared to spear her in the kidney, Aspect of the Hare washing over me almost as if by instinct. I caught the spear on the bottom of my foot and kicked it before it could pierce Vrawn, a gash opening up on her left side where the spear sliced through the shirt and skin.

She grunted but kept her eyes on the opponent before her while I guarded her rear. I was about to brain the little shit before me when a green and gray blur snatched it up by its bulbous neck and savaged and tore into it. Bea wasn't one to stay out of a fight long.

"Good girl!" I called and spun on Vrawn and her frogman. He laid on the ground with his head caved in and his legs spasming violently.

"Was that for me, or Bea?" Vrawn teased softly with a small grin. Blood seeped from her wound, but otherwise, we were hale. I reached out and cast Purify on her wound, then Void's Respite as we walked to the shade.

"I wouldn't treat you like that." I cupped her cheek, and her smile widened. "Let me clean this water, and we can see about swimming lessons, okay?"

"As you wish." She stood and watched our surroundings as I walked back toward Bea. Her muzzle was thoroughly bloodied, and her tail wagged happily.

Helped. She puffed her head out and called out an almost chirp-like challenge. *I killed it.*

"Yes, you did." I scratched at some of the feathers now growing from the top and rear of her head. "Good job. Just don't eat it because we don't know what these things have going on protection wise, okay?"

She nodded and went back to the water to drink some more, not really caring how grizzly the blood on her muzzle made her look.

I sent a wave of shadows through the pool of water, cleaning the bodies and any other nasty things from it, leaving cool and pristine water behind.

"Okay, Vrawn, we're ready for you." I took my shirt and breeches off. My boots already lay next to the water so I could feel it with my feet. It was nice.

She shuffled over, watching me disrobe until I wore only a cloth pair of shorts to cover my modesty, then began to undress. Which was distracting, but we had business to attend, and I was capable of control.

Pretty, Bea muttered beside me, staring at the orc as she stood in a loincloth and nothing else. *She has no scales, and the sacs of skin on her chest seem fatty. How does she survive? They slow her down.*

I snorted and looked over at her. *She's stronger than you are dear, and I don't have scales—what about me?*

She regarded me as if I were dumb. *You have me and sister. We are your scales. Your fangs. We are fast, so you do not have to be.*

I snorted again, and Vrawn cleared her throat pointedly. I shook my head and turned to see her almost pouting. "A woman hardly enjoys it when a man she likes laughs at her when she's almost nude and afraid."

"I was laughing at Bea, I would never mistreat you like that,

Vrawn." She looked from me to Bea, who stopped drinking and looked up at her. "She wondered where your scales were and how you survive without them. I explained that you're much stronger than she is and that I also don't have scales. Then she said that I have her and Kayda to act as my scales and claws."

Vrawn's deep laugh made me grin, and Bea nodded her head as if she understood and agreed; that it served me right that I doubt her knowledge.

I rolled my eyes and hopped into the shallow northern side of the pool and pressed on toward the deeper section to suss things out. It went well, and we had enough space for me to help her.

"All right, Vrawn, come on in." I watched as she waded into the water toward me. "Go ahead and get yourself accustomed to the water, dip your head under, whatever you need to do to get comfortable."

I shifted into my human form so that my tails wouldn't get in my way for this, and my claws wouldn't be an issue. My dark skin was jarring against the water, but I held on and dunked myself to get used to the cool, crisp feeling of the temperature around me.

Vrawn followed suit and fell back into the water so that her head and hair were soaked. She sputtered a bit, and a slight shiver overtook her, but she eyed me carefully.

"First, we get you comfortable floating." I walked until the water was chest height on me and turned to have her come along. "Now, lay on my hands and try to relax."

She frowned at me, so I took my right hand and held her still while I positioned myself next to her and explained again, "Lay back onto my hands, and I'll hold you. You have to relax so that you can float, though."

She took a deep breath and leaned back, her broad shoulders on my right hand and my left lifting her tailbone. She was thick with muscle, so floating was odd for her, and I could tell by her breathing that she wasn't relaxing at all.

"Deep, calming breaths, dear," my voice took on an

instructing, soft tone. "And as you try to find your buoyancy, gently wave your hands and feet in the water."

She thrashed a little in her attempt to get it, and I raised her upright. "Here, watch me."

I leaned back and let the water hold my weight, taking steadying breaths to send air through my lungs into my blood so I could relax. I gently waved my hands and feet with my eyes closed so that I would stay afloat.

"This is a serene practice, with more practice, you can float easier." I stood and shook myself, the vulpine habits of my fox-man form taking over my human body for a second. "I have you, so you can focus on learning. Once I feel you have it, I'll let you float on your own. No!"—I frowned at her worried look —"I'm right here, and I'm not going to let you fall and drown. I swear, I have you."

Warning!

You, as both a Knight of the Unseelie Court and a member of a dwarven clan, have given your word. While a broken oath will have dire consequences in either realm, failing to keep your word in this, will have extremely dire consequences. If you fail to uphold your word as a Knight, your court's honor will be besmirched, and your title in jeopardy. If you break your oath as a member of a clan, your clan can turn against you, or exile you.

Be careful.

She must have seen the same notification I received because she nodded once and did her best to obey my orders.

After about half an hour with gentle prodding, Vrawn damn near had it. She floated on her own, and I was able to let her go. I had to stay close because if I moved farther than ten feet, she lost her cool, but it was something.

"Okay!" I gave her a hug and scratched her back, affectionately. "You're doing great!"

"I have seen others swim, but that was not it." She looked me in the eyes. "Do I learn now?"

"You do." I leaned forward in the water and showed her how to doggie paddle, she took to it relatively easily as she moved from one side to the other. "Next, we use arms and legs."

She didn't do so well, her fingers splayed out as she tried to swim. I fixed her hands so that they were like paddles, and I held her stomach as she paddled and kicked through the water. Finally, I had her do it on her own, and she floundered a little, her even strokes becoming wild and unmeasured.

She stood and slapped the water in frustration. "I just don't get why I cannot seem to overcome this!"

"Maybe you need more of an incentive?" I raised an eyebrow, memories of my childhood washing over me. My mother in the pool calling to me with her arms open, her normally sun-kissed brown hair stuck to the side of her head as she smiled at me encouragingly. I would paddle as hard as my tiny, flabby arms and legs would propel me. When I caught her, she would give me the biggest hugs, and I would grin triumphantly up at her.

Those had been good times. Really good times. Times that I had unfortunately missed out on with my son, due to distance and my time away from him.

My jaded heart turned, the sunny summer day growing cold and barren. The pool filling with algae and leaves, then disappearing altogether, leaving me as the adult I was. Devoid of that warmth that so many people took for granted. The warmth that I'd had to turn to others for that had made my life both hell and happy.

I felt hands on my shoulders as I trod water and snapped out of my reverie to see Vrawn watching in concern. "Maybe we should rest?"

Suddenly, I felt much less like swimming than I had before. "Yeah, we can rest then get back to it in a while."

We trudged out of the water, the warmth of the breeze still managing to chill the two of us. With a flex of will, I summoned a small flame with my mana as the fuel and used it to warm the both of us.

"What was it that you remembered?" Vrawn's quiet question brought my gaze from my small magical fire. I mean, theoretically, I could have been doing this with flame all along, but I wasn't yet sure I could do with fire what I could with shadow. Maybe someday.

"My mom." Even as I spoke, I could feel the numbness of my past clambering up from the pit of my stomach and around my heart like a living shield.

"Was it not a joyous memory?" Vrawn tilted her head and continued, "I saw the way you smiled at the beginning, then when you stopped. So slowly as if something tainted it. What happened?"

I was quiet for a while, my silence making her fidget before finally, she put her larger hand over mine. "You needn't speak of it if it hurts you. I understand that pain."

"It's okay." I offered her a sad smile to let her know I appreciated it. "My childhood wasn't the best. I think you remember me telling you that things like this in my world aren't always safe?"

"I recall from our night on the plateau, yes."

"Well, people aren't either." I frowned, trying to get my thoughts in order before I fucked up. "My mom had me and my sister pretty young for my people when she was still basically a child herself. This was also in a time when she wanted to be with her friends and have fun. I never really knew all too much about it when I was young, but my aunts and uncles always took care of us. They were hard on her—tried to be, because she needed it. But it never really stuck. I was forced to watch, from a young age as alcohol and drugs consumed her, her focus and her drive. Made her get with people who were shitty and abusive to her, just so she knew where her next fix was coming from. Well, eventually, she married this guy she thought was perfect.

"Except he wasn't. They would get drunk, fight, and he would hit her. My whole family was really hard on each other, and sometimes, when she drank, she went after everyone. I had to watch all that while looking out for my little sister. My mom would try sometimes, like, it seemed like she really cared, you know? But it always seemed like her addictions took priority even as she called my sister and me her world. Eventually, she couldn't afford to have us anymore, forcing my sister and me to go live with two different sets of relatives. I can't complain, my aunt and uncle did their best to raise me to be a good man. But my sister and I grew apart, and then I joined the Marine Corps when I was old enough and ready to get away from everything."

Vrawn nodded as I spoke, my story was mine, and she wouldn't interrupt.

"Well, while I was away, my mom divorced the first asshole, and found herself another one." I shook my head, forlornly explaining the next bit, "She had cleaned herself up, was sober and as far as I knew, was off drugs too. I was really proud of her, this was about the time when my son was born. She wasn't around much for him—my fault, really. Lingering anger on my part and family drama, I think, but she was really there for my sister's two little boys. Those two were awesome. Well, they used to go and stay with her sometimes and they would for years! They had fun, I guess. Never was a problem until my sister caught wind that my mom's then-husband drank a lot and would yell at her and the boys. My sister told her she didn't want them around that because she knew what it could do to them, and that she wasn't sure what this guy was capable of doing to her kids. You know what my mom does?"

I couldn't help the tears of impotent rage that sprang to my eyes. "She accused my little sister of being on drugs and neglecting my nephews to try and get them taken away from her. So that *she* could have them." I punched the ground with my metallic hand, the earth giving in to my fury and hurt, leaving behind an imprint of my knuckles. "My sister had to prove to the people who would take her boys away that she wasn't on drugs, and the boys were taken care of. That was a long and arduous process that was borne completely out of my mother's need to feel like she could finally be a good mom. *Two kids of her own, and she had to try with someone elses?!*"

That last bit had brought me to my feet, my chest heaving, and the breaking in my heart coming about all over again. "I'm still not very close with my sister, and I only have my mother and myself to blame. I barely know my nephews because I feel like a stranger to my own family! What kind of monster am I? What kind of monster—"

Large arms encircled me from behind. "You aren't a monster any more than I am for foreseeing my brother's death, Zeke."

"You know, I tried to see her when I got out of the Corps?" I shook my head, chuckling darkly at my stupidity. "For more than a year, I tried to see her and get her side, but she never showed. I tried and tried. Because I was stupid and I wanted her side of things. To tell her that what she had done was wrong. And now I don't have a mother. Hell, except for a few aunts and uncles, I barely have a family. Because any time I see my grandparents they tell me I should go see my mom, and I worry she's going to be there, so I stay away. I've lost so much."

A scaled muzzle sniffed at my cheek, Bea trying to cheer me up a little. I could feel her mind pressing against mine sadly, trying to show me memories of her running to make me smile.

"You have your son," Vrawn offered softly. "He's adorable from what Maebe has shared. And you have your brothers, and friends, and Maebe. And me."

I turned in her arms and held her tightly for a moment as my anger and sadness slowly drained away from me.

"Thank you." She ran her hand over my head and back comfortingly. "For sharing that with me."

"Thank you for listening to me rant and complain for no reason." I sniffed bitterly. She pushed me back so that she could hit me with a severe glare. "Don't try to cow me, Vrawn, that was a lot. I'm sorry you had to endure it."

"I did so because I care for you." She grasped my chin and forced me to look her in the eye. "And that you shared that with me means that you trust me enough to know your pain. I hold that trust dear. But it also shows that no matter how broken by their circumstances one may be, they are capable of great things, as you are. As you have shown time and time again."

My lips twitched. "I don't even remember if I've ever told anyone here about my mommy issues. Not even Maebe."

"Then you should tell her." Vrawn cupped my chin and bent to try and kiss me. I stopped her by jerking my head back. "What? What is wrong?"

"You tell her, I want you two to share things, and it seems she's had to tell you more about me than I have." I pulled myself from her arms. "As for that kiss? You're going to earn it. Back in the water."

She growled, her tusks flashing as she frowned and stomped her way to the water with me. I ran and cannon balled into the deeper end where I wouldn't break my ass on the ground and came up to see her stepping into the shallow side.

"What now?" She crossed her arms under her ample chest and glared at me.

"You're going to swim to me, and when you get to me, I give you a prize." I grinned at her as she cocked an eyebrow up curiously. "Come catch me, darling."

She grinned and began to press forward through the water until it was hip-deep on her, and she dove in as I had shown her to. Her powerful arms rowed, over her shoulders and through the water like a green, newbie Michael Phelps. As she grew closer, I would back away and have her come further and further into the water. Her breathing grew slightly ragged, so I reminded her to breathe every time her head was above water.

After ten minutes of constant cat and mouse, I let her catch me where I stood in the beginning of the shallow end. She touched my abdomen with one hand and pulled me toward her with a call of pure animal victory.

"Finally, got you!" She lifted me above her head, my turn to panic as she laughed and pumped her arms up and down with me in them. "I will have my prize now!"

"Then put me down, damn it!" My feet kicked pathetically, and I scrabbled to hold on to her wet body.

"Oh, no." She *accidentally* threw me four feet into the deep water, and I came back up to leer at her. "Whoops."

"Oh, it's on now, mama." I snarled playfully and took my arm and whipped it into the water so that a wave of water splashed up against her chest and face.

Our war of watery torture began then and let me tell you, when a nearly three-hundred-pound muscled woman hits the water and sends a wave at you—you better fucking run.

I clambered out of the water at the side, completely soaked to the bone and still dripping water from her monsoon level splashing. She grinned happily as she joined me, rays of sunlight filtering through the treetops above us and warming her skin.

"You feel better about the ocean now that you can swim?"

She shook her head. "No, but I know that I can at least float, now. And that's a start."

I nodded proudly at her, "Good. Now about that prize."

I stalked toward her, and she grinned knowingly.

CHAPTER EIGHT

We both swam a bit more, taking a few hours to really get her comfortable with the water and the idea of swimming before we prepared to return.

I hadn't heard anything from the guys, so that had to mean that they were alright.

"You're worried about the others?" Vrawn toweled herself dry this time, the water having almost won this last time as she cramped up. I had warned her not to get into the water so soon after eating, but no, she couldn't listen. Now she knew and would be better prepared for next time.

"Yeah, a little bit." I called to Bea mentally, and she returned with a little more blood on her muzzle. I frowned at her, and she looked down in shame, like a dog that knew you knew they had done something bad. "What did you do?"

I glanced behind her and found a frogman body ravaged and torn apart. "What were you thinking? What if those things are poisonous?"

Tasty, and slime good for throat. Bea snorted and trudged forward.

"You could've been hurt!" I insisted, but she touched the gem on my collar and filtered into it.

I summoned her once more with a tug of will, and she came out of the collar looking around. "Look, I'm not trying to be an asshole; I just want you to be safe. I love you so much, what if something bad happened to you?"

You fix me. Her simple trust in me was alarming, but her thoughts were much more complex as she showed me memories of me helping her and caring for her. Giving her good food, the monster crystals to help her grow. *I love you. Means trust. I trust you, you need trust me.*

She licked my cheek before touching the collar again and filtering away.

"What am I going to do with her?"

"Love her and accept that she will be her own creature for the most part?" Vrawn's arms wrapped around my shoulders and leaned back against her. "She is very intelligent, and has a predatory instinct that you do not at times. I think she will be all right."

I sighed and shook my head, turning to ensure that Vrawn was decent. She wasn't, and while I was comfortable with her, I still blushed a bit. I didn't look away, but color deepened my cheeks.

She slid her clothes on, a small smile cracking her features a bit, then swayed toward me. "I'm ready when you are."

I grinned, and she grasped my hand as I cast Teleport to take us to our room at the inn once more.

…tching them for now, but when Zeke and Vrawn are back, we should discuss a plan of action on this. Balmur finished, and the others were quiet for a moment.

I scowled at the darkening room and reached out through my earring. *What the fuck is going on?*

Hey, Zeke's back. I could almost feel the shit-eating grin in Muu's voice as he spoke.

We were just about to call you, buddy. Jaken's mind-voice sounded strained.

You're a terrible liar, man. Bokaj sighed, then continued, *We have a bit of an issue. Nothing is wrong with us, but we found out that the syndicate may have a splinter faction that works with the Children of Brindolla. They've got some folks who may be aware of us watching our movements, and we think that there may be a warehouse here that they use to store some goods.*

And you guys are watching the watchers while waiting for Vrawn and me so that we might be able to make a move on the warehouse? I tried to keep the skepticism out of my voice, but I was concerned. How deep did these zealots have their fingers into things?

And how far were they willing to throw themselves toward the cliffs to try and get rid of us, even though we were trying to solve their problem for them?

A knock on my door shook me out of my thoughts, and Vrawn admitted James to the room, his lips pressed tight in thought.

"Bokaj has our two tails under observation and can lure them into a trap if needed," James explained softly so that only we might hear. "Balmur is at the warehouse with an operative from the syndicate now waiting for us to decide what to do."

"We aren't luring anyone into a trap." I sat on the side of my bed and thought for a moment. "If they have ties to the syndicate, then they're likely decent fighters, and if they have even remotely close to the same kind of enchanted gear that Asshole and Cudgel did, then we would be in for a hell of a fight. We can try and hit the warehouse, but we need to go in there knowing that this person with Balmur could be a plant, and it could be a trap. Or trapped at the very least. We all know what that little bastard Tarron is capable of, especially after the fiasco with the high elves."

My first and former enchanting trainer, Tarron Dillingsley, the little gnomish fucker, seemed to be heading a group of zealots with the intent to rid Brindolla of outsiders. Either by killing us, extortion, blackmail, and coercion—nothing was outside their purview—and they wanted to take care of War's influence themselves.

Which we knew was impossible, because they would know that they were coming because of their ability to kind of sense the populace of the world. They can't sense us because of the fact that we aren't from here, though there is the fact that one of the generals sent all of us some pretty nasty dreams. Seeing loved ones dead, and their corpses warning us to stop had driven us on.

"We can look, but let's not engage." I grimaced, remembering what we had come here to do. "And maybe before we leave, we figure out a way to get those tails off us."

"Sounds good to me, let's get out of here then." He shrugged, and I turned to look around the room for anything that might be hidden as a plant. Nothing, thankfully. Seems Katja had some pull here, or at least good enough service not to let anyone into our rooms.

James explained to the others through our earrings what had been discussed, and the others agreed with my thought processes.

"How do we wanna get out of here?" I glanced at James as we were on the way out of the room.

"Bokaj lured them toward the market," James pointed out the window at the end of the hall toward the north. "The warehouse is actually pretty close by, near a secret dock that the syndicate uses for secret things. Balmur is there now with the syndicate rep."

"Just because Bokaj has two of them on his back, doesn't mean that is all of them." I walked toward the window carefully, then eyed the outside past the curtain.

I didn't notice anything too conspicuous, but I did notice an old man rocking in a chair in a high window facing this one with a pipe in his hand. He had to be about eighty feet away from us, but his eyes were on this window and the front of the inn as well.

This place is under surveillance. I growled through the earring to the others and paced back to my doorway and the two who waited there. "Vrawn, will you wait here with Bea and keep her company? I'm going to need to shift into an animal form to get us out of here without being seen and have James in the collar to boot."

Vrawn agreed, and Bea filtered out of the collar to stand with her in my room. "Be good for Vrawn, okay?"

The raptor growled assent and plodded toward my bed with Vrawn fussing behind her.

James touched the collar and turned into a cloud of gray smoke that siphoned into it.

I glanced around then took a form I hadn't taken before because it was creepy as shit, that of a spider. This one was roughly the size of a chihuahua, like the ones that we had been fighting in the jungle after our battle with decay, but it had a special ability I wanted to capitalize on. The fact that it could walk on walls.

I stuck myself to the wall, taking a moment to get used to the new vision, then clambered up the wall.

Stick to the corners, pause and watch, then move slowly. The spider's instincts instructed in a deeper voice than I expected. Following its instructions, I crawled along where the roof and walls met, slowly. All I needed to do was find an open window, then I could turn into something else to be a little less conspicuous.

The tavern area below looked to be full up, Jaken and Muu sat watching the door with mugs of warm liquid in their hands. Their eyes seemed drawn to me, and I waved a leg at them and moved along. A window behind one of them was open near the rear of the room, so I made a b-line for it.

Zeke, if that's you stop right now. I froze at Muu's command. *We're being watched across the room by a guy who just came in. You may want to try and go through the kitchens.*

I turned and scuttled my way toward the rear of the room near the bar, carefully trying to avoid being seen.

"What in the hells is that thing, Katja?!" One of the bar patrons cried as his finger whipped up at me.

You've been made, run! Jaken bellowed through my mind and

stood fast enough to knock his chair back. "I'll kill it! I hate spiders."

Several patrons took off boots and began to throw them at me wildly as I crawled faster and faster. A knife sliced by my left foreleg, and I juked around it as best as my eight legs would let me.

"Get back here, you little shit!" Jaken howled and raised his shield in time to catch me when a boot dislodged me from the ceiling. "Ah, ha! I have you now!"

He shoved the shield toward the kitchen as his sword flashed forward, *barely* missing me and giving me a small head start. The chefs threw pots and pans, one of them belting my body with nearly boiling water that had living crabs inside. A small chunk of my health sizzled away, and I fought not to curl up from the brief pain of it.

Jaken took a pot on the shield as he bent to try and "crush" me with it, cursing loudly as he tried to get me. The door through what had to have been a pristine kitchen stood slightly ajar, and I put on an extra burst of speed. A spear shot over-head and rattled the door open even further.

"Don't worry, pretty lady, we'll kill the little bastard for you!" Muu cried, and made his way into the kitchen. "Aww man, this place has crabs!"

"Those are lobsters, you fool, and get out of my kitchens!" One of the men that had thrown pots at me snarled.

"Please, Muu, come back in here and look for more spiders here, I think your friend has it under control." I was too focused on getting out alive to see if he followed Katja's request, but once I hit the outside, I was up on the wall and the sound of chipping wood.

"Ah-ha!" Jaken screamed, and I paused long enough to see him take out a vial of something that he splashed onto his new shield that looked like a viscous green smear. "I got the little bugger!"

I snorted to myself as he toted his shield through the door

only to be screeched at to get out and go around with that bug grossness on his shield.

The things we do for friends. He sighed theatrically. *Zeke is out of the inn.*

I found a small dip in the roof and shifted to my human form and used the earring to get to Balmur. *What am I looking for?*

Opposite side of the bay area is a port with three docks, Balmur explained carefully. *We're on the roof of the warehouse next to our target, and we will be waiting for you. Try to be quiet so that you don't draw too much attention.*

I nodded before looking at the slowly darkening sky. Owl would be okay for this one, seeing as stealth was required. I carefully positioned my body, so it was low to the roofline and glanced around to see if anyone paid attention to my spot.

I couldn't see anyone, so I doubted if anyone could see me. I shifted into my owl form, the feathers of my right wing looking exactly as they did on my left, then took off toward my destination. There was a small covered entry from the roof that Balmur and another person waited on one side of, so I carefully dropped down and landed on the opposite side.

I shifted to my fox-man form and allowed James to come out of the collar, when he did, I hushed him with a hand to his mouth and pointed toward Balmur and the other persons' position.

We stepped around the small cover, and a dagger sliced toward my throat.

I grinned and grabbed the blade by the sharp edge with my metallic right hand, the vibration and soft sound of pealing metal so satisfying to my ears.

"Cool it." Balmur snorted, rolling his eyes at the other man who tried to take back his weapon. I just grinned wider and held on to it.

"Would you kindly let go of my blade?" A whispered snarl from the hooded darkness before me greeted us.

"You always try to stab friendlies?" I inquired as I admired the weapon in my hand. It was a black metal that looked like ebon iron, but I wasn't sure about the make. No matter what I did, the stats of it seemed to be hidden from me.

"Only when they sneak up on me," his response had been expected, and I let the weapon go with a shrug.

"Sounds like you need to be more careful." He stiffened at that and Balmur shot me an uncertain, questioning glance after my statement. *He tried to stab me. We've killed people for stuff like that.*

He's with me and the syndicate would come after us if we kill him without cause. Balmur sighed through my mind. *I would prefer not to go toe to toe against an entire criminal organization with whom we have little to no clue how deep they run in this country.*

And here I thought you knew everything about the seedy underbelly of this world? James coughed to cover his chuckle.

I know what my mentor was able to teach me; he works for the syndicate, so I had an in. Balmur sent, then growled, his glance James' way more menacing than he meant.

"Communication earrings, nice." The figure glanced at Balmur, then at James and me. The three of us stilled, eyed him critically. "Oh, don't worry, we have them too. One that gets us to the nearest members, and another that allows us to send word to our handlers who keep tabs on our movements. That way, if I disappear tonight, you all die."

I saw a flashing grin beneath the hood before it fell back to show me the cat-like figure beneath it. Slitted orange eyes blinked at me, whiskers twitching in delight. "You expected human?"

"I expected someone who could keep their identity more of a secret, but I guess a cat having my tongue is the least of my worries." I grinned at him, and his irritation turned to confusion as I offered him my hand. "Name's Zeke. You?"

"I am Calmyra." His voice had a purring tone as he took my hand in his. "And this other one must be… James?" The dragon elf frowned, and that only further satisfied the guest. "Our knowledge runs deep."

"I see." I smiled at him in return and turned my back toward our objective. "Fill us in then, Cal."

"Only my friends call me that." He harrumphed quietly as he sidled closer to my side and motioned to the building across the street. "Three floors, three entrances, two on the ground floor and one roof with fifteen windows—all secured from the inside. Guards patrol the outer perimeter on five-minute rotations, and the guard switches every four hours."

"Well, if we're gonna be working together, we should be friendly." I poked at him with a finger. "Spells, traps, or anything else that could be a concern?"

"Nothing on the outside, but we have had bodies inside that have gone missing. It's part of why I'm here," Calmyra explained in a low tone. "And just because we find ourselves temporary allies, does not mean we need to be *friendly*."

I turned a winning smile at him, making Calmyra snort disgustedly before casting a sideways cat-eyed glare at Balmur and James. "Is he always so insufferable?"

"Yup." James nodded with a sly smile.

Balmur fought not to laugh out loud. "Always has been. You get used to him."

The cat-kin rolled his eyes and shoved my shoulder gently. "At least attempt to be professional."

"Me?" I feigned being hurt, doing my best to bat my eyelashes at him. "You wound me, sir, I'm the model of professionalism."

"Okay, okay." Balmur still had to fend off being amused. "Time to pony up and get in there. How do we want to do it?"

I acted like I was thinking while I was really gathering shadows and bending them inside near the closest window. I watched as a dark blur crossed the glass pane, slightly obscured by the rough cut of it. I closed my eyes and grumbled as if thinking harder, really just throwing my consciousness into the shadows and using them to unlock the window from the inside.

I heaved a sigh and opened my eyes as I withdrew myself from the void. "I think we go in through that window."

Calmyra's head whipped toward the windows, and I used his minute distraction to wink at the other two with a hint of shadow manipulation to give them an idea as to why I suggested it.

"Seems like a valid point of entry." Balmur shrugged and began to prepare himself to cross the mere fifteen-foot distance.

"You want me to toss you?" I asked with a goofy, lopsided grin.

He shook his head and went to leap across only to be stopped by Calmyra. "Please, allow me to go first. I have ways of holding onto things, and a window is the least likely thing to stop me. Also, the guards are due right... about... *now.*"

I couldn't help but respect the fact that he had them timed so accurately. True to what he said, two guards walking toward each other overlapped on their rounds with barely a glance at one another before moving on.

A moment later, they were out of sight, and so was the cat-kin. He hung precariously on the outside of the window, trying it and finding it open. I hadn't even noticed that he was gone until I'd looked up.

We not worried about him? I asked Balmur and James.

Balmur touched my shoulder. *Two of the missing thieves are his sisters. He wants revenge as much as we want to know what is being planned under our noses. If we can help him, he will help us.*

I nodded once and watched as he melted into the shadow and stepped out of the shadows in the window. A muted crunch met my ears as James just hopped from the roof we stood on to the ledge of the window easily, whereas I took owl form and glided across with no issues.

We shut the window before our snooping and sleuthing truly began, sticking to the shadows so as not to be made from the outside. This section of the warehouse seemed to be holding a large variety of art. Paintings and sketched drawings of land-scapes and nobles encased in open wooden displays in some places with dried hay and paper packing supplies readily at hand.

I say nobles because these people looked aristocratic in nature, a certain degree of pomp and airs of wealth seemed to be included in the artwork. Snooping here gave us nothing of any use after circling the whole of the floor carefully and quietly. Even managing to get behind some of the art was difficult but manageable, though it yielded nothing.

We came to a set of stairways, thin with metal handrails that led up and down. "Do we go up or down?" Calmyra muttered as he slowly checked a nearby window.

The guards had done three rotations by now, and we hadn't heard anyone inside. Nor had we found any traps.

"Better go up, that way we can save the more dangerous bottoms floor for last," Balmur suggested, his gaze intently on the stairs, a pocket of dust that he blew onto it in his hand.

"How is the downstairs most dangerous?" I blinked at him.

"Guards can look into the windows at any time and see us," Balmur explained softly while observing his handiwork, then shook his head. "Wires on the stairs, we need to go up on the rails themselves. They aren't trapped."

He took a second to rest his hand on the rail before hopping up onto it with no sound whatsoever, then walked up with Calmyra stalking up the rail behind him.

I looked over at James, who shrugged and did the same just before I turned owl and flapped up to the floor above with no issues. Calmyra regarded me coldly. "Cheater."

"I prefer the term, gifted, thank you." It wasn't a joke so much as letting him know I was unbothered by his disdain.

This floor was jam-packed with boxes and crates, barrels with foul-smelling things inside that made my sensitive nose screech in protest to the proximity. Calmyra hissed softly, and I could understand why the scent burned noxiously.

Sulfur and chalk were in the air, and there was something culty going on here. We dropped into crouches and slowly explored, checking for traps and finding some of the boxes were trapped.

Calmyra and Balmur worked together to find the mechanism of one that would have released a noxious gas into the air, then opened the lid. Inside stood several thick rolls of paper, blank and black as pitch, with nothing else.

Several other boxes and crates turned up chalk, more traps, and various tomes on proper summoning etiquette. Nothing on a ritual itself, but whatever was going on up here seemed to point toward someone wanting to bring a shit ton of demons into play.

"Is there a way for us to ruin these materials?" I whispered to Balmur, who shrugged.

Calmyra reached inside one of the boxes with the books. "We can take these and put a damper on things. At least a little bit. The syndicate may take more once our investigation is done —summoning demons is something we expressly forbid."

I nodded and took one of them, the cat-man opting to take the other two in that crate as evidence to his people. Then I took some of the chalk and paper for Yoh, as well. Maybe he could shed some light on the subject.

"Let's move on," James suggested before nodding to an empty section of the room.

We moved close to it, the scent of copper and burnt incense thickly cloying the air. Red chalk glow in a pentagram of similar design to the one that I had seen in Maebe's study in the Fae Realm where Yohsuke had summoned his now patron Archemillian. The demon had been instrumental in us getting Balmur back from the Hells and had since then been a pain in the ass by ordering us to find a demon that a powerful human had summoned to our plane. But at least now we knew what was going on.

And it was likely here somewhere.

We need to be on high alert, James whispered through our earrings.

What's going on? Jaken replied quickly.

Balmur moved closer to the summoning circle, careful to avoid breaking it or coming into contact with it before answering, *I think we found the site of the demon summoning.*

You need us? Muu and Yohsuke asked in unison.

Let us investigate more, but if you can safely start moving this way, it may be smart. I advised cautiously. *Bokaj, you may want to keep your tails busy for a little while longer. This could get ugly.*

You got it. If you need me there, you'd better fucking call. His anger was understandable, especially since we could be facing a relic of his best friend's recent tumultuous past.

I took a steadying breath and whispered, "Hubris."

The scepter appeared in my hand quietly, and I felt a little better for the contact. Balmur had his blades, one holy and the other Sorrow, his sentient vampiric weapon that Maebe had given him.

James just stood there, casting his gaze about, and Calmyra turned and stalked about the room with us nearby. The rest of the boxes we opened held little more than what could be just more materials. We took what we could or thought would throw things out of whack for the assholes with the crooked schemes, then made our way slowly back downstairs.

The trip to the second floor was uneventful, though getting down to the first floor proved tricky.

"We need someone to disable this trap from below," Calmyra muttered softly.

The mechanism was a system of wires that intersected and wove together intricately like a spider's web, but they looked to be attached to a series of bells and pipes.

"Balmur?" I looked over at him and he shook his head. "What's wrong?"

"I'm good at these things," he started, but stopped and had to take several deep breaths. "But if there's a demon down there and I'm alone with it... I don't know what I'll do."

I frowned, *B... are you afraid?*

He nodded, and that was all it took. Sometimes, friendship is about helping your friends face their demons and supporting them as they overcame them. Other times, it's being willing to stand in the gap and face those demons for them.

I'd take that hit.

"Tell me what I have to do." I shapeshifted into my vorpal

viper form, my body condensing into a long, thick snake's form. The wires were warm against the cool air, and I could perceive them with my heat-sensing pits as my tongue tasted the world around me, as well.

"As you slither through, I need you to disable the bells as best you can." Calmyra motioned with his hands as he spoke, his eyes darting around the room. "This means potentially biting off the clapper so that it will make no noise. Once that is done, I can safely disable the other mechanisms."

"Why not use magic to just stop all of it?" James asked quietly, a look of consternation on his face.

"The wires are spelled to snap should they be magically tampered with," Balmur explained tepidly. "If it weren't for that, I would've been able to do it from this side."

How did you know that? James frowned at the dwarf.

Balmur flicked a finger to his magical eye. *One of the eyes I collected from that mage we killed had an ability to see magic. It's about twenty minutes from needing to feed again, and I'm not sure if I should do it now or not because the other eyes I have are drow eyes. They see heat signatures better. The abilities will switch once the eye consumes again.*

Makes sense, James muttered, making sure he glanced about. *Let's get this over with. Something about this place is giving me the willies.*

I made my way carefully up the rail, cautiously avoiding the wires, sometimes having to raise single sections of my long body just to avoid a cleverly wrapped section of railing. I bit and pulled out seven bell clappers before my mouth became too full to continue, and I had to make a choice—do I try to go back and spit them out? Or do I swallow them?

Get. Your brain. Out. Of. *The gutter.*

I took a deep breath and decided to slowly hang down the rail and reach out with my mind toward the shadows that pooled there. They responded sluggishly, with me having to strain immensely just to get them to respond, but seemed to be okay with me poking them to become a soundless depository for my current mouthful. I opened my mouth, a tinkling of bell clappers softly escaping as they hit my fangs, but nothing near as loud as the bells themselves would be. I sighed in relief and released my hold on the shadows. Thank the gods for that gift. Phew.

I made my way back up and started the process again. Two rounds of expelling later, we finished this portion of our escapades, and I was able to rest on the bottom floor while the cat-man rogue worked his way swiftly down the stairs with his tools almost flashing like blades. He would pin the triggers back with small barbed metal pieces and move on almost before the first one was set. It was an impressive sight to behold and with my work and his taking only fifteen minutes or so to boot.

Once they made it to the bottom floor, I shifted back to my human form and watched the shadows around us.

Something isn't right, I sent and growled to the others.

There's a goddamn demon here. Of course, something isn't right, Bokaj shot back with his weapons at the ready.

I found what had sparked the sensation of wrongness around us. This was a cooler of sorts with runes on the walls that would hide a presence and keep things cold.

At least that is what I can understand of them from this distance, Hubris explained. *If I were taken closer, I could attempt to decipher things a little more easily.*

I thought about it, but guttural growls and deep crunching noises reached my ears, and I turned toward the south of the building. In the center of the poorly lit room sat a large, flabby body of maroon flesh that held something in front of it like a baby.

The crunching didn't stop, but the beast threw something over its shoulder slightly away from us. Balmur went to go see what it might be and brought back the remains of an arm. The delicate wrist, and forearm had bangles and bracelets dangling from it.

Calmyra's eyes looked blank, dead, as he reached out and took the grim finding.

Oh, shit, that was likely one of his sisters—Balmur hadn't had the time to finish the thought before the syndicate representative yowled in fury and pain at the loss of his sister.

His blade flashed toward the hulking form before us as he sprinted forward. "Monster!"

The thing spun around, a grotesquely large arm lashing out and just above Calmyra's head as he skidded beneath the strike. His stabbing blade flashed into his hand, and he began to slash and gore anything he could reach. The creature took damage, but I was too far away to see how much or what level it was.

Hope you guys are close, shit's popping off in here, Balmur called to the other party members who were on their way.

James had already leaped into combat. *Level 37. The thing in his arms is level 40.*

The demon fought ferociously to protect the bundle in its other arm, the left-hand slapping at the two agile fighters as it tried to back into a corner to cut off routes of attack from behind him.

Fire wreathed its body, and it roared loudly, a crashing sound from outside somewhere off to the east of our position almost made me look away, but I would have to trust Balmur to watch my back.

"I'm going in. Balmur, you steer clear of this one, okay?" I saw him nodding before I let myself be taken into combat.

Your plan is sound, master, might I suggest that you use me to cast this spell?

I still found it vaguely irritating that Hubris seemed to know what I would do before I even did, but I sighed and used it to cast Falfyre. A slight mana sacrifice seemed to be needed, so it cost 250 MP rather than the 235 MP I had expected. Rather than the sword coming to my hand, the brilliant platinum weapon added its three and a half foot length to the end of the scepter, making it look more like a naginata, especially with the foot-long length of the hilt. The runes along the blade shimmered like the heat along hot pavement, and my connection with Hubris was slightly more amplified than before.

This is our power, master. Hubris couldn't hide the smugness in its voice, and I found myself grinning in excitement. I wanted to see how this would turn out with one of my new aspects.

Aspect of the Terran Gorilla – The Primal Warriors body grows denser, and their hide thickens to increase their physique and power like that of the king of the trees.

+20 strength, +10 defense, -5 dexterity

Muscle density increased, rage abilities deepened.

My body did exactly as the spell said it would, my arms lengthened, and every muscle fiber in my chest, back and core flexed at the same time, thickening immensely. My legs felt a little heavier as well, but not by much, and I could tell that my humanoid body had a smattering of the same grass-like fur over it that my buddy Frederick had all over his body.

I *whooped* and launched forward, the blade slashing toward the creature's throat.

Balzerus Demon Lvl 37

A flash of infernal flame formed a barrier between us and forced Falfyre to slow its deadly descent into the bastard's flesh.

"The baby is the caster!" Calmyra snarled as he moved within the barrier toward the little creature. The Balzerus demon backhanded the cat-kin into the flames, and he howled as his fur singed, and his health bar dropped 15%. I couldn't see his level, but that wasn't good.

Radiant golden energy poured over his body, and I knew that aura of healing—Jaken was here.

A rocket of green and manic energy pierced the barrier. "All this fun without me? What the hell?"

"Shut up and fight, Muu." Yohsuke's voice drifted over my left shoulder as I swung my weapon once more and found the demon's flesh, carving off 13% of its HP bar. A rush of cold air brushed against my back, and I knew that Kayda was behind me, a bolt of lightning tearing the ceiling apart to strike at the demon, shocking it and the creature in its arms. The demon roared in fury, a magical burst of flame and force buffeting us as we stood against it.

A glimmering from the depths of the bundle the demon held caught my eye, and I suddenly lost the will to fight. I was with Maebe and Vrawn, and their conversation with each other was just so enticing. We were in a house I didn't recognize in front of a large window peering outside over a large forest. Both of them sat facing each other in front of the window, moving and discussing something.

I couldn't help but smile at the contentment in my heart at their closeness.

Wait. I growled. *I'm in the middle of a fight, how the fuck is this possible?*

Both women looked over at me, and their eyes were dead, the portions of their bodies that had been on the side closest to the windows visceral with blood, bone, and pustules, their faces growing more skeletal and demonic as they stood to sway toward me. But the usual seductive swagger was gone from their bodies, replaced by an almost puppet-like shambling. The forest outside began to burn and glow with the pyres of flame that swept toward us.

"You should never have come snooping." Not-Maebe's voice came from a mouth that didn't move.

Not-Vrawn reached out to me as if to call me into a hug, and I balked at the idea. "Do you no longer find me attractive, my dear?"

This voice was off, and it was just the push I needed. I launched myself forward, and cracked both of them in the face with a spinning back kick. If this was a dream, I wasn't going to wait like some teenage lamb to the slaughter while my tormentor tried to kill me.

"This ain't Elm Street, you piece o' shit!" I bared my teeth as I landed, and bum-rushed Not-Vrawn while she was off-balance, knocking her to the ground only to have her disappear.

I turned to see Not-Maebe, no longer a monster, but herself, leering down at me where I crouched. "You'll learn to fear me, champion. You all will. And what I represent."

"Let me guess, you're a general, and you want us to give

up?" I rolled my eyes and stood. "Not happening, but if you leave this planet, now—I won't hunt you down and rip you limb from limb for fucking with the people I love."

She laughed then, the sound not even close to how her laugh should have been. "Even when I'm in front of you, you can't kill me. Come find me once more, and let's see who is stronger then."

Maebe turned to walk toward the window, clearly unbothered by my threat, so I lashed out how I thought might affect the creature. "Your brothers thought that they were stronger than us, as well. They died pitifully."

Not-Maebe stopped and turned, her face becoming even more angular and foreign as whatever this was continued, "Their pathetic existences are nothing compared to mine, and I will see you dead at my feet for thinking they could even amount to me for a moment."

I spread my arms wide in welcome with a grin plastered on my face. "Bring it, bitch."

Not-Maebe just winked and vanished in a cloud of smoke, the dream leaving with her, and I came to awareness, standing with Hubris in my hand.

Looking around, I saw that the others had yet to fully return from what was happening and that the demon and the little bastard were gone.

Calmyra lay on the ground, bleeding from his mouth but breathing. I cast Void's Respite on him, and the shadows enveloped him and settled into his skin. With how the spell worked and his location in the darkness, he would likely recover fully in a moment and need no other healing.

I can wake them if you wish?

I lifted Hubris to head height and examined it critically. "You can?"

I studied the magic that had been used against you, and I believe that I can nullify it with how little remains inside your friends' minds.

I nodded and did as the scepter explained, using small taps against each of them with my mana to scour the general's spell out of their minds. It took all of my focus, but each one only cost me 100 MP. I guessed I'd been down long enough for my mana to fully recover, which wasn't long. They could still be in the area, but finding them would mean having to split up, and that wouldn't do.

I got to Balmur, his left eye bleeding a bit, and tapped him. As he came to, he immediately groaned. "My eye."

He lifted out his jar of eyes and lifted one toward it, the spectral mouth lashed out, grazing his fingers as it devoured the orb hungrily, then disappeared.

"What the hell was with that?" I asked Balmur as his body was racked with spasms of agony. Watching what happened to the victim of the eye he stole was part of his price, the price to use the eye.

I paid experience one time, a whole level's worth, and I had a maintenance fee of the majority of my mana every morning to get my metal arm to act as a normal arm. I was used to it by now, but I didn't think I could ever get used to what he was going through.

"The eye starts to consume whatever is around it if the sacrifice isn't made on time." Balmur rubbed his eyes and spat angrily. I cast Void's Respite on him too, and he calmed greatly. "Thank you, man. And listen, I'm sorry I wasn't much help against that demon."

"Think nothing of it." I clapped him on the shoulder and rested my hand there. "You know, you saw a lot more shit than we did there, and you came out of it swinging for the fences. I can understand not wanting to face your tormentors just yet, but we're here for you too, buddy. You can lean on us."

"Just don't lean on me too much if you're bleeding like that." Muu punched the dwarf lightly with a wink. "I only want my scales dirtied by the blood of my enemies."

Balmur brightened up immediately, and then we all began moving through the lower area. I took Hubris over to the walls to have it look over the runes that had been used.

Cold and concealment. Looks like they meant to keep the demon and its ward concealed from scrying, magical detection, and the corpses from rotting overly much, as well.

"Come to think of it, how did I know that demon's type?" I glared at the wall, trying to discern what I could, touching it didn't do anything, and I was beginning to grow a little tired of that.

I shared that knowledge with you. If I have seen a creature while in the care of another master, I will share with you. As I will these runes.

I frowned in appreciation. "That's dope! But what do you get out of this?"

I serve you, I get that, and I gather more knowledge as we both go on. I crave knowledge, and so long as I can learn, I will be content to serve you.

"I see." I made to dismiss him, but stopped. "Where do you go when I dismiss you?"

I follow you in a pocket dimension, once you summon me, I reappear where I am needed.

"Very well, you may go." The scepter left my hand and vanished as it would, and I looked to my friends.

Yohsuke sighed. "Well, we lost her this time, you guys all have weird dreams, too?" We nodded and frowned. "Which one of you called her a bitch?"

I grinned, and raised my hand and so did the others. I looked over and even saw Calmyra slowly raising his clawed hand.

"I don't know who you are, but I like you." Yohsuke smiled. "I called her a bitch, too. Said that she was beginning to hate the word."

"That was a caretaker demon," Balmur explained. "They watch over powerful creatures, children, and other things. Protectors, if you will. And he was protecting the general."

"Do we know where they're going?" James looked around, and I shook my head.

"Across the sea," Jaken suggested with a thoughtful look on his face. "It looked like a ship in the background of my vision. I was the last to go under, and it looked like he was projecting images to all of us."

"Trees and a house," I stated.

"I was here," Balmur added.

Yohsuke had been near a large blackened dome of some kind, James near a cliffside overlooking a large amount of water. Muu had been outside a large house with animals everywhere.

"Bokaj is saying that he didn't see anything because he wasn't affected," Balmur relayed for us. "He's saying that his tails have disappeared after he followed them to the docks."

"He see the ships they're in?" I asked hopefully, but he shook his head.

"Okay, let's get back to the inn and recover from this." Yohsuke led us out of the building, I found the guards dead, their bodies husks on the ground up against the walls.

Jaken held up his hands. "I just knocked them out."

I shook my head, and turned at the rasp of a throat clearing behind us. We looked at Calmyra, who motioned to the building. "The syndicate will take over investigating here. Fear no reprisal from us or our fine city—we will see that witnesses remain quiet and that your stay here has no more hiccups than it has. Balmur, I will be in touch, and the rest of you have my gratitude for attempting to help me avenge my sisters."

I stepped forward and pulled him into a brief hug, him stiffening up against me. "I'm sorry we couldn't do more, Cal. We'll find those two and make them pay."

I didn't swear to it, but the words seemed to go a long way toward making the man feel better. He nodded his head. "Quite, thank you."

He turned and walked back inside alone, and we stayed for a moment in silence, watching his outline lean over and then kneel by his family's remains.

How many more would suffer at these monsters' hands? Hopefully, fewer and fewer as we grew stronger. I could hope.

CHAPTER NINE

Breakfast that following morning turned out to be a more somber affair as we still hadn't heard from Scar about our passage to the Continent of Beasts.

"Fiery one," Katja called as we finished our food, Balmur standing as she made her way over to him to speak in hushed tones.

He grunted and cursed. "No fucking way. Seriously?"

Katja nodded once and turned around to walk to the end of the bar and raised a bell, its chime rang out three times, and all the bodies in the bar stilled.

"Those of you affiliated and my guests may stay, everyone else must leave." When no one seemed to be moving quickly enough for her taste, she raised her voice and bellowed, "By order of the Wraith, *move!*"

A large crowd stood and made their way toward the exit as swiftly as possible. Some of the more normal-looking patrons stayed seated, but their demeanor changed, and one in particular stood and grasped at his neck. His flesh relinquished his shirt, and up and over his head came the mask that Calmyra had been wearing. "Pleasantly surprised to see all of you here like this, though I wish the circumstances were better."

"What the fuck is going on here?" I growled as the other people in the room moved to stand closer to the cat-man than I was comfortable with. Almost like we had been deliberately sold out. "I thought you would still be mourning the loss of your sisters?"

"I am, and I likely will forever, but there is a larger issue at hand, and I wanted to offer you all a spot at the table." His scowl deepened as he turned to Katja. He spoke in a language that I had no idea what it was, and she replied with a nod before closing all the slatted wooden blinds to the room around us and securing the door. "Thank you, Katja."

"It is no problem." She folded her arms behind the bar and watched all of us in the now-darker room.

"Well, spit it up, then, kitty." Muu stood and crossed his arms over his chest. "What's got the cat's tongue?"

"I despise you and the shapeshifter so much." He bared his fangs, and hissed at the two of us, his men snorting and chuckling to themselves quietly. "I came to see if you would be interested in assisting us with a slight... *issue*."

"The navy decided to make a move?" Balmur raised an eyebrow and crossed his arms under his flaming beard. Calmyra stared at him in open surprise, and the rogue just grinned. "I followed a group of naval grunts last night from the warehouse and figured that after their investigation, they may have decided to do something. I just don't know exactly what."

"Very astute," Calmyra said, then grunted, his tail flicking behind him. "They want to out the syndicate and kill us all. They'll call it 'fair trials,' but they'll execute us and anyone else that they possibly can if they think they're connected to us."

"Isn't protecting your people something that you'll take pride in doing?" Jaken cocked his head to the side, waiting to see what the answer would be.

"Of course, but we aren't exactly the stand in the streets and brawl kind of organization."

"I fail to see how this is our problem." James snorted and shook his head.

"The syndicate here directly maintains and oversees the criminal element in every major, middling, and minor city, village, and town on the continent," Balmur explained quickly. "These guys fall, a power vacuum opens up and there will likely be blood in the streets everywhere. Believe it or not, they keep things civil with their laws, knowledge of who is corruptible, bribable, and who can be blackmailed into supporting their cause. If we let this city fall, the kingdom falls into chaos."

"...And that makes it our problem." Bokaj stood up and glanced at the rest of us. "We can't screw over that many people."

"No, we can't, and since we're getting ready for some kind of brawl, we're going to need something in return." Balmur looked the cat-man in the eyes and the syndicate rep raised an eyebrow. "We have a group of friends who are going to be in Lindyburg; the Braves of the Thorn and the royalty from the capital. They'll be there rooting out the former governor's wife and her people. I want you to make sure that the *seedier* folks in the city assist them however they can."

"I can't promise that, but let me ask around." Calmyra stepped into a corner with a clawed hand up to his right ear, he spoke softly for a few minutes. Finally, he nodded once and returned. "The Wraith has given consent in exchange for your services with the protection of the citizenry, to include protection from the navy and their goons by whatever means necessary."

Balmur turned to look at us. "We in?"

"Pretty sure if we don't help, Jaken will beat our asses." Yohsuke sighed heavily. "But after this? It's straight to our destination. We can't keep doing this wild, off into nowhere bullshit. We have goals, and the longer we wait, the more likely things are to go wrong. That cool?"

All of us nodded our assent, and Yoh turned to Calmyra.

"One more question: how do we know that fucking with the navy here won't screw us over with the capital?"

"The naval higher-ups here send doctored missives and reports to the capitol so that they can maintain a vast majority of freedom from their control. They take bribes from us to stay out of our way, and they get to keep their front."

Couldn't we simply message the king and tell him what's up? Jaken sighed, and ran his hands through his hair before retying his ponytail.

And admit we have ties to one of the largest threats to the kingdom's organized rule? Balmur interjected before I could answer. *He would send forces here to try and subjugate all of them and us for knowing things. We should handle this quietly and ask for forgiveness over permission and risking our progress.*

"So then, what changed?" I glanced over to see Katja pulling out a bow, several long daggers, some small knives, some bandoliers, and setting them on her counter.

"We think that they may be acting in connection with the Children of Brindolla, and they're trying to pin the demon summoning gear on us," Calmyra explained, pulling out a small tube with papers inside. "This is a report to the crown stating that they will be acting against a mass summoning of demons orchestrated by the syndicate in an attempt to take this city and eventually the continent."

I whistled long and low. "So they meant to take this city from you as a possible base for themselves?"

"Potentially, but we think that there is an element of attempting to cut into our business as well." His explanation made sense to me. Greedy and corrupt people in power always attempted to gather more for themselves. Made sense to cut in on the local racket in an attempt to wrest control of the criminal element of this entire land.

"What do you need for us to do?" Yohsuke said, then growled, his eyes narrowing dangerously.

"I need you to be visible while we move unseen." Calmyra snapped his fingers, and the men and women behind him filed toward the back of the building and down a secret entrance. "I know that they have their people moving throughout the city while they pull the strings. We mean to go after the leaders as you all take on their men in your own ways."

"If it doesn't matter how it goes, I have an idea." Balmur grinned at us. "I say we go full-on with this thing."

"I'm listening." Muu smiled at the shorter man.

"Jaken, James, Muu, and Vrawn are going to be our bait." Balmur clapped his hands and rubbed them together.

"I hate this shit already." Muu harrumphed, and the rest of us grinned.

———

My breathing reverberated against the interior of the mask I wore, a long canine inspired thing that hid my vulpine features from the world. I watched from the roof as my friends crossed beneath me.

Eyes on the peanut butter, I joked to the other overwatches.

Seriously? Peanut butter? Jaken sounded uncertain as he said it.

Balmur grunted at us. *We're trying to attract the mice while the syndicate goes after the rats. Mice like peanut butter, so that's the code. Focus up!*

I hate you all so damned much, Yohsuke's laughter echoed in my head. *Sucks that they want us to leave these assholes alive if we can.*

It does, but it is what it is. Bokaj stalked along the rooftops across from me with his bow in hand.

As the peanut butter group moved along the ground toward the center of the city, we noted more and more white sailor uniforms belonging to the navy.

I listened as we went by, careful to stay out of sight until I was needed. The people in the street who had normally just ignored the navy's people eyed them warily and avoided them as they loitered in main areas. The more I listened, the less I liked what I heard.

"Yeah, that's what they said, Milfy, I swear it." One of the human sailors beneath me grunted to another as he eyed some of the stalls that had been set up further down the road. "The sun hits noon, we're to start the operation. Anyone we think has ties to the syndicate, we take 'em down."

Party starts at noon, guys. My warning made the bait group twitch except for Vrawn. She just looked around unabashedly at the city and smiled at people here and there.

You all know what to do when you get there get it started and be very careful to pay attention to what's going on immediately around you. Balmur's voice echoed to all of us, but the group below would have the critical role in this charade.

Muu and Jaken walked into the market area first with Vrawn in the center of the group as if she were a noble lady out on the town in her finer than normal clothes, a dress of bright and vivid red that made her arms look even beefier with her curves. James brought up the rear of the group at a slight distance as if he were watching her back for thieves or cutpurses.

As if on cue, one of the sailors in the shadows saw something he thought stood out and stepped closer to investigate. As soon as he was away from his friends, one of them stepped out closer to the street trailing behind his friend who walked from the shadows, I dropped silently into the shadows near the loner and put him in a headlock with my forearm over his mouth to mute his muttered cries of distress.

Naval Sailor Lvl 20

He passed out from lack of blood to the brain in seconds, and my next target began to turn toward me as I laid his friend down. I surged forward, my right hand flung forward to strike his chin as my left hand swiped forward to push on his right hip. I yanked his head toward my body, his balance completely lost, and since I controlled his head, I dragged him back to the other guard and knocked him out, too.

Mine are out. I broadcasted to the others and saw motion across the street where Balmur brutally clobbered one of the sailors there with his fist and slammed his head into the wall with a silent snarl. His gaze caught mine, and a little of his humanity returned before he nodded to me and melded into the shadows.

Sailors on the way to the market have been taken care of, Yohsuke informed us, then he added. *Bokaj is in position, and the distraction is on point. Fan out and get the closest ones like we discussed.*

The syndicate cleaners are here to take the ones we knock out with them to holding, let them do their jobs. Balmur's orders in this were as good as gold, and I hopped up a set of boxes onto the roof of the next house as a set of men entered the alley from the opposite side of the street to collect my work.

I dropped on the next set of sailors and smacked their heads together with thuds that may have attracted attention, so I called the shadows around me to block the view from the street and deepen accordingly. Sure enough, a curious man in a white shirt wearing old khaki-colored breeches came into the alley to investigate. I waited until he was close enough and reached through the shadows to grab him and pull him through the wall. I slammed my hand against his mouth before he cried out.

"Are you with the navy?" My voice had deepened to near beastly levels as I shifted into my hulking werewolf form. He shook his head wildly, and I sniffed near his face. The mask still covered my features, but my jaws were plainly visible from where he watched in horror. "Good. I'm going to move my hand, and you're going to listen carefully and quickly. You scream, and you'll end up like the two men at your feet. Do you understand?"

His eyes shifted down to the two unconscious men on the ground, and he nodded once more. I let his mouth go, and though his heart rate and breathing were like being near the speakers at a party, he didn't scream.

"What's your name, human?"

"Tr... Trent, sir." He whimpered, his lower lip quivering pathetically. "I swear I won't tell nobody you did this, I swear it on my auntie."

"Hush, human." I leaned on my monstrous side to intimidate him into silence. When he was quiet again, I glared down at him. "You are going to go home and stay there until a crier comes to deliver the good news. You get any people who aren't part of the navy that you can into their homes, and you do so *quietly*. Can you do this?"

He nodded, either because I had said to do so quietly, or he didn't trust himself to speak.

"Act as if nothing happened and leave this alley in one minute." I released my hold on his shirt and shoulder gently so as not to hurt him and rushed down the alleyway toward the house at the opposite end. I whipped around the corner into a sailor who had been drawn by the noise and decided that nothing was wrong since he was busy urinating on the side of the building. I rolled my eyes and leashed the beast inside me so that I didn't accidentally turn him and waited until he was at least finished peeing to attack him.

Look, it's not really out of any kind of respect, because clearly, he had none for the city he was in. It was more so he didn't pee on me while I was trying to put him under. If he peed on me, I'd kill him. And I had a mission to do.

Finally, he put it away, and I was on him instantly, my palm on the back of his head and shoving it into the wall with a dull thunk and the sound of his body slumping down onto the ground. A little blood was all that remained of our interaction.

We have a problem, they're starting to gather on the peanut butter, Bokaj's alarmed voice reached us, and I closed my eyes as I tried to remember the direction they all were. I leapt into the air and shifted into my eagle form and lifted into the air, moving toward the market with speed. My claws found home next to Yohsuke in an alleyway.

Vrawn, James, Jaken, and Muu looked to be surrounded by thirty sailors with one of them pointing to Muu and shouting something in a language I didn't understand.

There're more of them on their way here, Balmur explained, and I saw him at one of the higher points of the area before he stepped back. *Let's get in there and help them but remember to avoid killing. Bokaj, crippling shots only.*

An arrow severed one of the sailor's Achilles tendons, and the group converged toward our friends. I surged forward, falling to my hands and feet, shifting into my belgar form as I moved. I kept my head high to avoid goring anyone. Though several bodies bounced off me, and a cutlass streaked over my armored skin just before I shifted into fox form. I pivoted and turned toward the group once more. My body enlarged, and my fur grew shaggier as I took ursolon form and slapped the taste out of a sailor's mouth with the back of my paw.

I roared, spittle flung from my mouth into the face of a sailor before I crushed his foot with my paw and shoved him away from me. His howling was drowned out by shouts of anger from his friends as the melee fighters let loose.

Bodies flew away from Muu and James, their fists and feet moving rapidly and their strength leaving much to be desired from the sailors, their bodies unable to take the brutality being dished out. Vrawn refrained from using a weapon, simply punching and breaking limbs with her hands and feet. Jaken roared loudly, and his body took on a reddish hue as he called the sailors' attention to himself.

Arrows whizzed past us and into feet, shoulders, and knees to keep people from moving. By the end of the thirty sailors, only James had taken damage, and that had been from Vrawn whacking him when he got too close.

"I am so sorry, James, please forgive me," she earnestly begged, her frown and sorrow apparent on her face.

He rubbed his jaw, angrily. "I'm not mad at that, fuck. I'm pissed that there are more of these assholes coming. Come on, let's go."

CHAPTER TEN

Sure enough, there were another two full boats worth of sailors on their way. Yeah, we could take them if we were going to take it seriously and just massacre them, but that wasn't the plan.

Anyone have any ideas as to what we can do to get these guys to surrender? Jaken asked wearily. Trying not to kill anyone had been taxing on us, even though we did make it look easy.

How about a combo attack strategy? I offered as we moved along the rooftop toward where the platoon-sized formation of sailors marched toward the market. The rest of the party glanced my way, and I continued on. *My dragon form is black, right? With colored highlights, sure but it's black. What if we were to have me fly in, and Yoh and Balmur manipulate the shadows for me? Like, try to scare them off with a type of dragon they've never seen before.*

I mean, that could work. Muu grunted, a soft hiss leaving his lips as James shoved him aside, a small hole in the roof having almost swallowed his foot. *Thanks.*

If it will get them to lay down their weapons and surrender, I'm in. Yohsuke affirmed with a nod and glance at Balmur.

He nodded once, and I stepped away from the group, cracking my neck before I sprinted as hard as I could in the opposite direction they had been moving. As soon as I was next to a gap on the roof, I pushed myself into the air as hard as I could and shifted. My draconic wings and body felt much too large to be in the city, but I banked and turned toward where I would be needed.

To play up the theatrics of my appearance, I roared loudly as I beat my wings against the air. Dozens of men and women screeched, "Dragon!"

Luckily for me, none of the sailors appeared to have bows or crossbows as I flew above them, coming to a stop and landing in front of them with an earth-shuddering thud.

"Do you all mean to fight me?!" I howled in as draconic a voice I could manage, the men and women clearly taken aback by my sudden appearance and terrifying demeanor. "Surrender, and I will allow you to keep your pathetic, miserable lives. Scurrying about on the ground like mice."

Some of the men laid down their weapons and ran, a few of them tripping over the others in their hurry. Others drew their weapons.

One of them actually stepped forward and scoffed, "You look to be about adult age for a dragon, you've got a lot of nerve acting high and mighty in front of a whole mess of men and women who could kill you. Black dragons are evil creatures, sure, but you don't look so tough."

My fangs flashed as I laughed and held my clawed arms out before me. "You think me merely a black dragon? I am Daedrona. I am the black death. I am the very shadows at your feet. Witness my power and quake in fear as I fashion a lance with which to strike you *down!*"

I prayed that Balmur and Yohsuke had been paying attention to what I had said and held my clawed arm up next to my head. After a second, I worried that they had missed the cue, but the stirring in the shadows around me was almost haunting. They made it look like the individual shadows under each man and woman was being taken like it was a soul, the coolness of it brushing their flesh and gathering just above my hand.

Six of the sailors fainted then and there, while the shadows coalescing in the air around me shot forward and speared the speaker through the chest, his body falling back and hanging on the shadow spear like an insect stuck to a collection box.

"I no longer feel so generous," I hissed menacingly. "Put down your weapons and kneel, or I will eat some of you and feed the leftovers of your corpses to my shadows."

Black streaks of void energy crackled down from my claw tips like lightning, and the energy of it swirled around my body like I was calling all the shadows in the city to me.

"We surrender!" A woman who looked to be in her mid-forties came forward and dropped her weapon before kneeling. "They don't pay us enough to fight dragons and the shadows of hell. I'm done."

Within seconds the whole force knelt, and the syndicate's cleaners came through with irons and chains to take everyone away. Once they were all out of sight, I shifted back into my fox-man form and sighed.

A hand grasped my shoulder and swung me around, Yohsuke looking ready to kick my ass. "Seriously, 'Daedrona?' What the fuck was that?"

"It sounded like a decent dragon name, man." My cheeks burned slightly as a blush set in. "Balmur, how goes the top-secret stuff from Calmyra?"

"The higher-ups are on a ship heading somewhere, they made to escape on their own." He shook his head and motioned to the people around us. "He said that we're good and that he would see that they kept their word and helped in Lindyburg."

"Are they close enough to get to with me flying?" I stepped closer to him as he asked. "I can go out there in dragon form and sink those bastards."

Balmur added that and waited. "Unless you can carry us and some of them, they said no. They have accomplished mages with them on a naval vessel, and the higher-ups are all a little stronger."

"He did also say that thanks to this, the people can rest easier and that we're always welcome here now. I have full rights within the syndicate, as well." He grinned before looking at Muu and me. "He said to have some drinks on them, but that you two had to pay for yourselves since you want to act like idiots."

We laughed, the people around us beginning to come forward with praises and words of gratitude. Children played in the streets a little more easily, it seemed.

Finally, Yohsuke sighed. "I'm tired, time for a bit of sleep. Wake me up when our ride is ready."

We left the market and arrived back at Katja's in time to feed Bea and wait for word. It took several hours of waiting, but finally, Scar arrived with word and to collect his fee.

CHAPTER ELEVEN

"Okay, no seriously," Muu asked for the sixth time on our way from the barrel maker's shop to the docks to meet our contact with the ship we would board to cross the ocean. "It's called *what* again?"

"I'm not dignifying that with an answer," Balmur finally said, then growled at the other man.

We'd spent the night after the warehouse explaining our findings to the others before sleeping. Balmur had spoken to Scar's contact, who gave us the name of a ship and her captain crazy enough to take us to our destination.

We had been a little thrown by the name of our vessel, but it would sail, and the crew was reported to be one of the most competent to dock here in the city, so we couldn't complain too much.

The ship was the only one currently in the bay, the others had left as soon as the tide was high enough to get away from us. Scar having offered what we could do and were capable of, he seemed to scare away the others.

The navy's ships were gone as well, though no one seemed to know why.

But, back to the Pussy Willow. Yeah, no, you heard me right. The name of our ship was the Pussy Willow.

Naming conventions aside, the ship looked immaculate. From bow to stern she was cut fierce and lithe, the hull of her smooth and wet from the waves, with the sails tied tight above. The mast was thick, and the other, smaller masts, held smaller sails that spread wider than the mainsail to catch the wind.

On the dock before the ship sat a figure cloaked in green and gold, with bright yellow eyes watching our arrival.

"Be you Storm Comp'ny?" A voice sort of warbled across the distance to us.

"Yes, we be," Bokaj answered amicably. "Who, might I ask, are we addressing in return?"

The figure stood and lifted the stool that had been beneath him in a smooth motion. "I'd be the first mate o' this vessel and her crew. Mind your tone, and we'll be fine. I'll be your liaison between your group and the crew and cap'n."

Ouch, I hope he didn't think I was trying to be a dick. Bokaj seemed a little put off by the interaction. "Listen, friend, I didn't mean to come off impolite if I did. We're happy to be sailing with you and your crew."

"Weren't nothin' impolite at all, boy." The warble deepened, a small chuckle emanating from the hood. "That's just the way o' things. Respect goes far on a ship like this, and when someone untrained steps aboard, it be best to set expectations before that point. I'd hate to have to make any o' our payin' customers walk the plank for belligerent behavior."

"Seems a good policy." I nodded. "And how's the pay we've offered?"

"If you pay half up-front and half upon completion of our venture, we have an accord." The figure stepped forward toward us, twenty feet still between our group and him. "I hear tell that the lot of you can scrap? So long as you can hold your own in a fight and assist in protectin' the ship, we're good. Any of you sailors?"

James and I chuckled to ourselves, Yohsuke being hidden

safely in my collar for now. James nodded to me and pointed a thumb at himself. "The two of us are trained in amphibious warfare."

"You been on ship?" Muu raised an eyebrow at James, knowing my only stints on ships had been the USS Peleliu for a few hours and landing with helicopters for training. It was a wild ride for sure, but I had no real experience on ship other than being *on* them.

"Nope, but my training will see me through," James asserted cockily. "There's not a whole lot that we need to know, right?"

The first mate eyed us steadily, then, "Stay below decks when we're making way out of the bay, and once we're out to sea proper, I'll shout you on to the deck. Introduce you to the crew."

"Sounds good," I spoke before anyone else could offer a rebuttal. The figure motioned us onto the deck, and we made our way over the gangplank onto the vessel. Clean and ready for sail, as far as my untrained eye could tell, the Pussy Willow looked ship-shape and ready for the sea.

The first mate took us to an entryway toward the rear of where a raised portion of it stood a door, "Guest cabins," the man explained easily. "Two rooms, three beds. Just make your-selves comfortable as you can, and when we speak later, we can discuss watch and work schedules."

"Work?" Bokaj raised an eyebrow in surprise. "Who said anything about work?"

"You did when you agreed to take the safety of the ship and crew onto yourselves as part of our agreement to give you passage." The sailor seemed to have known this would come up. "It be nothing more than an assisted watch schedule. No hard labor unless you request it, or you're ordered to by the captain as some sort of recompense."

"Seems fair." Jaken smiled his easy smile and nodded to the rest of us. "Let's get to getting boys and girls. The day moves on."

We all nodded and filed into the cabins, two rooms separated by a thin wall, were no more than ten feet tall at the rear and nine at the fore. The three beds—really, they were hammocks hung from the ceiling with two ropes on each side, so they were wider and a little more stable—were tucked into the back of the small fifteen-foot long room. At only about twelve feet wide, the rooms weren't the largest, but Balmur had another plan,

"At night, I say we switch off on who has to be in the rooms and have the others go into the Happy Home." He looked around at our surroundings with distaste. "This isn't really meant to be where guests go, it's the upper echelon of the crew's quarters. Two people out at night, and if anyone needs anything by day, they can come in here to rest."

"What about Yoh?" James asked as he tested one of the hammocks. It swung slightly but seemed stable.

"He can have his coffin over by the window, and we put a thick piece of cloth or leather over the porthole," I answered after a second of thought to the layout of the room. We could make it so that his coffin was tied down in the day so it didn't move, and then during the night, he could take it with him.

We settled into our individual rooms. James, me, Vrawn, and Yohsuke in the room on the right side of the door looking in, and the others in the left. It was what they had, I'm sure, but they would soon enough realize that we had other accommodations. To be completely forthright, we could give them back a room and earn their trust and good rapport if we really wanted to.

"What if we have us all in here with that spell and just let them have that room?" I asked the others, who thought about it a bit.

"What would that accomplish?" Bokaj lay on his bed with Tmont snoozing lazily on his chest.

"We earn good rapport and save them the hassle of being cramped," I offered with a convincing grin. "Not to mention, they learn that we're powerful, and if they fuck with us, they die."

"Chances are good that they want the payday." Balmur coughed into his hand softly to clear his throat, then went back to looking over a small item in his hand. "They can try to loot our corpses, but they would lose a lot of lives over it, and that would leave them damned near dead in the water. If we can make them like us more, I'm all for it."

"So then, we just wait until they bring us on deck to let them know we're benevolent and then see what they say?" Muu asked as he fiddled with his work, trying to sew something together made of leather.

"Sounds good to me," Bokaj smiled easily and closed his eyes. "Wake me up when they need us."

It took about another hour and a half after that for one of the deckhands to come for us. A younger man with a bald head, he had tattoos everywhere of all kinds of fantastic beasts spoke, "First mate and the crew will be seein' ye now sirs and ma'am."

I gave a mental *whoop* to the rest of the gang, and we made our way into the bright sunlight. The ship rocked gently over the waves as we stepped out of our living quarters to come face to face with the crew. Thirty members of the large vessel's crew watched us steadily, some of them covered in grime and filth, others seeming cleaner and more concerned with their hygiene. Some of them even watched us from above within the sails and looping ropes along the mainmast. One such older sailor smoked a pipe, and treated some of the ropes as a makeshift seat, almost like a recliner, and watched us with leisure.

The cloaked figure we met on the dock stood before them and lowered his hood. Soft blue skin that reminded me of a fish's glimmered in the sunlight, his neck gilled with four slashes that opened and closed as he watched us. His bright yellow eyes staring at us as we took him in, he seemed to be used to this.

His ears and figure seemed to be cut similar to an elf's, but the pointed appendages had earrings and smaller pointed growths that spread along the bottom of them. His face was a little more fishlike, and his nostrils were slitted, though he had a slight point of a nose. He wasn't hideous or anything, but he wasn't a looker.

"You done gawkin'?" He asked pointedly, and I nodded before he turned back to the crew. "All right, you miserable bastards! These here are our guests, Storm Company. They be makin' their way across the sea to the Continent o' Beasts! Now, none o' you sorry dogs better be givin' 'em more a hard time than anybody, or expect to have to swim! They mean to help us protect the ship and each o' you, though why I don't know. You're all, the lot o' you, the sorriest set o' sailors I ever laid my golden eyes on!"

I looked at the others and thought. *Is there going to be a mutiny on this bitch?*

The first mate looked up and pointed up at the sailor in the rigging, the sailor's eyebrow raised slightly, and the first mate hollered, "Especially you, Taejon! I ought to beat you for your insolence!"

"Said the same thing to yer mother, boy," the older sailor howled back, and the rest of the crew laughed.

I expected the sailors to all be berated, but the first mate began to laugh with the rest of them and turned to us with a grin. "Sorry, all o' you, this is a little joke we like to play on people. We don't get many guests, so we try to have fun. The crew is as well-oiled and prepared for the sea as our fine ship is, you're all in good hands."

I could get behind a crew like this, I thought to the others, then added, "Well, you had us all fooled. Listen, we were thinking about something and wanted to run it by you, if you had a moment?"

"Of course, what is it?" He stepped closer while the crew milled about behind him curiously.

"We wanted to offer you one of the rooms back," Balmur stated before I could, looking over to Bokaj for him to continue the conversation.

"We have a way to create a space for us to rest and recover in." The first mate seemed surprised but remained quiet while the ice elf spoke. "With that, two of us will sleep out in the room itself, while the others will be in this space. That way, you can communicate with us and us with you, and your crew doesn't have to be completely cramped in their quarters."

He blinked at us. "Mighty kind of you all for a bunch of strangers."

"We're about to be cramped on this craft for a while, sir," Jaken explained with his normal easy-going tone. "Better that we try to make everyone happy and be as accommodating as we can so that it's more of a pleasant voyage for all."

"Well, I'm Joesa Webbost, first mate o' this ship, and I'd like to extend my heartfelt gratitude for that to the lot o' you." He reached a slightly webbed hand out for us to all shake before he turned and called to the sailors. "Get your asses in gear! Best sailors today get the swanky bunks!"

Everyone except Taejon moved with an urgency to get their work done, making Joesa snort and turn back to us. "We'll get this lot sorted out later. Tonight, you'll dine in the cap'n's quarters with the cap'n. For now, let's talk a watch rotation. Any of ye are more than welcome to patrol the deck at any time, just mind the sailors and their workin', and we'll be fine. We'll need a couple bodies at night, though."

"We have someone in mind for that." I grinned, knowing Yohsuke would be able to keep watch at night and likely would be fine. "He sleeps during the day, so he'll be good enough at night."

"Excellent." Joesa brought out a small piece of paper and pulled out a monocle on a small stick that he held in front of his eye. "I do believe that we were also promised assistance with provisions?"

"Yes, we have barrels that are enchanted to keep food fresh far longer than it should be, and a barrel that always has fresh water in it." The enchanting process for both had been surprisingly easy to come up with and the component I had used for the food barrel had been a finely cut piece of amber and a little ice magic from Bokaj. The water had been very easy, and little imagination was needed to make it.

I pulled both of them out of my inventory easily and set them down before the first mate to inspect, "There's no food in here."

"It will be full later on," I assured him, "Once our cook is awake for the evening, he will put our food stores in the barrel and seal it properly, as well."

"Very well then." He nodded and scratched the paper with a long fingernail before looking back up at me. "Would you be so kind as to take these into the cargo hold?"

"Certainly." I smiled at him and lifted one of the barrels before glancing at Jaken. "You mind grabbing the water one, bud?"

"On it!" Muu launched himself forward and grabbed the barrel before Jaken could. The other man just shook his head, and the two of us marched toward where Joesa had pointed us to. A large grate with a latch and a hook attached to it stood open as the crew pulled out several items they needed to clean and treat the ship with for maintenance. We walked the barrels down the wooden steps, they creaked and groaned a little under Muu as he walked, and I resolved to have Bokaj take a look at them when we got a chance.

I found the other barrels of food easily enough by the smell of salt and blood. But there was another scent mixed into the air that I wasn't quite as familiar with. It smelled of wildflowers, baked goods, and strawberries.

"You smell that?" Muu asked over the calls of the sailors above us.

"Yeah, what is it?" I found myself drawn to the back corner of where the food was.

They are close. The whispering wind of the Air Primordial flashed through my mind. *Find them for me!*

I shifted into my fox form and hopped onto the top of the barrels, Muu calling, "Hey, what the hell are you doing?"

I ignored him and set about sniffing my way toward the

object that I had found caught a whiff of. There was a scent of sweat mixed into it now, and I could hear a soft grunting sound. I launched myself over the last barrels and landed just above a small creature. Big, almond-shaped brown eyes looked up at me out of a messy batch of black hair before a cry of "Fox!" Echoed in my head. Hands snatched at my vision, and I was scrabbling not to fall into the child's fiendish grasp.

Muu tore his way through the barrels easily, shoving them aside until he towered over the small creature and reached down to lift her and me out of the cubby she'd tried to hide in.

I fought like the dickens to safely and gently extricate myself from her grasp, but she held on for dear life. "No! He's my fox, and you can't have him!"

"He's not a full fox, kid, and he wants to be let go," Muu tried to explain calmly. Her grip tightened around my throat, and I growled evilly.

She yelped and let me go, so I shifted into my fox-man form and regarded my assailant. A small girl with a button nose and a smattering of light freckles watched me curiously, no taller than three feet she had to be some kind of halfling or something.

"What are you, mister?" she asked quietly.

"I'm Zeke, and I'm a kitsune." I pointed from myself to Muu. "This is Muu, and he's a dragon-kin. And both of us are surprised to find you here. What are you?"

"I'm Odany, and I'm not sure what I am." She seemed to be more curious about me than anything, so Muu sat her gently on a barrel.

"Where are your parents?" I asked, and she shrugged. "What do you mean you don't know?"

"I was brought here by someone in a ship as a baby, spent about ten years tryin' to figure out a way back home." She shrugged and held up her hands in defeat. "I don't have none, I guess."

"Of course, the Wind Primordial picks a kid like this," I muttered angrily. I heard a grunt behind me and turned to find one of the sailors watching us intently.

"You found a stowaway?" She hollered and lifted her chin to look farther back. "I'll go let Joesa know, thanks!"

"Oh, no!" The girl squirmed and tried to escape our grasp; it was actually difficult to hold on to her she was so strong. What the fuck was she? "They'll throw me overboard to the sharks!"

"No, they won't," I assured her. "You are a very special person, and we will take care of you."

Muu nodded and mentally put out the call. *We need you guys on deck. We found a stowaway, and Zeke says she's the final elemental champion.*

Seriously? Balmur called out excitedly. *We're coming!*

"Come with us, Odany." I held out a hand, and she eyed me uncertainly before she grasped my fingers and hopped off the barrel she was on easily.

We escorted her up the stairs to the waiting first mate, who had a grim expression on his face. "I see you found a bottom feeder." He raised his chin and called out to the others. "We're still close to shore, get the plank ready, let's see if she can swim!"

The sailors around us hooted and hollered, all except Taejon, who shook his head sadly.

"Belay that." The first mate's gaze shifted to me as I only said it loudly enough for him to hear. "We'll pay her way, and make sure she's fed and behaves well."

"She's a child that you just found on a ship." Joesa narrowed his eyes at us distrustfully. "Unless you brought her on board to try and save money, or you seem to like children, which will get you cut here, I do not understand why she needs to be here."

I rolled my eyes. "No one I know likes kids that way, and the suggestion alone is call for an ass-kicking where I come from. We don't want to see her die, and she's also a key component to a quest that our group is taking on."

"Quest?" The first mate perked up. "You have a quest to find children?"

"We have a quest to find special people who will do great things." I nodded down at Odany, who looked both scared and excited to be above deck. "And I can prove that she's destined for greatness. Watch."

I motioned for the sailors to step back away from her, and knelt down in front of Odany, "Hey, I'm going to show you a magic trick, do you want to learn?" She nodded enthusiastically, and I smiled at her. "I want you to hold your hand up into the air and say, 'wind come, I summon you.' You have to really want it, though, okay? Can you do that?"

She frowned, and I could feel the presence of the Wind Primordial watching, waiting.

The little girl closed her eyes and let go of my hand, she frowned and her little eyebrows knitted together. She lifted her hand and cried out, "Wind, come here, I summon you!"

A gale-force wind slammed into the side of the ship from the aft and bow that rocked all of us almost onto the deck, the course we had been on slightly changing. Joesa bellowed loudly over the noise, "All hands, mind the mast and the sails! Rild! Straighten our course, woman! All hands to your stations!"

The gusting gale whipped around all of us, tearing at loose clothing and hair whipping around each person with Odany in the center of the small maelstrom. As I worried that the wind would see us wholly off course, it stopped and died down to a breeze. She opened her eyes in confusion. "No wind came."

She frowned up at me, and her hair whipped back and forth as a towering wind elemental formed next to her. It stood easily as tall as I was, and as thick. Holes in the concentrated gust were where the mouth and eyes should have been.

"You need to name it, Odany." I encouraged her as she stood rooted to her spot on the deck in shock. "It's waiting for a name."

Should we be concerned that it's so big? Bokaj asked from where he stood near the mast with his bow out and an arrow drawn.

Maybe it will explain? I hoped as I watched her.

"I'll call you Dusty!" Odany finally raised her hands and launched herself at the windy figure, and it silently caught her.

My child will speak to none other than her, for that is her choice. The whispering of the Wind Primordial in my mind became deafening for a moment in his victory. *You have completed your quest. I will speak to my brothers and sisters of this, and we will visit you together, soon.*

I found myself grinning and looked fully toward where Joesa watched us in shock and nervousness, then I pointed to where Odany and the elemental played. "The kid stays. You'll get extra gold with her passage as well. Talk to you in a bit!"

He just nodded, dumbstruck, while Muu and I coaxed Odany and Dusty toward the rear of the ship and the rest of my friends. It was time to fill them in on what could happen next.

CHAPTER TWELVE

The group of them stood in a small semicircle around both Odany and me with her large elemental friend dancing in the slight draft of air on the back end of the ship. Every now and again we would catch sailors watching us then scurrying back to work.

"Dusty says that you all are weird," Odany piped up finally, making me glance down at her. The funneling elemental simply stood there. "She doesn't like how all of you are staring at her, she's self-conscious."

Balmur blinked and glanced at me, and I shrugged. *She won't speak to me, but having Odany as a mouthpiece, for now, isn't too bad.*

"She says that the furry one is supposed to train me on how to use my magic?" Odany looked at all of us before everyone's eyes settled on me.

"I will, but wind isn't necessarily my forte, so I can really only teach you theory stuff until I can access the magic myself." I frowned at her, then at the elemental, "Why is Dusty so big?"

"That's not a nice thing to ask a girl, mister Zeke." Odany frowned at me angrily, then cocked her head to the side. "She says I was too strong to risk one of the older siblings coming here. My call tore her through instead of a design-ated one."

"How are you so strong?" Jaken asked, and I found myself wondering the same thing again.

"Dusty says it's cause my aff-nity with wind and magic both are real high already." She shrugged and left it there.

"But *why*," Muu asked as he dug into his pocket. "Listen, if you will tell us why I have something sweet you can have in trade. We have a deal?"

She eyed him steadily, then looked to Dusty, who just shrugged back, likely not knowing what sweet was. Did elementals eat? I'd have to ask sometime.

"Deal's goin' fast, take it or leave it…" Muu waved his hand in front of her face, and her head moved side to side along with it like a dog trying to scent for a treat.

"Fine!" She finally barked. "But the sweet thing first!"

Muu narrowed his eyes at her. "Promise?"

"I promise!" Odany smiled, and Muu relinquished her treat. A small piece of something tan and red in his scaled palm. "What is it?"

"Saltwater toffee." She seemed a little skeptical until he popped another piece into his mouth and groaned in delight. She did the same and immediately grinned and chewed loudly, making my skin crawl.

Yeah, I'm one of the people who hates noisy eaters. It's just a visceral reaction on my part, but it sucks. Gross.

"So spill, what's so special about you?" Muu pressed her.

Odany looked at Dusty intently for a moment and then turned back and shrugged. "She doesn't know."

She went back to chewing, and I had to stop Muu from freaking out by putting a hand on his chest.

"Okay, so like Dusty said, I'll be teaching you how to harness your powers." She regarded me as her teeth beat the toffee into a paste, making me close my eyes to rein in the fit of chills running down my spine. "To do that, we need to harness your mind and creative abilities. So we start with meditation."

"Whassat?" Odany bounced toward me, her eyes huge.

"It's where we sit and focus our minds so we can draw on our power." She frowned and shrugged, following me to the side guard-rail of the ship.

Water lapped at the belly and wind whooshed by as I explained the process to her, which made her sigh exasperatedly multiple times.

I opened my eyes to find her standing on the rail with her arms out to the side for balance with Dusty watching silently.

"What are you doing?!" She turned sharply to look at me and slipped, her arms waving as she pitched backward.

Time seemed to slow as I mentally ordered Kayda to swoop down and catch her if I couldn't get her myself. I pushed my body into overdrive and lurched forward, so slowly.

Kayda's sharp cry caught my attention as I frantically searched below the side of the ship and saw the child skipping on the air, almost like how Bea could. Kayda's blue feathers flashed across my vision as she snatched Odany up out of the spray of the surf by the back of her shirt.

The flailing girl smiled and howled excitedly as Kayda deposited her onto the ship's deck.

"Okay, none of that." I growled menacingly at her, but she just giggled and ran about some more. I focused on my bond with the Primordial Elementals and called to the wind, *Hey, what's with this kid?*

I felt nothing for a moment, then a breeze crossed my nose, and a scent of ozone reached me. *Her control is unlike anything you can comprehend, all you need to do is guide her. She needs no true teaching in meditation, or accessing her mana—she does it naturally. Teach her to harness her natural gifts and mind her until you make landfall.*

Out loud, I snarled, "You expect us to babysit for more than a month?!"

The Wind Prime's voice was chilling as it replied, *And your reward is coming,* druid. *My brothers, sisters, and I currently decide how to divide our blessings to you all. Or would you rather we abstain?*

I rolled my eyes and turned away, looking out toward the

sea. "I'm not going to train her anymore until I understand how your powers work, Wind, it's dangerous to expect her to understand what I'm talking about when you and I have no connection other than a shallow one."

There was a breath of air that puffed against my face. *That's fine. She will have my Dusty to guide her until our deliberations conclude. I only ask that you see to it she is not harmed.*

I nodded once, and the touch of chilling air in my mind was gone, then reached out to my brothers. *The primordials are discussing our rewards for the quest.*

I wonder what we're going to get! Muu's voice sounded like he was smiling at the thought of it all.

"Whatever it is, I'm sure we're gonna be stronger for it." Jaken grasped my shoulder and turned me to look at him. "You're doing a good job, man. Don't worry, I think between Kayda and me, we can manage the kid. Why don't you look around the ship and see what you can find until we have to go see the captain?"

I looked from his gentle expression of understanding to Odany playing with Kayda and Bea standing guard over Vrawn, where she stood by the cabins.

I pulled Jaken into a hug and nodded once. *Watch over her, baby.*

Kayda shuffled her feathers, and I moved to stand next to Vrawn. "You want to look around the ship?"

"I would be delighted." Her tusks flashed with her pleasure, and she took my hand before we went to see what our new surroundings were like.

The ship's wide deck was roughly thirty-five feet wide and one hundred and seventy long. Probably galleon sized? Maybe a little larger, but who knew. Sure wasn't my area of expertise, despite all the pirate fantasy I'd read as a kid. Ships were cool and all, but the water was *not* my forte. So anything on said water was extra learning I didn't truly care for.

"Whatever will we do for all the time we are here aboard this ship?" Vrawn's question brought me out of thinking of childhood-afternoons spent reading books about vampire pirates and Viking inspired teens sailing the seas.

"We can focus on leveling up our various crafts, training, and protecting the ship." I raised her hand and kissed it. "As well as spending time together. How are you holding up?"

"It is odd being away from the village, but the company is not displeasing." She watched the clouds above us moving by for a moment. "What happens once Maebe returns?"

"She comes to us, and we move on." I motioned to our route at the fore of the ship.

"No, I meant, with me." She turned to me, and I couldn't help but see the worry in her eyes. "Will I be returning to the village?"

I shook my head. "Nope. You're a part of Storm Company, now. You're a part of the team. And as such, I'm going to be working on getting you better gear, first and foremost."

She smiled. "I've never had an enchanted item before, what is the process like?"

"Not hard." I shrugged and motioned to the ones I wore. "Don't worry, I got you. I just think it would be prudent to wait for a little bit on doing it, so I have a little more juice to go on from the elements. Hopefully."

"I understand your desire to wait, and I appreciate your thought, thank you." She paused for a moment, "Might I make a request?"

I found myself smiling. "I have a pair of boots planned that will allow you to walk on water." She turned to me sheepishly. "I know that you're still fearful of the water, that's okay. But we have your back like you will have ours."

"Thank you." Her quiet acceptance was nice, though I could tell she was still worried.

"If you want to talk about it, we can." My offer was soft-spoken, but the weight of the words carried farther. She shook her head, and that was all.

Gather, all of you who helped with the quest. Gorumbal tumbled through my mind.

I nodded and sent the call to the group, *It's time. Meet at the rear of the ship.*

"If you'll excuse me, I need to go to the others for a moment, but if you need to talk, I'll be here for you." She seemed a little deflated, so I kissed her on her forehead and touched her cheek. "The elemental primordials are calling for us to gather so they can reward us. I'll return as soon as I can."

I made my way from where Vrawn and I stood by the middle deck where the gangplank had been around to the rear of the deck where I found the others, except for Yoh.

"Should we have Yohsuke come?" Muu asked with a raised brow.

"Kayda and I will take care of the sun for now," I advised and he turned to go and wake our brother while I turned my thoughts to my bringer of the storm.

She took my thoughts and used her powers to summon Blessed Rain, the clouds around her darkening, and the breeze quickening. A warm smattering of droplets flecked the area, sailors began to swear and move over the rigging around the sails fervently until they realized that the wind wasn't picking up.

The sun being safely covered by the clouds of the spell allowed our vampire brother to storm grumpily around the corner of the cabin area toward us.

"This better be good, man," Yohsuke said, then growled, his eyes casting about dangerously.

"Do you even sleep?" I found myself frowning at him as he crossed his arms.

"It's the vampire equivalent to recharging the batteries." Yohsuke shrugged and motioned vaguely. "If I rest anywhere else, the hunger gets to me, and I can't really get the level of relaxation I need to not be a raging asshole."

Jaken, Bokaj, and Muu all grinned and glanced at each other before they asked, "When aren't you?"

He stared at them coldly, until the world around us fell so quiet that the lack of sound unnerved me.

The view was as much the same as it had been, but the people working aboard the ship moved as if through molasses. *We have altered time and reality by our presence, we must be swift.* Gorumbal's voice greeted us all. All around us, motes of elemental energy grew from orbs the size of a nickel to the size of small suns that blotted out the world behind them.

Every element represented, for a moment, I worried that Yohsuke would burst into flame with the Light Primordial so near. His arms moved to protect him as the light intensified greatly, but nothing happened.

My light will not punish you this once, undead. The Light's voice echoed around us. *Though the sun will still harm you should you stand in it. Attend us.*

The energy of the elements pulsed around us, and a rush of energy crashed into my body, overloading my vision with notifications I dismissed until I could focus on them.

The Flame Primordial spoke first, *Your toiling for our gain has not gone unnoticed, and while we would reward all of you as greatly as we plan to do, few of you have the natural ability to become vessels for our strength.*

This is why we have chosen to bless all of you that we can, The Water Primordial's soothing voice washed over all of us. *In what way that we can. I have chosen. The living flesh of normal mortals cannot cope with the cold of the depths, this is why I bequeath my frozen gratitude to Yohsuke and Bokaj.*

Water rushed from her manifestation and covered their skin, pooling around their forearms, then sinking in.

Heat washed over all of us. *I have chosen to bless Balmur, at his request, and as a child of my realm.*

The flames on Balmur's body intensified, and he sighed as if stepping into a warm bath after being in the cold all day.

We have given the blessings we will give, as our price was paid, the Shadow Primordials low voice that sounded like a multitude of speakers made me shiver. *All three of you have proven worthy, pass on my adoration to my champion.*

I nodded, and so did Yohsuke and Balmur.

I choose to offer my freedom of movement to both James and Muu, The Wind Primordial moaned. Whipping tornadoes of green energy swirled from the tempest of primal wind and lifted the two melee fighters from the ground. They settled back down after a second or so and began to look themselves over in delight.

Light flooded the area around us, blinding all of us until it faded shortly after. A single glow was all that was left once the light faded to normal, and that glow came from Jaken.

You have earned this light, paladin. Her soft voice was warm against my skin, and I smiled at the pleasantness of it.

I nodded. This was as it should be. Everyone had worked so hard for all of this.

Druid, six voices drew my attention, and all eyes were on me.

The shadows swept forward. *Our beloved adores you, and your manipulation of our being pleases us. Continue as you are, and we shall see if you do not rival our beloved.*

Water, earth, wind, and light surged forward, striking me from several directions at once, and the same overload of information overtook me.

A burning on my chest where my tattoo was made me claw open my shirt and watch, as once more, the tattoo shifted and raised, the white line turning from white to solid gold against my black fur. The diamond mountain became a full-fledged piece of diamond in my skin, the tidal wave of water a sapphire in the same shape. The flame crown that showed the Flame Primordial's dominion solidified into a ruby version.

The green tornado became an emerald, and finally, the darkness of the pentagram's blank spaces filled with pure obsidian. The star-like flecks of golden light that dotted my fur filtered into the golden lines and created a nimbus of energy that swirled hypnotically. Once all the representative elements had mutated, agonizingly so, the mark sank into my skin, and I felt it breaking apart. Breaking down and spreading throughout my being.

It was weird not having my tattoo anymore, but I could feel

the bond with the elements was still there. Just… deeper. Then as I watched, the tattoo, marks and all, resurfaced as they had been.

We bestow upon you a power you have earned, Gorumbal's voice held a tinge of almost guilt while he rumbled at me. *While it will make you vastly stronger and more versatile, our combined blessings might interfere with each other.*

The Fire Primordial picked up after his brother finished. *It is rare that a body holds so many affinities, but your body is not purely mortal any longer. Where a trifling interest was safe, our full gifts now resonate with you wholly.*

This has never happened, finished the Water Prime. Her somber tone worried me almost as much as being in the depths would. *We… do not know what this could do to you, droplet.*

It is our sincere hope that your strength of will and the natural balance of our gifts will meld well with your Primal Warrior abilities, as a Druid keeps the balance between civilization and nature. Light pulsed warmly from her and I basked in it for a moment before she continued, *But it is a hope we cannot be certain of.*

"Are you certain I should have this power?" I did my damnedest to keep my voice steady despite the messy tangle of nerves roiling my gut. "Please, know that I hold your musings and decisions in high regard, but isn't this too much for one man? Am I even worthy of this?"

No, you are not, the Wind Prime seethed, wind whipping at my clothing. *But power comes at a cost, and the price for our assisting this realm and our resurgence was such that this was born of necessity. My brothers and sisters adore you, druid. This decision has cost them much, and I do not unders—*

Gorumbal's vibrating bass voice rumbled over his brother's, *Our friendship will cost you much, friend Zeke, but we believe you responsible enough to hold sway over our dominions. You have earned this.*

Your question shows humility, flame. The Fire Prime's crackling tone sounded more at ease. *It is your conscience and consideration for the ramifications of your actions and impact that we can trust you to hold yourself accountable.*

And strike at our foes, ridding this world of those who would subjugate us for their own machinations, The Shadow Primordial hissed darkly.

"I will do my best." I looked around at my brothers. "We all will."

Thank you, and good luck. They left us then, the Water Primordial's words of gratitude signaling the real passage of time. Sailors moved about and watched the clouds slowly drifting by above.

You can end the spell in a few minutes baby, I warned Kayda and looked to Yoh. "You can go back to sleep, man. We can discuss things later on, if needed. Thanks for being here."

He nodded and walked off toward the cabin entrance as I turned back to the others.

"These notifications could be trippy." I watched the others' reactions, and the gravity of it wasn't lost on them. "Anyone want to start?"

"I can manipulate fire now, like tinkering with spells," Balmur began and smiled. "This means I can add all kinds of cool stuff to my repertoire of spells!"

I nodded, and as I was about to speak, Muu and James grinned at each other, then us before James spoke, "Five points to dexterity. Nice!"

"I can tinker with Light magic." Jaken smiled. "I think it may add some *oomph* to my smite, too."

"Added ice manipulation, though I can make some spells with it if I try hard enough. I don't really have a ton of mana, so it may be harder for me." Bokaj seemed a little let down, but he was okay after a moment, letting it go. "It'll be worth it if I can figure out how to coat my arrows in ice."

"I can help you with that, I think," Balmur offered, and the two grinned.

"I take it that Yoh got the same kind of tinkering ability," I began. "I got it all, I think. The other elements, that is."

"Do you feel any different?" Muu asked with a spark of concern in his eyes.

I took an inventory of myself and shook my head. "Not really? A little stronger, I think, and kind of tired, though."

"Well, if anything happens or gets weird, let us know, okay?" Jaken took his hand and set it on my shoulder as he looked me in the eyes. "Seriously. Anything at all."

"Yeah, you got it." I couldn't argue with him on that, and I wasn't about to try.

The others cleared away to do various things for a little bit before dinner with the captain and I went to the room we had and sat on one of the cots to go through my notifications.

ABILITIES UNLOCKED!

Elemental Tinkering (Earth) – Earth now heeds your command unlike it had before, and new spells can be created and discovered within the proper elemental realm. Be warned that mana is consumed at a higher rate while tinkering with a spell, or discovering a new spell.

Elemental Tinkering (Light) – Light now heeds your command unlike it had before, and new spells can be created and discovered within the proper elemental realm. Be warned that mana is consumed at a higher rate while tinkering with a spell, or discovering a new spell.

Elemental Tinkering (Water) – Water now heeds your command unlike it had before, and new spells can be created and discovered within the proper elemental realm. Be warned that mana is consumed at a higher rate while tinkering with a spell, or discovering a new spell.

Elemental Tinkering (Wind) – Wind now heeds your command unlike it had before, and new spells can be created and discovered within the proper elemental realm. Be warned that mana is consumed at a higher rate while tinkering with a spell, or discovering a new spell.

That was all well and good, but the other notification was wilder.

ABILITIES UPGRADED!

With the collection of so many Elemental Tinkering abilities, your strength as a Primal Warrior has grown to reflect these new aspects.

Elemental Aspects now available!

Elemental Aspects! I wondered what they did, and I would definitely be checking into them sooner rather than later.

Watching the sailors working was cool and all, but I had some new power I could wield for enchanting, and I planned to use it.

I went out and found Vrawn, taking a sword that she had grabbed from the hoard as well as a pair of metal boots, a leather breastplate, and a couple rings.

"No other requests than the boots?" I raised an eyebrow at her, and she shook her head.

"Nothing from me." She smiled indulgently as Odany clambered about her waist and up onto her out-stretched arm. "If you have suggestions that might do well against creatures of the sea and beyond, I will take them."

I nodded and called Kayda to me for a moment, leaving Bea behind to watch over the two playing ladies.

"You're going to help me lay lightning into this weapon, sweetheart." Kayda seemed excited by the prospect, her grip tightening as she spread her wings in pride.

The sword was longer than most of the ones I had seen before, wider as well but not quite a great sword like the one Jaken would wield at times. The weapon was sharp at the edges, and the hilt was plain too. Definitely a weapon meant to kill and not shine too much in the eyes of others.

If I had to guess, the metal itself was something stronger than even mithril, but what it was exactly I couldn't say. Jaken may have known, but I wasn't going to interrupt whatever he was doing just to satisfy my curiosity.

I gathered the image of what I wanted to engrave in my

mind, and Kayda pecked at my ear angrily. *If I am to assist you, you must share your ideas with me.*

I glared at her for a moment, then acquiesced by spinning my mana out of my finger into the design I had in mind.

Lightning arcs more, and more here, here and here, she pecked places I should add bits of arcing power and the intense creative musings I had felt before took over again.

I pressed the centerline down in a sort of meandering path with the arcs from it stretching out. Then pressed all the way through it, while the arcs only engraved a bit from the line to the outside of the blade. Then, the same thing on the other side, but not uniform, because lightning varied and each strike was different.

The total mana I'd used for the design of the engraving had been intense—847 MP. Probably one of my most expensive engravings.

But it would be worth it, I hoped.

Add some of my feathers! Kayda offered and plucked some of her older feathers from her plumage. Five of the softly crackling items landed in my hands.

I thanked her by stroking her small head, and the feathers grew until they were normal sized in my hands, each almost as long as my forearm.

"Great idea!" I set them aside and dug around in my inventory for a decent kind of conductive metal. Which, if paying attention in science classes at all as a kid, had been silver. While it would be painful, I could add the metal with a glove, or have Kayda drop it on for me. The second sounded better since she wanted to be involved.

I took out about thirty silver coins and placed them into a small bag she put into her mouth to hold until I told her to drop them onto the blade.

"Hubris," I whispered, and the scepter came to me from its pocket dimension.

Enchanting more? This design seems interesting, how do you plan to make it more effective?

"I was going to add Kayda's feathers and silver, so it's conducive to electricity," I explained and ran my hand over the design.

Intelligent, and you wish for it to produce electricity? Like lightning damage? Wait.

A gentle warmth radiated down my arms and into my chest.

You have gained much since last we spoke, master. You will be able to make things much easier, now. Combining your air and fire mana into the blade will produce a stronger tie to the elemental lightning you wish to make.

"Can I even do that?"

Do you not do so to make new spells already?

"I use the concepts of forging to make new spells." I frowned and rubbed my head.

I will show you an easier way. Put the sword onto the deck, and take me in both hands.

"If I use two types of mana like this, I'll be too exhausted to keep channeling it. The enchantment might be terrible!"

Trust me, master.

I growled and then looked to Kayda, who stared at me curiously, so I sighed and let her know. "When I say so, drop the coins onto the sword. Oh, here."

I picked her feathers up and put them into her claw to help. Just in case I couldn't use my hands to do it myself.

I closed my eyes and began the process of using elemental mana, envisioning the mana leaving my mana pool in two separate routes, fire going down my left arm, and air my right. Both meeting inside Hubris.

I will control the flow so that you do not lose much mana, we begin now.

The two aspects swirled down the scepter and into the sword in a bright yellow arc that made me gasp, and Kayda tilt her head back and forth.

My mana drained steadily, more steadily than it ever had while using aspected mana like this, but it still drained swiftly.

I am controlling it so that loss is minimal, and I add ambient magic to it as well to bolster your work. Focus your intent and will, master!

I did as Hubris ordered and focused my mind. First the silver needed adding… *now!*

Kayda dumped the silver in, and as the last piece disappeared from view, Kayda threw in the feathers, a flash of azure light around us came as a result.

Have her strike it with pure lightning!

She must have been able to sense the need, screeching angrily she zapped the metal of the weapon steadily until the end of my mana transference.

Name the weapon, master.

Arc Cutter

+15 damage, +18 Lightning damage

Special spell: Storm Roc's Ire – caster invokes the anger of the mythic Storm Roc, calling lightning from the sky to smite their foe once. Cool down: 12 hours

Lo, unto the skies they eyed and saw her, wings spread far and her anger deeper than the oceans—they quake in fear of her rage and beauty.

Sword made by grandmaster smith Mikel Thornson and enchanted by adept enchanter Zekiel Erebos.

"Wow." I blinked at the blade and grinned widely.

The blade was beautiful, and the silver that was supposed to fill the engraving wasn't silver anymore, it was the same azure color as Kayda's lightning magic. The blue lightning enhanced metal arced throughout the weapon, filling the center with smaller arcing branches that touched the cutting edge, but not ruining it.

I noticed that my enchanting had jumped two levels, putting me at level 48. Closer to master level! Yes. But two levels? Seemed a high jump, but I'd jumped that high before, hell higher, even. Something about doing things I'd not done before, branching out in my skills.

I moved my attention to the boots after a rest, adding more elemental energy to them with small bits of advice from Hubris.

Then the rings, chest piece, and a set of bracers that I found in my inventory.

Four rings, one each for defense, mind protection, protection from the cold, and the final one to increase attack speed. Though the final ring took a little bit of mana to activate. I'd have to see if she had any since Muu did, I had to assume that she did too.

The bracers I enchanted to defend against elemental damage, a lesser version of the ones I wore since they couldn't empower strikes with the residual magic that was absorbed.

The chest piece was made to be as hard and sturdy as mithril while being lighter than the leather that it was made of. That had been fun and easy, I also gave it a little protection from water magic, so there was that.

I thought about calling to Bea so she could shepherd her to me, but I held off. Now, I thought, *what should I do about the kid?*

She should likely have a way to defend herself. A weapon of some kind. But I'd have to see what she thought.

Bea, will you bring Vrawn and Odany to me?

They're playing. Her simple response and lack of obedience threw me off. She had been herself this morning as well. *You come to them. They're having fun.*

I turned to Kayda, who turned away from me, her head bobbed up and down as if she were laughing.

I inventoried my work and stormed out onto the deck to find all three of the people I sought and found them all playing a game of catch. Vrawn threw Odany up into the air, and the child would step up higher on the wind, then float gently back down as Bea called up to her in an audibly excited kind of bark.

The indignity gripping me as I had walked outside melted away when I heard the child's giggling and saw her smile. Then Vrawn laughing and grinning as she was, relaxed and enjoying herself? I could get used to that.

Granted, I missed Maebe like crazy, but I knew she would be back as soon as she could. And I had to work on things here while I could, and patching things up with her would take some of the pressure off Maebe.

Not to mention, I wanted it too. I'd fucked up royally, and she had every right to be angry. I should focus on trying to fix things on my own.

I waited while they played for ten more minutes, the girl suddenly stopping and looking panicked. "I'm hungry."

I found myself laughing probably louder than I had in some time, almost doubling over as all three sets of eyes swung my way.

"We can get you something to snack on." I had some travel rations in my inventory that we hardly ever used, but it was edible, and it would hold her over, I hoped.

I took the brown square roughly the size of a pop tart and tossed it to her. She caught it and immediately tucked into it, eyeing the people around her dangerously.

"Vrawn, your weapon is ready, and I enchanted the gear as well." I stepped closer to her and handed her the items one by one. Small sounds of awe and surprise came from her that made me grin.

She put the boots on immediately, looking like she felt better already. The other gear she threw on as well, admiring how everything looked, then looked over at me. "You said you had my weapon as well?"

I found my boyish grin spreading almost of its own accord as I held the weapon out in both hands. She frowned and removed the shirt I had used to cover it, Kayda hopping off my shoulder to assume her full glorious size so she could watch with pride.

"Oh, my gods, it's beautiful, Zeke." She lifted the blade reverently from my grasp and held it aloft, the sunlight shimmering off it. Kayda pecked the weapon, and an arc of electricity jumped between them, making her shuffle her feathers as if it tickled. She brought it down and closed her eyes as she stepped back, the arc she swung it through ending abruptly as she spun and parried an invisible blade from an imaginary enemy. The weapon looked light as a feather to her, and she maneuvered it so expertly that I found myself enraptured in her form and force of will.

Seeing her moving like this, you could tell that she had spent years and years developing her martial prowess until it was as finely tuned as a rock star's guitar. She was the weapon, and it made me more than a little jealous.

"Woah…" Odany whispered as she shuffled closer to me, her eyes on Vrawn and Vrawn alone. "She's so pretty! And she looks like she's having fun."

"Yeah, she does," I admitted, and she grinned up at me. "I was going to ask—do you want a weapon?"

"If it's like hers I want two!" Odany danced with her arms up in the air before staring back at Vrawn and attempting to copy some of the larger woman's movements. Solidly planting her legs, the girl whirled her hand in a pattern similar to rolling your wrist and stabbing forward, then back again. She giggled, and when she "slashed" Dusty, the elemental threw her arms into the air and feigned death.

I watched Vrawn once more, and the sword itself began to glow an azure color as it wove a pattern of death through the air. Vrawn's closed eyes and mildly labored breathing made me frown, she jumped and struck out at the air behind her with her foot and spun to land on the railing, her sense of the battle she fought almost as real as her surroundings. She shuffled back and pitched herself to the right and over the rail of the ship.

I grunted as my body moved on its own, the wind whipping over my face as I dove over the side and shifted into my eagle form with Kayda hot on my heels. As she fell, she fought even more fervently, Arc Cutter glittering in the air around her as she flipped through the air, keeping me away for fear of getting cut in half. She landed on the ocean in a three-point, superhero-style landing that made me groan at how goddamn awesome she was and then she began to fight again. The world around her forgotten.

She bared her teeth, her tusks flashing angrily as she

grunted and snarled at the foes in her mind, and I had to work to stay aloft to ensure she didn't hit the ship. As she cut the air in front of her, she lifted the blade with a savage cry, and azure lightning crackled around the blade. The sky split in half, and a column of lightning sundered the air before us and crashed into the water twenty feet in front of me, spraying my feathers with water and bringing Vrawn to her senses.

Kayda chose that moment to swing down and lift her from the water toward the ship.

I worked my way up the side of the ship and landed on the rail in my fox-man form, grabbing the rail with a clawed hand as Vrawn looked around her in a near panic. "You okay?"

"I haven't had an inspiration that intense since before the war." Vrawn let the sword's tip rest on the deck as she looked at me, a grave expression on her face. "There's a fight coming, Zeke."

CHAPTER THIRTEEN

"Wait, what?" Muu took his clawed fingers and ran them over her head once more as we all stared at Vrawn on the back deck of the ship.

We'd gathered together after her prophetic vision, and she had explained what she had seen—experienced. It was a fight of downright epic proportions on the ocean with black creatures from the depths. The news was more than a little distressing to me as this whole thing was one of my biggest nightmares.

"They came from the depths in droves, and then something massive joined them, I cannot tell what it was, but it was larger than anything I have ever seen." She looked distressed, so I found her hand and held it. "I do not know what this will mean, or how soon it will occur, but it is coming."

"So, we need to prepare things." Jaken frowned, his eyes closing for a moment. "Give me a little bit, I need to pray and think."

I glanced askance of the others and mouthed, *pray?*

The others shrugged and mouthed *paladin* back, and that was that. I was going to need to do a lot of enchanting. If something was coming for us, then we needed to be ready, and we needed the crew to be ready too.

"Dinner isn't for another hour; the captain is currently in a planning session with the gunner, gunner's mate, first mate, and the quartermaster." One of the older looking crew members explained when I had begun asking after the first mate. "Best not to disturb them, the captain is a bit... volatile when disturbed."

"Very well, thank you." He nodded and walked off, whistling a tune I didn't recognize.

What're we going to do? Jaken asked at last.

We can enchant the ship to be sturdier, the sails as well. Maybe we can also enchant the cannons? Zeke, what do you think? Balmur was busily scribbling in his book when he glanced up at me.

That could work, we might also want to try enchanting their weapons if we can. Between you, Jaken and Bokaj, you think we might be able to make some ballistae?

Muu's head whipped over toward me. *You're talking about flinging harpoons? Like, Moby Dick type shit? At something that could likely swim off with us? Also, we look weird like this so let's talk out loud for now.*

"It doesn't need to be attached to the ship you goober." Bokaj rolled his eyes as he whittled something small. "Yeah, I have a decent amount of wood, though I don't know about the amount of metal that Jaken could have. Why don't you, Balmur, and Yohsuke, do what you did in the Great Below? With the shadows?"

"Because all we did was gather the magic for Maebe to shape and shoot." I had to admit, it was a good idea. "Bokaj, Balmur, and Muu, I need all of you to work together and start a blueprint for a ballista. We can start by making one of them and ensuring it works."

The three of them nodded, and Muu pulled out his little notebook for them to crowd around. James watched me expectantly, and I sighed. "I don't suppose you brought any books on the ocean and its creatures with you?"

"You bet your furry ass I did." James grinned. "I already started researching what was out here, and let me tell you—shit ain't pretty."

"Keep it up, when you find something that could be as big as Vrawn described, come let me know." I made to move away, but Vrawn stopped me.

"I would like to prepare, as well." She looked determined, and I nodded.

"I have a good job for you since you seem to be a good teacher." I motioned to Odany, where she spoke to Dusty with Bea and Kayda watching over her.

"You want me to babysit her?" She frowned deeply, and I shook my head, then she brightened up a little. "You want me to teach her how to fight?"

"You will instruct her on her martial development, and I will instruct her with magic," I raised my voice so that the others would hear me as well. "We bump it up to twice a day training from here on out so that we can be prepared. New shifts to watch the seas."

"And what is our fearless leader going to be doing as we all bust our asses?" Muu put his hands on his hips and glared at me.

I grimaced at him and motioned to the water. "I'll be going in to try and collect what forms I can for a couple hours a day so that we can fight back."

He visibly blanched at my statement and went back to what he was doing without another word. "That's what I thought."

I turned to Vrawn. "Can you figure out what type of weapon Odany would do well with?"

"Of course, I carry an assortment of weapons to see who would be most suitable for a weapon type." She smiled and left me standing there wondering when she had picked up sarcasm until she stood in front of Odany and produced weapon after weapon.

"Jesus Christ, she was completely serious." Pulling my jaw up off the deck, I went to go see where Jaken was.

The sailors nodded my way, their curiosity making them pause in their various tasks to wave or smile at me. I did my best to smile back and be as friendly as possible. We would be working with all of them soon to protect the ship, so it would be rude of me not to.

I found Jaken standing on at the front of the ship where the rails met, and the waves were cut. He stared out over the ocean with his back to me, his platinum armor glinting in the light of the afternoon sun.

I stepped closer to him, and he turned to offer me a small smile. "Hey, man."

"How you doin?" I reached over and ruffled his shoulder playfully, and he just shook his head.

"Wondering what Luna would think of all this." He motioned out to the world around us. "I find myself thinking of that question more and more often, wondering if coming here might not be the better option for her."

"Coming here?"

"Yeah." He frowned in thought then crossed his arms before him. "Like, if we do a good enough job here, maybe the gods could bring her and her mom over here. Maybe we could live here."

I hadn't thought of it like that. "Yeah, that would be pretty wild. But wouldn't you want to stay home?"

"That place sucks, man." Jaken groaned and shoved my shoulder as if to wake me up. "The planet is dying, the people there are so full of themselves that they let others die for no reason, and what is there to do about it? I can't do anything about it, I'm just one guy."

I let that statement hang in the air a little bit, silently contemplating what I could say to help him feel better. I found it hard. Harder than I might have before I met Maebe and Vrawn.

"You're right." I shrugged. "Earth sucks. The humans there are, for the most part, somewhat shitty. And though you're one man there, you're one man here, too. And one man can change someone's entire perspective. If you change one life for the better, you've made the world a better place. Think of Luna—if you were to raise her as righteously and wonderfully as you would love to, think of the people whose lives she could change."

His eyebrows furrowed over his eyes. "I guess I hadn't thought about it like that." He put his hands on the rail and leaned forward. "So, the fight is coming to us. What're the others doing?"

"They're researching, and working on trying to get a blue-print together for a ballista, what we need to know is how much metal we have, and that's where you come in."

He opened his inventory and frowned. "I have a good bit of iron, copper, a little steel, and bronze. I have a good amount of lead. Silver, too, if I can work with it. And… about twenty bars of mithril."

"Think we have enough to make a couple rounds of shafts for the weapon?"

He grinned. "Yeah, we should have enough. You going to enchant them?"

I grinned back. "Do you doubt me?"

He shook his head and clapped me on the shoulder. "Not in the slightest."

"Good, let's use that mithril to make a weapon for Odany, and then the less important but magically inclined metals can be used for the rounds." I shook myself out and grinned at our prospects. Now it was just time to convince the captain of what was to come.

We went back to the others and began planning as the sun set, the stars peeking out against the light made me smile and think of my wife.

"The captain will see you now," Joesa advised us and motioned toward the door at the back of the cabin that opened to a set of stairs that led up.

Once we all climbed the small set of stairs, we came to a

large room with a round table that looked like it would be capable of seating all of us comfortably.

A figure separated itself from the shadows near the rear of the room, the long burgundy coat swaying as she moved was almost trench coat like. A cream-colored blouse with ruffles at the chest covered an athletic build, and black leather pants scraped soft so they made little sound were tucked into tall black boots with no heel. Or, rather, one black boot and the black leather of a peg leg that clacked onto the ground as she moved forward.

Feline eyes the color of fire watched us curiously as she spoke, "I am Captain Holly Jennisovna, welcome aboard the Pussy Willow, Storm Company. I have heard little of you, and I hope to rectify this."

"As do we." Bokaj bowed at the waist and moved forward with a grin. "Forgive me, I had hardly expected the captain of such a fine ship to be so alluring."

A purring sound emanated from the woman as she smiled, her sharp teeth flashed in the light and her whiskers twitched in delight. "I like this one."

The rest of us chuckled, and she motioned for us to be seated. "Joesa, my dear, see to the men and have the food brought to us in twenty minutes. It is time for our acquaintances to be made before we fill our bellies, yes?"

"As you say it, Cap'n." Joesa smiled and backed out of the room, leaving us with the mysterious woman.

"As I said, I welcome all of you, but I did hear tell of a stowaway?" She raised a furred eyebrow, and the rest of us nodded. Odany raised her hand. "You may speak, urchin."

The little girl had been washed, much to her chagrin, and placed in a dress that was way too large for her until her normal clothes had been cleaned. Could I have done it with shadows? Yeah, but they would be weird, and she had needed a bath.

"I didn't mean anything disrespectful by it, ma'am, I just wanted to go home." Odany did seem contrite, and her downcast face helped, in my opinion. "When I learned you were heading for my homeland, I had to do it."

Captain Holly watched the girl in silence for a moment before she turned and walked back toward a cabinet on the right side of the room.

"What is your name, urchin?" The woman projected her voice to be heard, startling the girl.

"Odany, ma'am." We had spent a few minutes on our way over talking about manners and the appropriate way to address people with station. I was proud she'd remembered.

"I appreciate the manners, Odany," The captain said as she moved haltingly back toward the table with two bottles in hand. "But I've worked all my life to become a captain of one of the finest vessels on the Obvoran Ocean. To be called 'ma'am' by anyone aboard my ship is grounds for a thrashing. I'll let it slide because you're cute."

The captain grinned at Odany and poured a sweet-smelling liquid into a small metal cup in front of her while scenting the top of her head.

Before she could think to take it and drink, I snatched it off the table and took a deep whiff of it.

Holly gave me a throaty laugh. "Do you think I would poison a paying customer?"

I laughed in return, setting the cup back in front of Odany, who took it and sniffed it as well. "I didn't expect juice to be what you served."

"I have no aversion to alcohol, but my drinks are to be served with food." Captain Holly poured more juice, this one smelling more bitter and earthy than the other one. "This helps with digestion and keeps scurvy at bay. We have a couple barrels of the stuff below to keep my sailors healthy. A sip every few days keeps them ship-shape."

"Clever idea." Jaken growled appreciatively. "While we're on board, if your men and women need healing, tell them to come find me. I will be happy to help them."

"Noted, thank you." She reached across the table and

touched his face, then pulled her hand back and scented her hand. "What's your name?"

"Jaken, Captain." She purred at his deference and looked to James, who sat next to him. "I'll introduce the rest of them counterclockwise. This is James, Balmur, Muu, Vrawn, Zeke, and the guy next to you is Bokaj."

As Jaken named each person, the captain would touch their face before taking in their scent. Finally, Odany couldn't hold her curiosity anymore and blurted, "Why do you do that? Where's your leg? Why are you so pretty? Can I touch your tail?"

All of us would have been stunned if not for the fact that she was a child, and I had been slightly expecting the first and second question from one of us.

The captain's throaty laugh made the rest of us chuckle. "Oh, lovely Odany, I gather your scents so that I can tell where you are and who you are, when I travel the ship. I know each of my sailors by scent, and it helps me keep a better control of events."

"As to my leg, that is a grand tale of adventure and excitement! But I'll tell you that after I answer your other questions. I'm pretty because my mommy gave me all the best baths when I was little, and I look like her. And my tail? My tail is sensitive, so only if you promise to be gentle, and only if you ask first. Okay?"

The girl bolted out of her chair and careened forward until she was almost behind the captain and came to a halt. "May I?"

Captain Holly nodded once and lifted her twitching tail up so the little girl could stroke it softly with a look of shock and awe on her face. As she came to a finish, Captain Holly twitched her tail under her nose and tickled her, making Odany sneeze, and the rest of us laugh.

That's how you did it right there.

"Glad to know our captain is as personable as the rest of her crew." I chuckled, and she regarded me warmly. "Thank you for taking us aboard."

"Of course, money is money and protection a necessity." She frowned at all of us. "Though I was told there would be two others?"

"Our brother Yohsuke is asleep," James explained quickly. "Our other party member is currently not with us, but will join us as soon as she can."

"I see, and how does she plan to join us?"

"She's a very powerful magic user," I answered, and Vrawn pointedly glanced my way. "But we also bring other news. One of us experiences prophetic visions, and through one of these visions, we've seen a battle coming."

She stopped smiling immediately. "What sort of battle?"

"Something large and monstrous is coming, and we don't know exactly, but we wish to be prepared," Vrawn stated plainly.

"You've been kind enough to take us to our destination for money and protection," I reiterated for her benefit and ours. "That means that we will be preparing how we can. Enchanting the ship to make it stronger, weapons, cannons, making a weapon to use in the fight. Even enchanting weapons that your crew already has if necessary. Anything we have to do."

She frowned and nodded. "While this is concerning news, I have heard tell of a slew of ships being attacked. Sunk and destroyed with little evidence as to what happened. We came upon one recently ourselves. The ship's mast was completely gone, no bodies, just a ship floating aimlessly. Nothing else left behind."

"Do you think they could be connected?" Balmur asked before sipping his juice.

"Could be." She shrugged after a second. "I have not heard much, our broker only being able to tell me that you are of a capable sort of a Storm Company. Why don't you tell me of yourselves? Who are you? *What* are you? And how is it you can enchant an entire ship and every weapon on it?"

Bokaj leaned back and sighed. *Was only a matter of time. Let me talk, guys.*

He smiled his best and began to speak, "We're concerned people with powerful interests all over the globe. As to our name, Storm Company was only decided on recently, before that we had moved under no name and with no pretense of glory. It was recently that we decided a name might aid us. As to how we could do this? One of our own is an accomplished enchanter who likes to ply his trade in fascinating ways, and we have the means to do so. Is enchanted gear truly so uncommon?"

"It is not uncommon to have an heirloom or something passed from captain to captain, or from generation to generation in a family, but a whole ship?" Captain Holly shook her head and chuckled incredulously. "That is the stuff of myth and legend. Armor and weapons? Not so much but still costly and not common at all. If you mean no harm, then I suppose I can take you at your word for this."

She stood, tail flicking back and forth agitatedly before she spoke again, "We have a trade agreement with a local lord of these waters, we will see him in two days time. He will at least ensure that we have some security until our preparations can be made."

"What kind of lord is he?" Bokaj stilled as the door opened, and food came in.

The servers set steaks and cuts of various fish with steamed veggies on nice plates before us and left in a hurry. Joesa poured wine for all of us except Odany, and we ate peacefully for a few moments.

Finally, Captain Holly decided to answer us cryptically. "He is a fair, but greedy lord, and he's a bit thick-shelled."

"I take it that you're going to make us wait to find out?" I raised an eyebrow as I enjoyed my food. I tried the fish and found it mildly fishy, but I ate it anyway since I was hungry. She nodded, and I sighed softly. "Very well. What can you tell us of yourself then? What kind of ship is it that you run?"

"And what's the story about your leg?!" Odany blurted out, after swallowing a bite of food.

Captain Holly smiled and bowed her head. "I did promise this story."

She stood from the table and stepped back into the shadows a little before she spoke, "There we were, in the Magdaryi Strait, a place known for large fish so full of energy that they leap from the water. I manned the helm of the ship as Joesa steered, calling out coral reefs to avoid as we made our heading. So blue was the sky that the water reflected the clouds, and only my fierce gaze would pierce the water as we made our escape from some nasty fiends.

"We made our way out onto open waters after hours of running, our pursuers having floundered mere moments before, and our freedom was secured. As my crew and I celebrated, one such fish leapt from the water and speared my leg with its sharp nose. The bone shattered, and my flesh tore!"

Odany gasped, and raised her hands to cover her mouth.

"My men fought to save the leg, but alas, our foe had managed to sight us with their cannons." She took out her sword, a long curved saber that she used theatrically. "With no time to waste on the limb, I *cut* it from my body and had our poor healer staunch the wound so we could flee to safety once more. That night, under the peace of the stars and with the oceans as my witness, I cast my limb into the water as a sacrifice for luck and fair tides."

"What happened to the fish?" Vrawn whispered her question, and Odany nodded hurriedly.

Captain Holly grinned fiercely. "So hard had we fought that our bellies rumbled something terrible. My crew and I dined on the fish, and his head I preserve near the quarterdeck. A reminder that what the ocean gives, she will take—if you let her."

"An interesting tale." Bokaj grinned at her before observing, "Your crew seems well-disciplined and close-knit."

"That would be because they are." Captain Holly made to sit, but stopped herself before standing once more. "My crew and I are close because every day on this ocean is treacherous and dangerous. The people who sail it, sometimes more so. As to what we do? We ride the waves in search of adventure while transporting cargo, at times, providing protection to some merchants so as to lighten their loads and put their crews in less danger."

"So, you're like guards?" Jaken raised an eyebrow with an uncertain look on his face.

"At times," her grin seemed genuine. "Other times, we are a community funded research vessel. It depends on what adventure calls on us next."

Sounds kind of suspicious to me, James grumbled through our minds.

Does what they do really matter? Muu shot back pointedly. *We need to get across this ocean, and with us here, they will likely decide that something odd may not fly. Leave it alone for now, and we can focus on getting shit done.*

That's surprisingly wise for you, Muu. I raised an eyebrow at him, and he just sighed, looking up at the captain.

"You guys sound wonderful. I think my brothers and I will start on the ballista tomorrow, so we have a head start." He motioned to me. "I'm not sure what Zeke will need to enchant the ship, but he will start tomorrow too."

I nodded, and with that, the rest of our meal passed in peace and with minimal talking. Vrawn carried Odany back to the room, and we put her to bed outside the Happy Home at first, then decided that she should be inside where it's safe. Vrawn would keep her company and I would stay out to be available with Muu.

As we both laid in the beds, the sound of the waves washing over us, I listened to the waves for the barest while before finally. "You know, I'm glad that you're here."

"Of course, you are." Muu snorted, his voice teasing. "I'm amazing."

"You are, but mainly since you kept us from doing something regrettable earlier. And you took charge when you might normally let someone else."

He was quiet for a minute, then he finally sat up and got out of bed so that he could look at me. "You ever miss home?"

"Sometimes, yeah. When I think about my son? Every time." I sat up but didn't get down out of my bunk. "You?"

He frowned. "I miss some of our friends who aren't here, sure." He turned around and walked over to the porthole in the room and sighed. "Otherwise? No. To be completely honest, I've been thinking about… staying."

At first, I laughed, but when I looked over at him and found a sad smile looking back at me, I was stricken silent. "You can't be serious, man."

"Why not?"

"You would miss playing video games too much." This time I did stand up and move toward him.

"Zeke, I'm an *actual* dragoon." He motioned to his body. "I'm the strongest I've ever been. And here, I can do some real good. Be the real me."

"What about your family?"

"John? Please, he'd barely notice I'm gone." He shook his head at the thought. "My sister and my nephew have their own lives, and I never get to see them, but I think I'd miss mom. She would want me to be happy, though. I think she'd be proud of us."

"You know damned well what I mean when I ask you that fucking question." I growled at him, trying to hide the hurt by masking it with anger. "What about your friends? Your real family?"

"You mean what about you?" His knowing look was enough to make me want to hit him, and I wish I didn't have the control that I did at that moment. "I know you would miss me, man. And I'd miss you too, of course. But other than a few people that I'm really close to, I don't have the ties to home that you do. There's nothing to hold me back here."

My mouth opened, closed, and then opened again before I found I didn't know what to say. One of my best friends was thinking of staying behind, and I might never get to see him again.

Numb, I looked away. Suddenly the room was much too warm for my comfort, and I needed to be anywhere but here. I stood, turned and marched out the door, Muu's shouting falling on deaf ears. Kayda reached out to me with her mind, but I just shut down our connection and threw myself over the side of the ship so that I could turn into an owl and fly for a bit. I heard feet scrambling to the rail and a raised voice calling something, a crew member pointing at me before I was too far gone to hear. Rather than flying off and leaving the ship, I flew circles around it, turning to thoughts and plans for crafting to dull the throbbing ache in my chest.

I would likely need to use a lot of mana to protect the hull. Unless I used the same kind of idea that Vilmas had used with the wall around Sunrise. If they had overlapping fields of protection, they could keep things from penetrating them. But to do that, the source of power would have to be insanely strong.

…or constantly present!

I could use the ocean to power it! The idea was kind of complicated, but I could do this. I fluttered to the rail and shifted, going into my inventory to see what sort of goodies I had available. I didn't want to place anything too shiny on the bottom of the ship to attract any sort of attention from below. But I did have chunks of iron. It would be stupid to use that since Maebe might be joining us soon, and I didn't want to bother the others, so I took dozens of copper coins and began to heat them before smoothing them into thick plates until I had more than twenty of them.

"Hubris."

I reached back into my inventory and found two quarter-sized sapphires, then added a set of copper grips to hold them in place, then engraved a small symbol into the copper side around it. With Hubris guiding me, we made it so that the two gems would use water to power nine of the other plates that held protective runes on them. Each one would strengthen the wood in a radius of up to ten feet around it. They would overlap slightly, but that was for the best. I reached out to her with my thoughts and plans so that I could get a little more guidance or permission.

And this only steals mana from the water of the ocean, and not the creatures? The Water Primordial asked me skeptically after I'd explained my musings.

"As far as I am aware of." I shrugged. "Any living thing within the ocean isn't water unless it's an elemental, so it'll be fine."

Very well, you have my permission to do this thing. Before her presence left me, and I could turn back to my work, her cool presence amplified in my mind, and I could see her standing on the deck. *You do me proud, droplet. Continue to grow and wash away your enemies.*

Her smiling figure faded, and I was alone with Hubris once more.

I sighed and got to work, placing the different copper placards into the wood of the ship.

That one goes on the other side of the ship, master. Hubris' correction startled me and I almost lost my grip on the wood.

"Thank you." I lifted it out and placed the right one in, and this side was completed. It was a quick matter to finish the other side, and once they were all in place, I moved to the final step—the power sources.

I do not need to be held for this portion, master. I will simply be near you. With the enchantments laid already, the power sources being placed will simply empower the other spells. It will take a small amount of time for them to become fully charged, but by tomorrow at dawn, they should be at full strength.

"Thank you, Hubris." I let the scepter go and held on to the rope I had tied around my waist. I leaned back like a scuba diver and turned in a single motion so that I could guide my descent. My head dunked into the water just below the waves, and I saw the spot that I had clawed a mark into.

With my breathing limited, I dug out the necessary spot around my marking and slid it into place. Casting Regrowth to grow the wood back around it until only the sapphire was visible to the water was where I stopped.

I could feel the pulse of the magic being taken from the water and used to power the others immediately. I grabbed the rope and switched to the other side after pulling myself up onto the deck.

After the job was done, I felt like I could finally rest, half the night having been eaten up already. Though it had been worth it with another level gained in enchanting, pumping me up to level 49 in the craft. But I wasn't ready to go back in and face Muu just yet.

I cast Shadow Speak, and Maebe formed of the shadows around us, the darkness of the sky doing her well.

"Hello, my love." I smiled at her, and she nodded her head. It was hard not being able to touch her. "How are you feeling? How long has it been?"

"Much improved." Her smile seemed tense, but she did sound less tired. "It has been another two weeks for me, but how go things in the mortal realm?"

"We found our ship to the Continent of Beasts and prepare the ship for a battle that Vrawn saw coming." Maebe stiffened up. "Something big is coming, and we aren't quite sure what it is."

"I see." She turned slightly to my left and frowned. "You seem different."

I nodded. "A lot has happened. We found the final elemental champion, and she's going with us to our destination. It's her homeland. We received our rewards, but the quest is still active. I think once you return and receive your reward, it'll be completely done. Speaking of, how is returning looking?"

"We found the spy, and are interrogating him as we speak." Her look of concern turned to one of malice. "He is surprisingly glib, but I have tasted the lies spewing from him and know that he should break soon. Once he does, I will require little time to return to you. How long has it been since last we spoke?"

"About a day?"

"Then, the dilation seems to be fluctuating, as it has been two weeks here." I frowned, and she seemed to pick up on my coming question. "I did not reach out due to how busy I have been. My mother sends her regards, and have you called to the other creature I mentioned?"

I frowned. "Other creature?"

Maebe sighed. "Yve. She expressed an interest in serving you, and I am inclined to send her to you, anyway."

"Oh! I remember her name now." I frowned deeper at Maebe. "Why?"

"We have uncovered a plot," Maebe began apprehensively but continued when I moved closer. "The Seelie have sent operatives into the Prime Realm to capture you to use as leverage. They know that if they do anything else, a war could break out and with how strong we are now, they will lose. But if they have you, they can use it against me."

"I'm in the middle of the ocean, dearest." I motioned to the water all around us. "They'll have a hard time getting to us out here."

"They are not above alliances, Zeke," she whispered pointedly.

My eyes narrowed at her. "You think they could be working with the Children of Brindolla?"

"Summon her to you, Zeke, right now. So that she can watch over all of you, my husband and precious friends." She looked behind her. "I must go, they believe he will be ready to speak again soon. I love you. And I long to see you once more."

"I love you too, be safe." She nodded, and the shadows dissipated where she was, leaving me with the night crew who moved on thinking I was probably crazy for speaking to myself.

I moved to a more secluded portion of the deck before closing my eyes and whispering, "Tan'rbleth."

"Finally!" The drain on my mana barely registered as a

crawling, creeping cold sensation reached out from behind me that made me shiver. I turned to find a tall, thin woman wearing a white dress that looked like spun moonlight standing there watching me with eyes so red they could have been blood, but they glowed on their own. I glanced about to see that no one had spotted us before turning back to her curious expression.

"Yve?" She nodded, her features a little less defined as she stepped closer to me, invading my personal space. "Little too close, don't you think?"

"You'll have to forgive me, it has been so long since I was near a king, and one so interesting as you." She smiled, all of her teeth looked sharpened and serrated. "Yes, I am Yve. I am to be your guard while you are here in the mortal realm. My darling younger brother speaks highly of you."

"Servant?" She nodded again and stepped back. "Do you take animal form as well?"

"I have many forms." Her mischievous grin was unnerving. "But like my brother, I prefer a feline form to that of most others. Would you prefer that?"

"I think so." I was still a little put off at how quickly she had come and with no real effort on my part. "Why are you so interested in me?"

She shook herself out, the short hair on top of her head growing longer. She then fell to her hands and feet in feline form. She stood nearly shoulder height on me and her canines were as long as daggers and just as sharp.

"I find you fascinating because you are mortal, and yet you command the respect of many." She plodded around me, her huge paws barely registering on the deck. "You have even ensnared the mind of my queen—the only Fae to ever earn my name. I knew if you were important to her, you might be worthy of my interest. So I told her to give you my name. Imagine my delight when you finally called."

"What are you?" I found myself reaching out to her, and she pressed her head against my palm. "You and your brother."

"We are the spirits of the Olde Fae, those who fought in the

war between the two courts more than a thousand years ago."
She purred against my hand, rubbing her teeth over the butt of
my hand just like a cat might. "I was among the first to die for
our cause, and so strong was my desire that I returned to the
realm in animal form. As each form grows, we consume and
grow stronger until we either regain our memories or the Wild
Hunt claims us."

"So, the members of the Wild Hunt aren't all demons?"

She shook her massive head.

"Once we reclaim our memories, we continue to serve
ourselves and whomever we choose to, because then we regain
our immortality."

"So, no one knew your true name before Maebe did?" I
found the story too enticing to give up asking questions, and she
seemed the talkative type.

"That is correct." Yve purred and lay down only to roll
lazily onto her back to show me her stomach. "I watched her
growing up from a babe, already hundreds of years old by this
time. I was there when she entered the dungeon for the first
time, and on the first floor of it, she wiped out all of the guards
that had been sent with her who intended to betray her. Their
blood turned the ice crimson and coaxed me out of hiding only
for her to trap me!"

"No way!" I whispered, and scratched her stomach as she
rumbled with laughter.

"I felt much the same." She batted at my hands playfully
and turned to her side. "She gave me the ultimatum, serve her,
and reveal my true name, or die."

"You had to have figured a way out of the trap, right?"

"I did not!" She assured me. "It was made entirely of
shadows and try as I might to batter them away, she kept me
there for more than a day and a half. Finally, I thought that
serving her would be more entertaining than stalking her. I have
been her faithful servant since."

"That's an amazing story." I sat back on my heels and
smiled. "She is pretty awesome."

"Indeed." Yve stood and shook herself out once more. "Come then, my King. It is time that you rested."

I raised an eyebrow at her. "You're here for all of a few minutes, and you're already bossing me around?"

Her face was suddenly very close to mine. "I have orders from my Queen to ensure that you are safe and taking care of yourself. It is time for all the good little kings and queens to be asleep."

I rolled my eyes and figured it would be better to do as suggested than fight her and ruin my work out here. I walked back to the cabin door, then paused to look out at the crew. They moved on and did as they were meant to, glancing at me and then away as if there was nothing out of the norm.

"They can't see you, can they?" I looked over at Yve, and she shook her head. "I see. Probably for the best."

I walked into the hall with her close behind and then into the room, only to find Muu waiting for me.

"Now listen here, you ignorant bitch." He rounded on me and stepped forward to get into my face.

Yve surged past me on my left and knocked him back into the wall, visible to my friend as she placed her paws on either side of his body against the wall.

"Yve." I sighed with a warning tone.

"I am intimately familiar with what each of your companions looks like, my King." Yve sounded cheerful as she spoke, still menacingly covering my friend's view of me.

"I take it this one is like Servant?" Muu droned, pressing a hand against her bulk and shoving lightly. She moved, but not by much.

"I am nothing like my darling little brother, morsel." Yve bared her teeth, then licked Muu on the face. "I am much more ancient and difficult to please. Do not approach my King so aggressively again."

"It's between him and me, so you can butt out." I snapped my fingers and flexed my will much like I would with the shadows around us.

She stiffened, backing away from Muu and sitting by my side, a contented expression on her face. "I do see why she likes you so."

I rolled my eyes and turned my gaze on Muu as he wiped his face and spat. "I think her tongue got in my mouth."

"I get it." He looked up at me in confusion. "I get why you think the way that you do. I don't agree in the slightest, but I get it. It sucks that I do, but if you're going to stay, then I have no choice but to support you. Because I can't have that bad blood on either of us."

He was quiet for a moment until I walked the distance and pulled him into a quick hug. We patted each other's backs, and he lay in his bed before I lifted myself into mine above his.

"Is she going to sit there and stare at us all night?" Muu's voice drifted up to me.

A purring chuckle filled the room as I closed my eyes, and Yve answered, "Why would I stare at you both all evening?"

"Oh, thank god." Muu sighed in relief, then yelled in surprise.

"I will only be watching *you*, morsel." Her laughter made me grin, and I drifted off to sleep.

CHAPTER FOURTEEN

The sun crept lazily through the hole in the cabin wall, brushing against my face. I woke up, blearily grateful for a peaceful night of sleep.

It stood to reason that the creature we had fought had sent us these dreams and likely needed to recover from hitting us all with a vision like that mid-combat. Not that I would be complaining honestly.

I cracked my back and rolled off the side of my cot and landed unceremoniously on top of Muu, who was trying to get out of bed himself.

"So full of grace, Majesty." Yve purred on in delight.

"You can take that shit for a walk." I snarled at her, feeling much less royal than I should have likely felt at that moment.

She simply purred some more and watched me untangle myself from my friend.

"Good morning to you too," Muu grumbled as he stretched and stood up. "Yohsuke came in about ten minutes ago, so I'll be taking the next 'shift' of watch. Really we'll be working on the ballista and glancing around. What about you?"

"I enchanted a good chunk of the ship after our spat last night." He rubbed his neck and I smacked his arm. "Don't worry—we're good. I just had to get it out of my system."

He nodded and we left it at that, he pointed to a plate left out for me and I gobbled down the biscuits and gravy with a side of delicious bacon.

"The creature who cooks for you smells... dead," Yve observed cautiously.

"Well, he's a vampire, so I would think so." She nodded sagely, watching me as I consumed my food, then I paused. "Do you need to eat?"

"I will hunt when I can." She arched her back languorously and yawned. "I do not need to eat often. Though if I stay on this plane too long, I will need to eat something large."

"Thank you for letting me know." I tossed her a piece of my bacon, and she sniffed at it curiously before picking it up delicately with her teeth.

The rumbling of her chest as she consumed the morsel seemed odd at first. "Swine?"

I nodded. "Bacon."

"I adore this *bacon,* your chef is quite talented." She padded closer to my plate and began to sniff at it. "What is the white blood on the plate?"

I laughed at her simplistic view. "It's called gravy. You can make it with a little bit of sausage in it to give it zest and consistency. Here."

I put some on my finger, and a rough, sandpaper-like tongue washed over it. "Mmm." I offered a piece of bacon with gravy on it, and Yve moaned low in her throat. "This is truly masterful cooking. Has my Queen eaten this?"

"It's been a while, but she likes Yohsuke's cooking."

"I must speak with him soon." She decided and padded over to the coffin on the ground. "You may slumber, for now, vampire, but I *will* learn your secrets."

I had to laugh at that, and she turned to pace toward me.

The remainder of my plate was hers which she delighted in, commenting on the light and flaky biscuits the gravy had been slathered over.

"What will you do today?" I asked her as she devoured her newly-given food.

She licked her cheek to get at a speck of gravy and eyed me. "I will search the ship for Seelie. And then I will protect you."

"Can you swim?" She nodded then turned back to her food. "Good. Then you and I will go into the water today."

She ignored me to finish the plate, then blinked at me sadly. "I have known many pleasures, King Zeke, but I would know the name of this one. Please?"

I snorted and rolled my eyes. "Biscuits and gravy with bacon."

She repeated the words with her eyes closed as if memorizing it. I shook my head and used shadows to clean the plate before leaving the room.

The sun reflected off the water, almost blindingly at first, but my eyes adjusted. I could see that Jaken, Bokaj, and Muu gathered around a spot on the foredeck and muttered over their blueprints with a thin man who had a belt of tools around his waist.

Best leave them be, for now. Vrawn and Odany trained with a small sword made of wood that had been stained dark.

Bea and Kayda watched next to Dusty, who seemed to be kicking up a pleasant breeze for the two of them.

Vrawn took the girl through several different motions with the sword, and Odany seemed to be having difficulty paying attention until Vrawn swept her leg out from beneath her, sending the poor girl sprawling.

"You are already strong, Odany." Vrawn sighed heavily as her student collected herself from the ground. "You must give that strength purpose."

"But I know I want to fight with two weapons!"

"You must first master one," Vrawn replied patiently. "I

want you to do twenty-five vertical slashes, just like I showed you. Bea will watch you and let me know if you slack off."

Bea plodded over to stand in front of Odany and hissed at her before barking at her to begin.

"Okay!" Odany shouted angrily and began to chop with her sword, her form leaving much to be desired.

Vrawn stepped closer to me and smiled softly. "She has potential, but it's not with any of the weapons I have. What will you be doing?"

"I'm going to be going into the water to acquire new aquatic forms." I grinned at her with a bravado I wasn't feeling, and she relaxed a little. "I won't be down there long, and then we can get some sparring in later, as well."

That was something she found exciting, her face lighting up a little before she turned back to correct the girl's form.

"Did I just hear you say you would be going into the ocean?" Captain Holly limped toward us with a bright smile, though she seemed worried.

"Yes, you did, Captain."

"Do be careful down there," she warned. "We're close to the lord's territory, and there are all sorts of nasty creatures out in those waves."

"I'll make sure to watch myself down there." I smiled at her, then waved to Vrawn and my babies as I sprinted over the side of the deck and jumped into the water below. I heard a second concussion near me and saw a long eel that winked at me.

I rolled my eyes and turned back toward our destination. I cast Water Lung on myself rather than taking fish form. I wanted to lure predators to me.

The shadow of the boat above me played tricks in the water around us, the motion making me think there was more to the area than there truly was. I couldn't focus like that, so I made my way further from the ship, finding a school of fish to follow.

Their yellow, black, and green scales seemed to blend into the ocean around them as they surged around me curiously. I cast Nature's Voice and noticed that there was no longer a timer to it.

Huh.

"Can you all help me find a predator?"

The fish seemed put out that I could speak to them at first, startled by the noise, but one of them answered, "Why would we do that? They eat us."

"Sorry, I'm a Druid, see?" I motioned to myself, and they didn't seem to care. Tough crowd. "I was hoping to find one or two to collect their forms."

"Try swimming deeper, to the east," another fish suggested as they swam forward to eye me carefully. I reached out and tapped it, scaring them all off, but acquiring the form.

I shifted, then swam with my new tiny body down into the darkness.

This is wrong! We shouldn't be swimming alone, where is the school?! I rolled my eyes and ignored the fish's instincts as I pressed on with Yve hot on my tail. Light was scarce here, but I could still see slightly thanks to the heightened aquatic vision. Any light was useful to a fish, and this was enough for me now, as well.

The ocean floor was still quite a ways off when the instincts suddenly quieted, like a sudden jolt of silence.

Something's out there. I growled and swam in a slow circle, then saw it, a set of eyes. Peering out of a cold darkness, a silvery glint to them as the creature moved forward. It looked like an eel, but it was some kind of water snake. It had to be with how it moved. I couldn't get a bead on the color or look of it as it stuck to the shadows.

I'd need to lure it out. Thinking on it, I swam downward again. Just toward the stalking serpent at an angle and waited.

A rush of primal fear seared through me as I twisted and shapeshifted just in time to catch the fangs that would have pierced my fish-like skull if I had hesitated a second longer, on my metal arm. The snake tried to recoil, but I shot my arm forward and called the shadows to my aid. They wrapped around the snake to hold it still while I looked it over.

Dark scales mottled green and black covered the thick hide with small dorsal fins on the sides and top of its back and then a small barb at the tail. It writhed and squirmed, but my control over my magic was flawless, and touching the cold scales allowed me to obtain the form I desired. Thinking on it, the thing could be useful, so I took my clawed hand and rammed it into the beast's throat. Blood as black as pitch poured into the water around us.

"You struck as ruthlessly as my Queen said you might." Yve watched from where she swam, her voice quivering for some reason.

I ignored her and watched the shadows around us, this couldn't be it, could it?

After waiting for a couple minutes, I sighed heavily and began to haul my prize toward the surface. The hide seemed like it would make decent armor, and I wanted to give Muu something to help level his crafting. I was a little way from the kill site when I caught a glimpse of motion off to my right.

"Are you a whale?" I asked rhetorically as the massive creature swam close to us, within about thirty feet. Its gigantic bulk displacing the water slightly before passing out of visible range. "That was beautiful. I wonder if this is what it feels like to whale watch?"

"Move!" Yve snarled as she slammed her eel body into my side to shove me out of the way as the same whale swam directly toward me and my prize. The wide mouth opened, the film it had there being cast aside from the lips to reveal rows of sharp teeth as long as my leg pointed my way.

Fuck me!

I shifted into my belgar form, the weight drawing me into the depths and out of the way of the carnivorous whale's trajectory. It nicked the serpent's corpse, the razor teeth shredding the tail a bit and taking some with it. I shifted and rushed back up in time to run my fingers across the creature's stomach, then used my shadows to collect my serpent corpse before legging it out of there.

The whale turned, and another one of the monstrous creatures soared from the depths toward us with a third coming.
Three of the bastards and their levels varied only by one.

Carnivorous Whale Level 63

Yve slithered through the water before me. "Get out of here,
I will distract them!"

"What if you fall?" I labored to get myself out of there, but
I worried about her.

"Then I fall for a worthy cause—*go!*" She turned and
barreled past me toward our pursuers with a battle cry that
made the hair on my neck stand.

Kayda! I shouted mentally as hard as I could after slamming
open our link. I could feel her surging toward where we moved,
but she wouldn't make it in time.

I pressed the serpent toward the surface once more and
turned around. "Move Yve!"

She turned and swam away, clearing my line of fire as
quickly as she could.

Pouring mana from the core of my being the same way I
had to enchant Arc Cutter, I called Hubris to me with a flex of
will and cast Lightning Storm through it. The power flexed,
and the spell doubled in size and intensity, the cylindrical
shape of it concentrating as soon as it left me into a slightly
smaller cone that slammed into the whale swimming straight
at us.

Dark whale flesh blackened immediately, and the creature
thrashed violently where it floated in the water, forward motion
suspended as it fought the pain. I had managed to hit it for a
quarter of its health in one blow, but the mana cost to alter the
spell and amplify it had been enormous. About triple the 250
MP cost, and some of it had escaped into the water around me,
making my fur stand on end.

The other whales were coming, so I grabbed Yve with some
more shadows, my mana reserves trickling slowly away. I
pressed us toward the open air in bursts and saw motion
above us.

The serpent broke the water first; Kayda grasping it precariously in her claws. *I have it!*

My shadows fled from the catch and used some of them to send slicing attacks at the closing whales. The attacks did minimal damage, a couple percent here and there, but they kept coming.

Once I broke the water, I threw Yve into the sky and shifted into my green dragon form. Using my powerful wings, I lifted myself into the air and gathered the location of the ship off in the distance by about a mile or so.

Water broke beneath me; one of the whales surged up, clearing the waves by almost twenty feet to try and take a chunk out of me. My wings worked to move me aside, and the creature fell back onto its friends.

We can lift that creature and take it to our lair. The dragon's instincts grumbled. *We would eat well, and it would give us strength.*

I raised a ridged eyebrow as I wondered. "Think we could lift it?"

Try.

Good enough for me, I grinned and muttered, "Pie" Before diving at the one still trying to get its bearings below me. The crashing weight of its friend had stunned it for a moment, the blackened flesh on the nose giving me a thrill, *that was the one we wanted!*

I raced around and swooped down, digging the claws of my feet and hands into the creature and heaving. It barely budged at first, but I worked my wings harder and harder until it lifted, and we moved forward.

You are weak for a dragon. The instincts spat.

I rolled my eyes and noticed that my load lightened slightly. I turned my head to find Yve carrying the tail as a giant eagle, her powerful wings flapping as much as mine were, while Kayda struggled with her cargo.

The whale struggled mightily, bucking one of my hands free, and almost making me drop it before the instinct in my head took the reins.

My head reared back as my chest filled with fresh, sea-salt filled air and exhumed a venomous gas straight into the blow-hole of the creature. It struggled more, but I watched in morbid delight as its health bar sank, a small skull popping into existence beneath it to show the poisoned status.

Our poison is potent, though the difference in your levels will only account for a small amount of damage from you.

"It takes mana to do that shit, though!" I had recovered a decent bit while flying, but that attack had eaten through 507 MP!

If you would prefer to drop it, then by all means. The dragon growled through my head. I rolled my eyes and continued on as my muscles strained.

Zeke, we think we can see you, what're you doing? Bokaj asked in alarm.

I told Bea to find him and tap his leg with her tail to get his attention.

You using her to talk? She nodded at him, and he continued. *Is that thing alive?*

She nodded her head once more and smacked her lips excitedly.

Why the hell are you bringing it here, then? Jaken howled through our earrings.

Bea growled and slashed with her clawed hands, and the others seemed to get it.

We'll be ready to light it up once you're in range. Be careful.

A crashing splash below us reached my ears, and Kayda's screeching anger spiked as a crash of lightning split the air beneath the whale and me. I could almost hear the angry calling of another one of the whales below us before a secondary splash sent a fount of water up toward me, splattering my wings.

It took all we had to get the whale over to the ship and close enough for my friends to do some damage. Hopefully.

The violent retort of a cannon preceded a force that nearly tore the whale from my grip. The damage amplified by the fact that it wasn't a cannonball that had hit, but a batch of thin balls that shattered against the hide and loosed shrapnel that seemed to burrow into the fat and bled the creature well.

I whipped my head back and let my chest expand before spewing more poison into the monstrous whale's blowhole and snarled as it expelled some of it back into the air.

"Hold your breath, Yve!" The Fae creature growled and must have consented to the order because I didn't hear any more coughing than that of the whale trying to clear its lungs.

Another volley of cannon fire came and rocked our prey from my grip, dropping it into the water. Arrows sprang from it, my friends joining the fray, with Vrawn leading the charge on the water with Arc Cutter at the ready. She slashed the creature on the way into the water, and when I was certain I wouldn't hit her, I dropped from the sky in a deep dive after it. With the water disturbed, I took no damage from the impact, shifted into my fox form, then into my own newly-gained whale form to lift it out of the water and into range.

It thrashed wildly and slapped me with a surprisingly sharp fin, slicing into the large fatty section of my forehead. I slammed into it as hard as I could to keep it from fleeing the area, and as far as I could tell, we had escaped the rest of the pod, as well. It was at less than half health when it began to wail and moan in a cadence that underwater made me feel as though I was going to get sick.

What the hell is that noise? Balmur cried. *It's driving the sailors mad. They're fighting each other!*

All of you get over here so I can cast Water Walk on you! Bokaj called to the others. After a few silent seconds, *Go! Kill the damned thing. I'll get these guys.*

I couldn't see much of what was happening, but the fight with the whale turned into a massive struggle. I bit at it, my vision slightly impaired as my eyes were on the sides of my head. I could sort of tell where it was just by the sheer mass of it, but it was going poorly.

Use your sense of smell, child. A gentle voice urged me through my mind. *Our sense of smell is sharpest.*

I took a deep inhalation of water, the salt burning slightly, and a sense of panic filled me. *Breath, there is a sac of fluid in the nostrils that filters the salt and hydrates our body. We do not actually breathe this way, so you will need to rise for air soon.*

I fought on and could tell that the creature was injured by the amount of blood scent in the water. I pressed it back up with my huge head and pushed out of the water and took a deep breath.

Bite it! The voice wailed, long and low, sudden motion on the left side of my head sending a rush of adrenaline through my veins.

I lunged forward and bit the fin before me, the sharp object bloodying my mouth a bit, taking 7% of my HP, the salt stinging mercilessly.

I could hear my friends fighting with it, their weapons and attacks striking it mercilessly. A burst of lightning struck it and me as well, sapping 15% more of my life away.

Luckily it did a lot more damage to the creature. Between all of us working on it, we managed to kill it before it killed anyone. I let go of the fin in my mouth and shifted into my normal form to wade out of the water onto the massive corpse.

Chests heaving, the others looked at me with Muu leading the charge. "The fuck did you bring that thing here for? Are you nuts?"

"We need the experience, and as far as I know of, this thing was twenty plus levels higher than us." I poked the hide. "Look at what we're capable of! We can do this."

"But did you have to put all of us at risk for it?" Jaken reprimanded me gently. His consternation was evident on his face, and I blushed a bit.

"I didn't know this thing was capable of that." I looked at the others as they stood and glowered at me. Everyone except for Vrawn. "What's on your mind?"

"I leveled up." She smiled at me and then the others. "Did you all not gain experience from this fight?"

They glanced at each other, frowning, Balmur nodding. "Well yeah, I got a little over five hundred experience from it. Think we share with the crew as well since they fired at it with the cannon?"

The others just shrugged and seemed to deflate a bit. "I get that my bringing it here was risky, but if we have to fight something big, we need to go into the fight stronger. The reason I grabbed that snake was more instinctive than anything, really, but I wanted to see if we could use anything from it. I'm not sure about this whale, though. Muu, is the hide salvageable?"

He set to work looking it over and began to cut into it with his blade, frowning as he separated the flesh from the muscle and fat below. "There's some kind of poison in here, I think. Everything is ruined."

I snarled at the dragon instincts mentally before ducking my head. "My bad, man. Sorry."

"I get it." He punched my shoulder lightly. "We can still look the serpent over. Let's go back to the ship."

I checked on Yve, who looked to be fine and took flight to get back to the ship before the others.

Spots of blood covered the deck here and there, some of the sailors coming to on their own where they lay in piles together with weapons drawn.

I cast Mass Regrowth on as many of them as I could and healed the others as well. Jaken and Bokaj had already started to heal them, their wounds swiftly knitting shut. I joined after that and aided where I could.

"I hope there was a decent reason for that episode of stupidity." Captain Holly crossed her arms over her chest as she regarded me coldly.

"Yes there was, Captain." I panicked inwardly and hoped she would believe me. "I brought it here to help us and your men prepare for what is to come. I know it wasn't much, but every little bit does help, and we want your people to survive this if they can. That means we need to prepare."

She eyed me steadily for a few heartbeats, limping toward me finally and leaning close to whisper, "You will do nothing of the sort again without prior authorization from me, am I clear?"

She leaned back, and I made to answer, but she hushed me with a finger to my lips. "Because if you do, I will throw all of you to the sea and be rid of this business. Money be damned. You may speak now."

I just nodded, keeping my nearly-mutinous mouth shut for once.

She left me to see to her men, and I breathed a little easier, turning my mind to my brothers. *You all okay?*

Other than smelling like sloppy tuna and gout-ridden slippers? Muu grumbled. *Fine. We're on our way back up to the ship. Vrawn too.*

Calm as hell, Vrawn clambered over the side of the deck with her chest heaving. Yeah. Perfect image of calm.

"That was fun," she panted with a slight grin gracing her features and a flush on her cheeks.

"I'm glad it was." I smiled back before surveying our surroundings some more. The sailors seemed to be coming back to their own again and their eyes fell on me. So I had a decision to make.

Whatever you have to do to keep us from getting shanked—do it. Bokaj snarled, his animosity surprising me.

"Agreed," Balmur's voice surprised me. "That was a little dumb of you, man."

Crestfallen, I stepped away from him and addressed the crew, "Ladies and Gentlemen of the Pussy Willow! I apologize for my actions, I merely wanted to ensure that we would be prepared for the fight to come."

Looks of disbelief and discontent colored the faces of the men and women watching.

"You the one what made the ship magic?" The older crew member Taejon wandered over to me. "Made that there sword that the young lady be usin'?"

"Yes sir." I frowned at him, but he nodded his head excitedly.

"You make my blade do magic, I'll call us even." He winked at me and handed me his saber. It was finely kept with a simple basket hilt to protect the user's hand from attack.

"How you magic it'll be up to you." He waved and turned to walk away, then stopped and turned to the others watching intently. "Y'all got somat better to do? He magicked the ship, he can magic our gear."

Oh, I'm gonna make sure his is great, I assured myself.

"Give me time, and I'll ensure that all of you have magical weapons." The crew clambered forward, but the captain surged forward and snatched me back.

"There will be no enchantments placed on your weapons all at once!" She bellowed, her own blade clearing her scabbard at her hip. "Joesa will call the roll, and you will come to have your desired *weapon* enchanted. One and that is it. If our friend here has more time, we will think on some more options, until then —get back to work you mangy curs!"

They all roared back at her, Taejon winking at me as he slid by.

"Is this an acceptable deal, master Zeke?" Captain Holly raised a well-manicured brow in my direction.

"We have an accord." I nodded to Taejon's weapon and then motioned to the cabin with it. "I'll be in my cabin. I trust that your first mate will be able to return the weapons I enchant?"

"He will manage." She smirked, and Joesa just rolled his eyes. "Can I entrust my weapons to you?"

"Of course." We walked to the cabin together, and she handed me her blade, of similar make to Taejon's as well as a small crossbow and a dagger. "Give me some time, and I'll have them out to you."

She smiled and turned to leave, but I stopped her. "Your leg."

"What about it?" She scowled at me, her eyes narrowing.

"Give me your leg." I motioned at it and made a grabbing motion. "I'm not the absolute best, but my friends and I can make you a better one if you'll let us."

"You may take a look at it tonight." She frowned thoughtfully. "I have need of it now. Go about your business, master Zeke."

She turned and stalked away from me, so I went into the cabin and set to work. Taejon's weapon I took my time with.

It wasn't nuanced, by any means, but his blade would be the sharpest weapon I could muster, and it used wind aspected mana, too. If he swung it fast enough, it had a chance of about 35% to form a wind blade that would slice a target up to thirty feet away, and that was only if he was actively trying to make it happen. Not the best, but it was all I could manage. Hell, I even used a small amount of diamond to increase the blade's sharpness and durability.

Overall? I was happy with it.

I considered being cheap with all of the other weapons, though, but Jaken would hear nothing of it.

Better to ply your craft here and now and grow from it so that we stand a chance rather than save some cash. We're liquid, man. Let's do it right. He paused, then asked, *You have enough mats to make it through? I know you can add components to things. You need anything?*

Yeah, any precious or semi-precious stones and metals you guys have would be greatly appreciated. It makes my life easier if I have more components.

A few minutes later, Jaken came to me with a collection of components from the others. Rubies, pearls, sapphires, emeralds, agate, obsidian, topaz, and other somewhat precious stones. Then he pulled out several small bars of metal. "These are test bars that I was using to check what kind of metals we find to them. Think of them like references. I don't need them anymore because any new metals I find I take to the dwarves. Like that hunk we found in the dungeon."

"Thanks, man, I really appreciate it." I frowned at all of it. It would last, I hoped. "I'll work on breaking them down as I go. I'm high enough level now that I'm almost to master. Hopefully, this does the trick."

"We can hope." Jaken grinned and stepped out of the room to give me space to work.

I turned my eyes on the captain's weapons and grinned. Time to play.

CHAPTER FIFTEEN

I wiped my brow, sweat building up in the fur there from the amount of time I'd spent hunched over the items brought to me. I felt like it had been days, the ache in my skull made my vision blur slightly, and I had to stop.

Everything I had touched, I'd infused with magic to the best of my ability.

Shadow Swallower's Saber

+14 light damage to attacks, sword beats back shadows and brightly illuminates the immediate vicinity around the wielder.

Darkest night meets the stars and fades from their mighty light.

Sword created by adept smith Deannie Busch and enchanted by adept enchanter Zekiel Erebos.

Heart Piercer

+15 to piercing damage, 10% chance to cause critical damage multiplier if target is shot in the chest.

Aim true, fighter, and there's a chance you might not have to fight too hard.

Weapon created by adept woodworker Brolm

Brighthelm, and enchanted by adept enchanter Zekiel Erebos.

That's enough of that. The rest of the people who made these weapons are hardly of note, and you guys really just want to hear what they do, right?

I thought so too.

Fae Step Stabber

+13 damage, +15 damage to non-Fae creatures

Once daily, this dagger will allow the wielder to step into a place they can see within 30 feet.

That last one I was proud of. When the captain had claimed them, her grin let me know that I was almost forgiven. The rest of the crew got weapons befitting their service. I tried to keep things tied to requests and elements that *wouldn't* catch the ship on fire. Of course, that greatly upset the kid who wanted a sword made of only flames, but he got over it when I handed him a hammer that would freeze enemies if hit enough.

Exhausted and overtaxed, I checked the notifications I had.

CONGRATULATIONS!

You have ascended to the rank of Master enchanter!

Cost of components used will be halved.

Damage outputs for weapons increased!

Spell types increased!

Be warned: in order to use the items you make to full advantage, the wielder may need to meet certain criteria, or the weapon effects will be diluted to match their level. This can be negated only in certain circumstances!

Good luck creating out there!

I grinned, that must be why when a grandmaster gave us gear, it always seemed like their work was improving. Realistically, we were, and we could finally see a little more of a weapon's true capabilities.

Interesting, I thought to myself. I tapped my cheek in contemplation with a frown. I pulled out Storm Caller, and the stats were the same. Well, there was that gone. Must have been because the second I touched it, the stats solidified. Was it a way to ensure that enchanters and smiths had a way to continually make money as someone improved? They would have to come back for better gear as they grew.

I made it to master enchanter, I advised the others.

That's great! Muu's whooping from outside made me grin, and I heard the door open.

A gigantic wood splintering crack echoed through the air, shaking the boat. I was on my feet and heading toward the exit when Balmur piled into the room with Bokaj hot on his heels, both of them a little more grim than usual.

"What's wrong?" I asked knowingly. "You guys, okay? The ship, okay? What happened?"

"The fucking limbs for the ballista snapped, and took part of the rail with it," Balmur snapped, rubbing his temples in irritation. "We used the metal and wood that we had, even some of the wood that the wainwright had on hand to make it, and it *fucking snapped!*"

"I told you there was a chance it might happen!" Bokaj growled back.

"So we're fucked on that front." I sighed and sat back on the bottom cot. I looked at the two of them, fuming and being goofy. "The hell is going on with you both?"

They looked at each other, Bokaj looking askance of his friend before the other man nodded, and he could answer, "We're scared."

I stayed silent, watching them until Balmur decided to speak up, "It's the level of the fight. We can walk on water, breath it, fighting on it and in it—but we can't know what the hell is coming. And that's getting to us."

"I can respect that." I dragged my nails through the fur on my head. "I'm worried about not having Maebe here. But if anyone should be safe, it should be her. Would that I could make it so Vrawn weren't here for this, too."

"You and your ladies." Balmur snorted, a wry grin gracing his face. "You'd keep them safe before you would us."

"I'd keep them safe because I trust both of you to fight with me," I corrected him. "We walked through the Hells and back for you. And I know you would've done the same."

"Yup." Bokaj slapped his back, joining me on the cot. "We'll get through this. It's just going to be a lot harder without our weapons."

"Ship on the horizon!" A dull voice bellowed from above us.

We glanced at each other, then scrambled to the door and outside.

I looked to where the others all gazed and saw what they saw. True enough, a ship was there. But I couldn't quite make out what kind of ship it was.

Joesa swore. "What's a damnable naval vessel doing this far out?"

The three of us perked up. *Navy ship? Think it could be the one that our tormentor could be on with her demon caretaker?*

I glanced at Balmur after his question and shrugged. *It's possible.*

"We need supplies, if we can raid theirs and check them out to see if they're on board, we might stand a chance in this fight." Bokaj frowned, he tapped Joesa on the shoulder. "Think we can catch them?"

He turned and regarded us coldly. "You want us to close with a naval vessel, potentially accost them and steal from them?"

"You guys don't have to do anything if you don't want to," Bokaj reasoned. "Our thoughts are on our combined survival."

The first mate snorted and turned on his heel, walking away without another word.

Think the captain is going to try and kick us off the ship? I rolled my eyes, trying to envision her reaction to all of this.

Everyone, be on the lookout for the captain, Balmur called to all of us. *We just suggested piracy.*

Booty? Muu perked up immediately. *Swashbuckling and buccaneering?! Can we? Can we please? I'll eat all my veggies!*

Shut up! James snapped, his voice making all of us flinch. *She's come out of her quarters.*

"Did mine ears deceive me?" Captain Holly shouted as she moved through the crew with a serious glare on her face. "Did I, Captain Holly Jennisovna, hear that *piracy* has been uttered aboard my Pussy Willow?"

"We merely meant that we think that vessel might harbor a threat to the continent, a demon, and possibly more." Bokaj spread his arms and tried to make himself seem more suggestive. "Not to mention, more supplies for the ship and ballista. It could be beneficial."

"The benefits of *piracy* are death!" She howled, her hand falling to the saber I had enchanted for her. "They hang pirates from the gallows. My brothers dangled in the wind for just serving aboard a vessel accused of the act!"

"Okay, we won't raid them." I stepped forward.

She turned to me, her eyebrow raised. "Who said that?"

A slow grin spread across her face, whiskers flicking back and teeth glinting in the mid-morning light.

Joesa stepped out from behind the captain with a tricorn hat that he passed to her and raised his voice, "Mister Taejon! Hoist the colors!"

The crew roared and set to motion as the eldest crew member pulled the rope with a red flag on it. As the wind caught the flag and pressed it forward, dual sabers crossed beneath a snarling cat's visage.

"Let the sea have what she desires!" The captain bellowed loudly.

"And we keep what we can carry!" The crew returned even louder as they spun around and went back to their stations.

Are we seriously on a pirate ship? Jaken groaned, looking thoroughly defeated.

Would you expect anything less? Balmur chuckled. *We need to catch them sooner rather than later. Zeke, think you and Odany can get the wind on our side?*

I nodded and spoke aloud, "I'll reinforce the sails to keep

them from splitting from the pressure." Balmur nodded and made to leave, but I grabbed his shoulder. "I'll need your assistance for a moment. Let's do what we can and then get started."

Balmur and I climbed toward the sails, and I summoned Hubris. He narrowed his eyes at it, but I calmed him with a look. "I'm strong, but even I run out of mana. I need you to bolster my strength."

The child, bring her and have her assist as well.

I frowned. "And Odany, I guess."

Balmur melted into my shadow, a cool chill running down my spine that made me shiver. He returned a second later. "She's coming."

The ropes shifted beneath me and I saw her climbing with a huge grin firmly in place. "You needed my help, too?"

"Yup!" She smiled harder, and it was too hard not to grin back. "You two are going to help me enchant the mast and cross beams to strengthen them, then we will enchant the sails."

I instructed Balmur and Odany both to touch Hubris and focus on feeding it mana. It was a little more natural for Balmur, but Odany struggled with it.

"Think of the mana in the core of your being like a lake, and as you reach for it and pull it out of you, you're just digging little rivers through your arms and fingers to the outside." She glowered at me. "I'm serious, it's how I do it."

"Is it like playing in the mud?" I raised an eyebrow at her, and she barreled on ahead. "You wanna draw a pretty picture, and you gotta use all the wet to draw the lines, so when it dries, it looks pretty?"

Between you and me? She had me stumped.

"Sure.," She grinned and closed her eyes, focusing on what she was doing after I answered her. "I want you guys to think really hard about giving me your mana for now, okay? Let's hop to it."

I closed my eyes and wove the engraving I would use to carve into the wood before us. Funneling the mana from the two of them through Hubris and shaping it with my will was different and much more difficult. Still, the gift I'd earned from Fainne, god of the dwarves, held out. A swirling, looping pattern formed over the mast and the other portions of the wood, all of them wisping toward the sails and their respective goals.

We bottomed out our combined mana after a moment, the desired engraving having just been placed.

The edges farthest from us may need to be deepened slightly to be safe.

"Thank you, Hubris," I muttered and glanced at my two helpers. Odany seemed heavy-lidded in the eyes, and Balmur was rubbing his temples. "You two rest and recover, I'll be back and we can begin enchanting."

"That wasn't enchanting it?" Poor Odany almost sobbed. Balmur took pity on her and patted her hand, speaking to her softly as I escaped to check my work.

Sure enough, some of the engraving needed to be deepened. I used my claws with Hubris to guide me and made short work of the job on the right side of the ship. That took about ten minutes. The left side was a little worse, so I took twenty for that side, but otherwise, it was fine.

I joined Balmur and Odany back in the center mast's rigging, where they waited.

"You both ready?" My question sparked a hint of ire on Odany's face, her scowl joined by her crossed arms let me know just what she thought of my asking her help. "What's the issue, kid?"

She lifted her chin slightly. "You were supposed to be teaching me. And that was just you using me, like the people who brought me from my home had planned to have happen."

"Use you?" I tested the waters skeptically. She seemed justified by my reaction to the word, her arms crossed tighter. "Listen, Odany, my leaving you in Vrawn's care is so that *you* will survive the coming fight. Us enchanting this ship is so that we *all* can survive this trip so that *you* can get home. If you want to survive with us and live to learn how to use your magic, there needs to be a willingness to accept a give and take. I need you to give me your strength and mana so that I can give you a chance to survive. Do you understand?"

She thought on it for a moment before she nodded once and pressed her hand over to rest on Hubris, "Fine. I'll help you to help myself. But our training needs to happen."

"It will happen, Odany," I assured her. "We all want you to survive. You deserve a chance. We're giving you the chance to fight for your future. You have to help us with that. And I will definitely be helping you train your magic soon. Besides, hasn't Dusty been helping you?"

She frowned and waved a hand down at the elemental who floated ten feet below us. "She tries, but she's hard to understand sometimes."

Balmur rested his hand on Hubris silently and waited for my instructions.

"I want you both to think about making the wood stronger and more resistant to the wind. Okay? *Just* the wood." They nodded and screwed up their faces with concentration. I did the same, and the enchanting began. Halfway through, I used a full amount of agate to keep things solid, and the total cost put us over 2,000 MP. It wiped me out completely, my ring, and drained Balmur and Odany both a little more.

The agate and mana mixed, glowing a slightly seafoam color before settling and flashing once.

I saw no enchantment notification, but I *knew* that it held.

"Good work, next, we enchant the sail." Odany looked mutinous, but she calmed down when Balmur held up a hand to get my attention. "Yes?"

"While we wait on our mana to recover." He motioned to Odany. "Why don't you explain the process of enchanting to us and allow Odany a chance to learn her magic?"

The little girl perked up, and I chuckled. "Sure. Which would you like to learn more of, right now?"

"My magic!" She howled and almost fell out of the netting below her.

I snorted, and Balmur clapped his hands delightedly.

"Then let's start with the basics while we wait." I clapped my own hands and waved to the air around us. "With many forms of magic, you can attune yourself to them. Balmur and I can send our thoughts into shadow. What I want you to do is attempt to focus on sending your consciousness *into* the air and wind around you. It's a little hard at first, but you can do it. You seem to have a natural gift for magic."

"I do?" She seemed pleased as punch to be complimented like that.

"Sure do. The wind primordial himself seemed to think very highly of you." She giggled and clamped her eyes shut.

"What do I do now?"

"I want you to focus on your element around you." She focused a little more, her eyebrows knitting together in concentration. "Use all your senses except sight to take it all in. Taste the air as you breathe it in. What scents do you smell? What do you hear? Feel it moving across your skin and in your hair. With each interaction between the wind and you, let it take you further from yourself."

She took in deep drafts of air through her nose. "I smell the salt of the waves, and taste the sweat and toil around me. I feel... warm. I can feel the albatross on my shoulders and hear her breathing."

The wind around me shifted slightly, filling the sails to my right.

"I feel the waves lapping at my feet, the sprites playing in my hair." I frowned at her, her hair transforming as we watched from black to gray and lifted strand by strand into the air around her head.

Panic took hold of my chest, icy fear gripping my ribs as I watched the gray at the top of her head beginning to lighten and turn white.

"Stop!" She didn't seem to react to the sound of my command, so I reached out, grasped her shoulder, and shook her. Still no response.

"WIND!" I howled into the air, feeling my connection to the element with my mind. I blinked, and I stood in an airy palace of clouds solid enough to move about on.

You have a lot of nerve howling at me, dog. A voice filled to the brim with cold hatred berated my back.

I turned to see the maelstrom given life, a large elemental at least fifteen feet tall towered over me with an opening twice as tall behind him.

"I'm 'howling' at you because your champion is connecting to your magic and it is *changing* her!" I couldn't lose the fear in my voice, no matter how hard I tried. "For all I know, it could be killing her."

My magic will not kill her, mortal. The Wind Primordial snickered, the gust buffering my clothes and fur angrily. *Come.*

The sweeping funnel of an arm motioned me closer, and the buffeting aura died down a little.

I stepped closer and looked out of the large opening into the vast reaches of my host's domain. Sprites and ariads, wind dryads—strange creatures that looked like clouds given human form—floating and flitting about on the breezes and gusts. There, floating in the center of it all, Odany bobbed up and down with her eyes open.

She smiled and whispered to herself.

Her connection to my realm is uncanny, her ability to adapt to my power is almost worrisome, and the best part is? The creature paused for what seemed like forever, giving me time to truly take in what I was seeing. All of the creatures playing around the little girl and her just taking it all in delightedly.

"Your people love her."

My people adore *her, mortal.* He corrected slightly less angrily. *If I were not smarter than that, I would swear she was one of us.*

"Is it possible?" I raised an eyebrow at him, and he turned to regard me.

It is not possible, the lines to the Eriments dried up long, long ago.

I blinked. "The what?"

The Eriments, a people whose bloodlines mixed with our own. The swirling hand of the prime lifted up to his chest and stayed there. *Theirs was an ancient race we loved, and their passing was... difficult.*

"What happened?"

Human mages, mortals whose hubris couldn't be contained, hunted them to extinction to study them. Enslaving our beloved children and grandchildren to have them perform tricks and minor magics so that they could perfect their own. Using their blood to experiment for their own... sick fantasies. His voice took on a howling hiss as he spoke through my mind. The breeze that had wafted around him flickered into a turbulent whirlwind that slashed at my flesh painfully. *When the last of them fell, my brothers and sisters wailed for months without end. The pain we felt severed our ties to the prime realm shortly before the high elves struck them down.*

"Sounds like you hate mortals still for what those ancient assholes did." The wind turned and glared down at me with the small holes in his face that had to be the place it saw from. "Hey, there are a lot of people out there with hate in their hearts over things that ancestors did. I can't say that they're all wrong. Seems a common thing. Human, elf, Fae, and now elemental? I can't say that I would put it past anyone."

Do not compare me to those mortals when my pain is immortal. I will live until the universe fades and know the pain of our loss until my last breath.

"But did you really *feel* that loss?" I asked quietly.

A painful slap into my chest flung me up against the cloud wall behind me. The raging winds slapped against me, my health beginning to fall slowly, small slices developing all over my body.

I mourn still to this day, druid! His fury beat along my body.

"I'm just saying that maybe all of *your* children may not have been taken!" I roared over the gusting noise. "What if your lineage was smart enough to hide? What if they left the continent to get away from all of that?"

The wind died down immediately. I floated gently to the

ground and watched as the elemental equivalent to a god turned its gaze toward the little girl playing in his domain.

... I do not know, druid. His bluster seemed to leave him. *Do I dare hold out hope? Do I want for them to live as I did in the past, knowing that they may be sought out once more for something perverse and terrible?*

"I wouldn't claim to know." He was a dick. A big one, and helping him wasn't something I wanted to readily offer—but I did owe his champion my aid. That helped bridge the gap that his dickishness and my anger had created. "But what I do know is that little girl needs my help to harness your power. If she's one of your people, then I need you to let me know what to expect."

You can expect that she will continue to progress more swiftly than she has on an instinctive level, he went contemplative for a moment. *I will need to think on things, but for now, she will need one of my smarter children to guide her. Unfortunately, Dusty cannot teach her and guide her the same as my eldest child can. She has a name already, and you will help her to summon her. Her name is Sylphy. You may go.*

His dismissal slammed me metaphysically back into my body, and my eyes opened even as I jumped and fell backward. Time slowed immensely, and I forgot everything I knew for a moment and forgot how to shift forms. Luckily, my foot caught in one of the openings in the netting and stopped me, albeit painfully as my hip was displaced violently from the drop.

I shifted into my owl form and fluttered back to the mast and hobbled closer to Odany before shifting back. She was still stuck in his realm, so I smacked her shoulder, and she popped out of it with a look of betrayal.

"Ouch!" She huffed petulantly. "I was doin' what you asked, mister Zeke."

"Yeah, yeah." I growled over my aching limb. "Listen, I need you to dismiss Dusty and call Sylphy to us from the wind realm. Okay?"

"No." She refused stubbornly, her arms crossing automatically.

"Then, I'm not teaching you any magic." I began to limp

my way down the ropes even though I could have... you know what? Yeah. I'd do it big.

I cast Teleport and landed jarringly on the deck of the ship next to a crew member carrying a length of rope. The man cried out, and dropped the rope onto the deck as I hobbled down the wooden planks of the ship.

A swift wind halted me, and Odany landed in front of me. *Fuck, she's learning faster than I thought she would. This is bad.* I growled.

"Why won't you teach me?" She huffed, her hands out to her side.

"Because you refuse to do as I instruct." I shrugged and went to walk around her but a wall of wind erupted in front of me. "You better knock off this childish tantrum, kid."

"I have a name!" She roared, her eyes flashing turquoise just before the wind whipped even more into a frenzy.

"Yeah." I rolled my eyes, stopping to look at her. "And a temper too. If you can't rein yourself in, you can't learn magic."

"But I'm better at it than *you!*" She shouted, a look of... was that competitive nature on her face?

I took a calming breath and reached out to the shadows around me, pulling them to me as effortlessly as she had the wind and gathered them in an orb the size of a basketball in my right hand. In my left, a blazing fire roared to life, and I twisted it until it also floated in an orb over my hand.

I solidified my grasp over it, then lifted them into the air over my head. I pulled the stone from the dirt on the deck, lifting it into an orb the same way I had shadow, and did the same with water. Light filtered into my hands, and then wind came to my will. My mind ached at holding all of them in tight, precise balls over my head, spinning each of the six orbs like I was a planet and them, my moons.

"You got raw power, kid," I spoke gently to her, almost a whisper over the wind she controlled. "And that can be a heady thing. But I have you beaten in control and experience. My control and expertise can be yours someday if you work *really* hard. But it can be yours sooner if you listen to me. And you don't seem to want that."

I relinquished my control over the elements floating over my head, their return to the various places they belonged as spectacular as one might think, and the sailors around us clapped vigorously at the show. I kept my eyes on the kid, though. Her scowl had only deepened.

Finally, her walls of wind dropped, and she looked up at me. "Dusty, go home. Sylphy, come to me."

I felt a slight pop as the large elemental dissipated from this realm, and a smaller one formed to Odany's right side. It was basically a smaller version of the same elemental, but this one had wider eye holes and a mouth.

"Thank you for summoning me." The smart little voice echoed almost hollowly from the being. "It took some time longer than had been expected."

It looked at me. "Did you have trouble teaching her my name, idiot druid?"

You have got to be shitting me, I snarled.

CHAPTER SIXTEEN

I huffed once as we finished the sails. Weaving my mana through them had been difficult, so we only went one at a time. We strengthened them, and then when we finished that, it was time to teach Odany how to use her magic.

And put her little smart-ass self and her little smart-ass elemental to work.

Look, I'm all for spunk and originality in people. People are as different to me as the voices in my head are—belay that. She's allowed to be herself, is what I mean to say. But herself has just *so much attitude.*

And it's just so unconstrained by manner or fear, that she just has it all over. She'd been such a happy child until she realized she had power. What was that saying? Absolute power corrupts absolutely? Well, there should be one about little girls and being able to try and cut a grown man in half with wind when she doesn't want to work on her magic.

"Why do I have to make the air go into the sail again?" Odany whined for the tenth time in almost as many minutes.

"I told you six times ago—to learn to control your mana

usage." I rolled my eyes as I was doing the *exact* same thing as she was.

"But we know I can control it!" She pouted with her lower lip quivering intensely, I snorted and laughed. "What's so funny?!"

"You, thinking the lip quiver will work." She growled, and I snapped my fingers loudly to get her attention. "You do well on this for another twenty minutes or so and maybe—*maybe*—I'll teach you how to make a spell. But you have to try, and you have to pay attention. Deal?"

She nodded, and I knew that she would try because learning spells was all she wanted to do. Honestly, she could probably make them herself, and she likely would, but it would be a while before she did it well enough to be trusted to do it without guidance either from Sylphy or me.

Who, by the way, was nearly as mutinous and dastardly as her summoner. The little wind elemental chided and rebuked me any chance she got and doubted my training *loudly* to boot.

"Really?" The echo came, and I shuddered, the near-murderous desire almost winning out, from my left side. "This is purely labor that will make the ship travel faster. How does that help her?"

"By putting her to work on a ship she damned well could have been thrown off of?" I sarcastically shot back. "Not to mention, she's learning constant control and what it feels like to focus on a task with her magic. Why do I have to defend myself to you?"

"Because, idiot druid, it is my duty to oversee Odany and to see that her strength grows, and not to see it wasted as it is now." The little wind elemental crossed her arms before her.

"Getting really fucking tired of you dickhead wind elementals," I muttered to myself and focused as I silently summoned Yve to my side. I'd called her back shortly before enchanting to be sure I didn't end up killed by the surly little child or her elemental pal.

The large Fae strode forward in her saber tooth form and

loomed over the elemental. "I've never devoured one of these before, my King. May I?"

"No, but you can bat her around if she keeps trying to distract Odany." Suddenly, I knew that the Fae had made herself visible to Sylphy thanks to the audible gasp from her. "Yup. You come to Odany, and I got someone who comes to me. You keep talking shit and we play harder than we are now. I don't care who you belong to, you and the kid are my responsibility now. Hear me?"

The elemental went to move away, and Yve sprang over her head, leaning forward into a low crouch. "My king spoke to you, little wind thing. I would *suggest* you answer him."

An echoey reply of "Fine" reached my ears and she went to her master's side.

Sometimes it's good to be the king.

True to her word, Odany did put forth an effort to use her magic well and focus it as she was told to. Finding the appropriate carrot for the student, and the right stick for her servant was great. I could work like this. But I'd need more eyes.

"Yve, you sure it's okay to summon Servant?" I glanced at the Fae, and she nodded visibly as she watched the little elemental hungrily. I covered my head in shadows the same way Maebe had before when I first summoned him and muttered, "Milnolian."

The shadows at my feet deepened perceptibly, and he stepped from them with hardly any draw on my mana. "My King."

"Hello." I found myself almost reaching out to him like he was a dog and stopped myself. "Ah, sorry. How fare things in the Fae realm?"

"Well, my Queen's interrogation techniques seem to have improved in her time here among the mortals." He sounded overjoyed at that, and I wondered what kind of interrogation moves she had learned here. That sent a chill up my spine for no good reason.

"Do you think she will join us soon?" I wondered a little more hopefully than I maybe should have.

"As soon as she can, my King," he answered politely before scenting the air. "Sister."

"Hello, little brother," Yve purred from her spot on the deck. "Good to see you again."

"You tried to eat me the last time I saw you." Servant eyed her mistrustfully. "Why are you here?"

"I chose to divulge my name to our King," she answered simply. Her feline smile not threatening in the slightest, the Cheshire like lilt to it making me freeze. "I find him interesting, as I am certain you do."

"I find him trustworthy," Servant replied, though he made no move to say anything else.

"You two going to behave yourselves here?" I asked warily, with the two of them staring each other down.

"Yes." Yve relented after staring at her brother a moment longer.

"I will." Servant answered, and I knew they would. Their word had given me notifications. Good. "What would you have of me? Queen Maebe told me some of what she suspects, but nothing has changed, has it?"

"The kid is my charge now." I pointed to Odany as she played with Sylphy while waiting on me. "You're going to watch my back at all times while Yve watches her."

"Four thousand years old, and I'm relegated to nursemaid." Yve flopped onto her side and lifted her legs into the air. "However will I live down this shame?"

A barking laughter came from Servant that made me pause, he gathered himself and coughed once into his paw before looking up at me. "She can be entertaining at times."

I grinned at him and shook my head. Time to teach the kid.

"I want you to close your eyes and focus on what you were just doing, and I want you to pour your intent into it." Odany frowned at me when I gave the order. "Yes, I want you to make a utility spell. This is going to help us travel faster. And since we will be traveling a little more quickly, we can make sure we get you home *faster.*"

"And you'll still teach me how to defend myself?" She narrowed her eyes at me, distrustfully.

"I will." She received a notification of my oath and nodded.

"And all I have to do is focus on making the spell?" I nodded at her, and she closed her eyes, her hair lifting from the sides of her face as she concentrated. She opened her eyes, then cast her spell.

"Continuous Gust," she shouted and made a small symbol with her hand and blew through it softly. The soft hush of air became a mighty gust filling the sails nearly to bursting and pressing the vessel forward hastily.

"Great work!" I hooted and hopped up and down. "Now, we can catch that ship in no time!"

"Why are you after that ship?" The echoed voice of Sylphy whipped up behind us.

"Because we have reason to believe that ship might belong to an enemy of the realm, one who we seek to bring peace to this land." I glanced down at her pointedly, then back at the ship in the distance. "I'm sure your father told you about my group's mission here in your world and why it's important that we destroy these enemies to the realm?"

She was still, silently listening to something but then turned back and stated, "That checks out."

"Glad to know I have your approval." I rolled my eyes and faced forward with my shoulders squared. "Part of what is to come will be combat. You seem comfortable making barriers of your own. Let's see if you can do it with any kind of strength."

"You said you would teach me how to def... oh." She seemed to deflate slightly.

I turned my steady, mirthful gaze down at her. "You're starting to catch on, Odany. There's hope for you yet."

She scrunched her nose in distaste, and I snorted at her. "Make a barrier."

She motioned before her and brought wind into a small

whirlwind in front of her, the clothes around her frame billowing.

"Strengthen it," I ordered softly. She scowled and compressed the winds until they swirled thinly, but they were compacted and seemed dense as I smacked them with my fist.

"How?" She grunted both hands pressed forward to try and add more to it.

"Imagine it denser, like a maelstrom, or storm contained in a small jar." I condensed a bit of shadow in my palm and made it grow smaller, like a smith folding iron until it was small but hard. I cast Void Shield in front of her and knocked on it. A *thunking* sound rang out. "Like so."

She focused on the construction of my spell, touching it and prodding it. She held her hands together in front of her, palm to palm, and slowly spread them before shoving them in front of her body.

A shimmering wall of solidified wind popped into existence, and sweat beaded from her forehead with the exertion of it.

"How's your mana bar?" She looked at me weirdly. "If you look in the corner of your vision, just under your health bar, you'll see a blue bar that shows how much mana you have."

She frowned at me and opened her status screen, she fiddled with some things on her own, and I had to fight the urge to just have her show it to me.

"It's almost empty." She frowned again. "But it seems to be going back up a little. Is that normal?"

"Yes." I nodded at her, and she smiled as if relieved. "Your intelligence dictates how much mana you have, and your wisdom decides how fast your mana regenerates. If you touch the names of the stats, you can actually see what they do."

She did so, and her small smile brightened.

"That's weird then." She grinned at me. "Because you're wrong."

I blinked at her, confused, and a little irritated. "Well then, your magic may be faith-based so it could be that your wisdom needs to be higher, so it dictates how much mana you have. That's how it is for Jaken."

"Nope!" She giggled and planted her ass on the ground with her arms and legs crossed.

"What the hell are you talking about, Odany?"

"I get mana from intelligence *and* wisdom!" She giggled. She touched something, and then a small filtered screen popped into my vision that looked like it had been redacted with question marks.

Name: Odany
Race: ???? (?????)
Level: ??
Strength: ???
Dexterity: ???
Constitution: ???
Intelligence: 27*
Wisdom: 13*
Charisma: ???
Unspent Attribute Points: 10

"What in the actual fuck?" I tapped on the asterisks and found out that her mana was indeed affected by both, equally. But her mana regeneration was still only affected by wisdom. So the little shit had 400 MP already.

"That's a bad word," she tutted at me with a stern look. "Vrawn said so."

"Yeah, yeah." I groaned. "What level are you, Odany?"

"Dusty and Sylphy said not to tell you." She closed her eyes and turned her head as she crossed her arms mulishly. "Because it's dangerous."

"Look, I get that, but I'm here to *help* you, not harm you," I insisted, which seemed to only make her buckle down harder. "Okay, you don't want to tell me? Fine. But you have ten points to spend and if you're going to spend them anywhere, I would suggest constitution and wisdom."

"Why?" She quirked her head at me, inquisitively.

"Because your constitution will make your health go up and raise your endurance a little as well." I rubbed my stomach as if it would show her what I meant. "And your wisdom will make your mana higher and recover faster."

"Is yours high?"

"Yes, it is." I smiled at her, and she looked ready to pop until I sweetly explained, "But I can't tell you how high because it could be dangerous."

Her harrumph made me think of an old-timer, and I actually laughed for a minute, almost pitying her, but I sighed and patted her shoulder. "Spend your points how you feel is best. My friends and I will try to help you, but unless you've got a lot of health, to begin with, you're in danger every time you get into a fight. Okay?"

Her brow furrowed again, and she tinkered around with it. "Seven in wisdom and the rest in constitution."

I held out my fist and winked at her. "Good job."

She tapped my fist with her own and giggled. We rested for a short time longer so that her mana could recover, and then we went right back into practical applications of her shield spell.

She was so adept at it by the time we finished a couple hours later, that she could mold the winds to suit her needs and almost effortlessly as I flung spells at her from all directions. We also kept her Continuous Gust spell up, too. She was tired after, but beamed with pride as she strutted through the crew to the cabin to wait with Muu.

He was going to protect her since Vrawn refused to let the rest of us board the naval vessel without her.

"Maebe would destroy me if I were to allow that." She was right, of course, but the stubborn set of her jaw stated she would be joining us one way or another no matter what. "Leaving you alone again to potentially fight a demon? And a general? I will not fail in my duty to her, or you."

"I appreciate your strength of will." I bowed my head to

her, a wry grin stretching across her face. "Captain, how would you like to do this?"

Captain Holly eyed the ship as we closed on it, only a mile or so away by now, and grunted. "We follow the accords."

She turned and clapped the eyeglass closed, eyeing us. "The accords are law to the pirates of the oceans, and without them, the already chaotic and merciless waters would be even worse. We will announce ourselves and allow them a chance to surrender after we board. Should they wish to fight, they will be dispatched with minimal casualties if possible."

"And if it's not possible?" James asked quietly from behind me, making me turn and stare at him for a moment.

"Then, all but those who surrender die." She sighed as if having to relive seeing something similar before. "We can take on extra hands if needed, accommodating them and their lives until we make land. At which time they can choose to stay aboard, or leave the seas forever. That is our way."

She snapped her fingers, and her crew moved by us with practiced ease, weapons prepared, and the sails pulled taut with the wind. The ship pulled closer to the naval vessel, the Harbinger, and our crow's nest watcher bellowed, "Battle stations! They've rear cannons trained on us, Cap'n!"

Cacophonous booms shattered the sound of the swelling waves around us, whistles that reminded me of munitions falling back home. My first reaction was to try and find cover before remembering that I was the cover, casting my senses to where Kayda watched from on high to check the trajectory of the projectiles in time to block the first one with Void Shield. My mana drained, and I grunted with the impact, my knees flexing as I brought the slightly heavy object down onto the deck. No sense in wasting ammo.

"They've disregarded the accords!" Captain Holly bellowed, her saber sliding free of its sheath with metallic whoosh before she held it aloft. "To battle!"

The men and women around us cried out raucously, and we set to work. The vessel's attempt to escape was thwarted by us making ground on her and cutting her off, Odany canceling her spell for us with a mental command from me through Muu. The anchor for our ship dropped with us three or four football fields away from the incoming naval vessel. The men and women on board cheering as they thought to ram us.

I reached out to the element of water and ground my teeth as I solidified it using the shadows of the depths. The water froze in place like a glacier before us and lifted the ship out of the water entirely. Hubris appeared in my hand to assist me with the finer mana control needed to avoid completely destroying the ship.

"Should we board first?" Jaken called over the grinding of wood against ice.

"No! You'll go with me after the strikers' board." Captain Holly whistled a shrill note over the din, her ears flattening against her head. "Strikers!"

Taejon and ten other crew members whipped out grapnels and ropes, slinging them over onto the ship before us, the bow of it only a foot away with the large figurehead of a knight with a lance striking forward towering above us.

Kayda, keep an eye on things for me baby. She screeched, and flitted over to the other ship swiftly on the breeze.

I watched through her eyes as the strikers clambered over the rail and onto the deck to meet the sailors on the other ship.

I've got eyes on too, these sailors are well equipped. Bokaj warned the tension in his voice was palpable. *Should I start with cover fire?*

"Bokaj wants to know if you want him to fire on the men attacking your strikers?" I asked the Captain, her surprise quelled when she noted the ranger on the side of the crow's nest. She nodded, and I passed her permission on to him.

Arrows soared through the air, and cries of pain rang out over the edge of the railing of the ship before us.

Father, these people we are with will need help soon, something is wrong with these other people. A crash of lightning punctuated Kayda's words of caution.

"Cap, we gotta get up there, your men are in danger." I

started forward, but she grasped my shoulder, her claws digging in a little as I made to move by her.

"We will wait for *my* word," she snarled. A horrendous shrieking scream pierced my ears, making me flinch. A figure crashed onto the deck, his neck snapping as he hit the wooden deck head first, the skull cracking and caving in from the weight. Taejon's once capturing eyes gazing lifelessly at us from his shattered face.

"Come!" Captain Holly roared and sprinted forward. She was up the rope almost as fast as I could shift into my eagle form to fly up. I fluttered up to the rail and surveyed the area.

Sailors in white with mottled purple and red skin savaged the bodies of the strikers who had fallen. The others fought bravely against the line of barely human enemies with arrows sticking from the bloated bodies barely registering the projectiles' presence.

I shifted out of my eagle form and shouted to the others. *We got some weird shit going on here, y'all. Kayda! Bring the storm, Yohsuke, get your stinky ass out here.*

I was trying to sleep, you stupid bastard, his half groggy voice cut through the din around me. *The fuck is going on?*

We have darkness inbound, we need your help out here with these assholes! Jaken called. I felt a hand on one of my tails and turned with a snarl to find him struggling to get up with one of the enemy sailors on his waist, trying to bite him. I pulled him up even as he battered the sailor's head for all he was worth, the damage just not even calculating on his health bar. His attacks did nothing.

What the fuck are these things? James grunted, I saw him bounce off the main mast of the Harbinger and kick one of them in the head, its neck snapping gruesomely, but it continued trying to attack him. He blasted a hole in it with his ki, the chest smoldering before it crashed to the ground and began to thrash violently.

"Go for the chest!" he roared to everyone in earshot. He seemed to rethink that when he tried to shove his hand through the right side of another sailor's chest. "The heart! It's the heart!"

"We got it!" Yohsuke appeared to my left freshly shifted from bat form, Kayda's healing rain beginning to fall around us and darkening the sky. "You better get to fighting brother, save me some."

Vrawn flung me out of the way as one of them came at me with a clawed hand and snarling open mouth. I spun and pulled my claws across its throat, warm blood gathered under my nails just before Yohsuke's astral blade pierced the man's heart, and he tossed him over the side of the ship.

"Game time." I shook my shoulders out and rolled my neck, reaching into my inventory for Magus Bane. I cracked my neck before twisting the axe in my hand familiarly.

I planted the haft of it into a sailor's chest, knocking his feet out from under him, and used the axe to pin him down. I cast Aspect of the Ursolon and roared loudly, shoving the spike at the bottom of the haft into his heart. The thrashing began, and I moved on to the next enemy, a woman foaming at the mouth with wild hair trying to grapple Vrawn from behind.

I went to assist her, and her blade whipped around behind her, the sword passing through Vrawn's attacker's neck. The body fell backward but rose again in time for me to slash the body through the back and spine.

The heart flopped out of the corpse, sloshing onto the deck with a noisy squelching, and I stomped on it with a satisfying splash and splatter.

I growled in delight and moved past Vrawn, her weapon flashing just behind the small of my back to cut down the severed upper body of one of the strange sailors that had tried to grab onto my lower back to bite my ass.

"Thanks!" I growled, and she just grinned my way as lightning danced along her sword.

I grabbed one of the chomping sailors by the throat and felt a pull on my being from the sails, an aura of sulfurous rage emanating from above me drew my attention. I glanced up in time to see Tmont scaling the rigging to try and get to a human-looking man muttering and waving his hands.

We have a caster! I bellowed to the others and felt a couple jerking impacts on the body in my grasp. Bokaj had fired arrows into the back of the creature before me, and it still tried to claw at me, the nails on its body dragging down my armor. The nail clipped my shoulder, and a pulse of sickening energy seeped into my body like venom.

I snarled and threw the creature from me bodily, and cast Purify on myself. The spell didn't do much, and I had to hold it for another five seconds to get it out of my body completely. *Don't let them bite or scratch you!*

Arrows screeched through the air and clattered into something in front of the mage, that looked like a barrier.

Zeke, take Magus Bane and get up there, Yohsuke barked as he fought through a crowd of beefier looking sailors, his blade slashing and carving a path for him. *James, you too. Jaken, get the hate for us, man, these guys are spreading thin and ganging up.*

Got it! Jaken clanged his sword against his shield and shouted for all he was worth, "Come and get me, you demon bred pieces of *shit!*"

A glowing red aura burst from him in a wave and everything in the area took an interest in him. The caster created a symbol with his hand toward the crowd that stormed forward toward the paladin, and they stopped cold.

Each one began to shake and grunt as if they were in pain, the backs of their shirts tearing and bursting as wings sprouted. The caster fell to a knee with a smirk and blood dribbling from his mouth. His dark robes and body my target as I jumped for all I was worth toward him. My body lifting twenty feet into the air and my left arm snatching some of the rigging beneath him. I felt a hand on my leg and turned to find one of the flying sailors latched onto me.

I kicked out once, twice both landing in the face loosening his grip a little bit, doing nothing to actually damage him. Frozen lightning struck him in the spine, and he shook furiously as the electrical agony surged through him. James appeared on his back, his own wings flaring as condensed ki covered his clawed finger tips. Flesh tore, and the crazed sailor cried out in pain, sharp teeth flashing as James carved the wings from his back and stabbed into his ribs from behind, ending the sailor's life. His ki blade caught my hip, 9% of my health bar falling instantly, but the rain helping to regenerate it swiftly.

"We gotta kill him fast." James stayed and clambered up over me as if I were so much netting on an easy obstacle course.

James beat against the barrier with it cracking a little by the time I reached the crossbeam and swung Magus Bane, activating Cleave to give my swing a little boost. The barrier shattered into millions of pieces, and the caster's eyes began to bleed from the backlash of the spell shattering.

"You'll never win against my masters," he gasped, a victorious grin splitting his face as he hissed, "This ship will be the last thing you interlopers ever see. You and your pet pirates."

"Where are your masters?" James grasped him by the back of his cloak, the man choking slightly as the monk lifted him.

"I'll never tell you that." He cackled and licked his lips, his dark eyes shifting about. "The three remaining generals are plotting against you as we speak. Oh, Razmerdil will be *quite* upset he didn't get to devour you as he planned, but who cares. Die."

He lifted his arm and revealed a long dagger that he brought toward his chest to try and kill himself. James stopped his arm, and I grabbed the blade with my metal hand snapping it in half.

"Don't kill him." James nodded at my order and put him in a blood choke before I could turn away. The others fared well against the creatures down below, but Kayda had two of them attempting to bring her down to the ground, and Bokaj was trying to give her covering fire, but they kept weaving away from his shots despite leads and wind working in his favor.

"I'll get him to the others and take care of them, you go protect Kayda." James shoved me toward her then dropped to the ground slower than what should have been possible. Had to be some kind of slow fall ability that helped him defy gravity so well.

I took off toward the edge of the crossbeam and dove off before shifting into my eagle form, powerful wings lifting me aloft and toward my baby. I didn't dare make myself much more of a target than I already was, and I couldn't trust the dragon form to hold to my will.

The two-winged sailors, one male with a hulking figure and a lithely built female, harried her as she flew. She clawed at the female as she flew beneath her claws, but the larger figure tried to break one of her wings. Static burst around her feathers and a ball of electricity attached to his face, but he seemed undeterred by it.

I rose above her and dove down to use my claws to bloody his face, the creature's arm flailed and struck my left wing, the bone holding up, but the nails pierced straight through to the other side making flying a risk. I shifted as soon as the nails had come out, luckily the venom didn't have a chance to enter my body, or I might have been hurting.

I growled and shoved my metallic hand into his back, but the wind up here was insane, and I wasn't able to penetrate his ribs. So I cast Lightning Bolt and hoped that it fried whatever was inside him. The electrical arc crashed into him and his body went rigid before he collapsed, and I was able to dig in and actually crush his heart.

I tossed the body aside, and it fell toward the water, I shouted over the wind. "I'm here now, baby."

This small one annoys me father, she is too agile for me to strike, and my rain does not harm her. I could hear the irritation in her voice, and the small wounds healing on her body ignited my ire as well.

I melded my shadow with hers, and the second the flying fuckass passed within range, I used that chance to cast Shade's Prison on it. With her momentum halted and her wings frozen, all she could do was fall as Kayda turned and dove at her. The storm roc caught her tormentor and speared her with gigantic beak and claw, tearing off her head and wings before plucking out the beating heart and casting it aside.

By the time we landed on the side of the ship, the others had finished the crew off, and my mana was full once more.

"We all good?" Yohsuke groaned. "I'm pretty tired."

"How is a *vampire elf* tired?" I raised an eyebrow at him in disbelief.

"The fact that I'm a vampire and actually need to sleep in my coffin to rest, dog breath." He rolled his eyes and turned to walk away, stopped, and turned back. "You know I can't not look for loot up in here, man. Let's go."

I chuckled and walked with him to the cabin. *Balmur, you wanna check for traps ahead of us?*

Balmur moved forward quietly and began to scan the area ahead of us for traps as we entered the cabin area.

You've gotta be fucking kidding me. Balmur swore violently and backpedaled into the rest of us. His chest heaved, and I made it out of his way just in time to avoid him retching onto my feet. I peered around the corner into the doorway, and it wasn't the bloodied remains all over the hallway that made my stomach churn, surprisingly.

No, it was the glyphs and set up in the room at the end of the hall that caught my eye. And the visage of the grinning demon staring out of a mirror on top of what looked like an altar.

CHAPTER SEVENTEEN

"Hello, boys," Archemillian purred from his side of the mirror, his face pressed closer until only one of his eyes was visible. "Ah, and lady as well. How *are* you all?"

"We'd be better knowing that you weren't cavorting with the enemy, demon!" Yohsuke snarled and marched into the room.

"Brave words, wait." The demon's manicured eyebrow lifted slightly before his almost beautiful features twisted in rage. "You've been *defiled*! By whom?! Who dares claim what is mine?!"

"Shut the fuck up," Yoh said, spat and grabbed the mirror in both hands. "Explain why we're seeing your ugly ass here where people are trying to kill us."

"Well, my pet." Archemillian laid it on thick as he batted his eyes. "I followed a lead to a rebellious faction of Demi-demons to this... place. I had seen the deal made for power with a cloaked figure in return for... sacrificial rights. It was not what you mortals would call pleasant. Is that the champion nego-tiator I hear retching in the hall? My kindest regards to him, if you would be so kind. Tell me, any news of the demon you've been told to hunt?"

"We found it," I muttered at him evilly, his warm and almost jovial gaze making me want to choke him.

"Ah, but he escaped you, didn't he?" The demon *tsked* and wagged a finger as if chiding a child. "So, rather than giving in to my baser urges and crushing the demonic blood vials I promised to hold like I so want to, I shall abstain. For two boons, of course."

"What's the price?" Yohsuke sighed tiredly. "No souls."

"No souls." Archemillian pouted theatrically, his usual charming smile returning. "One, you will tell me how you came to be a vampire—in-depth and unfettered so that if it was unwilling, I might take my vengeance. Two, you find the ones who are taking the blood of my demons and destroy them."

We glanced at each other for a moment, and curious delight dawned on his face. "You had no idea that this is what can happen when mortals ingest the blood of demons?" My brothers shook their heads, and that seemed to bring even more joy to the demon's features, a sparkle of mirth entering his eyes. "You should know all about it by now, why—your *brother* Balmur should know all about it. The tainted blood I collected wasn't merely from exposure to our realm. It was a catalyst for greater change. To make him stronger, more aggressive, dangerous."

Like a steroid made of demon blood. I choked myself on the thought, imagining them holding him down and pouring the disgusting stuff down his gullet.

"We found him, he's not dead yet, though." Jaken hauled the unconscious caster to the front of the group. "Operative word being *yet.*"

"That is not him." Archemillian shook his horned head. "He was here, certainly, but the one who made the deal was a great deal more… charismatic. And he offered many souls."

I frowned. "Gnomish?" Archemillian regarded me as I spoke and motioned a familiar short height. "'Bout yea tall, old as shit and speaks like he has the biggest dick in the room?"

"Dude." James smacked my shoulder, but my hackles were raised as the demon squinted at me.

"I am not familiar with that last description, and the second one not so much, but he was gnomish." He tapped his chin thoughtfully. "Tell me, does he carry a staff covered in runes? Capped in blackened metal?"

"Mother*fucker!*" I bellowed as loud as I could, the rage in my heart dulling all the rest of my senses as the world shrank.

The little bastard was trafficking *souls* now? Distressed screeches from the sky and barking from outside the door brought me out of myself to the sensation of hands around my body, holding me down.

"If only I had spoken to him when our deal was made, he would have made a fine use of my power." Archemillian tutted and turned back to Yohsuke. "Time is of the essence, pet. I will hear this tale soon, and my vengeance related. It is not a quest, merely something to stay my hand. Do you agree?"

"Fine." He threw the mirror across the room, and it shattered with Archemillian's laughter ringing out around us. "Let's loot the place and get the hell out."

"You all go ahead," Bokaj muttered as we walked out of the room. "I'm going to see to Balmur."

We nodded and piled outside, then a strong hand grasped my shoulder and turned me. Vrawn frowned at me. "You hate him that much?"

"I hate anyone like him that much." I growled, a heavy sigh heaving from my chest. "He's selling souls out of spite, Vrawn."

"Who?"

"Tarron Dillingsley." The name tasted like ash on my tongue and almost made me gag. "He was supposed to be my mentor, and when he shot me down and taught me wrong on purpose because he was hurt that we were supposed to be saving his people instead of people born and raised here, he took up the cause in his own way. He will lie, cheat, kidnap, steal, and apparently sell souls to do what he thinks is best."

She frowned. "Other than the selling souls portion, which I despise myself, is that so bad?" I stared at her, but she just watched me back, so I motioned for her to elaborate. "How is it any different from what you would do if you knew that your own situation was hopeless?"

"What?" My hackles rose again. "Are you defending him?"

"No." She shrugged, motioning to herself. "I'm merely offering a perspective from someone outside the situation. You have power gifted to you from the gods. All of you are uniquely trained to fight in our world despite having not been raised here and creatures who would normally spurn mortals actively seek to aid you in your fight. If someone else came to your world where you had once been revered and seen as powerful to do the same things you are now, would you not do what needed to be done to protect what you love? Would it not be important for you to try and maintain some semblance of control over your steadily worsening situation?"

I paused, stopping myself from lashing out, or telling her that she was wrong, and instead looked at her. Really looked. There was a hint of what she had said there in her eyes. Truth.

"You feel the same way, don't you?" She didn't look away, but a small amount of pain seeped onto her face, her eyes pinched at the corners for a second too long. "You do."

"I do." She motioned to me, then her weapon. "You've studied enchanting for months, and are already at the level of a master. You and all of the others fight like men possessed and have skills and abilities normal people like me can only gain through deadly training, and even then, you all still far surpass us. Surpass me."

She stepped out into the gentle rain falling from Kayda's spell. She stopped and let it bathe her, clearing away some of the gore that had spattered onto her from the fight. "You all are legends forging your names in this world, saving us and taking our plight onto your shoulders, and we cannot do a thing to stop it. You, or the generals, or even the damnable minions. We are vulnerable, and those of us who know what is going on are terrified. Because we have no say in what befalls our home."

"Of course you do." I stepped closer and reached out to her. "You're here, right now, fighting with us."

She pushed my hand away, suddenly angry. "Because I forced you to let me. Because I gave you no choice. If you had a choice to bring me along for this, would you have?"

Dangerous territory here, Zeke. I sighed to myself.

"Honesty," I muttered to myself, and she seemed taken aback by it. "You deserve honesty. I trust you, so you should be able to trust me. No, I would have chosen for you to stay with the village to protect them. Because I know what a great asset you are, how brave and courageous you are, and how you would be willing to lay your life down for the people we care about. I wouldn't have brought you because I would save you from the hardship of being here with us where things can truly kill us. Because if I had to choose, I would die alone and save everyone I could."

She stayed silent, almost eerily so. So I spoke on, "Is that some sort of god complex? Taking the brunt of the blow for the glory of it? Because no one else is capable? Please." I snorted at myself and rolled my eyes. "I do it because I constantly think that I'm the only one who should because everyone else is better suited than me. Because I've tried my best to be a shield against misfortune for others my whole life. It's all I know how to be. Protecting others because I'm not worth it. So yeah, if given the chance to choose whether you get a shot at living or not, I would have you live."

She walked away from me then, her shoulders rigid, and her weapon at her side. She grabbed a rope on the side of the ship and hopped over the rail out of view.

"That was smooth," Captain Holly remarked with her arms crossed as she leaned against the wall of the cabin. "I had plans to go see what I could find in the captain's quarters, but this was... enlightening."

"Forget you heard it, and we'll be okay." I sighed and ran my hand through the fur on top of my head. "You're better off not knowing anyway, it seems."

"She wanted you to tell her that you would have her fight at your side rather than be anywhere else." She pressed, bouncing off the wall behind her with a press of her shoulder blades. "You have no mind for romance, my friend."

I couldn't bring myself to fire back at her, so I just rolled my eyes. "I'm pretty incapable lately, it seems."

"Don't you try and press that pitifulness at me, master Zeke." She punched my shoulder, and it ached mildly. "I saw you fight. All of you. You were amazing, and so was she. No one touched her, and the one who came close died at your hand because you had her back. I dare say, if I had let you all board first, my men might be alive now, and that is something I must live with. Poor Taejon."

"Yeah, but we didn't know either," I shrugged, it was the best I could do at the moment. "Your crew's sacrifice is noted, thank you."

"Noted?" A coughing laugh burst from her mouth. "Noted? Really? Have you, 'the shield' grown so callous that lives mean nothing to you anymore?"

"No, but I can imagine that monetary compensation will come out of our payment to care for any of their families back home." I turned to face her. "The coming fight will be worse, that's why we're preparing ourselves and the ship for what is to come. Will this person we're meeting tomorrow be able to help us more if we give him more? Or are we just paying to pass through?"

"More the latter," she grumbled. "But we can ask about the first. You might want to go after her then because we will need every hand we have."

I nodded and moved away toward the lattice-like grate that covered the portion of the deck that led below.

We got wood and other supplies down here, nothing metal other than what the carpenter would use to make minor repairs, but it should be enough to make at least another ballista if we're careful. Bokaj seemed to take a moment to go over the findings he'd spoken of again. Then shouted, "There was a hollow wall! We found some metal!"

I grinned, then shook my head and went to find my way below deck. There were barrels of rotting food and some of water that had been heavily poisoned. Seems they had hoped to make us sick if they couldn't kill us. I was a little pissed off that our prey wasn't here, but that just meant that they were further ahead, right?

I surveyed the goods, as well, and found that they would work. The ship moved and listed slightly to the right, the deck shifting with it, and we decided it would be a good time to get the hell out of there. We loaded up and left.

Once we were clear, my ice wholly melted, and I shot a fireball at the ship, burning it to cinders there on the ocean. No point letting it float there uselessly. The sailors mourned their dead together that night as we plodded along in the water back on course. Some, if not all of them, drank a little to the memory of the fallen.

Muu joined them, muttering something about how Taejon had only had two weeks to retirement. He looked genuinely saddened at the loss of the old man, and I couldn't really blame him. He had been nice.

Bokaj, Balmur, and Jaken worked through the night to get the ballista ready. The base had been made previously, it was only a matter of bending the limbs for the weapon so that it would launch projectiles with enough strength. It was slow going, but worthwhile when they filed into the cabin with grins on their tired faces. I wanted to help; I could have if I had been allowed to melt metal down, but we had a limited supply, and they weren't sure how it would all react. Poorly made metal being mixed with decent metal was bad.

"It'll work now." Bokaj yawned noisily and smacked his lips. "I'm gonna sleep forever."

"If you wouldn't mind enchanting it, we'd appreciate it," Jaken added a little tiredly as he walked past with a wave.

"Balmur wait." He blinked at me tiredly, and I sat up so I could talk to him. "I'm sorry about what happened on the ship. I know that had to be hard on you."

"It was." He scratched his head. "I'm sorry that I hid on the ship while all the rest of you fought those guys."

Recalling the battle, I hadn't seen him. I just thought he had been elsewhere. Shit. "You want to talk about it?"

"Not particularly," he kind of joked back, more hopeful than anything else. "What happened... happened. I'm trying to get over it. I was lucky enough that exposure to the drug was all it was. It never fully took me over, and they weaned me off it after a time because it would have killed me. Couldn't lose their negotiator."

His tone took on a bitter note, and his nose wrinkled in disgust as he spoke that last sentence. I nodded at him, and he seemed to take it as our conversation was over. He opened the door to his dimensional home away from home and closed it softly before looking back at me. "Thanks for trying to be there for me, man."

I nodded once more, and he stepped through the door, and I was alone again.

I stood and stretched out before going outside to take a look at their work. It was to the right side of the bow and would turn almost fully three hundred and sixty degrees. Their work had been great. Though the line that they had given me to work with was leather that Muu supplied, it was workable.

I enchanted it to be tensile, but unbreakable, using some Faerie iron shavings to assist in that. Once that was done, the line attached to the front of the limb, and I bent it back in place only to realize that I had no idea how to set it, and I didn't want to break it.

A strong pair of hands grasped mine and held the limb of the right side in place, and Vrawn ordered, "Place the drawstring under that little lever there near the front of the system."

I did as she said and waited while she had me take the limb from her then went to the other side of the machine. She bent the limb back and attached the line to the other side of it easily. Once that was done, she slowly let it come to a rest before reaching over and flipping the little lever with her finger so that it became a ring that held the line solidly.

"I'm sorry that I was so volatile earlier." Her apology

seemed sincere, her face hidden from me slightly in the darkness. It was the later hours of the morning, and I hadn't really slept well.

"It's fine, I'm sorry if I sounded petulant. Or like I was trying to play down your desires to help defend your world." I scratched my neck and sighed. "I'd be lying if I said that my caring about you didn't sway my words, but it's mainly that I'm just an idiot who would rather see his friends and loved ones taken care of before himself."

"That's not so bad." She smiled over at me and patted the rail next to her. "I spoke to Muu. He supported what you had said, and he also pointed out that it may have sounded like I was supporting what Tarron was doing. I do not. I just think it better that you know there are people out there who would help you. Like me."

"I know you would." I joined her. "I mean, you're here now, right?"

"I am," She chuckled, her tusks flashing a bit more. "But I would be lying if I told you that I hadn't come because I was jealous of Maebe and how much time away you spent with her. Now I know what it's like, and I cannot begrudge you having little time to send messages to me when in the grand scheme of things, you were likely even busier then than you are now."

"At times," I ceded, but I reached out and took her hand and pulled her closer to me. "But there were times that I should have *made* time for you. And I didn't. I'll never be able to make that up to you, and I'm sorry for that."

"I understand." She grasped my hand and squeezed once. "Are you tired?"

"A little, but I need to enchant this first." I patted the ballista. "Are you?"

"I am, but I will wait for you." She let me go and stepped back so I could get to work.

I spent some time thinking about what I wanted the ballista to be able to do, and that was act almost like a rifle, but to also have the highest amount of piercing damage and probability that we could manage. So, that left me with a couple options here. What did I do? I engraved the side of the weapon's wooden body with a rune for endurance that Hubris showed me, it looked kind of like the symbol for infinity but had a line in the center going directly through it. How it correlated, I couldn't tell you, but the scepter hadn't steered me wrong yet.

Next, I engraved symbols for power and strength on the limbs that looked like a mountain and river flowing over it. Once that was done, I affixed a metal plate to the front of the weapon just under where the projectiles would be launched and added a large cut opal to it. The opal gave a bonus to accuracy somehow.

When the light shines on it, master, you and all others will understand.

I shrugged and went back to work. I figured I might see if this would help and used Vulpine Casting to help keep from not having enough power since I was on my own. After powering the enchantments, I once again felt the pull of inspiration and added multiple components to the enchanting. Equal parts diamond on the body of the weapon and then faerie iron to the limbs. Finally, Hubris encouraged me to add some of my blood.

Even that made me a little leery of the scepter at that moment, but with the risk of failure looming over me, I bit my left thumb and pressed it onto the centermost portion of the ballista where the projectile would sit.

The final siphoning of my mana stopped, leaving me with only a single point of mana left and a splitting headache.

Shapeshifter's Ballista
+20 to attack, +19 piercing damage
Shifter blood – Each item used as a projectile for this weapon will be changed into that of a giant bolt. Upon impact, the normal damage will apply, but added damage is possible.

When a fox comes to you in a strange forest, be wary of them, for you never know if the shape before you is the truth, as will the target of this weapon always wonder.

"Oh, my god," I muttered to myself under my breath. Vrawn touched it and gasped as I checked my enchanting level and saw that I had gone up by one.

"Zeke, this is amazing!" She whispered to me. "How is this possible?"

"Hubris helped me." I frowned and noted that the scepter had indeed done so, but was nowhere to be seen.

I am here, master. I am just in my pocket plane. Our bond has grown with your trust, and that allows me to assist you even from here.

"Well, thank you for your help." I could feel the pleasure at my surprise, and I left it at that.

Vrawn and I walked into the cabin and found Muu snoring blissfully in his cot with Yohsuke sitting in the bottom one.

"I finished telling Archemillian what happened." He seemed a little tense. "He says that since I was force-fed the blood, I'm not in any kind of infraction of our contract, but he's going to insist on trying to collect something in recompense. He just doesn't know what would be the most advantageous thing yet."

"He wasn't getting your soul to begin with, so I can't see what he has to gain from trying to get you killed or anything. Besides we already did him a favor." I was starting to get a little angry that people seemed to be coming out of the woodwork like this. It was still suspicious that he was there, to begin with.

"Right, but he could insist on me trying to pay him back," Yohsuke insisted. "I hadn't even seen that there was an issue in the contract, but it was right there, three paragraphs in, third-page subsection six: the obtainee of any demonic power shall not willfully or negligently become a member of the undead for any reason upon which time the patron finds out the contract can be considered null and void."

"Wouldn't the negligently portion cover being bitten?" Vrawn asked curiously.

"I thought the same thing, but he said that it was intended to be there so that people couldn't just not fight back and become one. Since I had been fighting when I was bitten by one, the contract is still in force. And since it was Zeke acting of his own volition by shoving the vial in my mouth and not me, me telling him to didn't count either. Especially since you stopped me from spitting it out and forced me to swallow it. We got lucky there."

"Yeah, we did." The relief I felt at that moment was immense, and I was suddenly much more exhausted than I had been before.

"Get some rest, man. I'll be up a little while longer to watch things. Dawn is in a few hours." He gave me a side hug and headed out the door.

Vrawn and I walked into the Happy Home and found my room, one that I had previously only been in with Maebe, and my heart ached for her absence. I wrestled with the idea that I should reach out to her to see if she was okay, but I knew that if I did, I might interrupt her in something really important, and that could be deadly. I opted to lay down on the now-bigger bed with Vrawn and tried to get some more sleep.

CHAPTER EIGHTEEN

I woke up to Muu shouting inside the door, "Up! Everybody get up!" I stumbled out of bed with Vrawn grumbling evilly behind me as I opened my door.

"What is it?" I yawned, I had finally been able to get a few more hours, but I had to imagine it was still early.

"We made it to the edge of the lord's territory, and he should be showing up soon. Cap' wants us all on the deck." Muu explained as he stepped outside the door. "Yohsuke is still up, but he's a little pissy about it, and I had to feed him."

"I'm fuckin' tired, you bastard!" The vampire snarled. I walked out onto the ship to find him wearing his cloak's cowl up, even in this room. "My coffin has my name on it as soon as we meet this stupid fucker."

"Well, let's get dressed, and we can all get out there and be presentable," Bokaj muttered and turned around to go do as he had said. I did the same after passing shadows over myself and Vrawn to clean the two of us up. I dressed in a green shirt with some brown breeches that tucked into my black boots. Vrawn wore a similar outfit, but her shirt was gray and the breeches a deeper brown.

I smiled at her and shifted into my human form to give her a kiss before we left. I walked out, and Odany grumbled as she stepped out of her own room. I passed shadows over her to clean her, and her clothes, and she shouted at me, "That felt weird! Don't do that!"

I just laughed at her as she eyed her clothes, then smelled them and dropped them in surprise. "They're clean?"

"Yeah, maybe someday you can have that much control over the wind?" I raised an eyebrow at her, and she gasped, much more alert and happy than before.

The rest of us piled out of the room, and Balmur dispelled the doorway to it so that we could use it again that night. The sun was near its zenith, but what caught my eye was the island we sailed directly toward in the distance.

"Why has no one called that out?" Balmur wondered out loud, the island seemed a few miles out, but still, it was interesting. Maybe the guy lived on the island? It would be nice to step onto solid land once more.

I found myself smiling at the prospect of moving my toes in the sand, and it put a little pep in my step.

Captain Holly stood up by the bow of the ship watching the horizon line carefully. "Ah, welcome to the land of the woken," she teased, eyeing all of us, her eyes lingering on where Vrawn held my hand. "Glad to have you all here to meet with the lord of these waters."

"I'll be glad to walk on land!" James grinned and stretched enthusiastically as if getting ready to go running.

"You landlubbers." Holly rolled her eyes and turned back to her watch. About forty-five minutes later, we had come close enough to the island to make landfall, but instead of doing that, they dropped the sails and anchor.

"What're you doing?" Jaken asked curiously as the captain pulled out a long horn.

"Contacting the lord of these waters." She smiled back before blowing a long, deep, blasting note out over the water.

"Oh, so we just wait until we hear something, and then we

can make our way in?" Muu asked excitedly, then began to watch the trees on the island as if looking for something. "Or they give us some kind of sign?"

"You will see." She purred, her tail twitching slowly back and forth.

Water began to move around the area before the ship on the port side, and several of us muttered, Muu being the loudest, shouting, "Oh! Secret entrance! James Bond supervillain shit going on here!"

Then a large head almost the same size as the ship erupted from the waves, and large greenish-blue eyes opened and peered down at us. It was almost draconian in shape, the beak-like tip a jaw like a dragon's, and the ridges on the top of its head had several horns that burst from the tan skin atop the head.

"Oh, what the fuck is *that*?" Muu screeched noisily, and I rammed my elbow into his ribs, making him gasp and double over.

"Lord of these waters, Eldarna the Great and Wise Tertle, we of the Pussy Willow beseech you grant us the boon of passage through your territory, and we request aid in battle to come. Will you assist us?"

A loud booming voice that was impossibly deep returned, the mouth moving as it spoke, "What... do... you... offer... in... return?"

"We offer you shinies, and shimmers to add to your hoard, and continued tales of your benevolence and might." Several sailors moved, bringing a large chest forward and placing it on the deck next to the captain so that she could open it and motion to the coins and gems inside. She pulled out the weapons of the sailors who had fallen and held it aloft as well. "We offer the weapons of our fallen, enchanted, and pristine for your aid."

The head dipped lower, the large eyes looking at each of us in turn. "Do... they... know... my... rule?"

"They do not, Lord Eldarna." Captain Holly bowed her head but reached out to us. "He will need to collect your scents and a portion of your lives. This portion is only a drop of blood, freely given."

"Blood is a powerful thing to give to anyone." I glared at her angrily. "Is that why you never told us?"

"It is." She crossed her arms. "It is partially nourishment to him. He gains time for his own life from it, and he's never done anything wrong to us in the years I've sailed these waters."

"Fine," Jaken answered as he stared at me pointedly. "What do we have to do?"

"Go to the side of the ship and reach out your bloodied hand." She made motion to do the same, but Yohsuke charged forward and did it first. He pricked his finger with a sharpened nail and offered his hand out to the tertle.

Eldarna dropped his massive head to the side of the deck and touched the hand offered to him with the space between his giant nostrils. He inhaled deeply, and our clothes moved toward him with the gust of his partaking. After he inhaled, he lapped up the offered blood and grumbled, "Undead... you... pass."

And so we continued, all of the new members of the crew and the guests to the ship making their own small offerings in accordance with the rules. I was wary of it at first, but when all the others did, I wouldn't have wanted to start a fight with the draconic-looking creature myself.

I slashed my thumb with my right hand and offered it up to the creature. Doing the same as the others had, though, I was curious as to whether or not I was strong enough to claim this sort of form. Was he mythical or legendary? Did he have a class at all?

He touched my hand with his beaked face and gasped, "Mother's... chosen?"

"I am he, I suppose." I tried to hide my pleasure at gaining his form but failed miserably.

"If...I... had... known... you... were... in... my... domain... I... would... take... you... myself... to... anywhere..." He licked my entire body, wetting my clothes and all. "You... are... beloved... by... all."

Dozens of creatures separated themselves from the trees on his back, animals, and other mysterious types of creatures watched us. "What are they, Lord Eldarna?"

"My… wards." His head craned back into the air, and he turned to look at them, slipping into a watery tongue that I understood perfectly due to my tie to the water elementals. It seemed that he no longer considered his words carefully, so this must be his native tongue. "They are weak or injured. I protect them in their time of need, so they will come in my time of need. Now. They say you need my aid?"

I responded to him in his preferred tongue, the sound feeling weird to me. "Yes, we will likely be fighting a general of War in the ocean, and I am not as well versed in water combat as I would like to be. My brothers and I are in danger if we can't come up with a way to fight him and the creatures he will likely bring with him."

"Many evil creatures have gathered in the waters around my territory, and some have even approached me about joining with a fell creature who wishes to rule all of the oceans and depths. I refused and have been threatened. Do you think these creatures one and the same?"

I nodded, fear gripping my chest. "It does sound familiar to something they would do."

"Then, I will offer my aid, as it is what the Mother would wish," he replied, and a sort of turtle-like smile crept over his face. "I have many I oversee on my back who would happily aid you in learning water combat."

He turned and offered his side. "All of you who wish to learn water combative techniques, come and climb aboard my shell. I will have you speak to some of my little friends."

I passed the word on to my friends, none of them could understand him except Balmur, who had a language spell that let him understand things others said.

The boys and Vrawn with Odany hot on her heels scrambled over the deck of the ship onto the water below and sped toward the shore of the shell.

Odany splashed into the water, and I realized I hadn't planned on her getting off the ship until now. So I would be equipping her with a water walking ring as soon as I could. Vrawn pulled her from the water and carried her to the shoreline.

"I... will... pull... your... ship... do... not... fear," Eldarna spoke directly to the captain, and then we were off. Waves surrounded the ship, and the tertle began to move on his way to where he would. "Continent... of... Beasts... is... your... heading."

"Yes!" Captain Holly shouted, and he turned back to his direction of travel.

On the shell, we moved toward the creatures who watched us fearfully from behind the trees. "Hello, all of you," I tried in a friendly tone. They shrank back, some of them looking humanoid with gills on their necks and ribs, fins on their arms and legs.

They moved further back from the tree line and seemed to be leading us toward the center of the shell. It was quite the trek I led us on, trying to get to the center and keeping them in sight. An hour at a swift pace, as if they were fleeing for their lives in a deadly game of chase. When we finally thought we had caught up to them, there was a large humanoid figure with a shark-like upper body holding a large spear facing toward us with a scowl on his face. Behind him was a bowl-like indent in the shell of the creature we rode that held water in it that looked like a large lake.

The shark-man spoke a guttural version of Aquan. "Why you chase my friends? How you get past great one?"

"We're here at the great one's consent," I replied in Aquan, the language of the water elementals. "We're here so we can learn how to fight in the water for an upcoming battle."

"Why should we teach you, land walkers?" A lighter voice asked rudely. I turned to a stone in the water and saw a small woman poking her head out from behind it, grasping the stone as if it was all that kept her there.

Balmur translated for the others as we spoke, and I felt a hand on my shoulder.

"Well, that's up to you." Jaken shrugged next to me. "If you don't mind something truly evil taking over the ocean and destroying it and everything you love? There's no reason because if we lose, that's what will happen."

"Things already pollute these oceans!" she screamed, her face coming out from behind these one, part of it blackened, the eye a sickly yellow with a red pupil. "Things that had no place being there."

"What happened to you?" he asked for me to translate.

"I was swimming near a set of islands, and the waters turned to poison and changed me. I swam as far away as I could, but the poison had taken hold, and the only thing keeping me something close to normal is this water." She stared at us with sheer hatred and loathing on her face. "This is *likely your fault!*"

"We killed the dragon that had been poisoning the waters of a set of islands with his presence," I explained softly. "We cleaned the area of his body so that his taint could be cleansed by the water elementals."

She stared at us hard, finally challenging, "You could be liars."

"What proof can we give her?" James scratched his head, and Yohsuke rolled his eyes.

"How quickly we all forget that we're knights of the Unseelie Court." He stared at me, and I felt the urge to punch him in his smug chin before or after facepalming.

"I, Zekiel Erebos, King of the Unseelie Fae, swear to you that by quest of the Elemental Water Primordial, my brothers and I went to a series of islands to rid the waters of the tainted influence of a black dragon called Riktolth." I saw the notification for my word pop into view. "We dispatched him and cleaned up his body so that the waters would be purified."

She frowned and read the notification, her lips moving as she did, the words brought a sad smile to her lips. Looking a little more closely, she would have been exquisitely beautiful except for the monstrous black patch of scaring marring her face and shoulder on the right side.

"I see that you speak truth." She frowned, her hand finding her scarred cheek absently, "Would that you could have been there sooner."

"Maybe we can fix that for you?" Bokaj asked out loud, looking to Jaken and me.

"I don't know. We didn't really get the chance to try and cure anything affected by the taint." Jaken looked at me. "I have magic that heals, but that's not something I could handle, I don't think. Maybe use Purify?"

"You heal her," the shark-man ordered loudly, brandishing his spear at me. "You heal her, or me no teach fight."

Well, there's that. Balmur thought to the rest of us.

QUEST ALERT!

Scarface – A mysterious sea creature has demanded you heal his scarred friend in order to learn how to fight in the water. Reward: Unknown, Training from the creature. Failure: No training, and likely made into chum.

Do you accept? Yes / No ?

I rolled my eyes and accepted it readily before addressing the others, *We may have to overkill this thing to keep it from returning. Or somehow getting into the water or anything else here. I need Bokaj and Jaken as well as Balmur.*

Me? Balmur seemed shocked at his inclusion. *I kill things, I don't have healing spells.*

"Come on, I'll explain as we do it." I motioned all of them toward the water, and the shark-man snarled at us. His spear closed the gap between me and him, the sharp edge of it almost in my throat. "Look, we want to get this over with and make sure she's okay so we can learn. It may take all of us. Relax."

"It's okay, Blinthil," the woman called as she pressed away from the rock and toward the water's edge. She wore no clothes, and the guys except for Bokaj blushed furiously and looked away.

"Bokaj, you want to try and see what Purify does to it first?" I offered as the woman lay on her back in the sand.

He did so and the darkness on her face flickered and ebbed before returning to what it had been.

"Okay, how much magic can you amplify, Balmur?" I asked and watched as he did some figuring, stopped, opened his book and ran his fingers over several lines of words I had no understanding of.

"I can multiply any magic cast in front of me, if I know the premise of the spell, by a minimum of two." He frowned a little more. "If I know how the spell works, I can make it up to four times stronger, and if I can perform the spell myself, it goes up to five or more depending on how well I know it."

"Fucking wizards…" I groused half-heartedly. He smiled at me, and the others for me to decide what to do. I summoned Hubris, and they eyed me skeptically. "It's going to help us amplify this further. I'm a little worried that we may not be strong enough to do it, but we can give it a shot. Jaken, you're going to pump radiant healing magic into the scepter. Bokaj, you cast Purify for all of your mana, once you're out, stop. I'm going to hold my own Purify for fifteen seconds and see if that helps. Balmur, I want you to amplify the purification magic."

"Can you explain how it works?" He looked to Bokaj and me both.

Bokaj started it, "Think of the mana coming in and eating away the tainted energy and darkness of the thing."

"Almost scouring it out completely and setting it to right," I finished. He closed his eyes as if envisioning how the spell would go down.

"I think I have it." He growled. "Sorry, gotta feed the eye."

We blinked at him as he turned away and fed his eye once more. We tried to ignore his discomfort, and once he returned, he seemed a little more focused.

"You cool?" Bokaj asked him softly. The dwarf merely nodded back once and refocused on the task at hand.

"All hands in," I ordered, and three other hands grasped Hubris. "I'll cast first and hold the spell, then when I say now, you all join in. Hubris will tell you when to cast your spell Balmur."

He nodded, and we all fell silent. The sound of the waves broken by the giant entity we rode on drowned out by the thudding of my heart as I held Purify. One ding. The second. Finally, the third. "Now!"

800 MP siphoned from my body into the scepter and melded with Jaken's healing energy and Bokaj's less powerful Purifying spell. The nimbus of golden and green energy swirled down the length of the weapon growing larger and more focused until it reached the gem at the end and met Balmur's magic. The muted beam of surging energy shot into the woman below the four of us and zapped her directly in the chest.

Her shriek of anguish and cries to make it stop coupled with the look of angry boiling that roiled along the left side of her body made my entire body run cold until something pierced my right shoulder, and the sound of shouting and violence erupted behind me.

I couldn't take my eyes away from the mermaid, her fin splashing us with water as she writhed as if tortured from the inside. Finally, just below her left-most rib, her skin split open, and a geyser of black, brackish liquid splattered out onto the ground. The sludge almost living as it did what it could to get away from us and the damnable light that had outed it.

I summoned the shadows around us as Jaken saw to her healing, and let the void delightedly gobble it all up. Like a child with candy and a voracious sweet tooth, the ooze was gone.

The woman stilled almost like she was dead, for mere seconds before Jaken, Bokaj and I buffeted her with healing magic. Her body was still a moment longer, so I decided to give in to my first aid training and ensure she got air the old fashioned way.

By force.

I tilted her chin back, and went to ensure her airway was clear when a small glimmer caught my eye in her throat. I sent shadows into her mouth to try and dislodge it, and it worked, but she still wasn't breathing. I grasped her nose, covered her mouth with mine and blew twice, her rib cage inflating as I did so. Then I clasped my hands together and began compressions to the tune of Stayin' Alive.

Three rounds of this and she coughed up some more ooze that screeched and tried to work its way toward me, but I nuked it with Fire magic. She coughed and sputtered, her hands cupping together close to her chest. I cast Regrowth over her and she began to shake a little less.

"What was that brutal thing you did to me?" She glared at me distrustfully.

"It's a resuscitating technique I learned for when someone stops breathing." I glanced at the others, but they seemed content to let me speak. There was no more arguing or sounds of fighting behind us, and I was curious to see what had happened.

"You could have just pushed me into the water." She complained, but a small smile came to her lips as she sat up and looked into the water. "It's true. It's gone."

"We're glad to have been able to help." Bokaj smiled at her, and I turned to the others behind us.

Vrawn sat on the shark-man's back with his legs up over her waist in some kind of weird wrestling move, and he looked like he was about to pass out from the pain. She blinked at me. "He stabbed you and tried to stab the others. He earned this."

"I'm sure that he means well now, right?" Balmur tried to get his attention, but the man seemed to be blanking. "Let him go, Vrawn, please?"

She released his legs slowly before standing and walking over to me. "How does a kiss resuscitate someone?"

"It wasn't a kiss." I rolled my eyes. "It was me forcing air into her lungs, and keeping her heart pumping blood until her body could start back up on its own. If it would have started back up that way."

"So, there was no certainty in that?" She frowned and cocked her head to the side. I shook my head, and she frowned more. "You will teach me this."

There was no arguing that point with her, so I just shrugged and nodded my agreement.

It took a moment for the shark-man to stand on his own, and see to his friend before he turned to us and grumpily snapped, "Fine. We teach to fight in water."

We grinned at each other and got started immediately.

Shark-man, Tony as we began to call him, was a gangster. Literally. Well, formerly. See, his family had been part of the original owners of this stretch of the ocean; they oversaw the peoples and creatures in the area, taking portions of the treasure from passing ships and those that sank. It had been lucrative until the Great One had come along and eaten half his people and mortally wounded the rest.

"Only reason I survive was fighting style." He lifted his chin and gnashed his teeth. "Bit Great One on his fin and surprised him. Earned respect and life. Became protector of shell garden."

"That's a great story, Tony, but can you teach us something a little more practical than trying to bite?" Bokaj groaned at our would-be trainer. "The only ones that would help are Zeke and our Vampire buddy, Yohsuke."

He grumped a minute more before pulling out his guitar and strumming a melody to distract himself from our glares and pointed looks of anger and indignation.

"What melody is that?" The mermaid asked, with her head poking out of the water toward Bokaj.

"It's just one that I came up with." He shrugged and started to play a little more surely than he had been before. The song was soft at first, then crescendoed into a loud burst that made me smile. It was almost like the breakdown of a metal song, but not quite there.

"You have a talent for music," she observed with a smile. "Would that my sisters could be here to hear you play. Can you sing?"

He blushed. "Yeah, I can sing a little bit. But when it comes to lyrics, I don't have the greatest head for them. The melody is where I flourish."

She came up out of the water until she was up onto the sand, and once her tail fully cleared the water, the scaled appendage rapidly molted and fell away until a pair of legs sat in the debris.

Master, collect the molting. It is a powerful magical component!

I cast my shadow forward as she stood on shaky legs to take herself toward the still-strumming bard. She wobbled her way to him, his music stopping suddenly as she came to his shoulder. "Don't stop playing, I will teach you how to sing even better."

"But you've never heard me sing," he refuted as he looked at her feet, his cheeks turning a slight shade of purple.

"Why does that lady have no clothes on?" Odany's suddenly shrill voice scared the hell out of all of us. "She's naked!"

I turned to see her giggling and pointing, Vrawn grabbing her and pulling her aside for a moment.

"I'm nude because it is the way of my people," the mermaid seemed confused. "How else are we meant to lure sailors into the depths to mate?"

"Lure sailors… I thought that was sirens?" James looked confused and pulled out a small notebook, readying his quill. "Is there some kind of difference?"

"Oh, yes." She smiled and motioned to the water. "If a siren were to come out of the water, she would transform into a hideous half-serpent creature with wings. Their bodies are scaled and their claws sharp. They eat the men and women they mate with. We do not."

Bokaj looked up at her, his eye stopping to follow every curve of her body, "What do you *do* with them?"

She smiled, her perfect teeth flashing in the light as she

looked down at him with her hand stroking his shoulder. "Other things."

I snorted, and Tony cleared his throat. "We train now?"

————

We trained for a few hours, Tony going through how to use our ability to walk on water as an advantage rather than leaving us as sitting ducks.

"Must watch the image if you can see, ocean is unforgiving and thick at time," Tony motioned to where a large snake watched us from below. This creature was like a large coral snake, but super friendly. He would shoot out of the water and slap us with his face to show us how to dodge incoming attacks. "Image is lie, sometimes creatures use this lie to kill. You must be smarter. Move completely out of way, and use their contentment to your advantage."

He stood on the water and watched below himself as the snake shot out, dancing away from the creature and tapping it in the back of the head effortlessly. "Dead. You do."

We practiced, some of us getting it a little easier than others. James and Balmur got it on the first go around and Yohsuke on his second. It took my third try, and Jaken just didn't seem to get the hang of it at all.

"Damn," he growled as the others took turns chasing the snake and Tony through the water. We sat on the shore so I could help him out. "I just can't seem to get it."

"You just have to move further back, that's all." I thumped the plate armor pauldron on his shoulder, and he grunted inarticulately. "Seriously, all it really is, is a refraction of the light off the water, then the snake."

"What does that even mean?" He threw his hands into the air, exasperated.

"It means that the light is bending by the time it hits what you see, so it looks like it's somewhere it really isn't." I showed him by putting my fists out in front of me. I lifted one and put it next to the other but slightly overlapped them. "What the light hits is really below the reflection, or slightly off from it."

"So then it could be even further away?"

"Yeah, or a little more to one side than the other." He nodded and stepped out onto the water.

"Let's go again!" He barked at the snake, the large creature swimming toward him and slinking into the water. He waited patiently and watched the water beneath his feet. Taking a deep breath, he peered into the water and hopped back and to the right as the snake just cleared the surface of the water where he had been. He smacked it on the back, and the rest of the observers cried out in triumph.

Jaken looked back at me, and I gave him a thumb up in support. We carried on with our training.

Underwater fighting was difficult, but we knew that already, the only way to really combat that would be to attempt outguessing your opponent or tricking them into giving you their back.

We worked on that for a little while, then while we rested, Bokaj took lessons from our new mermaid friend.

"You must focus mana into your voice," she coached from her spot slightly behind Bokaj's shoulder, her hand on his throat near his voice box. "Here. I have also heard stories of accomplished musicians using mana to stimulate and add to their playing as well. Let us try it."

"Could you show me how to?" He raised a brow and motioned to her, then the rest of us. "We would all love to hear you sing, I'm sure."

"Very well, but I cannot be held responsible for anything that happens due to my singing." She stared at all of us for a moment then, looking each of us in the eyes until it had been bumped up to an uncomfortable silence.

"What can happen?" Vrawn asked softly, just as the mermaid made to open her mouth.

"A mermaid's song is meant to enthrall and entice; once you hear me sing, you will understand what I mean."

"Is there a way to counteract it?" James asked, nervously rubbing the ring on his finger.

"There is, but this is an important lesson, and I wish for this one," she touched Bokaj's shoulder as she spoke and smiled softly. "To learn the full scope of what he could be. I will reward you for your assistance after."

Then she opened her mouth, and her voice filled the world. I could feel my mind slipping at the beautiful tones of her voice. The pitch was lilting, the wordless symphony that was her voice lulling us into an alarming sense of ease. Even with the blue-bathed area around us from the beacons on our hands, I wanted to be near her.

To hear her sing her song for me and only me for all time.

Vrawn and Odany shuffled closer to her, their faces pleasant but slack, somehow less themselves. The ethereal waves of warm, welcoming sonorous vocalizing came to a halt, the emptiness afterward making my heart ache so fiercely that the world itself seemed gray for the loss of it.

The two ladies' eyes welled up, and I felt that in my soul.

"I have to learn how to do that." Bokaj sniffed. His eyes were red as if he had wept, and he pawed at his face. "Please teach me."

"I will teach you." She touched the faces of the two women, whispering something in their ears and kissing each of them fully on the mouth. "I will need to do the same for all of you. Come to me."

We all stood without a second thought and came straight to her, lining up behind each other so that she could address each of us in turn.

When she came to me, she pulled my chin toward her and leaned against my chest so that she could speak into my ear. "Change your shape, shifter." I did as she ordered and came out in my human form. "Thank you. My voice and the voice of my sisters will no longer hold sway over you. You are free to sail these seas as you have before, unmolested by my touch. Be at peace."

She pressed her lips to mine, and it felt as if I had kissed sea foam. A chill ran through me, and I knew without a shadow of doubt that I would never need to worry about her song touching my mind or heart again.

I wasn't sure if I would be better off for that or not. But listening to her teaching Bokaj how to do what she had done, I was grateful.

CHAPTER NINETEEN

We fought for two days, learning how to combat creatures of the deep, and it was hard. Not only that, I had also been delving into the depths of my elemental control. I hadn't made any new spells, but I was much more comfortable combining the elements in different ways.

Our path and rate of travel over the last couple days had seen us moving well beyond Eldarna's territory into open waters that were neutral territory. This had been a designated area for the creatures of the oceans to come and meet others of their kind for mating rituals or other reasons. This could be for anything from schools of fish to tertles like Eldarna.

It was afternoon and we rested, the fur along my arms and the back of my neck stood on end.

Something changes the weather, father. Kayda warned me from the sky. Our bond opened up further, and I could feel the change in the atmospheric pressure around us.

Eldarna, who hadn't spoken to us in days, called out, "They... come!"

We listed forward as the giant tertle came to a stop in the water.

Tony and Mertle, that's what Bokaj had called her, not me —blame him for the weird name—waved to us and wished us luck as we booked it to the ship.

"Calling an audible here, we have no clue what's coming for us," I bellowed to the others as we ran, speaking aloud so that Vrawn and Odany could hear me too. Thinking of it, I cast Water Lung on everyone, then added to my previous thought. "Boys, we're taking the fight to them. Vrawn, you can fight too, but I need you to stick closer to the ship so that Odany is safe."

"I want to help!" Odany cried out angrily. She had been learning to fight too, and she was definitely a strong caster.

"You will be!" I snarled, her interjection only keeping her from hearing the rest of the plan. "You're going to help keep the ship mobile so that we can keep harassing whatever comes at us with ballista fire. Balmur, you want to handle that?"

"Got it." Balmur sped past all of us. His dexterity was the highest of all of us, and we struggled to even keep up with the dust he left behind.

"I'm going to be providing whatever help I can." Bokaj pressed forward, his stride only slowing to pass his message. "But I may be doing song buffs this time around."

"Be open to suggestions," Muu said as he ran by. "Don't just play the hits."

The two of them sped off in the same direction, and I looked to the others.

Jaken grinned. "I'll be in the thick of things."

"Same!" James hooted as he sprinted past me. Bea followed him closely, carrying Odany and Vrawn on her back, her red eye glaring angrily at me. Even under the effect of the dragon's anger, she still loved the two ladies more than me.

"We communicate the whole time," Yohsuke ordered. *For those who can't hear me because you jackasses ran ahead like assholes, communicate during everything. Got it?*

Who is you? Muu asked teasingly, and we all rolled our eyes.

"Eyes in the sky?" Yohsuke asked me, flicking his head up as we ran. I nodded and shifted into my eagle form and lifted up into the air as it grew steadily more turbulent with winds threatening to topple me where I flapped my wings.

I strained against the winds buffeting my body, bending my wings painfully. I opened my mind to Kayda and found her flying above the majority of the turbulent winds. *You going to be okay?*

She screeched and responded coolly, *I am in my element, father. They will regret attempting to take my birthright.*

My beak quirked at the corners in an attempt to smile.

Banking toward the left, I found my way toward the ship and the roiling waters before it and Eldarna.

I landed on the ship and shifted back to fox-man form so I could look over the others who were there. Odany and Vrawn huddled behind the mast away from the winds.

"It may be a good idea to figure out how to nullify the winds, Odany." I said and growled at her so she could hear me over the din of the aerial onslaught.

"I will try!" She howled and closed her eyes. Suddenly Sylphy and Dusty popped up, her smile growing. "They're going to help."

Rather than screeching angrily at how she can do that, I just nodded once and moved toward the bow of the ship where several shapes and creatures were breaking the surface. Humanoid figures carrying tridents and rough-looking weapons pointed our way. Then a larger figure burst from the ocean, several smaller things surfacing with it.

"Welcome to your death!" The creature cackled in common so that all could hear. "You ruin our plans *no more!*"

I rolled my eyes, this was definitely a general, he continued on in his tirade. "My sister was right in sending us here as swiftly as she did, you're weak, and your friends will not stand a chance against me!"

I smiled as Kayda fluttered over his head and sent me the information that made me smile.

He's only level 41. I passed the word through our earrings, and I laughed as the others did.

"He's in for a rude awakening then." Yohsuke climbed over the side of the rail and grinned at me.

"Well, no reason to give him or the other guys a chance to get any kind of plan together." Jaken frowned. "Let's get going at 'em."

Kayda struck first, but a gout of flame ate away her lightning as a large figure dropped from the sky. A copper-colored dragon flapped his wings in a tempo that allowed it to take a place next to the larger creature in the water.

"I think they sought to end you more swiftly, Baranzil," The dragon droned lazily, looking at a clawed hand. "Good thing sister sent the two of us as she did. Treacherous little beasts, aren't they?"

"Yes, Breggil, they seem to be," the massive creature rolled his bulbous eyes. "This kraken body is a vast disappointment, but the oceans will be mine, and we will drown the world. I envy your draconic form and your apparent *level*. Come, time to kill them and take this world for our own and our master, War."

As soon as he turned his eyes back to us, a projectile slammed directly into it and zapped him for about 10% of his overall health. A tentacle rocketed toward us from the water, and Jaken leapt up to deflect it with his shield while shouting, "Game time!"

Two more projectiles launched from the ballista toward the copper dragon, and it ducked under them with ease. The ship dipped dangerously, the sound of splintering wood surprising me. I turned and saw the others looking into the sky and figured out that Muu had taken to the sky to live up to his self-styled class.

"Let's get to the killing," Yohsuke grinned and dove over the side of the ship, and I followed suit.

Bea, keep Odany safe! I ordered her, she barked her reply loudly, and I grinned as I dropped down onto one of the weirdly humanoid fish people who tried to stab my best friend as he fought two others.

I grabbed him with my left hand, the slick thing almost slipping from my grasp before I stabbed my right hand fully through the back of the tough skin at the base of his skull. I grabbed his spine and ripped it back toward my body and tossed the corpse aside.

Yoh dispatched the two in front of him. "They're low level, but there are a lot of them. We need to be cautious. AoE spells need to abound, if anything."

I got the hint and turned while pulling Magus Bane out to attack the monsters that had thought themselves sneaky enough to come after me. I slashed them and bashed them, wondering when something more exciting would happen when the world shattered around me. The sound of explosions from Yohsuke and Balmur attacking almost covered the thunderous *kabooming* of the cannons. Each blast toward the massed creatures and scattered them handily before the ship was moving away from our position swiftly, trying to get into a more favorable position possibly further from us and danger.

There were some of the creatures attempting to board it, but Vrawn kept them from making it onto the deck. More lighting crashed in the sky, and I saw Kayda fighting with the dragon, the two of them whirling in the air, the dragon painfully gripping her.

I'm going to go save Kayda! I roared to the others.

A stupendously loud crash echoed out from in front of me as Muu landed, he grunted under the pain from it, but luckily he didn't take fall damage if he landed on his feet. "I'll come with you. No one fucks with my niece."

I sprinted forward and leapt up into the air, shifting into my draconic form, green highlights along my black scales flashing through the lightning that had started gathering in the clouds. A thud on my back between my wings let me know Muu had come along for the ride.

I snatched up one of the fish-men in my clawed hands and lifted his struggling figure into the air fifty, a hundred, two hundred feet before dropping him like a sack of potatoes.

"Here's hoping he doesn't evolve and grow wings!" Muu whooped, and I found myself grinning.

Kayda looked to be doing better at fighting the figure off as the lightning built around her, but he was dogging her for every flap of her wings. Her beak was bloodied, and she looked slightly tired. I could tell that her mana was low, and I didn't dare risk adding rain to the mix and giving the sailors an even harder time.

Aerial combat between dragons is usually deadly, your best chance at coming out on top is to allow the bird to take his attention and to tear his wings. The guttural voice of the dragon's instincts echoed in my mind. *Her sacrifice will win the day.*

"I sacrifice *nothing!*" I roared back at it, surging forward even harder than I had been before. It tried to grapple control away from me, but I opened my mind to both Kayda and Bea, and their presence helped me beat back the monstrous will.

I began to get snippets of information from the dragon's instincts, as if I were tearing bits of how to move from the incorporeal voice, my wings beating harder as I used my longer neck and tail to assist me in navigating through the air.

Get me close, and I'll get on his back and take care of him, Muu ordered me. I liked that plan more than the dragon's and sped along.

Kayda, shock him again if you can, baby. Then get to the ship and lay low to heal.

She acknowledged me with a screech of her own and clawed at Breggil's face just as multiple arcs of electricity crashed into him from the nearby clouds.

He cried out as the elemental energies fried him, his health dropping by about 12%.

Breggil Lvl 54

That wasn't as concerning either, why were these guys so weak? Melvaren had been stronger than them. Hell, a *minion* had been too.

Breggil dipped in the sky, his wings not working so well, and I got an idea. I shifted into my fox-man form and rolled, grabbing a confused and slightly startled Muu by the arm. *I'm not going to have you jumping and missing.*

I cast Regrowth on Kayda before shifting into my dragon form again to close the distance between us and Breggil. I tossed Muu on his back as I bit into his neck from the side. Kayda dipped below us in an attempt to flee, and the fight was truly on.

Claws skittered across my scales ineffectively, Muu and I stabbing and gashing where we could, wings, back anything in reach. A sickly green energy covered Muu's holy spear before it stabbed into Breggil's body six times before I could blink. The dragon roared in agony.

We're winning! Muu cackled delightedly as I grabbed the other dragon's open mouth with my clawed hands and arched my neck back, inhaling. The stored breath and intent mixed with the glands in my throat as I exhaled and spewed poison into the other dragon's open maw. It choked him, and his chest began to expand as his own breath weapon charged.

Muu was there instantly to wrap his legs and arms around Breggil's snout and yanked it shut with a giddy shout of, "I saw this in a cartoon once!"

With nowhere else to go and the particles of my poison still in his throat, the gas ignited, and a burst of smoke emanated from Breggil's throat. Most of his life was gone by now, and his wings were shredded, our descent to the water imminent.

"Come on!" I urged Muu, pointing toward the ship and the others.

Eldarna fought the kraken called Baranzil valiantly but seemed to be having a rough go of it for some reason. His bloodied beak attempting to bite at the tentacles slapping him and sucking him into the creature's grasp. I could see a couple of spots along his shell had been blackened and saw what looked like some kind of casters around his body standing on the water and touching him.

Muu jumped lightly and cleared my back as Breggil fell

further toward the water, his health at a quarter, and plummeting. "I'll go help from the ship!"

"I got a plan!" I called and flapped over toward where the kraken fought the tertle. I shifted and fell slightly, then grinned and took my newly acquired tertle form. My body was nowhere near as large as the island-sized Eldarna, but I was at least half his size and heavy as fuck. And plummeting toward the kraken!

I collided with him, my head and neck pulled into my shell protectively, and I felt him slide out from beneath me so as to avoid the majority of the damage, but the water beneath me wasn't so bad when I was this size. I peered out into the deep, and hundreds of fish-men swam through the water toward us. I shifted, bounced out of the water, and onto it like it was land, and booked it up onto Eldarna's shoulder.

He was hurting, and before I could cast a healing spell, the kraken rocketed out of the water, catching him on one side of the shell and launching that side over the other.

I lifted up into the sky and changed into a dragon, watching as the kraken dragged his dying brother out of the water and into the air, he was in the final dregs of his health now and rather than trying to heal him, the kraken opened his giant, beaked mouth and consumed him bite by bite.

None of us collected any experience from that, but he did. His level jumping up twice, his wounds closing before our eyes. Over his formerly squid-like skin, a shimmering coat of scales burst forth.

"Oh, what kind of home-brewed bullshit is this?" I roared more to myself than anyone else.

The kraken just lifted his tentacles triumphantly, calling out to the world, "My brother's sacrifice means a lot, but it will pay off when all of you die!"

Then, water boiled before his face and a whirlpool opened up, the hundreds of fish-men that had been coming to try and kill us all floundering and fighting for their lives to get away from his greedy gullet to no avail. Screeches and cries of anguish met our ears as they died in his jaws. Their lives fueling his gain.

We need to get the fuck out of here—now! Yohsuke warned us, I turned in time to see him getting onto the ship.

I glanced down on the water and saw James running against the ever-widening current of water being sucked toward the general. I arced from the path I had chosen for my flight to the ship and pumped my wings powerfully toward his struggling form. I lashed out with my leg, and he grabbed on to it with ease, kicking one of the fish-men who tried to join him away from us both.

Once you guys land, all of us are accounted for, Odany is already gearing up to help us get the hell out of here, Balmur yelled into our heads.

Already the ship lurched toward what I hoped would be our destination and getting there through the rising cloud of spears thrown from those lucky few survivors of the gluttonous rampage of Baranzil.

Six of the little bastards got lucky, scoring my wings to the point that my right wing tore slightly, and my equilibrium was askew. Rather than landing fully on the deck of the ship, I had to shapeshift into my humanoid form, smash my right shoulder on the rail and deal with hitting the mast with my gut to boot. My forward momentum carried me around to the other side of the large wooden stop, my pained groaning only abated by a healing touch on my injured shoulder.

"Thanks, man." I smiled weakly up at Jaken and stood with his help, his sure strength bolstering me a little.

The ship lurched forward as Odany cast her spell, and the sailors brought their full skill to bear so we could try for a clean break. I hated to do it, but I watched as the kraken grew to an immense size, lifting Eldarna's shell slightly and sending his tentacles into it to drag the creature out from his hiding place.

"We have to go back and protect him!" Odany cried, her tears of anger and indignation surprising me. "He helped us fight he should get to live!"

"There was no way we could take all of those fish-men *and* the general on top of that," Jaken tried to comfort her, but she wouldn't listen and clung to her idea.

Finally, her tirade had been enough, and Captain Holly marched over to her and lifted her in a single hand, laying the other across Odany's cheek in a brutal open-palmed slap to get her attention. The wailing child hushed and stared in open horror at the feline woman who had tears in her eyes.

"We bought his sacrifice!" Her voice sounded rough even to me, and I didn't know her as well as her crew did. They all looked distraught, but their eyes were glued to their Captain. Their leader. Their hope. "He knew he would face something he might not be able to beat someday, and that was his duty to himself, and the ocean! The ocean is harsh, what it gives—it takes back as easily!"

She dropped Odany, a rush of wind from Dusty stopping her fall as Captain Holly looked about the ship as if daring anyone to speak out against her. "I plan to survive. I plan to earn my money and mourn the loss of a friend by *surviving* this journey so that I can keep my word. Anyone who plans to stand in my way can walk the damned plank. Aye?!"

Her crew snarled back, "*AYE!*" Their fervor doubled as they scattered to do their best to keep us afloat and on our way.

Odany and I made the ship go as fast as we possibly could. Her gusting winds filling the sails, and my occasional use of the water to drive us further by manipulating the waves to give us a little headway. We all took turns sleeping in shifts, I plopped onto the cot and passed out immediately. The entire time I slept in a pitch-black, coma-like state, I wondered if we would get away. If that bastard hadn't gorged himself on his followers and started our way.

Luckily, I was able to get some rest, because there would be little more from then on.

CHAPTER TWENTY

"Kraken, hard to port!" A shouted warning shattered my peaceful rest, my bleary eyes shaking as I tried to make sense of the bright light around me after sprinting outside the room into the hall with the door to the cabin open already.

The ballista fired ahead of me, a large metallic spike sailing toward the beast only to glance off the copper scales covering his body.

He raised his tentacles and brought them down at us, the ship taking a hard right to *just* barely keep it from sinking the ship in a single blow.

Kayda screeched and fired a bolt of azure lighting straight at him, the jolting electricity shaking the kraken for a moment, allowing us to get slightly ahead of him.

I took a steadying breath and did something I hadn't done before, I took light and fire mana and swirled them together and gathered them like a spear before launching it directly at the bastard. It hurt him, minutely, with only a small percent of his health going down. I didn't dare get closer to him to give him the evil eyes to look at his level. That was just stupid if you asked me.

Though one of the sailors *swore* the beast was in the seventies by now. His continued eating and gorging making him bigger and more deadly.

The glancing blow irritated me, but it would be better to get to land where we could stand a real chance against him than stay and risk death on a tiny ship compared to him.

Arrows and more ballista fire covered our exit from his grasp, and that's how we spent the next six hours, barely missing his attempts to catch us thanks to creative use of some spells and elemental magic to keep him away. Eventually, he grew hungry and sucked more water into his gullet. Hundreds of fish and other creatures fell victim to his avarice.

Odany and I kept the ship going, and I started to truly help her go through a litany of potential attack spells.

"So, I rotate the wind at the front and focus on it piercing?" She asked during one of our impromptu lessons. I nodded, and she focused again, motioning with her hands so that a small whirling bit of visible wind built before her in a shape vaguely like a mushroom before sharpening like an arrow.

"Exactly." I smiled tiredly, then pointed to the kraken who trailed not too far behind us. "Shoot him."

She eyed me carefully, then shooed the spell toward the kraken, and it just irritated him.

I rolled my eyes. "You should put more intent behind it." I did the same thing that she had, but I added a higher rotational force to it, then pulled it back like an arrow. Once I felt like it was spinning fast enough and had eaten enough of my mana, I launched it. Rather than taking my magical delivery head-on, he ducked it, and it slammed into the pointed part of his head, taking a small sliver of his health away.

"We can't last like this, man." James groaned quietly as we ate a quick meal. We didn't dare eat too heavily so as to make us groggier than we already were. The bastard wouldn't let us sleep, and we were now four days into our mad dash toward the Continent of Beasts from when we had met the fucker.

Having been on the water more than a week, we were closer

to our destination than we should have been thanks to Odany and me, but all of us were exhausted and starting to flag. Just that morning one of the sailors had fallen from the rigging into the ocean. I had grabbed him with shadows in an attempt to pull him back aboard, but I lost a visceral game of tug of war against the kraken, and the poor man had been seafood. Literally.

Bokaj had tried singing him to sleep, failing that, he played a song of rest every few hours to keep us all standing and functioning at a base level. Even my two Fae comrades were beginning to flag under the constant onslaught of danger.

"We have few options left." Yohsuke brought us some food and looked at Jaken and me. "If this doesn't qualify for some divine intervention, I don't know what would."

"They told us a while back that it needs to be something truly needed." Jaken yawned and blinked at the rest of us. "The gods are fighting their own battle up there, and they need all the help they can get."

"We're fighting for our lives down here!" Bokaj grunted, smacking the deck before him angrily. The bags under his eyes a deeper purple than some of the rest of us. Even though the elves could take a four-hour meditation to rest, they could barely even get that.

We ate in contemplative silence while the kraken attempted once more to try and capsize us, but with no luck. The game of cat and mouse continuing, though he did almost turn us off course. Captain Holly's quick thinking and complete control of her crew saved us from another swipe of his tentacles, and finally I broke.

"Fine—I'll summon a fucking celestial!" The others cheered, and I closed my eyes, focusing on reaching out to the holy I cast the spell Summon Celestial.

The air before me rent in two and a large angelic being I was familiar with stepped out. Samu, Torchbearer of the Seventeenth Celestial Squadron under Lady Radiance Herself.

Wind whipped at the golden feathers of his long, luxurious

wings, his ten-foot-tall Greek stature dwarfing me, and a familiar soft smile greeted me. His halo of spun gold above tightly curled hair that looked like it could be blond dipped as he took a knee in front of me. His wings flared to the sides of his body as his golden gaze met mine.

"King of the Unseelie, friend of the elements and the only living mortal to claim dominion over them." He bowed his head once before standing and looking all of us over. "How can I assist such a powerful being?"

"Hopefully, by being an even more powerful being?" I said, his golden eyes narrowed. "Three generals have fallen, and two remain. One of them is chasing us. He's done so for the last four days, and we're beginning to fall. He doesn't seem to tire, and he doesn't seem to care how far he has to go to get us. If we don't get some rest, or to shore soon, we will die and our mission will be a failure. All will be lost. I don't know what you can do, but any help you can give us would be appreciated."

"This is why you called me?" He asked skeptically, I was too tired to tell if there was sarcasm in his voice or not. He reached down and touched my head, some of my fatigue melted away, physically at least. He did the same to the others of our party, opting not to do the same for the crew, but leaving a pile of feathers at his feet. "Use these to rejuvenate the sailors. I will go and attempt to stall him for a while—all of you rest."

"Thank you, Samu." I sighed heavily in relief.

"Do not fear reprisal from me, master Zeke." Samu turned slightly so I could see the smile on his angelic features. "This is the reason we are here. If it is of this magnitude, we will come."

"Thank you," I whispered as I fell to my knees. Suddenly, the overwhelming urge to rest overtook my survival instincts. The soft sound of flapping wings, then the ensuing battle between a general and a heavenly agent the least of my worries when all the pretty sheep began to jump a small fence in front of my face.

———

I blinked, the lack of light the first thing I noticed as the waves moved around us. Adrenaline surged through my veins, and my feet came under me in a flash. I whipped my head back and forth to see what I could and noted that the ship still sailed on. I stood where I had fallen, my fur warm, and my being refreshed at last. I noted that the others were stirring as well, but what truly surprised me was the lack of pursuit.

"The angel insisted that I tell you that he did what he could, he put the creature far from us so we could sail on," Captain Holly explained with a grin and a yawn that shook her whole body. I noticed one of Samu's fallen feathers had been tucked into her hair. "You like it? He said that it would assist in sustaining us. Half the crew is down sleeping—the ones who've survived at least. The fight between the angel and the kraken was short but fierce. The angel—yes, Samu, thank you—beat him back for a moment, then touched it, and they both vanished."

"He must have teleported him somewhere." I frowned, it couldn't have been far, the spell I had only let me do it when things were willing. If I could go far with them that way, it stood to reason that the distance might be significantly less for someone who didn't wish to be taken.

"Let's get us going on." I shook myself out and reached for the mana within me, pushing it out as wind and filled the sails. "We gotta get to land, sooner."

"I'm aware, master Zeke." Captain Holly rolled her eyes and kept her attention on the horizon line. "If memory serves, we're roughly two days from shore at the rate we're traveling. The sea bears us well, and the skies are clear—this is a good sign. We should be there soon."

I nodded to myself and went to the ballista to work on some of the remaining ammo we had for it. We had been using cannonballs for the shots at first because we had more of them to spare, leaving the actual ammo for us to use as we would.

I spent time enchanting them to pierce dragon scales with Hubris assisting me, using some of the broken shell I had managed to nab from when the little dragonling had hatched with Ampharia.

Each shot cost me roughly 657 MP, but the design was such that it would pierce scales and burst in a shocking bit of magic thanks to adding some of Kayda's azure feathers to the item too. Being a master enchanter helped now.

We had three shots with that enchantment, and I made one other that would freeze the target in place both with ice and shadow magic. That had been a little more interesting, the idea similar to the cage Maebe had used to trap Yve when she was younger.

Speaking of. "Yve, Servant." Both of them separated from my shadow in a single bound, their heads bowed. "You've both been quiet, how are you?"

"We watched while you rest, and since the threat was more to the ship and less Fae in nature, there is little we could do for you, my King." Yve's jaws stretched wide with her tongue stretching out almost lazily.

"What my sister means to say is that we could fight that kraken and buy you time, but it would likely result in our demise and leave you without protection from the Seelie should they strike." Servant flared pointedly at her while he stood there in his tiger-like shadow form.

"Very well." I sighed, thinking for a moment before looking at Servant. "I need you to go check on my wife. Can you do that, then return?"

"I can if you dismiss me, but you should know that she will likely be busy." I nodded and he didn't say anything further after seeing the look of worry in my eyes. "I know that you have been trying to keep your mana reserves replenished to keep the ship going and that calling to her is a distraction that could well get either of you killed... very well, I will inquire after the Queen for you."

"Thank you. Servent, go home, for now."

He faded into my shadow, his connection to this realm gone.

"You do that so well," Yve observed dryly, making me turn

to look at her questioningly. "Worrying over someone who doesn't need your worrying. Queen Maebe is the strongest Fae we have had in the Unseelie line since before even my time. Stronger even than the originator of the line. She doesn't need your aid in everything."

"She may not, but she has it anyway." I shrugged, lifting the final ballista bolt to look over.

"Why?" Yve padded closer so that she could sit in front of me. Her presence cool against my skin, and it felt a little much in the breeze of our traveling.

"Because that's what love is sometimes." My simple explanation seemed to puzzle her more, so I just chuckled. "You aren't used to love. It's a selfless emotion. I don't send Servant to check on her because I worry she's incapable of handling her business. I send him because I care enough to know that she's all right. And so that she knows I'm thinking of her. That she's important to me. Even when my brothers and I, Vrawn, and Odany, are all fighting for our lives, I still think of her. How she is, and if she's happy."

She pondered for a moment in silence as I engraved this one to do pure piercing ice damage, icicles pointing down the length of the whole bolt.

"You love her." It was a statement from Yve, and I just nodded to answer her. "What does this emotion afford you? What do you gain from it?"

"Her love in return." I snorted, remembering I was talking to a particularly ancient Fae. "Love is selfless. It's a feeling you get inside you that makes it so that being apart from the person you care about is almost physically painful. Like missing a part of yourself, but the part that you really care about. Their well-being sometimes trumps your own. You care more about how they are at times than you do yourself. They don't consume you, they just make everything better."

"Like slavery?" She cocked her head to the side and I laughed. "I take it, that means no? I find this puzzling."

"Love is knowing that the person you care about is all right when you're bleeding out and finding that you are relieved." I ran my finger over my work to check for imperfections. "It's hard to explain to someone who has never experienced it. I'm sorry if I'm confusing you."

"Mortal," Yve said suddenly. I blinked and glanced up to see her looking at me intently. "Love. Explain it to me."

"I know we were kind of discussing it, but I'm not really in the right mind space for a lesson on emotions right now." A large hand cupped my shoulder and I looked up at Vrawn.

"Love is the deepest feeling of affection you can hold for a person who is not your blood," Vrawn said. Her gaze fell to me with a soft smile on her face. "It can start from a friendship or a chance meeting with someone who shows you that you are worth more than what you thought. Or it can sprout from a fondness for someone else who compliments you in ways that you never knew you needed. It's wanting to share in the joys, hardships, and meandering paths of life with that person, or persons, whom you care for. Love can be burning passion and a cool breeze. Love is worth fighting for. Worth protecting. I love Maebe. I love Zeke."

I reached up to pull her down for a kiss, whispering, "We love you too."

She grinned and looked over at Yve. "Does that explain it for you?"

"You mortals and your attachments." She rolled her eyes and scrunched her feline nose as if in distaste. Then seemed to ease herself out of the mood she was in. "Do you think there is love for *everyone*?"

"I think if you will it to come, you may find it, or it may find you." Vrawn sat down next to me, closer to Yve than should have been comfortable, but she seemed fine. "But don't ever settle. I'm glad I didn't."

"I see." Yve frowned, not hard for a gigantic cat. "What is it that you are making?"

"I want to make a spear of ice that will freeze the ocean around a target, and will hopefully impale them as well." I frowned and then looked up at her. "You have a good deal of experience with the cold, do you not?"

"I am… adept with it, yes." She seemed to be a little wary of my curiosity. "Why?"

"Do you think you could help me with this?" I pointed to the bolt, and she raised a brow, her whisker flicking curiously.

"I have never been part of an enchantment before, I fear I would only hinder you," she stated uncertainly. I had to admit that was a little strange for her. Normally so certain of herself.

"Nonsense, Hubris will help us with it." I summoned the scepter and held it out before me over the item. "I have the intent in mind, all I need is for you to cast the ice magic into it. The material is conducive to magic, so it's not too bad or likely to fail anyway. Please?"

"You're giving me a choice?" Yve seemed almost as startled by that as the explanation of human emotion.

"You can either choose to help me, or not." I shrugged and she frowned. "Look, I'll be the king that is needed, but I want to work with my people. I'll order them when necessary, but I could do this myself. I just want to make a stronger product. You going to help me or not?"

She shifted into her elven form and put a hand on Hubris, stating, "Purely because I am curious as to how this works."

"Good enough." Vrawn patted my shoulder, and I agreed readily. Of course, she was just curious. Got it, just help me damnit.

Hubris controlled her mana output, and I provided the intent for the spell, adding another of Kayda's feathers as well as a bit of ocean water to it as components.

The engraving frosted over light blue and I could see my breath almost instantly. "Thanks for the help, Yve!" I lifted it and had to set it back down, my hand aching from the cold instantly.

This'll work, I smiled to myself.

The others came to, finally, and I could see their confusion.

"We'd better see to the others and get to working on our escape plan."

"Run." Bokaj scratched his head. "That's all we can do."

"He's right." Balmur yawned and rubbed his eyes. "Not unless we can make the ship fly, and even though we have a decent amount of mana between us all, there's not enough to make this thing take off. Right?"

I found myself laughing at that, and so did the others. It was nice to have a small moment of levity to cut the tension a bit.

"We keep trucking." Yohsuke sighed and began to pace a bit. "You know, with what we've done with Maebe, why not get adventurous?"

"How do you mean?" James sat back where he was, eyeing the stars above us.

"We could make wings with the shadows since it's night." He motioned to the sides of the ship. "Not normal wings, but like additional sails, and Zeke can use those to push more wind into to give us a little more speed. What you think, Zeke?"

"Seems like it would theoretically work, but what if that bastard catches up to us?" I looked over the others, and the apprehension on their faces.

"It would be better to be closer to land." Jaken stood up and stretched himself out. "No reason not to go all out."

That was fair thinking. We all stood and had something swift to eat before the two of them posted up on the sides of the ship. Odany cast her gust spell once more on the mainsails, then I made my own version of it.

Trade Wind – Caster uses his magic to control the winds around them for travel. This spell can be manipulated at will by adding more mana. Duration: 4 hours (or until canceled). Cost: 400 MP. Range: 120 feet. Cool down: 2 hours.

Balmur and Yohsuke closed their eyes and focused just before the shadows around me shifted and pooled in two different locations. I closed my eyes, and I felt them shaping the shadows like children molding sandcastles.

Balmur, make it a little wider toward the rear of it? He did as I asked, and I mentally probed the shadows on Yohsuke's side. *Make it a little shorter bud, there you go.*

I cast Trade Winds and split the spell in two, filling the makeshift wings.

The ship lunged forward, knocking me, Jaken and Muu off our feet. "Jesus Christ!" Muu shouted.

Odany giggled fiercely and clapped.

"I need to hire six of you!" Captain Holly bellowed with a ferocious smile. The crew cheered and clambered down to the deck with nothing left for them to do.

"Should we try and prepare some new spells?" The others looked my way as Balmur asked the question, and I shrugged, wondering what they were all looking at me for. "You've been making new spells the longest, man. We're still new to it."

"Oh!" I couldn't contain my surprise as it dawned on me that they were asking for my help. "Uh, sure—I'll help you make some, what're you trying to do?"

"I've got a little bit of an idea on how to do it from listening to you teach Odany," Jaken began, shaking his head and motioning to the full sails and then to the shadows on the sides of the ship. "I don't have the control yet to do the things you guys do with my magic, but I can learn. I was just thinking of making some sort of attack spell with light magic. I think I'm going to try it on my own, though."

My chest puffed up with pride at my friend's desire to push his learning on his own, and I grabbed him into a quick side hug, whispering, "Slow and focus on keeping your mana flow steady. You'll get it, I promise."

He nodded my way, and the others began to suggest types of spells they wanted to try making. Yohsuke wanted to make something that had shadows pulling health from a distance, which was going to be wild if he could manage it. I wasn't sure how to help him do it, but I coached him through my process of spell craft, and he seemed to pick it up readily before going to meditate on his idea.

Balmur had ideas for some spells that would allow him to mix fire and shadow together and have the shadows stick to the person like Napalm. I had a similar spell that I hadn't used yet due to the ease of access to water we had here, but I could see it being useful. I gave him some coaching as well, but with his wizardly understanding of magic, he was almost better at it than I was.

James and Muu just eyed us from the sidelines before shrugging and going to watch over the rails of the ship. They were faster now, that was all that mattered to them, and there was no jealousy I could pick up on.

"You aren't going to make anything new while you can?" Vrawn asked quietly from where she watched Odany concentrating on her own improvement. Bea stood with her head rubbing up against the large woman's arm affectionately as she watched me.

"No." I shook my head, turning my eyes to the waves around us. "I have a lot of spells I don't even use these days, and if I go creating something now, I take some of my mana out of the fight if something attacks us. It has a place, but we need to focus on staying alive."

She nodded, and Yve bumped my hip with her head. "Wise words, young King."

I took the small jab in stride and kept a lookout while the others worked.

CHAPTER TWENTY-ONE

Dawn cracked in the eastern sky by the time the others stumbled toward me, Jaken had managed to create a light spell that acted as a buff for his weapon attacks, which was awesome.

"I am so proud of you, man!" I smirked at him and shook him by the shoulder, and he took it in stride grinning back at all of us.

Balmur still scribbled in his spellbook and Yoh had given up on his spell entirely, muttering something about, "...goddamn pitching and rolling ship ass fucking stupid ocean makin' me all weird when concentrating bullshit fuck this stupid ship I hate the water, wet ass..."

I stopped listening after that with a snort and noticed Bokaj strumming his guitar. He'd been trying to figure out how to use his mana while strumming like his newest mentor had suggested but seemed to be having a little bit more difficulty with it than he had with his voice. He took a deep breath after strumming an off note and sighed heavily before setting his guitar on his lap and staring at it.

"You good?" I sat next to him on the stairs to the upper deck, where the first mate Joesa navigated the waters before us.

I'd had to cast my spell once more about an hour back, and according to him, we would be in sight of land by mid-morning if we kept traveling as swiftly as we had been.

"Yeah." He sighed and touched the wooden neck of his instrument affectionately. "I just never thought that my music would be so important like this, you know? Every musician wants to change the industry, and make songs that will touch peoples' souls, make them feel like we do, but this? This is insane. Sometimes I wonder what it's going to be like if we—when we—make it back home. You know?"

"I can understand that." My own mind wandering to what it would be like to feel like I had no power again. "I know you'll do good things, man. There's always that chance that you'll go big, you know? What's the name of that band from where we grew up? Boba-something?"

"Bobaflex?" He smiled at the name. "You mean one of the few bands from the Midwest to have made a living out of going state to state and rocking out? I love those guys. Yeah, maybe someday I'll get that big or bigger. Just seems like a lifetime away."

"Yeah, I understand that, too." A hand grasped my shoulder and Bokaj stared me straight in the eyes, a sad look on his face. "What?"

"I remembered that you'll be leaving Maebe and Vrawn behind." A mrow from his hood and a paw swat made him grunt. "Kayda, Bea, and Coal, too. I mean, I get to take T' home with me because she came here with me in the first place, but they're all stuck here."

I nodded, a little more robotically than I meant to. "Yeah, but they'll be okay. They all have each other. And maybe someday I can come back? Who knows. But I can agree with Maebe. I want to have what I can with her here while I can. Vrawn, too."

"You're a good dude, Zeke." He patted my back and pulled me close. "Always have been. Glad I have you here to watch my back with Balmur."

"Me too, buddy." I patted his knee, and I heard a whistle.

I turned and looked at Muu's silhouette, the sun behind him, making me strain my eyes.

"You two gonna make out or what?"

I rolled my eyes and flipped him off, his laughter cut short by a titanic wave rocking the ship hard enough that it listed to the side dangerously.

"Kraken to port!" Several crew members shrieked, cannons firing the few balls we had left at it to distract it.

The sky darkened instantly, a funnel cloud reaching down toward the water between us and the land that had just come into view. Winds whipped at us and threatened the ship's course and integrity as the weather system picked up intensity.

Kayda, can you help stop that thing? I asked uncertainly.

I will try if you ask it of me father, but I do not know if I can. I am not strong enough to take on a hurricane yet. Her mind raced alongside mine, and the only thing I could think to do was to try and send wind at it to disrupt it, but where the hell were we going to get that kind of power?

"James, man the ballista!" Yohsuke howled, turning to me and the other. "Muu, you help him! All casters to Zeke and me!"

I frowned at him, and he motioned to the storm and then mouthed *scepter.* My eyebrows shot up, and I summoned Hubris.

"You're going to funnel all of our magic into this spell to help me stop that funnel cloud from reaching the ocean," I explained, and the scepter understood.

Balmur, Bokaj, Yoh, Jaken, Odany, and I all grasped the staff and pointed it at the funnel cloud before another, lighter hand joined ours. I turned to see Yve, who smacked my arm and motioned toward the cloud. "I can't guard you if you die!"

Fair point. I thought to myself. I brought Bea into my collar with a tap from her snout on my shoulder to protect her and then opened my link to Kayda wide. Mana funneled from all of the hands on the scepter and down into the brightly glowing gem at the top of it.

I willed the magic to disperse the wind, the mana built and built until our arms vibrated painfully, but none of us dared let go.

I ground my teeth, changing the angle of the shot to meet the slowly descending wind cell and let the magic burst forth in a bright, glowing globule of energy, just as the ship lurched upward.

The shot arched just right, scattering a slight portion of the dangerous mass of rotating wind, but not enough to get rid of it.

"Fuck!" Muu snarled loudly, my throbbing headache-encompassed mind agreeing with his sentiment.

"You will not beat me again!" Baranzil cried happily. "I will kill you all and claim these oceans for my own in the name of War!"

"What do we do?" Bokaj looked around at all of us, his breathing too fast to get enough oxygen to his brain.

"We nut up and fight, man." Jaken shoved him, reaching into his inventory for a medium mana potion. "Let's get to it!"

You need to flee! The water primordial screamed into my mind, the tide of her voice like a tsunami hitting my brain. *He has incurred their wrath!*

I watched for some kind of sign as to what she could possibly mean, but all I saw was the asshole we had been running from.

The ship listed again, this time from behind, large tentacles reaching up over the end of it and sweeping several sailors into the turbulent waters and depths below.

The kraken was close enough that we could see his level now.

Baranzil Lvl 78

"Fuck me." I wished I could've cursed more, but wasting breath like that would do me no good. I used a couple potions of my own, getting me enough mana to cast Aspect of the Owl for the heightened mana regeneration that the raised wisdom would give me. "We need to get out of here! The water prime says something pissed off is coming!"

I took out Storm Caller and kissed it before running to the side of the deck and activating cleave as I swung for the fences at the tentacle. A wave of light rippled over my weapon, Jaken's buff, Glaring Smite, covered it and it sank deeply into the bastard's flesh, barely taking a percentage point of his HP bar with it. I hoped that would help distract it so I could get Odany to fill the sails when there was a scent of brine, and a musty odor of dead fish reached my nose and made me gag.

The ship listed again, and a ballista bolt slammed into Baranzil's head. "Argh!" The piercing aspect to it helped it to bypass the scales covering the body, and the burst of electrical energy took a couple more percentage points of health from him. The metallic bolt sticking out of the flesh like a lightning rod.

Kayda took my thoughts and ran with them, lightning flashing from her and into the creature, one of the freezing shots for the ballista smacked into its body and the right half of it froze as Kayda's Lightning Ball latched onto his head near the two protruding bolts.

A tentacle crashed into the hull of the ship; it didn't burst, likely thanks to the shields that I had made via enchanting, but another strike like that would break the ship apart, and it would do us no good.

The scent intensified and then was gone as soon as it had come. The water stilled, and I worried that the kraken was trying to stop us from fleeing when lightning crashed all around us in a circle. The fur on my body stood on end as it continued to pulse, crashing into the water and electrifying it painfully for Baranzil.

"Is that you and Kayda?" Yoh called out to me, a look of uncertainty plastered to his face.

"No!" Panic rose in my voice as the water beside the ship exploded upward with enough force to make the nearly ship-cracking attack from the kraken look like a fucking love tap from a high school sweetheart. The ship split from port to starboard with a splash and eardrum-shattering force. My health dropped 20% from the concussive blast alone, and my body flew twenty-five feet over the starboard rail into the cold ocean. My eyes opened beneath the water only to see a long body writhing beneath the surface.

A pair of serpentine eyes opened more than a hundred yards below me, and I thought I was going to die then and there. Whatever it was rushed up and by me hard enough that it launched me into the air and sixty feet away with ease. I hit the water with a grunt that threatened to pull water into my lungs, and I fought on, just trying to get to the surface, but the damned thing was so long and moving so violently that it was all I could do not to be sucked toward it.

Eventually, my head broke the surface, and there I was just treading water as best as I could, but what I saw flowing from the water damned near stopped my heart. A long, scaled body similar to that of a sea serpent's, floated out and stood as if it were the most natural thing in the world. The body twisting and turning back on itself in loops that shifted hues of color from black to green and then blue to seafoam green. The small, clawed arms growing from the length about sixty feet from the ocean's surface grasped at the air, and the funnel cloud ceased to exist.

The wind dissolving up by the new creature's massive head reminded me of dragons from Japanese lore. His whiskers looked almost like that of a catfish, and his head was draconic in shape. His piercing red eyes filled to the brim with primal hatred as another section of his huge body rose from the ocean and split the ship even further apart.

Kayda! I barked through our mental connection. I could feel her flying nearby, but I wasn't sure where exactly due to the presence of this magnificent monstrosity. *Get Vrawn and Odany to the shore, now!*

*But what about yo—*she began, but the large dragon roared so loud that my HP bar plummeted again, leaving me at 35% health.

Go now! I screamed, pulling myself out of the water and

trying to scramble and find my friends as the behemoth dragon fell on the General with a fervor only a true ruler could. I couldn't see his level, but every smack from one of the sections of his long, sinuous body brought the kraken's health down steadily in five to ten percent chunks.

Tentacles wrapped around the dragon's massive body as I moved to get out of the area, and a massive wave slammed me from my feet into the water, the current kicking me further away as the two wrestled for supremacy. Ichorous blood dribbled into the water, acidic and sulfurous as soon as it touched the ocean's salty body. The dragon's screech of anger and rage only seemed to make it fight harder, its large mouth crashing around the body easily, crunching through the copper scales as Baranzil screamed.

I took a pot shot with a Lightning Bolt that slammed into one of the general's many arms, only shocking it and minutely the dragon as well. I would have assumed it would barely notice a small attack like that, but his immense tail lashed out and just barely missed me, the water around me lifting me and carrying me further away.

Run! Fuck all this, get out of here! Muu urged us. I could see him springing out of the waves and into the sky, just barely missing the majority of the clouds that now spewed lightning toward the dragon. Multiple strikes crashed against its back, and it snarled, letting go of the kraken for a moment to rear back its head and inhale.

Breath weapon! Yohsuke howled, I could just make out some of the others sprinting away on the water as fast as they could. A gold and blue-hued energy blasted out of the dragon's mouth and hit the kraken directly in the eye. He screamed, his tentacles sharpening and punching out at anything they could, but the cutting energy from the dragon's mouth hit the water, and as soon as it did, a tsunami-like wave more than two hundred feet high shot out all around the two of them. The water buckled beneath me somehow, sucking me down and back before my mana drained and my body rose. I was in the wave with no mana, and my lungs longed for a single breath. I was just barely strong enough to get out of the water's surface for a second—long enough to gasp once, and then I was back in.

The dragon clawed the front of the kraken's body, lifting it from the water slightly so that the bottom of the kraken dangled over the waves and shook it violently. Tentacles wrapped around the dragon's throat, and it bit down on one of the coiling appendages violently. The limb detached easily, and it tossed it aside like a child with a broken toy before roaring again. The dragon slammed his adversary into the ocean and lashed out at it with his tail.

Suddenly, I felt two somethings dragging at my armor and turned to see both Servant and Yve fighting the water to pull me closer to shore and out of the depths. I had ordered them away, what were they doing here? Another fierce cry caught my attention as the two began to flag in their struggles. I urged them to go home, and they disappeared as my head broke water.

Another stabbing tentacle pierced into the dragon's lower coils like a blade, his blood leaking further into the ocean, bringing cries of rage and thrashing, making the waves around me chop and grow dangerously. They crested over my head, forcing me into the water as I fought for everything I had.

I closed my eyes, my lungs burning. *Mother! Mother help us. Please! Help… help… save my friends.*

This happened two more times, the water beating me down and sucking the air from my lungs before my vision blurred and faded to black as I called to the ether for someone to save my loved ones.

CHAPTER TWENTY-TWO

Pressure on my chest brought me out of my limbo-like dream of Maebe serving me a mojito on the beach while wearing a bikini, Vrawn playing volleyball with a group of seagulls. I was delirious, obviously.

How would seagulls hit a volleyball?

More pressure and a concerned squeaking noise before something cold and wet slapped me in the face, and something hard socked me in the stomach.

Water rushed from my lungs in coughing fits, bile rising with it as I puked and coughed up all the seawater I had inhaled. I looked to my savior and found a furry face that reminded me of an otter. Only the size of a horse. With... purple and gold eyes.

"Thank you, Mother Nature," I whispered hoarsely.

"It was Milktongue who found you, I just convinced her not to let you die." Her voice was tight as she spoke through the otter. Dire otter? "Many of my creations perished in that battle, my child. And the great water dragon, Orlow'thes was injured."

"I'm so sorry for your loss—our loss." My skin felt hot, and I wasn't recovering mana like I should have been. "What's going on with me?"

"Orlow'thes' blood is a toxin. When it touches something, it eats away the magic inside it." Panic gripped my heart, my limbs running cold and my vision suddenly narrowing. "It is not permanent, thankfully. But every item you wore on your person or that wasn't in your inventory is now inert. No longer magical or enchanted. The creatures in this area of magical origin are also in danger. Many lost their lives when Orlow'thes woke from his slumber, and his blood met the ocean."

"How?"

"The toxin in his blood is the same that flows through all of the ocean guardians." She sounded tired, and there was more than a small tinge of worry to her tone as the large otter looked over me with her eyes. "I am afraid that you will be without magic for a while. And it seems that fever is setting in."

Fever? I felt cold if anything. I tried to shift into my fox form; it was natural, and I should have been able to do it easily, but I couldn't. The world spun, and I puked again, only bile rising past my lips.

"It will be best that you do not attempt any magic for a while. At least a week, while you recover, and then until it returns after that." She patted my leg with the massive otter's paw. "I have asked the animals nearby to assist in caring for you while you recover. It is all I can do for you."

"But wait, what about my brothers?" She looked away from me. I stood, fighting the dizziness that threatened to engulf me. "Where are my brothers? Where's Vrawn? Kayda? What about Bea?"

I pulled the collar from my neck, and it turned to dust in my palm. "Bea? *Bea!*"

"Be at ease, Zeke," Mother Nature barked, tears filled my eyes as I stared at her, bereft of words. "I was able to pull her from the collar before the magic was fully gone. But she is… not as she was. She will need to recover as you will." I saw a small creature lying on the sands fifteen feet from me, a smaller version of my Bea—unconscious but alive.

As I finally realized that my metallic arm had slumped off

my ruined forearm—the scar tissue still ghastly—I threw it around Mother Nature's neck. I rested there, sobbing and thanking her softly for the small mercy she had given me. Given us.

"As for your friends…" She frowned, an odd facial expression for an otter. "I do not know exactly where they are, or what shape they will be in. My gift to you cost me greatly, and I cannot seem to find them. You will need to search for them on your own. I must leave you now. Trust Milktongue, and learn to work with nature in a new way. Recover swiftly, Druid. Your fight is only beginning."

———

Crashing waves rocked the beach before me, wind buffeting the trees and sands, making small tornadoes of silica as they came into view. The dragon and Baranzil continued their battle. Their howls of pain and rage driving the world around them to lash out with their fury. Echoing calls of the same rage and anger, maddened calls and blood-curdling screeches and roars rang out far behind me that made my blood run cold.

Milktongue grasped me as gently as she could in her teeth and dragged Bea and me toward the cover of a small hollow in a cliffside by the ocean out of the wind and rising fury of the waves. Our surroundings really only being beach, water, this cliff, and a dense-looking tropical forest.

I continued to watch for hours until finally, the two behemoth monsters tired, the kraken having sacrificed another three tentacles to finally get away, a geyser of ink slamming into the dragon's face and eyes as it fled. I was too weak to see if the dragon was okay, unable to truly move. But that didn't mean it didn't come closer to the land. Slowly, his long body writhed and thrashed, oceanic water covering his face, washing some of the graying ink from his eyes. He looked in my direction before opening his mouth and roaring in one long, ragged call before he flopped into the water and sank slowly down. I thought his massive bulk would hit the shelf by the beach, but apparently, it wouldn't as the last I saw of him was his tail slithering into the waves.

The darkened clouds outside slowly dissipated and cleared, leaving warmer weather behind. Milktongue stayed with me for a time, her warmth keeping my shivering at bay before I fell asleep for a little bit. I woke up to find several fish laying next to Bea and me.

Milktongue was kind, nosing them our way and encouraging us to try and eat, but we were both so tired that we could barely keep our eyes open. After a while, she brought us a rock that had been baking in the sun—slowly because it seemed to hurt her paws to touch it for too long. She nudged it between Bea and me, where it radiated a delicious warmth that helped both of us rest a little bit easier.

Before darkness and this blasted sickness threatened to claim me, I swore then and there that I was going to find my brothers, Vrawn and Kayda, and kill that last general. I would survive this. *We* would survive this.

Or I would die trying.

AUTHOR'S NOTE

Hey y'all

Hasn't this been a crazy experience? Book five! I cannot tell you how much it means to me to be able to share these exciting stories with all of you the way that I have been. (read: I love telling you all the stories that *I* tell him and *never* sharing the royalties.) **We've laughed, we've cried--hell I even pounded my chest at some of the thi-** -(Can you believe this yutz? "I pounded my chest!" What're you, an ape? Wannabe.) **... Zeke, did you have something to say to the nice folks?**

Damn straight I do, the *real* author of these stories is more than enough. Get back to writing for me bookworm. (**Now who's the jerk?**) You say something? I'll show you writer's block... That's what I thought. Anyway, thanks for your support, my brothers and I, as well as Kayda, Bea, Maebe, and Vrawn, all really appreciate your time and interest. Spoilers: We ain't down and out yet, and I wanna let you know that the boys and I will be back to struggling real soon. In the meantime--feel free to hyuck it up with the big guy until he gets the lead out on another book for you lot.

Sincerely,
Zeke (**And Me**) shut up, no one likes you, bookworm.

And then Zeke died from the poison flowing through

his veins, the sickness too much for his substantially weakened body to take

P.S. I'm really sorry, big guy. Did I tell you how mighty your beard makes you look? hehe hehe … okay, but please don't kill me. It's *my* story.

You'll have to read the next book to find out whether I feel merciful or not.

Fuck!

ABOUT CHRISTOPHER JOHNS

Christopher Johns is a former photojournalist for the United States Marine Corps with published works telling hundreds of other peoples' stories through word, photo, and even video.

But throughout that time, his editors and superiors had always said that his love of reading fantasy and about worlds of fantastic beauty and horrible power bled into his work. That meant he should write a book.

Well, ta-da!

Chris has been an avid devourer of fantasy and science fiction for more than twenty years and looks forward to sharing that love with his son, his loving fiancée and almost anyone he could ever hope to meet.

Connect with Chris:
Twitter.com/jonsyjohns
Facebook.com/AxeDruidAuthor
Patreon.com/StormCompanyandBeyond

ABOUT MOUNTAINDALE PRESS

Dakota and Danielle Krout, a husband and wife team, strive to create as well as publish excellent fantasy and science fiction novels. Self-publishing *The Divine Dungeon: Dungeon Born* in 2016 transformed their careers from Dakota's military and programming background and Danielle's Ph.D. in pharmacology to President and CEO, respectively, of a small press. Their goal is to share their success with other authors and provide captivating fiction to readers with the purpose of solidifying Mountaindale Press as the place 'Where Fantasy Transforms Reality.'

Connect with Mountaindale Press:
MountaindalePress.com
Facebook.com/MountaindalePress
Twitter.com/_Mountaindale
Instagram.com/MountaindalePress

MOUNTAINDALE PRESS TITLES

GameLit and LitRPG

The Completionist Chronicles,
The Divine Dungeon, and
Full Murderhobo by Dakota Krout

King's League by Jason Anspach and J.N. Chaney

A Touch of Power by Jay Boyce

Red Mage by Xander Boyce

Space Seasons by Dawn Chapman

Ether Collapse and
Ether Flows by Ryan DeBruyn

Bloodgames by Christian J. Gilliland

Wolfman Warlock by James Hunter and Dakota Krout

Axe Druid and
Mephisto's Magic Online by Christopher Johns

Skeleton in Space by Andries Louws

Chronicles of Ethan by John L. Monk

Pixel Dust by David Petrie

Henchman by Carl Stubblefield

Artorian's Archives by Dennis Vanderkerken and Dakota Krout

APPENDIX

THE GOOD

Zekiel Erebos (Zee-key-uhl Air-uh-bows) – Marine who loves gaming as a civilian with his buddies who are still in. Class: Druid. Race: Kitsune, has tails.

Yohsuke (Yo-s'kay) – Zeke's best bud/brother from the Marine Corps. Overlord, yeah, you read that right. Class: Spell blade. Race: Abomination (halfbreed drow and high elf) also, he's a vampire now. Big whoop!

Jaken Warmecht (Jay-ken) – Zeke's friend who typically needs help catching up in the games the group places together. Class: Paladin of Radiance. Race: Fae-Orc.

Bokaj (Bow-ka-jh) – A friend from the gym who loves video games and is in a pretty wicked band! Class: Ranger. Race: Ice Elf.

Tmont (Tee-M-on-t) – A panther with a taste for tails who happens to not just be a walking bag of assholes, but is also Bokaj's pet. Mainly that first one, though.

Balmur (Ball-mer) – Bokaj's best friend, and another good buddy of Zeke's who loves to game! Class: Rogue. Race: Azer Dwarf (Fire dwarf) HIS BEARD IS A FLAME!

James Bautista (Really?) – Another Marine that Yohsuke and Zeke know and game with often. Class: Monk. Race: Dragon Elf.

Muu Ankiman (Moo Ahn-key-men) – Dragon beast-kin with green scales and Zeke's roommate on Earth. Liiiiittle crazy, but he's okay. Class: Fighter. Race: Dragon-kin (it's shorter!)

Kayda (Kay-duh) – A pretty little bird with a shitty past, and hopefully, a bright future. Recently turned into a Storm Roc. Very protective of a certain flame wolf. And raptor now.

Coal – A flame wolf that Zeke took care of for a bit on behalf of the Primordial Flame Elemental. He's got a good temperament, a little heated at times, but he's a cool pup. He's home now and hopefully happy.

Bea Arthur (Bee) — A gust raptor and royal pain in the ass, but *man* does the group love her! She's a big scary, scarlet baby who loves Vrawn almost as much as she does Zeke.

Sir Willem Dillon – Owner of the tavern in Sunrise Village (the starter town) and Paladin of Radiance. The first guy the group meets and doesn't try to kill. (Or do they? MUAHAHAHA— No, really, do they?) Jaken's trainer.

Dinnia (Dih-nee-uh) – An elven druid who takes pity on poor Zeke and brings him into Mother Nature's good graces. Zeke's trainer.

Sharo (shah-row) – Another panther who assists his partner in crime Dinnia in training her student. Not a walking bag of assholes.

Kyra – Queen of the bears and good friend of Dinnia's. We like her.

Marin (mare-in) – We, uh… we don't talk about her. 10 out of 10, though. Kickass dire bear.

Rowland – Blacksmith in Sunrise who decides he likes the travelers, especially the one with the tail—no bias.

Maebe (may-buh—soft buh—if she hears you talking shit, I'm not responsible, yeah?) – Unseelie Queen of Winter and Darkness, who somehow gets thrown into the mix. Also, Zeke's wife. I know, right?

Thogan (ThO-gun) – Champion of the Unseelie Fae, and a rather clingy dwarf with a rough complexion.

Titania – Queen of the Seelie Fae, who has a predisposition of being a raging bitch to anyone and everyone she doesn't like. Like outsiders.

Craglim (Crag-limb) – Rowland's cousin. Racist piece of shit—but he's a good fighter.

Zhavron (Zah-vrun) – Orc fighter with a sordid past. Muu's trainer in all things fighting. A little intense at times.

Pharazulla (Far-uh-zu-la) – A bard of some renown, though a bit of a stuck-up asshole.

Vrawn – A lovely orcish woman with a soft spot for our local druid. She's built like a busty, brick shit house.

Sam – Mayor of Sunrise village. A fair man whose bear-kin wife and half bear-kin children believe in him wholeheartedly. Prefers to hunt for the village rather than govern.

The villagers of Sunrise – Great people who recently went through a lot of bullshit. Go easy on em, yeah?

Set – A decent little Fae-orc kid, doped into hunting a Belgar.

Ampharia (Am-far-ee-uh) – An elder green dragon friend of Mother Nature's who gives Muu her blessing and teaches him how to fight dragons.

Natholdi, Granite, and son (Nath-ol-dee) – A good, humble dwarven family that both Muu and Zeke love dearly. Newest additions to the Light Hand Clan.

Farnik Mugfist (Far-nick) – Leader of the Mugfist clan and good friend to the party. Loves a good cup of mead and song.

Shellica Light Hand (Shell-ih-cuh) – Leader of the Light hand clan and a Grand Master Enchanter. Crazy as shit with a diabolical wit. Zeke's trainer, unfortunately.

Silvannas (Sill-vahn-us) – Queen of the High elves on the prime plane of existence. Sort of a role model to Maebe.

Questis (Quest-ihs) – A high elf Druid enchanter who has a soft spot for kitties and bait. Pretty awesome guy. Seriously loves cats, though.

Fern (Like the plant) – A sabertooth cat that has a *serious* god complex. Loves to be fed and worshipped. Gives his druid Questis hell all the time.

Telfino (Tell-fee-no) – Son of Queen Silvannas, and inheritor of the throne. He's a good kid with a seriously strong class.

Manly Warbottom – A rascal bounty hunter halfling with a weird motley crew of badasses. Good lady likes money. A lot.

Braves of the Thorn – Manly's peeps and party, consisting of

Dawn, Nick, Nic, Bonnie, and Manly's best buddy Humphrey. Quality people.

Milnolian (Mill-Gnoll-Ian) – Goes by Servant, but he's a loyal servant of Maeve's who she passed to him as a gift.

Eiran'a (Ee-rahn-ah) – Maeve's momma and a *highly* skilled ice mage. She doesn't really care for the loving protagonist, but hey —beggars and choosers, am I right?

Westwind Royalty – The royal family of Zephyth, good people with a lovely daughter. Aboiye (A-boy-Eh), the king, and Chareen (Shareen) his wife.

Villeroa Westwind (Vill-er-oah) – Princess and water mage, with her elemental friend.

Zygnal (Zig-nahl) – Water elemental assigned to protect and help train Villeroa.

Jafrik (Ya-frick) – A Drow boy chosen by the Primordial Light Elemental to become the first of a new race, the dawn elves.

Vlegen (Vleg-ehn) – A dwarf of the Mugfist clan who didn't know his place. He learned the hard way that xenophobia isn't right.

Katja (cat-yuh) – An in owner and quite a nice lady of a little stoic for her own good. Has great booze though.

Calmyra (Cal-Meer-uh) – A cat man rogue with the Syndicate in a certain city who helped flush out the evil in his own people as they were working with outside factions against them. He's cool.

Captain Holly Jenisovna (Jenny-sohv-nah) – Captain of the

Pussy Willow and her crew. A nice feline lady who doesn't play to anyone's tune but her own.

Joesa Webbost – First mate of the Pussy Willow and a sea elf. He's also a pretty cool dude, a little goofy at times, but kind.

Taejon – A wily old man who worked for the Pussy Willow. His influence and carefree style helped the crew and the party integration a little more. Rest In Peace buddy.

Odany (Oh-danny) – A precocious little girl chosen by the Wind Primordial Elemental to be his champion. Her magic is insane, and her ability to control it even more so. She's naturally better with the elements than anyone ever imagined.

THE BAD

War – Galactic conquerer who probably suffers from only child syndrome. Probably needs a hug, or he will keep trying to take over the universe.

Minions of War – Not the lovable minions everyone loves. You know, not the yellow ones, or that fish from that one Will Ferrell animated move. These guys seek to undermine the strength of the gods by eroding the world around them slowly. And serve the other assholes in this list.

The Generals – A Number of War's better warriors capable of taking out the strongest people on the planet—and together they did. Dick move.

Rowan – I'm not gonna say much about this guy—read the book, then you'll know what a dickbag he is. Haha, was—sonofabitch is dead, now. No, seriously, he's dead. General of War? You forgot him already? Not worth knowing? I know it.

Pastella (Pahs-tell-uh) – Crazy elven woman with a taste for torture and violence.

Tarron Dillingsley (Tair-run Dill-night-slee) – Gnomish enchanter who—let's face it shall we?—sucks as a teacher for various reasons and lest we forget, the asshole in charge of the Children of Brindolla.

Children of Brindolla – A group of misguided citizens who believe they are the only ones who can truly save their world. They found themselves on the receiving end of an ass-kicking— but was that all of them?

Decay – A greater Fiend who held his own against the party and Maebe. Fell due to a brilliant plan and a little bit of finesse. Okay, the plan was half-cocked, and the finesse resulted in some bullshit—happy now?

Spiders – just a bunch of overgrown pests that needed an ass-kicking. Nightmare fuel FOREVER.

Lothir (Low-theer) – Big ol' wanna-be snake goddess who has a village of elves, orcs, and Fae-orcs under her command and demands sacrifices to restore and keep her beauty. All of that means that she's coo coo for Cocoa Puffs.

Melvaren (Mel-vah-ren) – General who took claim over Balmur and tortured him in the Hells for his entire tenure there. We killed the shit out of him. But not before he whipped our asses. Still dead, though.

Archemillian (Ark-em-illion) – The demon who Yohsuke summoned and gets his warlock powers from. Has a huge hard-on for souls, but he helped us this once. Didn't mean he was a fucking good guy, though.

Riktolth (Rick-talth) – The great black dragon who killed a mother red in a bid to die in combat. Yeah, you guessed it. We kicked his ass.

Governess Belltree – The lady leader of Lindyburg with a *series* distaste for magic. Like genocide level crazy.

Lilith – Drow queen and crazy manipulative, also a spider lady —creepy as hell.

Vampire Lord – Vampires, right? Yeah, she was on some serious minion shit but had beef with her sister that saw her die.

Xaenth (Shane-th) – drow guide and a general dickhead.

Breggil (Br-egg-Ill) – This dipshit took the form of a copper dragon and attacked Kayda rather than us—that was a huge mistake. We whooped that ASS, and then he got eaten…

Baranzil (Bar-ahn-zill) – An asshat of War who decided to take the body of a Kraken. He chased the team for days eating everything he could to power level so he could take the team. He ended up summoning the wrath of the water dragon. He dead… or is he?

AND THE UGLY

Insane Wolves – Think crazy wolves, but you know, crazier and angrier for some reason. Due to proximity to a minion of War, the minds of these animals have eroded to nothing but the drive to kill and eat anything that is not them, or another wolf.

Undead creatures – As you can imagine, due to proximity to a minion of War, these poor bastards rose from the dead in order to protect their alien masters. Even the stronger versions are worthy of a small bit of sympathy—they sure as hell didn't get any, but they are worthy of it.

Bone Dragon – I mean, pretty self-explanatory, right? It's a bone dragon! No skin, no muscle—all bleached bones and hate for the living.

General of War (Blight) – The asshole who did some truly terrible things, sent us on a supposedly one-way trip to the Fae Realm and got his ASS kicked. Yeah. That guy.

Ursolon – Think of a giant, striped bear with an anger management issue the size of North Dakota. Yeah. Now go fight one.

Werewolves – The hero's in some tales—but not this one. Oh no. These guys suck, big time! Hairy, needy pieces of crap.

Alpha Werewolf – The jerk in charge of the other jerks above. Bigger, badder, stronger, and usually way more cunning and ruthless.

The Wild Hunt – A flock of assholes (read demons) who patrol the realm of the Fae and take out anything they believe doesn't belong there.

Order of the Prime – A bunch of human wizards bent on controlling the elements and restoring mankind to their rightful place as rulers. Some real xenophobic asshats, these ones.

Spiders – Oh, I mentioned these already? Because there were a lot of them. With fangs. And all the feet. Seriously, I need to book an appointment for therapy now.

Belgar – A rhino-like Fae creature with a surprising sense of honor and code that it lives by. Big as shit, and it will run anyone in its way through.

Dofilnarr (Dough-fill-nar) – A Fae creature thought to have been hunted to extinction that takes the forms and abilities of creatures it touches while in its base state. Highly vulnerable to Fae Iron.

Vampire bats – ugly bastards that looked like man-bats that did a number on the party.

Hulking vampires – Vampires on steroids that would make the Dr. Banner feel normal.

Dungeon baddies – Doing what they were designed to do, right?

Demon Nanny – I don't really know what the hell this thing was, but it was taking care of something, a general perhaps? We aren't sure, but this thing was strong.

Fish men – these guys sucked, slimy little bastards that ended up being cannon fodder and a snack for a general. Garbage.

And other random jerks too unimportant for now to mention— they know who they are. Bunch of assholes.

www.ingramcontent.com/pod-product-compliance
Lightning Source LLC
Chambersburg PA
CBHW032230010726
47494CB00002B/431